GREY KNIGHTS

ON THE PLANET Khorion IX, daemonhunter Mandulis of the Grey Knights is locked in a titanic battle with the daemon prince Ghargatuloth. In a fight that costs his life, Mandulis manages to banish the foul daemon back to the warp for a thousand years.

A millennium later, Justicar Alaric of the Grey Knights is recuperating after bringing the renegade Inquisitor Valinov to justice. Amongst the artefacts recovered is the sacred Book of Days, which tells of the imminent return of Ghargatuloth. Leading an elite team of Grey Knights, Alaric must uncover the fanatical cults paving the way for the foul daemon's return. But with time running out, the daemonhunters must unlock the secret that will again banish the dreaded Ghargatuloth!

A WARHAMMER 40,000 NOVEL

GREY KNIGHTS

Ben Counter

To Helen

A BLACK LIBRARY PUBLICATION

First published in Great Britain in 2004 by
BL Publishing,
Games Workshop Ltd.,
Willow Road, Nottingham,
NG7 2WS, UK

10 9 8 7 6 5

Cover illustration by Philip Sibbering.

A CIP record for this book is available from the British Library.

ISBN 13: 978 1 84416 087 7
ISBN 10: 1 84416 087 4

Distributed in the US by Simon & Schuster
1230 Avenue of the Americas, New York, NY 10020, US.

Printed and bound in Great Britain by
Bookmarque, Surrey, UK.

See the Black Library on the Internet at
www.blacklibrary.com

Find out more about Games Workshop
and the world of Warhammer 40,000 at
www.games-workshop.com

IT IS THE 41st millennium. For more than a hundred centuries the Emperor has sat immobile on the Golden Throne of Earth. He is the master of mankind by the will of the gods, and master of a million worlds by the might of his inexhaustible armies. He is a rotting carcass writhing invisibly with power from the Dark Age of Technology. He is the Carrion Lord of the Imperium for whom a thousand souls are sacrificed every day, so that he may never truly die.

YET EVEN IN his deathless state, the Emperor continues his eternal vigilance. Mighty battlefleets cross the daemon-infested miasma of the warp, the only route between distant stars, their way lit by the Astronomican, the psychic manifestation of the Emperor's will. Vast armies give battle in his name on uncounted worlds. Greatest amongst his soldiers are the Adeptus Astartes, the Space Marines, bio-engineered super-warriors. Their comrades in arms are legion: the Imperial Guard and countless planetary defence forces, the ever-vigilant Inquisition and the tech-priests of the Adeptus Mechanicus to name only a few. But for all their multitudes, they are barely enough to hold off the ever-present threat from aliens, heretics, mutants – and worse.

TO BE A man in such times is to be one amongst untold billions. It is to live in the cruellest and most bloody regime imaginable. These are the tales of those times. Forget the power of technology and science, for so much has been forgotten, never to be re-learned. Forget the promise of progress and understanding, for in the grim dark future there is only war. There is no peace amongst the stars, only an eternity of carnage and slaughter, and the laughter of thirsting gods.

ONE
KHORION IX

It was a heaving sea of hatred, an ocean of pure evil.

Far below, the surface of Khorion IX was covered in a seething forest of torture racks, crosses and squares and stars of bloodstained wood on which were broken hundreds of thousands of bodies, mangled and wound around the wood like vines around a cane. It was like a huge and horrible vineyard, with rows and rows of crucified bodies spilling a terrible vintage of blood into the earth. The victims were trapped between life and death, their bodies exsanguinated but their minds just lucid enough to understand their agony. They were the servants of the Prince of a Thousand Faces, the cultists and demagogues summoned to their master's planet in the hope of an eternal reward that was all too real. Their bodies were merged with the wood that had grown as the seasons passed, twisting their limbs into canopies of fleshy branches and deforming them until there was barely anything human in them save for their suffering.

They said the screams could be heard from orbit. They were right.

At an unheard signal, the ground began to seethe. The crucified of Khorion IX began to wail even louder, their agony supplanted by fear, as the sodden earth burst into fountains of bloodstained soil and a hideous gibbering rose up from beneath. Iridescent, shifting creatures crawled up to the surface, some with long reaching fingers and torsos dominated by leering, huge-mawed faces, others with bloated fungoid bodies that belched multicoloured flame. There were ravenous swarms of tiny, misshapen things that gnawed at the roots of the crucified forest and immense winged monsters like huge deformed vultures that spat magic fire. Every one was a shining multicoloured vision of hell, and each was just a pale reflection of their master. The Prince of a Thousand Faces, the Forger of Hells, the Whisperer in the Darkness – Ghargatuloth the Daemon Lord, chosen of the God of Change.

A tide of daemons burst like an ocean from the ground and flooded through the crucified forest, shrieking in anticipation and hunger, the greater daemons marshalling the lesser and the lowest of them, forming a mantle of daemon flesh that covered the ground in a sea of iridescence.

The daemonic tide poured onto the surface until from far above it looked like an ocean of daemonskin, the lesser daemons sweeping between the rows of the crucified and the greater crushing Ghargatuloth's slave-victims beneath clawed feet. The will of Ghargatuloth resonated through the very crust of Khorion IX; every single one of the Tzeentch's servants felt it.

The next turning point will be here, it said. Thousands of the Change God's plots were coming to a head in this battle, a tangled nexus of fates that would set the path for the future. It was fate that formed the medium through which Tzeentch mutated the universe to his will, and so this was a holy battle where fate was the weapon, the prize and the battleground.

The cackling of the daemon army mixed with the screams of the crucified and the air vibrated with the din. For light years in all directions the insane babbling and screams of desperation gnawed at every mind, whispering darkly and shrieking insanely. Though the space around Khorion IX was largely devoid of human habitation, many of those few who heard the call of the daemon lost their minds in the prelude to the battle.

But the minds that mattered, the minds of those who would face the horde of Ghargatuloth, were unwavering. They had trained since before they could remember in resisting the trickery of Tzeentch himself and the creeping corruption that had brought so many to the fold of Ghargatuloth. They were armed with the best weapons the Ordo Malleus could give them, protected by consecrated power armour hundreds if not thousands of years old, shielded from sorcery by hexagrammic and pentagrammic wards tattooed onto their skin by the sages of the Inquisitorial archives.

They were ready. Their very purpose was to be ready, because when the time came to fight something like Ghargatuloth, who else could do it? They were the Grey Knights, the daemon hunters of the Adeptus Astartes, tasked by the Ordo Malleus of the Inquisition and hence the Emperor Himself to fight the daemon in all its forms. They were just a handful in number compared to the trillions of citizens making up the Imperium but when a threat like Ghargatuloth was finally brought to bear, the Grey Knights were literally the Imperium's only hope.

There were three hundred of them bearing down on Khorion IX to have their say in the confluence of fates. And Khorion IX was waiting for them.

THE FIRST THINGS Grand Master Mandulis saw of Khorion IX were the thick bands of cloud, white and streaked with red, as they rushed past the viewport of the drop-pod that plummeted through the planet's lower atmosphere. The screams from below sounded even through the din of the descent and the pod's lander engines, a million voices raised in praise and anticipation, calling out for blood and for new spirits to break on the anvil of Ghargatuloth's sorcery.

The Grey Knights' briefing sermon had told them that an ancient pre-Imperial barrows complex was their landing zone, but the plans they had to go by were from exploratory records three hundred years old. There could be anything on Khorion IX. It had taken more than a century to track Ghargatuloth to the planet, and the daemon prince would know the Grey Knights were coming. It would be savage. Very probably, nothing would survive. Grand Master Mandulis knew this and accepted it, for he had sworn long ago that the destruction of the daemonic was of greater importance than his life. He had decades of experience in the ranks of the Grey Knights, he had fought across a hundred worlds in the unending hidden war against the horrors of the warp, but if he had to die to see Ghargatuloth banished from real space then he would gladly die.

But it wouldn't be that simple.

The drop-pod's proximity alarms kicked in and filled the cramped interior with deep red light. It picked out the face of Justicar Chemuel, whose squad Mandulis was accompanying in the assault. Chemuel was as good a soldier as the Grey Knights had, and Mandulis had seen how he led his Purgation squad. His Marines carried psycannon and flamers and Chemuel had drilled them until they could lay down massive pin-point fire. It would be Chemuel's task to help clear the path through Ghargatuloth's servants so the veteran Terminator assault squads could close with the greater daemons and even with the Prince of a Thousand Faces himself.

That was the plan, but plans never lasted. The Grey Knights could fight the battles they did precisely because every one of them was trained and psycho-doctrinated to survive in the forge of battle alone if needs be; Chemuel like his battle-brothers would fight alone when the battle broke down into a slaughter.

That was when, not if. That was the way of daemons. They wrought bloodshed and confusion because they enjoyed it. Ghargatuloth had surrounded himself with an immense army of such creatures, and if the Grey Knight had to fight them all at once, then they would.

The restraints holding Mandulis and Squad Chemuel into their grav-couches wound in suddenly for the impact. Blood-streaked clouds rushed past the viewport and then they were gone. The pod's lander engines fired and again the pod decelerated suddenly, swooping as it came in to land. For a moment Mandulis was looking out on the twisted nightmare that was Khorion IX – the landscape shattered as if struck by a giant hammer, row upon row of tormented bodies staked out or nailed to crosses and arranged in terraced fields stretching between horizons. A waterfall of blood poured into a churning red sea in the distance.

A network of pre-Imperial barrows, the only recognisable landmark from the ancient maps of the planet, was ringed with banner poles from which hung innumerable flags of flayed skin. And worst of all, the daemon army seethed, hundreds of thousands strong, surrounding the closest barrow in an unbroken sea of daemon flesh.

Mandulis had been a Grey Knight since before he could remember. He had fought the Chaotic and daemonic from the heart of the Segmentum Solar to far-flung daemon worlds, from the halls of planetary governors to the endless slums of hive cities. Mandulis had seen so much that volumes of his battlefield reports filled shelves of the Archivum Titanis, and yet still in all his days he had never seen anything like the horde of Ghargatuloth.

He was not afraid. The Emperor himself had decreed that a Space Marine shall know no fear. But Grand Master Mandulis's soul still recoiled at the sheer magnitude of evil.

'I am the hammer,' he intoned as the landing jets pushed even harder against the drop-pod's descent. 'I am the right hand of my Emperor, the instrument of His will, the gauntlet about His fist, the tip of His spear, the edge of His sword…'

The Marines of Squad Chemuel followed Mandulis as he led them in the final battlefield prayer, intoning the sacred words even though they could barely hear them above the scream of the drop-pod's final braking jets.

The impact was immense, like slamming into a wall. The grav-couch restraints jolted back as the pods ploughed through the branches of wood and bone, into the middle of the daemon throng. A great scream rose above the din of the impact as daemons were vaporised by the impact, and the viewport was suddenly covered in their many-coloured blood.

'Pod down!' yelled Justicar Chemuel. 'Blow the restraints!'

The servitor-pilot controlling the pod's systems responded to the pre-programmed order and the bolts holding the pod's sides together burst with a series of sharp reports. The sides of the pod burst open and Mandulis's restraints fell away. Baleful reddish light and a truly appalling stench of decay flooded in, so thick it was like plunging into a sea of blood. The screams of the engines were replaced by the unearthly and hideous keening of thousands of daemons, like an atonal choir howling out a wall of sound. The weeping sky was scratched by the reaching branches of crucified limbs, the forest swarmed with daemons, the pure hatred of Ghargatuloth's army was like a wave of pain pouring into the drop-pod.

Mandulis had a split second before the daemons closed in again. The pod had blasted a crater, thick with daemon gore, ringed by broken crucifix-trees. Blood spurted from tears in the ground as if from severed arteries. The stench that got through Mandulis's helmet filters was of burning and blood, and the howling of the daemons hit him like a gale.

'Squad, suppression fire!' called Chemuel and his Marines, their psycannons already loaded and primed, thudded off a single, huge volley that blasted apart the daemons scrambling over the ridge of the crater.

Mandulis saw another pod hitting home close by, throwing up a foul rain of blood and daemon body parts. 'That's Martel!' voxed Mandulis. 'Chemuel, give him cover and link up!'

Two Marines ran up the crater ridge and their incinerator-pattern flamers poured gouts of blue-hot flame into the tide of daemons pouring towards them through the woods. Mandulis stomped after them, the servos of his ancient Terminator suit whirring, his wrist-mounted storm bolter barking as he sent blessed bolter shots streaking into leering daemon faces. He reached the lip of the crater and saw the army for the first time from ground level – gnarled limbs of iridescent pink and blue, bloated creatures that belched flame, the lopsided shapes of avian greater daemons lurching towards the drop zone.

Mandulis drew his Nemesis sword from its scabbard on his back. The blade leapt into life, its power field calibrated to disrupt the psychic matter of daemons' flesh, the stylised golden lightning bolt set into its silver blade glowing hot with power. He lunged forward and cut a wide arc through the daemons clambering through the burning remains of their brothers; he felt three unholy bodies come apart under the blade's edge.

It was a good blade. One of the Chapter's best, given to Mandulis when he first attained the rank of master. But it would have to drink more daemon's blood than it had ever done before if he was to succeed in his mission now.

Psycannon fire from Chemuel was shrieking past, the modified bolter shells exploding in spectacular starbursts of silver that shredded the attacking daemons. The flamer troops moved up and were beside

Mandulis, pouring more fire into the attacking daemons as Mandulis's Nemesis sword carved through
any that got within range.

Martel's Terminator squad cut their way towards
Mandulis, the huge tactical dreadnought armour battering aside the crucifix-trees as volleys of storm bolter
fire cut through the forest.

'Brother Martel,' voxed Mandulis. 'Chemuel will
cover you. We are close to the first barrow, follow me.'

'Well met, grand master,' replied Captain Martel as
he speared a daemon with his Nemesis halberd. 'Justinian is close behind us. I think we are cut off from
any of the others.'

'Then we will carry the attack ourselves,' voxed Mandulis. 'We knew it would come to this. Give grace to the
Emperor for our part in this fight and keep moving.'

'In position!' came the vox from Justicar Chemuel.
Mandulis turned to see the Purgation squad lined up
on the lip of the crater, surrounded by the dissolving
remains of charred daemons, ready to send volley after
disciplined volley from the psycannon into Ghargatuloth's horde.

Grand Master Mandulis could feel, thrumming
through the bloodsoaked earth and cutting through
the screams of the crucified, the deep angry growl of
something waking. Below the ground, huge and
malevolent, making ready to play its hand if the time
came. The pre-battle guesswork had been correct – it
was beneath the barrows and would be surrounded by
the deadliest of its servants.

Mandulis mouthed a silent prayer to the Emperor as
the daemon tide came again, gibbering and screeching
as they swung through the trees and loped along the
ground, shining with flame and foul sorcery.

Mandulis pressed down on the firing stud in his gauntlet and sent a stream of bolter shells ripping into the advancing daemons. He hefted his Nemesis sword ready to strike and, with Martel's Terminators at his side, he charged.

THE GREY KNIGHTS' strikeforce that attacked Khorion IX was the strongest the Ordo Malleus could assemble. Compact, fast, led by three grand masters of the Grey Knights and composed of the best daemon-hunting warriors the Imperium had, it was nonetheless far from certain that the force would succeed. It had taken a century to hunt down Ghargatuloth, the power which, through dozens of avatars and aspects, directed thousands of Chaos cults in acts of depravity and terror.

Ghargatuloth's purpose was to spread chaos and carnage in the name of its god Tzeentch, following an infinitely obscure plan that was all but impossible to trace. The Ordo Malleus had fought long and hard to find out that it lived on Khorion IX, an uninhabited and largely unexplored world deep into the Halo Zone of the Segmentum Obscurus where the beacon of the Astronomican barely reached. All that time Ghargatuloth had prepared and the Ordo Malleus had no choice but to send their troops into his trap, because they might never get another chance. Khorion IX was too isolated for a planet-scouring Imperial Navy assault and normal troops would last a matter of seconds on the planet. Even the Exterminatus, the ultimate Inquisitorial sanction, would not be enough – someone had to see Ghargatuloth die and, even with a devastating strike from orbit, the Ordo Malleus could not be sure.

It had to be the Grey Knights. Because if anyone could survive long enough to face Ghargatuloth in battle, it would be them.

The fast strike cruisers *Valour Saturnum* and *Vengeful* carried over two hundred and fifty Grey Knights, as large a force as could be moved quickly enough through the vastness of the Segmentum Obscurus. Lord Inquisitor Lakonios of the Ordo Malleus was in ultimate command but once the drop-pods were launched and the atmosphere of Khorion IX was breached, it was the Grey Knights themselves who gave the orders.

Grand Master Ganelon, who had personally killed the Vermin King of Kalentia when still a justicar, landed well off-centre in the thick of the daemon army. With nearly a hundred Grey Knights under his command he fought a valiant battle of survival against wave upon wave of daemons, back-to-back and completely surrounded. Marine after Marine died under sorcerous lightning or the talons of rampaging greater daemons and Ganelon himself began the Prayer of Purification, readying the souls of his men for the inevitable journey after death to join the Emperor in the final battle against Chaos.

The Marines under Grand Master Malquiant smashed into the edge of the crucified forest and formed a fearsome spearhead of seventy Grey Knights, tipped with the Terminator-armoured assault squads and ultimately the sanctified lightning claws of Malquiant himself. Huge portions of the horde swarmed to blunt the attack but those who bypassed the Malquiant's Terminators were cut to pieces by the massive, well-ordered crossfires from the Purgation and Tactical squads that followed. Malquiant's assault drained vast numbers of daemons from the forest, bleeding Ghargatuloth's horde dry in an awesome display of sheer bloody-minded aggression. But the horde was too vast and the broken terrain slowed the assault – Malquiant knew he would not reach the objective, and could only do what he could for his battle-brothers by forcing the bulk of the horde away from the barrows. As the assault ground to a halt Malquiant turned it into a killing zone, overlapping fields of fire and launching counter-assaults into anything that got through.

Grand Master Mandulis had landed closest to the barrows. Along with Squad Chemuel and Squad Martel, and Squad Justinian's tactical team who arrived in time to help cover the advance, Mandulis made the first strike into Ghargatuloth's lair. Over the static-filled vox he learned of Ganelon's sacrifice and Malquiant's relentless but bogged-down assault, and knew as he had somehow always known that it was up to him. Those who could told him that the strength within him was the Emperor's and that with His will he would prevail. Then Mandulis led the charge up the slopes of the barrows and all contact was lost, as sorcery flickered like lightning in the clouds ahead and the daemon horde began to sing the praises of their master.

THE CREST OF the barrow was lined with bodies whose skeletons had been deformed into tall spears of flesh and bone from which hung pennants of skin rippling in the hot, blood-damp breeze. The pennants were emblazoned with symbols that would have burned the eyes of lesser men – Mandulis recognised the same sigils that had been carved into the skin of

Ghargatuloth's cultists and written in blood on the floors of their temples.

Beyond the crest of the barrow, something huge roared. Mandulis, his gunmetal armour now black with blood and smoke coiling from the charred twin barrels of his storm bolter, turned to see the Grey Knights who had followed him. One Terminator from Squad Martel was down, along with several from Squad Justinian who had followed in the path blazed by Mandulis. Justinian himself had lost an arm and his helmet had been wrenched off by the gnarled hands of a daemon – his face was streaked with grime and his breathing was ragged and bloody.

Further back, Chemuel was forming a cordon to protect Mandulis's men from a counterattack. Mandulis had no doubt that Justicar Chemuel would sell his life at the foot of the barrow, holding back the daemonic tide with flamers and psycannon. It was a good and honourable way to die, but it would mean nothing if Mandulis could not press home the attack now.

'Martel! With me!' voxed Mandulis. The captain ran up the slick earth of the barrow, his Terminators following. 'Grace be with you, brother. Over the top.'

Under cover from Justinian, Mandulis and Squad Martel charged over the crest of the barrow. Before them stretched the whole barrows complex, a series of concentric circular mounds surrounding a ruined stone tower like the stump of a huge tree. Twisted trees, once Ghargatuloth's most loyal cult leaders, grew in tormented tangles everywhere, forming knots of screaming, blackened flesh. In the depressions between the mounds, blood had drained into deep moats, blood that churned as something massive writhed beneath the ground.

As Mandulis watched, the ground seethed and he saw pale shapes clawing their way from the earth. Stone coffins broke the surface and spilled mouldering bones and grave goods onto the ground. So massive was the evil beneath the barrows that those who had originally been buried there, thousands of years ago before Khorion IX had ever been discovered by the Imperium, were clawing their way from their graves to get away from it.

Mandulis led the charge. As he ran full pelt down the reverse slope of the first barrow there was a titanic eruption of earth nearby and something pale, towering and monstrous burst from the surface. A wave of daemonic sorcery washed over everything and the wards tattooed onto Mandulis's skin burned white-hot as they fought off the daemon's magic. He saw a hunched, twisted body, with a foul distended stomach, rotting skin sprouting feathers, and a long neck from which hung a wickedly grinning beaked head. Wings of blue fire spread from its back as it lunged and stamped down on Brother Gaius, shattering the Grey Knight's leg with a taloned foot. Storm bolter fire streaked up at it and Brother Jokul's psycannon punched holes into its decaying chest, but it just shrieked with joy as it picked up Gaius and tore him in two with its beak.

'Press on!' yelled Mandulis into the vox. 'Brother Knights, with me! Chemuel, Justinian, move up and give cover!'

Mandulis heard Gaius die over the vox, the Grey Knight's last breaths gurgling prayers of hate as he hacked at the greater daemon with his Nemesis weapon. Brother Thieln, Justinian's flamer Marine, died a moment later, cut in two by a huge rusted metal glaive wielded by a second greater daemon that tore itself out of the slope of the barrow.

Ghargatuloth's inner circle of daemons – Lords of Change, the cultists called them, generals of the Change God's armies – were bursting from the barrows to slaughter the Grey Knights who dared attack the Prince of a Thousand Faces. This was the heart of Ghargatuloth's trap. Mandulis had known it would end like this – a mad charge in the faint hope that the Grey Knights would reach Ghargatuloth in enough numbers to stand a chance of defeating him.

A daemon erupted from the ground close by, showering Mandulis with blood and earth. Captain Martel lunged in with his halberd, spearing the avian daemon through the thigh. Mandulis ducked the staff it swung, sorcerous lightning arcing off his armour and pushing his antipsychic wards to the limit. He swung his sword into the heart of the iridescence and the daemon's head was sheared clean off, the severed neck spewing viscous, glowing blue gore onto the ground.

Mandulis strode on as bolter fire and lightning streaked everywhere. He waded through the waist-deep gore of the moat and scrambled up the crumbling earth of the next barrow, crunching through ancient graves.

He could hear voices whispering and screaming inside his skull, a babble of madness that would have swamped a lesser man's mind. But the mind of a Grey Knight was built around a hard core of pure, depthless faith. Where other men had fear, the Grey Knights had resolve. Where others had doubt, Mandulis had faith. An Imperial guardsman, no matter how courageous or pious, still had that unprotected hollow of despair, greed, and terror at the heart of his soul. A Grey Knight did not. Ghargatuloth's mind tricks broke against Mandulis's mind like waves against rocks.

That was why it had to be the Grey Knights assaulting Khorion IX. The Lords Militant could assemble armies hundreds of millions strong, but not one of those Guardsmen would have kept his mind for a minute under the gaze of Ghargatuloth. So it was up to the Grey Knights, and now it was up to Mandulis.

Glowing hands were reaching from beneath the soil, large enough to pick up Brother Trentius and hurl him so hard that his body smashed into the stone tower at the centre of the barrows. One of the daemons held a staff of bloodstained black wood, pink lightning spilling from the bundle of skulls nailed to its top, arcing off power armour, blasting Marines off their feet where the other greater daemons could move in for the kill.

Squad Chemuel were buying time with their lives. They were surrounded, the towering avian daemons ablaze with blessed burning fuel and smoking from holes blasted by psycannon rounds. Chemuel himself had drawn his Nemesis weapon, which the artificers on Titan had fashioned into a spear, and was stabbing at the nearest daemon even as it tore off his other arm.

Squad Justinian had tried to keep pace with Mandulis and Martel but their charge had faltered. Justinian himself died in a sea of pink fire that boiled up from below, dragged down by daemon talons and torn apart. His Marines were scattered by the daemon that rose from the fire, wielding a great spiked metal block on a long chain that scythed through two Marines before their battle-brothers could turn and riddle the daemon with storm bolter fire.

Mandulis scrambled up the slope of the final barrow. Martel's Terminators, only a handful of them left now,

turned to cover Martel and Mandulis. The swarm of
lesser daemons broke over the far barrow and poured
into the complex to join their master in a waterfall of
daemons' flesh. The last sight Mandulis had of Justicar
Chemuel was of his body being thrown by a greater
daemon into the advancing tide, to be played with and
torn apart like prey.

Mandulis pressed on. The ground itself was fighting
him, collapsing beneath his feet into great fissures. The
tower loomed overhead, ancient stones spilling off its
ruined walls, and beneath him the pure hatred reached
a screaming pitch as Ghargatuloth tried to force his
way into Mandulis's mind.

The daemon prince would not succeed. That meant
he would have to stoop to defending himself personally. And that was Mandulis's only chance.

The tower was shattered and thrown into the air in a
shower of stone. The ground tore open and Mandulis
dug his feet into the crumbling earth as the storm tore
over him.

The sky rotted and turned black. A shockwave of corruption ripped outwards and turned the landscape of
Khorion IX into tortured, screaming flesh. Mandulis
glimpsed Captain Martel being picked up by the howling wind and thrown into the sky and out of sight, fire
still spitting from his storm bolter.

In the centre of the storm a huge, dark column shot up
from the site of the tower, so tall it punched through the
black clouds overhead. It was a spear of twisted flesh,
something living but never alive, and it was accompanied by a seething chorus of pure madness that tore at
the barriers of Mandulis's mind with such frenzy that
Mandulis, for the first time in his long life, felt a spark of
doubt that he would hold out against the assault.

He crushed that doubt and held his Nemesis sword in both hands, storm bolter forgotten because not even holy bullets could harm something like this.

The eyes of the storm swept over Grand Master Mandulis and suddenly the air was calm, the cacophony of screams clear and horrible, the assault on Mandulis's mind a pure keening.

The true face of the Prince of a Thousand Faces looked down on Mandulis. The grand master of the Grey Knights mouthed a final, silent prayer, and charged.

TWO
TETHYS

ONE THOUSAND YEARS passed. The Imperium endured – men and women died in uncountable numbers to ensure that. Armageddon was lost to the orks. The Damocles Gulf was conquered and strange new species were encountered. The Sabbat Worlds were overrun by Chaos and an immense crusade launched to reclaim them.

Stratix died in screaming plague, Stalinvast in the fiery extremes of the Exterminatus. The Eye of Terror opened and hell poured out through the Cadian Gate. The Inquisition continued to torture itself for the good of mankind, the Adeptus Terra tried to unpick laws and declarations from the will of the Emperor. The warp created new hells outside real space. Whole systems were lost in madness and new ones settled in their hundreds.

There were only two constants in the galaxy. The first was the Imperium's bloody-minded refusal to die beneath the weight of heresy, secession, alien aggression and daemonancy. The second was war – an unending, merciless, and all-consuming tide of warfare that formed the Imperium's bane, function, and salvation.

One thousand years of hatred, one thousand years of war. Enough time for a great many new horrors to rise, and for old ones to be all but forgotten.

WHEN THE FIRST shot had hit, Justicar Alaric had thought of the final days – the days when the Emperor would be whole again, when the heroes of the Imperium and the soldiers of its present would be led into war as one, and the final reckoning would come.

With the second shot, the one that punched through his leg and tore up into his abdomen, he had realised that he was not dead and that the final days would not come for him yet. He remembered red runes winking maddeningly on the back of his eye, telling him that his blood pressure was falling and both his hearts were beating erratically, that two of his lungs had been punctured by the shot to the chest and his abdomen was filling up with blood. He remembered dragging himself into cover as overcharged las-shots ripped into the stone floor beside him.

He remembered the shame as his consciousness drained into a dim grey oblivion, willing his limbs to move so he could loose a last volley of shots against the cultists who had wounded him so badly.

That was what Alaric felt as he awoke again. Shame. It reminded him of how young he was compared to some of the grand masters who had walked the halls of Titan. He had the crystal-pure mental core of a Grey Knight, that was certain, but wrapped around it was a

mind that still had much to learn. Not about fighting
– that knowledge had been sleep-taught to him so
deeply that it had displaced any memory of Alaric's
childhood – but about the great discipline that meant
not even shame, rage, or honour could get in the way
of a grand master's sense of duty to his Emperor.

Alaric was all but submerged in a vat of clear fluid, a
concoction of Titan's apothecaries that helped flesh
heal and kept infections at bay. He felt tubes snaking
all around him, feeding medicines into his veins and
sending information back to the cogitators he could
hear thrumming and clicking away around him. He
was bathed in light coming from lumoglobes arranged
in a circle on the stone ceiling above him. The whole
of the Grey Knight fortress-monastery was carved from
the same dark grey living stone of Titan, snaking deep
beneath the moon's surface in layer upon layer of cells,
chapels, training and instruction halls, medical facilities, parade grounds, armouries and, deepest of all, the
tombs of every Grey Knight who had fallen in battle
during the Chapter's ten thousand year history.

Alaric turned his head to see the brass-cased cogitators quietly spewing sheet after sheet of paper onto
which were scribbled the long, jagged ribbons of his
life signs. The medical facility was one he had been to
before – it was here that he had received the hexagrammic wards that formed a thin lattice of blessed
silver beneath his skin. Medical orderlies were moving
quietly between other recovery tanks and autosurgeon
tables, checking on the patients – some were troops or
other personnel from the Ordo Malleus. Others were
the inhumanly tall and muscular forms of Alaric's fellow Grey Knights. The facility was like a vaulted cellar,
the ceiling low and oppressive, the stone cold and

sweating. The lumoglobes casting pools of light around the patients, surrounded by shadow where cogitators and hygiene servitors hummed gently.

Alaric recognised Brother Tathelon, one arm blown off at the elbow and his body covered in tiny shrapnel scars. Interrogator Iatonn, who had accompanied Inquisitor Nyxos in the assault, lay with his entrails exposed as the dextrous metallic fingers of the auto-surgeon worked to knit his innards back together. Alaric had seen Iatonn fall, a blade plunged through his gut. Nyxos, as far as Alaric knew, had made it out unharmed, but of course Alaric had not seen the final stages of the assault.

One of the orderlies, one of the blank-faced, mind-scrubbed men and women the Ordo Malleus used for menial work, saw Alaric was awake and came to inspect the life signs streaming from the cogitators. Alaric stood up in the tank, pulling electrodes from his skin and needles from his veins. The black carapace, a hard layer beneath the skin of his chest and abdomen, had a large ragged hole in it where the first shot had broken through his armour and Alaric could see through the crystallised wound to the surface of the bony breastplate that had grown together from his ribs. There was another hole, larger, in the meat of his thigh, with a tight channel of internal scar leading up into his abdomen. He could feel the wounds inside him but they were almost healed thanks to his internal augmentations and the Chapter apothecarion. He was covered in smaller scars, burns from where his armour had become red-hot from the weight of las-fire slamming into it, cuts and gouges from shards of ceramite, newly lain over the old scars from previous battle wounds and surgical procedures.

Apothecary Glaivan was hurrying over from the far end of the facility. Glaivan was ancient, one of the few Grey Knights currently in the Chapter who had reached the extended old age a Space Marine's enhancements could grant him. Glaivan's hands had been replaced long ago with bionic armatures that gave him a surgical touch far finer than human hands, with splayed fingers tipped with scalpels and pincers. Grey Knights usually wore their power armour when outside their cells or at worship, but Glaivan had long since left his battlegear behind. Beneath the long white apothecary's robes his body was braced with steel and brass, and his redundant organs had been removed to leave Glaivan a shell of a Marine. His face was long and so heavily lined it was hard to believe there had once been a younger man in there. Glaivan was more than four hundred years old, all but the first handful of those having been spent in service to the Grey Knights and the Ordo Malleus.

'Ah, young justicar,' said Glaivan in a voice lent a faint buzz by his reconstructed throat. 'You heal well. A good thing, borne of willpower. They were high-powered las-burns, justicar, very deep. I am surprised that you are awake so soon, and very little surprises me.'

'I didn't see how it ended,' said Alaric. 'Did we…'

'Seven dead,' said Glaivan with a hint of melancholy. 'Twelve were brought to me here, most will be made well. But yes, Nyxos was successful. Valinov was taken alive, they have him on Mimas.'

Alaric climbed out of the tank, feeling the tightness in his muscles. Alaric had seen Valinov, just as the storm of las-fire had ripped out of the underground temple from the cultists under Valinov's command. He had seen a tall slim man with a sharp face and shaven, tattooed head, barking orders in a foul warp-taught language. His cultists – the mission briefing had suggested several hundred of them in the underground temple complex – were hunched and pallid-skinned, wearing tattered robes of grimy yellow, but they had been well-armed and perfectly willing to die beneath the storm bolters and Nemesis weapons of the Grey Knights. Alaric had been one of the first in, leading the squad he had recently come to command.

Now the assault was over and the survivors were back on Titan.

'How long?' asked Alaric. The orderly handed him a towel and Alaric began to wipe off the fluid – the healing fluid was cold and sticky, and pooled on the cold stone floor around his feet.

'Three months,' replied Glaivan. 'The *Rubicon* made good speed back. They wanted to make sure Valinov was placed in Mimas as soon as possible. That man is pure corruption.' Glaivan spat on the stone floor, and a tiny hygiene servitor scuttled over to clean up the spittle. 'To think. An inquisitor. Radicalism grows ever stronger, I fear.'

It was a measure of the respect in which Glaivan was held that he could voice such concerns freely. The Grey Knights were technically autonomous, but the Ordo Malleus were in practice their masters, and they certainly didn't want the Grey Knights harbouring seditious opinions about the Inquisition. Radicalism was, officially, a non-existent threat, and that was all the Malleus would officially say to the Grey Knights about it.

Alaric sifted through his last memories of the raid – gunfire streaking through grimy underground tunnels, battle-brothers charging in a storm of explosions. If the *Rubicon* had indeed made good speed then Alaric had probably been in Glaivan's care for a couple of weeks. 'Who was lost?'

'Interrogator Iatonn will not survive.' Glaivan glanced sadly at the interrogator's body, opened up beneath the autosurgeon. 'LeMal, Encalion and Baligant died in the assault. Gaignun and Justicar Naimon died on the *Rubicon*, Tolas and Evain in my care.'

'Encalion and Tolas were my men.' Alaric had attained the rank of justicar three years before, and he had lost men before – but he had seen them die. It was part of the bond between Alaric and his squad that they had all shared in the deaths of their battle-brothers, but this time Alaric had not been there.

'I know, justicar. There is a place for them in the vaults. Grand Master Tencendur has decreed they will be interred after your debriefing. I shall tell him you are fit.' Glaivan picked up one of the long sheets of parchment and passed it through his metallic hands, reading the patterns in Alaric's heartbeats and blood pressure. 'I should not say much until Tencendur has had his say, but from Nyxos I hear that your battle-brothers did you proud. When you fell they pressed the attack for revenge instead of faltering in despair. I have seen many leaders in this Chapter and what marks them out is that whatever they do, even falling to the Enemy, they inspire the men who follow them. Your Marines thought you were dead, and they fought on all the harder. Remember that, young justicar, for I feel you shall not remain a mere justicar for much longer.'

Alaric pulled out the last of the needles from his skin. 'I need to get back to my cell,' he said. 'There are rites of contrition for my armour before the artificers can repair it. And I must have missed out on much prayer.'

'Do as you see fit. Soon you will be ready to fight again. Chaplain Durendin is receiving confessions in the Mandulian Chapel and it sounds as if you could use his counsel before debriefing. I shall have the servitors bring you a habit.'

Glaivan waved an order and two of the menial servitors rolled off through the cellars of the apothecarion on their tracks to fetch Alaric some clothing so he could walk through the corridors of Titan with suitable humility. There was a great deal Alaric had to do after any battle, let alone one where he had been both severely wounded and been exposed to potential corruption. He would have to confess, receive purification, have his battlegear repaired and reconsecrated, see his name entered in the immense tomes recording the deeds of the Grey Knights, and be debriefed by Grand Master Tencendur and the inquisitors who had been ultimately responsible for the attack.

The life of a Grey Knight was ritual and purification punctuated by savage combat against the foulest of foes – just a few days of it would break a lesser man, and sometimes Alaric was grateful he could not remember anything else. But this was not the time to skirt the edges of heretical doubt. Valinov was captured and his cult shattered. There was a victory to celebrate, and there were fallen brothers to remember.

INQUISITOR GHOLIC REN-SAR Valinov had been a member of the Ordo Malleus since his recruitment as an interrogator by the late Lord Inquisitor Barbillus.

Barbillus was an old-school inquisitor, the kind of man sculpted into the friezes of Malleus temples and used as exemplars of righteous valour in sermons. Barbillus had worn armour covered in gold filigree depicting daemons crushed beneath the Emperor's feet and wielded a power hammer with a head carved from meteoric iron. He had ridden his war pulpit into the deepest pits of daemonic horror. He was a soldier, a fighter, a smiter of the foul and a scourge of the heretic. When the citizens of the Imperium heard rumours of the Imperium's secret defenders in the Inquisition, they imagined men like Barbillus.

Barbillus had an extensive staff, mostly of warriors who rode with him into battle, recruited from martial cultures all over the Imperium. But he also needed people to get him to the battlefield. Investigators. Interviewers. Scientists. Some of Barbillus's rear echelon staff went deep undercover for him, infiltrating noble houses suspected of daemonancy or vicious hive-scum gangs sponsored by hidden cultist cells. They were disposable and exposed, both to the violence that would follow discovery and the madness that could result from seeing too much of the Enemy. They did what they did because it was their way to join the fight against Chaos.

Very few of them survived to advance in Barbillus's private army. One of them was Gholic Ren-Sar Valinov.

The Ordo Malleus's records of Valinov's origins were patchy, mainly because he erased or altered most of the information held about him in Inquisition archives. He came from the Segmentum Solar, that was certain, from one of the massively industrialised worlds of the Imperium's heartland where only the sharpest and most ruthless could hope to gain recognition from off-world.

His birthplace was not recorded but Barbillus recruited him during a spectacular purge of the debauched naval aristocracy on Rhanna.

There were some suggestions that Valinov's position in the Administratum on Rhanna gave him access to the statistical information that, in the right hands, led Barbillus to cells of sorcerers and pleasure-seekers in the planet's nobility. Other inquisitors had been adamant that Valinov's skills could only have been honed in the Adeptus Arbites, or the Planetary Defence Force, or even the criminal gangs that ruled huge swathes of Rhanna's underhive. But Valinov's most useful skills were clear from the start – he was an arch manipulator of people, capable of flattery and coercion alike. He could draw the most sensitive information out of the wariest suspects.

Valinov was just the man for Barbillus's rear echelon staff, joining noble families or wealthy guilds or criminal cartels to hunt down sources of heresy and forbidden magic. Over six years, Valinov's work led Barbillus to the heart of K'Sharr the Butcher's criminal empire, the hidden cults that had seeded the dockyard world of Talshen III with heretics, the savage pre-Imperial human tribes of Gerentulan Minor, and a dozen other pits of corruption. He was good. Barbillus saw promise in Valinov and marked him out as senior interrogator. It was expected that Valinov would become Barbillus's advisor, coming out of the Imperium's underworld to ride at Barbillus's side.

Then came Agnarsson's Hold. If Barbillus did not die fighting the Daemon Prince Malygrymm the Bloodstained on that planet then he certainly died when the Exterminatus was brought to bear. It was not the first time Barbillus had ordered the death of a world. This time it was his personal staff who launched the cyclonic torpedoes from Barbillus's fleet of warships, having been ordered by Barbillus to destroy Agnarsson's Hold if he didn't return from the daemon-infested surface. Senior Interrogator Valinov had watched from Barbillus's flagship as the verdant agri-world was swallowed up by the magma welling up from its ruptured crust. Malygrymm was destroyed, but Barbillus never returned to his ship.

Temples were built in the name of Lord Inquisitor Barbillus. Statues of him, grim-faced and battered, invariably smiting some indistinct horror with his ensorcelled hammer, adorned Inquisitorial fortresses throughout the Segmentum Solar and beyond. His name was inscribed on the wall of the Hall of Heroes in the Imperial palace and written in the pages of Imperial history.

The Inquisition's files were clear on how Barbillus's staff and resources passed into the control of the Grand Conclave of the Ordo Malleus, and how Valinov served a second apprenticeship with a dozen inquisitors. No records remained, however, to indicate under what circumstances Valinov was recognised by the Ordo Malleus as an inquisitor in his own right, though doubtless it happened. He was active somewhere near Thracian Primaris during the brutal campaigns around the Eye of Terror, and probably played a part in the subjugation of Chaos-infected species discovered during the tail-end of the Damocles Crusade. But there were no details. Valinov had been thorough. Probably he had turned by then, and would have covered his tracks as he went in case another inquisitor found clues of his changing allegiances.

There was almost no information at all about Valinov's biggest mission. He went to the hive world of V'Run with a division of storm troopers from the Lastrati 79th, a coven of sanctioned psykers from the Scholastica Psykana and a squadron of Sword class escort starships. He was officially following up reports of a devolution cult that ruled large swathes of V'Run's underhive and ash wastelands, but afterwards it was concluded that Valinov had created the threat to give him an excuse to intercede.

All that was known about the V'Run mission was that two weeks after Valinov arrived the planet was swallowed up by a boiling, lightning-scattered veil of incandescent stellar cloud, a warp storm so localised and complete that it could only have been deliberately created. The hive world was drowned in the nightmare dimension of the warp. The storm was impenetrable and no one could be sure what happened to the nineteen billion men, women and children who made up the population of V'Run, but astropaths reported hearing screams emanating from the planet for light years around.

Valinov left a trail of atrocity across the Segmentum Solar. He immolated the capital of Port St Indra by overloading the city's heatsinks. Chaos-worshipping pirate ships wiped out a pilgrim convoy off the Nememean Cloud and named Valinov as their leader. As if desperate to commit depredations in the name of Chaos, Valinov wreaked indiscriminate havoc. The Ordo Malleus had by now deployed several inquisitors to trail him and anticipate his next moves, and they tracked him to the plague-stricken communities of the Gaolven Belt. Valinov had joined up with a cult formed from plague survivors who believed they owed their survival to the pantheon of Chaos, and welded them in a matter of weeks into a well-armed and fanatically motivated army manning a fortified asteroid.

The Ordo Malleus concluded that Valinov was preparing for a last stand. If that was what he wanted, then that was what they would give him. The Conclave approached Grand Master Tencendur, and he agreed to send a force of Grey Knights to spearhead the assault on Valinov's fortress.

The first man out of the boarding torpedoes and into the breach had been Justicar Alaric.

THE MANDULIAN CHAPEL was a long gallery with a dizzyingly high ceiling, thick with columns and with statues in niches running along the walls. To reach the huge, three-panelled altar at the front of the chapel, a Grey Knight had to walk past the unwavering stone eyes of hundreds of Imperial heroes. Some of them were legends, some had been forgotten, and they represented every part of the web of organisations that kept the Imperium together. Closest to the altar was the statue of Grand Master Mandulis himself, who had died a thousand years before – his figure was carved into one of the pillars as if he were holding up the chapel's ceiling.

The message was clear. Mandulis, like every Grey Knight, kept the Imperium from collapsing.

Alaric walked down the centre aisle, the filters built into his nose and throat picking out particles of incense that billowed from censers high up in the shadows by the ceiling. Flickering candles ringed the columns and were tended by a tiny servitor that hummed through the nave lighting extinguished wicks. The faltering light glinted off the gold on the altar, wrought by Chapter artisans three hundred years before. The centre image depicted the Emperor in the days before the Horus Heresy, his face turned away as if in recognition of his near-death in the closing days of the Heresy. The scene was flanked by scenes of Grey Knights – not crushing daemons or heretics but kneeling, their arms laid down. It was an image of humility that formed the centrepiece of the Chapel to remind the Grey Knights that no matter how strong they were, they could only prevail with the will of the Emperor.

Alaric had not yet had his battle-gear returned by the artificers and so he wore a simple black and grey habit. He felt naked in that place of worship, his bare feet against stone worn smooth by centuries of armoured boots. His wounds still hurt and he could feel the channel of rapidly healing scar tissue where the las-bolt had burned through his abdomen. His skin felt raw from the healing tank. But worse, the idea of helplessness was hot and angry in his mind. He had not been there when his battle-brothers died.

Chaplain Durendin was waiting in the otherwise empty chapel. The chaplain wore his enormous suit of Terminator armour as he always did when he was seeing to the Chapter's spiritual health. One arm was painted a glossy black to signify his office as chaplain and the rest was the traditional gunmetal grey. Durendin wore the same pair of ornate lightning claws that had been passed down since the Chapter's earliest days.

Alaric reached the altar where Durendin stood, and quickly kneeled before the chaplain. Then both men kneeled to the Emperor's image on the altar.

'Tencendur told me you would wish to see me,' said Durendin as they stood again. The chaplain's face was mostly obscured by the cowl he wore, and like any good chaplain he was a difficult man to read.

'You know what happened, chaplain. I was wounded and unconscious. Encalion and Tolas died. I have lost men before, but I was always at their side. I wasn't there this time.'

'I will not absolve you of those deaths, justicar. Every one of us must accept responsibility for the deaths of our battle-brothers. You have not been a justicar long, Alaric. You clearly have capacity to lead but you have only taken a few steps on the path.'

'That is what worries me, chaplain. I have never felt this doubt. Everything I have learned as a Grey Knight has told me that once the core of faith is breached then I am worth nothing as a warrior.'

'And you think that if you cannot forget that feeling of helplessness you felt when Valinov's men shot you down, you cannot trust the purity of your soul?' Durendin turned and somewhere under that cowl he stared deep into Alaric's spirit. 'Remember it, Alaric. Remember what it means to be broken and laid low. The mark of a leader is not whether you can avoid such misfortune, but whether you can take it and turn it into something that makes you stronger. Your battle-brothers are dead, but you can ensure their lives had meaning. That is what it means to lead.'

'I knew it would not be easy, chaplain,' said Alaric, 'but the size of the task has never been more obvious. I know that this will not be the first test, and certainly not the hardest. I am only just beginning to really understand the sacrifices the grand masters must have made for the Knights to follow them. Their faith must be absolute. I do not think there is a higher aim in the

Imperium than to be trusted as a grand master by the Grey Knights.'

'But you can do it?'

Alaric paused. He looked at the slices of polished red gemstones that made up the armour of the gilded Emperor, at the shadows covering the ceiling far above, and at the figure of Mandulis holding up the Imperium on his own. 'Yes. Yes I can.'

'That is the difference, Alaric. You cannot believe anything else. What you call doubt is the pain of learning a hard lesson. That you learned it at all proves what the Chapter has always thought about you. You have curiosity and intelligence, and at the same time the trust of your men. You represent a rare combination of qualities that means you will never be satisfied until you see your duty done at the highest level.'

Alaric stood and bowed quickly to the gilded Emperor. 'Tencendur will be waiting for me, chaplain. I will think about what you have told me.'

'You may not have that luxury, justicar,' said Durendin as Alaric turned to leave. 'Given what was found at the Gaolven Belt, catching Valinov may have been just the first step.'

THE ORDO MALLEUS had taken the rings of Saturn shortly after the inception of the Inquisition, and had turned them into its own unofficial domain. The lord inquisitors of the Ordo Malleus ruled Saturn's moons absolutely, because that was the only way they could ensure the security of their facilities. The Malleus controlled some of the most dangerous artefacts, texts, and people in the galaxy. The immensely complicated geometry of Saturn's rings means it was all but impossible for any enemy force to penetrate the thousands of turbo-laser defences that bristled from asteroids captured by Saturn's gravity. The ordo controlled the only reliable way in and out of the rings, the naval fortress on the outermost major moon Iapetus.

Mimas, the closest major moon to the vast swirling mass of Saturn, was disfigured by an immense impact scar covering a quarter of the surface. Built into that crater was the Inquisitorial prison where the worst of the worst were held in complexes of isolated cells with psychic wards woven into the walls, guarded by gun-servitors and a regiment of Ordo Malleus storm troopers.

Encaladus, the next moon out from Mimas, housed the Inquisitorial citadel, a vast and imposing palace where the lord inquisitors of the Ordo Malleus held court and the most senior of the ordo's inquisitors maintained personal estates.

Tethys was the location of the Librarium Daemonicum, the repository of dangerous knowledge gathered over thousands of years of fighting the darkness. The Librarium was completely hidden from the surface – thousands of void-safe cells and galleries of crammed bookshelves filled a sphere hollowed out of the moon's core. Untold millions of tomes, data-slates, scrolls and pict-recordings were refrigerated to preserve delicate pages and unstable datacores. Access to them was given only on the authority of the lord inquisitors themselves, and the more restricted sectors formed some of the most sensitive locations in the galaxy.

Titan, the largest moon, concealed beneath its thick orange atmosphere the immense fortress-monastery of the Grey Knights, covering the surface as if the whole moon had been carved with a pattern of towers and battlements.

The docks of Iapetus, the furthermost major moon, extended kilometres out into space and were always hosts to whole roosts of cruisers, escorts and battleships, including the strike fleet of the Grey Knights and enormous Imperator class battleships requisitioned from the Battlefleet Solar.

It was only by controlling this miniature empire that the Ordo Malleus could ensure the safety of the terrible knowledge it collected and the dangerous individuals it captured and imprisoned. It was this security that meant Valinov's possessions could be isolated and contained. It was here that Inquisitor Briseis Ligeia could examine them properly.

A THIN, PALE blue-grey light filled the research floor, weakly illuminating the reams of books and dataslates that filled shelves lining walls one hundred metres high. Spider-like archiver servitors scurried up the walls on thin metal legs, the fleshy once-human parts scanning book spines and labels for the Malleus research staff who spent their lives poring over ancient texts for their Inquisitorial masters. Many higher-ranking Malleus inquisitors had a personal researcher or two on Tethys, whose sole purpose in life was to find obscure and potentially vital information on the enemies of the Emperor.

The many floors suspended between the immense cliffs of bookshelves were mostly empty. A few pale, large-eyed researchers were hunched over crumbling tomes, gun-servitors hovering over their shoulders in case the knowledge they were exposed to overcame their minds. Their breath coiled in the air and they all wore close-fitting thermosuits; the temperature was kept too low for a human to survive more than a few minutes.

Inquisitor Ligeia preferred it when it was quiet. It gave her more room to think. A tiny guide-servitor droned on ahead of her, weaving through the various workstations and down a couple of flights of steps to where Valinov's possessions had been assembled for her. Ligeia wore bulky furs and an overcloak trimmed in ermine – she affected the clothing of an extravagant Imperial noble because that was who she was, or at least had been. She wore rings outside her tharrhide gloves and her boots were of the finest pygmy grox leather. She had been pretty once, but that was a long time ago and life had hardened her soul enough for it to show on her face. She was still imposing, and she liked the fact that people would react to her appearance first. It meant that she would be underestimated – a fact that had saved her many times.

Ligeia was not a born fighter, although she had seen her fair share of scrapes. She was an investigator, a scholar, schooled by the best institutions noble money could afford. The Ordo Hereticus had taken her directly from the nobility of Gathalamor, finding that her skills with information overcame the unease some of them felt at her growing psychic abilities. The Ordo Malleus had headhunted her because of her facility with ancient or cryptic texts. She had stayed, becoming a more and more valued assistant to various Malleus inquisitors until she had attained the rank herself, all the time honing her psychic power. The Ordo Malleus were mostly typically bull-headed deamonhunters with weapons and armour to rival the Grey Knights themselves, charging into battle with the unholy, but Ligeia's weapon was knowledge. A psychic Malleus inquisitor was supposed to hurl bolts of lightning or banish daemons with a word, but Ligeia's powers were geared towards understanding and perception.

Without Ligeia, untold atrocities would have unfolded without the Ordo Malleus even suspecting them. Perhaps Valinov was planning something that would not be stopped with his capture.

Ligeia took a seat and the guide-servitor flitted off again. No gun-servitor approached, because one of the privileges of Ligeia's office was the trust the lord inquisitors placed in her willpower. A suppressor field she carried switched off the defences in her immediate vicinity, so the signature of her psychic abilities would not bring sentry guns out of the walls. In front of her were lain the items found in Valinov's personal chambers and upon his person when he was captured, much of it still bloodstained or scorched by bolter rounds. Valinov's clothes, deep red robes extravagantly trimmed with silver, had a large ragged hole in one arm. Ligeia remembered from the briefing that Valinov had been wounded. It was a measure of his strength that he had survived the shock of a bolter round against unarmoured flesh. All these items had been assembled by the research staff at her request, in the condition that they had been found on Valinov's asteroid.

Valinov had been armed with a custom hunting las, a holdover from when he worked within the auspices of the Ordo Malleus. It was a beautiful weapon, the casings and barrel enamelled in deep blood red with the details picked out in gold. The power pack was similarly custom-built and was heavily overcharged going by the scorching on the barrel. Valinov had carried a wrackblade, too, a sneaky little weapon that looked like a combat knife but hid a neurowhip processor. The same blade had turned Interrogator Iatonn's entrails to mush. All very expensive and very rare.

Ligeia ignored the weapons. They had been checked by psyker séance and were free of any taint. What interested Ligeia were the documents. There were a couple of data-slates, a handful of scrolls tied with what looked like lengths of sinew, and a large book. The data-slates were schedules and inventories for the fortress – they indicated how well Valinov had organised what amounted to a benighted band of fanatics, but little else.

The scrolls looked more interesting. They were covered in cryptic messages in cramped handwriting, complex diagrams of pantheons or magic spells, transcriptions of chants and descriptions of ceremonies. Ligeia held her hand over the tattered parchment and let her perception bleed out of the inside of her head and down into the paper, weaving around not just the shape of the letters and diagrams but the meaning that infused them. She had discovered the power while in the schola back on Gathalamor when she was still a child, and though the Sisters who taught her had told her it was witchery she had been lucky to be recognised not as a threat but as a strong and useful psyker. It was one of the paradoxes at the heart of the Imperium: the Imperium was terrified of psykers, men and women whose powers touched the warp and formed a bridge for dark things to come through into real space; but it also depended on psykers, like the astropaths who transmitted telepathic messages or psychic inquisitors like herself who did with their minds what no man could do with weapons.

The meaning on the scrolls was a faint, flitting thing, vague and frustrating. Ligeia suspected it might be some complicated code but the deeper she reached the more she came across a barrier of meaninglessness. The scrolls meant nothing. Their only purpose was to look impressive. True rituals of the Chaos gods would have lit up her psychic perception like fireworks.

Though Ligeia spent some time examining them to be sure, she quickly came to the conclusion that the scrolls were meaningless. Valinov had probably faked them up to give to his cultists and make them think they were doing the work of the dark gods. It meant they were not ready for Valinov to introduce them to the true worship of Chaos. Probably he never would have taken them that far – they were just bolter fodder, men he could manipulate into dying instead of him. And they had died, every one of them.

Ligeia left the scrolls and pulled the book towards her. It was old and all but ruined with damp and mould. The pages were thick parchment but the bindings were ragged – Ligeia guessed that the volume had been rebound several times. There was no title. If there had been one previously, it had disappeared as the original binding peeled off.

Ligeia carefully opened the book. Even with her perception withdrawn it tingled her fingers when she touched it, as if its meaning was struggling to get out and be understood. Archaic High Gothic covered the page in front of her.

Codicium Aeternum.

Beneath the title were written lines in an elegant hand by some transcriber-servitor hundreds of years ago.

Being a full and faithful account of the deaths of Dae-mons, Monstrous Prodigies and the Lords of Darkness, and accompanying extrapolations of their return from Banish-ment.

The seal of the Ordo Malleus was emblazoned below.

Ligeia caught her breath. This was something she genuinely had not expected. She leafed through a few of the pages. Monstrous names looked back at her. She recognised the name of Angron, the Daemon Primarch who had once been banished from the material realm in the first Battle for Armageddon. She saw Cherubael and Doombreed, N'Kari and hundreds of others, with the dates and predicted durations of their banishments noted beside. Some of those names alone would have corrupted lesser minds.

The *Codicium Aeternum*. By the Throne, if it was real...

It had last been seen in these very halls decades before. It had been thought simply lost, hidden some-where in the bowels of Tethys where it had become a victim of the secrecy supposed to keep it secret. Many volumes had slipped through the gaps like that, and the Malleus had specialised knowledge hunter squads who roamed the lower recesses finding vital texts that had previously been forgotten. But that had not hap-pened to this book – Valinov must have stolen it from the Ordo Malleus's collection when he was still in the employ of Inquisitor Barbillus, earlier than any of the signs of his corruption. He must have been working towards some terrible plan for longer than the Malleus suspected. The *Codicium Aeternum* was one of the most valuable reference works the Malleus possessed, listing thousands of daemons banished by the Grey Knights or the Inquisition. Emperor only knew what Valinov had meant to do with it.

Ligeia stood and waved over the guide servitor, which was hovering at a polite distance.

'Ligeia to Librarium command. We have a sensitive text, possible moral threat. Send down a containment team and let the Conclave know it's the *Codicium Aeternum*. Ligeia out.'

The servitor thrummed off carrying Ligeia's message to the Librarium's overseers. They would know how to contain and secure a book of such power and value. As Ligeia turned back to the table she noticed that the book had fallen open at a seemingly random page, stained with age and damp, and barely legible. One word, one name, jumped out at her, scratched in red ink by an elegant, looping hand.

Ghargatuloth.

THREE
TITAN

The gathering was called in the Fallen Dagger Hall where Grand Master Kolgano, centuries before, challenged the Grey Knights under his command to an unarmoured dagger duel and promised his jewel-encrusted Terminator armour to anyone who could beat him. Kolgano was long gone, buried with his fighting dagger deep in the heart of Titan's catacombs, but the hall remained lofty and echoing.

It was used for drills, close combat training for newer recruits and sometimes, as now, for meetings between the Ordo Malleus and the Grey Knights.

A large round table of dark hardwood stood in the centre of the hall, flanked by rings of Malleus storm troopers in parade dress, their faces hidden by silvered masks. Inquisitor Nyxos attended most official functions with this silent, sinister honour guard, their faces never shown. He sat at the table flanked by two

49

standing advisors, one an astropath of almost impossible age, the other a brilliant young woman rumoured to have been poached from the finest officer academy of the Imperial Navy. Nyxos himself was an old leathery warrior, wearing simple black that served to flaunt the silver-plated brackets and servo mounts that lent his frail old body immense strength and speed. His bald, liver-spotted head jutted forward like a hawk's, sharp little eyes always scanning for prey.

At Nyxos's side sat Inquisitor Ligeia in impressive noble regalia, looking more like an elegant family matriarch at a society ball than a hunter of daemons. She carried the mouldering *Codicium Aeternum* in a small portable void-safe to keep its delicate pages from crumbling.

Grand Master Tencendur entered, wearing his customised Terminator armour. He had removed his helmet, revealing a face with a broad, strong jaw and plenty of frown lines. He was accompanied by his own squad of Terminators and by Justicar Alaric, reunited with his repaired wargear and walking behind the squad.

Alaric had been fully debriefed by Tencendur and had briefly spoken with his squad. They had begun the process of mourning for their fallen battle-brothers. Encalion and Tolas had been allotted niches in the catacombs of Titan where their bodies would rest, shrouded until the time came for the Emperor's servants to join him once more. Brother Lykkos was undergoing intensive training with the psycannon that Tolas had once carried. The other Marines would carry their battle-brothers in the funeral parade, and Alaric would have to speak in their remembrance. He had spoken for fallen brothers before, but this time would be harder than the others.

In time, new recruits would be picked to join Alaric's squad, and eventually they would replace the fallen. But that would not happen soon. Until then Squad Alaric would be two men short as a reminder of the threats they had always to face.

'Grand master,' said Nyxos, rising from his seat in respect. His servos whirred slightly. 'My apologies for the short notice. Many protocols had to be waived.'

'I understand that sensitive material was recovered from Valinov's possessions,' said Tencendur, his voice inhumanly deep and gravelly thanks to the ruinous throat wound that had nearly killed him back when he had been a justicar. 'Were it not suitably important I am sure you would not have asked to meet me here at all.'

Nyxos indicated Ligeia, who placed the book on the table and pushed it towards Tencendur. She ran her thumb along the gene-lock and the void-safe snapped open, revealing the mould-blotched cover of the *Codicium Aeternum*. The grand master walked up to the table and reached over, picking up the book in his surprisingly dextrous gauntlets and turning over the cover carefully. He read the title off the first page.

'We believe Valinov stole it before his treachery became obvious,' said Nyxos as Tencendur leafed through the stained pages. 'In itself it is not dangerous, hence we can remove it from the protections of the Librarium. But the information it contains is of a most disturbing nature considering it was possessed by a Radical.'

'Do you know why he stole it?'

'Valinov has not yet told our interrogators anything,' said Nyxos. 'Mimas has the best excruciators in the ordo and he may crack in time, but that will not happen overnight. We can make some guesses, however. Ligeia?'

'The *Codicium*,' began Ligeia in a knowing, upper-class voice that contrasted with the hard-bitten growls of her fellow daemonhunters, 'contains the names of many thousands of daemons along with descriptions and dates of their banishments. As beings of pure energy many of them cannot be permanently destroyed, only sent back to the warp until they can re-form; we believe the *Codicium* was first compiled in an attempt to systematically monitor their returns. Of course, the ways of Chaos are anything but systematic but the authors were thorough, at first. Many of the entries are incomplete or damaged but there is one in particular that I have determined was of particular interest to Valinov.'

Ligeia had placed a marker between two of the pages. Tencendur opened the book to the right page and stopped.

'Ghargatuloth,' he said simply.

'Ghargatuloth,' repeated Ligeia, 'was banished from the material realm a thousand years ago on Khorion IX by Grand Master Mandulis.'

'And he was banished,' said Tencendur as he read, 'for a thousand years.'

'You understand why we thought this was of such importance,' said Nyxos.

Tencendur closed the book and placed it back on the table. 'What do you need?'

Nyxos consulted a data-slate handed to him by his advisor. 'We all know what is happening at Cadia, Grand Master. The Eye of Terror has opened and Cadia could fall. The ordo needs me there to conduct

interrogators still operating on Chaos-controlled territory, so I cannot lead a response myself. Inquisitor
Ligeia will have authority over this operation. On her
behalf I am requesting that you assemble a Grey
Knights strike force with all possible haste for her to
use as she sees fit in investigating the possibilities this
information suggests.'

Tencendur did not look impressed. He glanced at
Ligeia. 'The galaxy is a large place, inquisitor. Do you
know where Ghargatuloth will return? Khorion IX was
destroyed by exterminatus.'

'We have an idea,' said Ligeia. 'The Emperor's Tarot
consulted at the time along with visions suffered by
astropaths in the vicinity of Khorion IX suggested that
Ghargatuloth would return somewhere in the Trail of
St Evisser.'

'How certain are these predictions?'

'They were recorded in the *Codicium* at the time.
They are the most certain we have.' Ligeia's voice was
admirably level as she indicated the final paragraphs of
Ghargatuloth's entry in the book. The Trail of St
Evisser was a set of systems to the galactic east of the
Segmentum Solar, linked by association with an Impe-
rial saint. Tencendur didn't recognise the name – the
Imperium was a vast place and it had more than
enough near-forgotten corners for Chaos to hide.

Tencendur shook his head and pushed the book
back across the table. 'Not good enough, not if this is
all you have to go on. You have said so yourself, Nyxos,
the Eye has opened and we may all be called upon to
stem the tide. We have companies on their way to
Cadia already and I will soon be among them. I cannot conscience ignoring such a duty to follow your
guesswork. Valinov could have taken the book for any

reason. He could have stolen it out of spite, to test our defences, for the challenge. And even if he was hoping to bring Ghargatuloth back, we have him locked up on Mimas where he will be tried, broken and executed.'

'Do you know,' said Ligeia calmly, 'what Ghargatuloth was?'

Tencendur bristled. Alaric imagined he was not used to being talked back to, even by an inquisitor. 'Of course. A daemon prince.'

'It took the Ordo Malleus more than a hundred years to find out its name. Not even its truename, just the name it used to create cults all over the Imperium. Then it took decades to track it to Khorion IX and when they finally cornered it, they sent three hundred Grey Knights to banish it. Not one of them came back. Mandulis was the only one we were even able to bury. If Ghargatuloth is to return, he will need help. He could still influence the weak-willed from the warp but until they can bring him fully into real space he will be comparatively vulnerable. It will be the only chance we have to strike at him before he becomes too great for us to deal with. The ordo tried to count how many citizens died as a result of Ghargatuloth's cults but the even the logistitian's corps couldn't come up with a number. If there is a way we can stop that then we must take it. I will go alone if I have to, but I have a duty to the Imperium and it will be fulfilled.'

Tencendur paused. 'I cannot lead them. The other grand masters are needed elsewhere, as are our force commanders. I can spare you a small taskforce but officers…'

'That is why I asked for Justicar Alaric to attend,' said Ligeia, looking suddenly at Alaric. 'I understand you cannot spare battle-leaders. Justicar Alaric has distinguished himself and, as the first into Valinov's fortress, was there from the beginning. Alaric and his squad, a Terminator assault unit, two more tactical squads and the *Rubicon*. I know it is still a great deal to ask when the Enemy is pouring from the Eye, but you understand that the possibility of Ghargatuloth's return means I cannot ask for anything less.'

'If Valinov's interrogations reveal...'

'Grand master, Ghargatuloth will already be calling to his followers. In four months he will have been banished for a full thousand years and he will be able to create new cults and instruct them in drawing him into real space. Valinov will take too long to break. We must go now.'

Tencendur turned to Alaric. 'Justicar?'

Alaric had not expected this. He still had the feeling he had failed at the Gaolven Belt, and he could still feel the wounds that had nearly killed him. Durendin had told him how far he had to go before he could be trusted to be a leader of the Grey Knights, and now he was being asked to join Ligeia on a mission she evidently believed was vastly important. For a moment, he floundered. Should he refuse? A servant of the Emperor should show honesty where he had doubts about being able to fulfil his duty. But if he didn't go, who else would? What Tencendur said was true – the Eye of Terror would soon be using most of the Grey Knights' resources and all of the senior brother-captains and grand masters would need to be there.

Alaric walked over to the table and picked up the *Codicium Aeternum*. It was heavy and decaying. Daemon's names marched across its pages, foul and terrible names along with descriptions of their atrocities and the circumstances of their banishment.

Ghargatuloth's entry took up several pages – the Prince of a Thousand Faces created benighted cults all over the Imperium, each distinct and ignorant of the others, each working towards grand plans of atrocity that only became visible as their final horrific moments were played out.

A daemon's banishment was a complicated concept. The strength of the daemon, the method of banishment and sheer luck determined how long the daemon would have to languish in the warp. Mandulis must have dealt Ghargatuloth a fell blow indeed to banish the daemon for a thousand years. The *Codicium Aeternum* had been written in an attempt to catalogue all those factors and predict accurately when and where daemons would return, but Chaos by its very nature refused to be categorised so neatly and the book had been left half-finished – but not before Ghargatuloth's return had been predicted.

If Cadia fell, a spearhead of pure Chaos could punch deep into the Segmentum Solar. The Grey Knights, the only soldiers who could face Warmaster Abaddon's daemonic allies, would be needed there. But if the Grey Knights were all deployed at the Eye, and something terrible arose to strike at the Imperium's undefended underbelly…

It was Valinov who had taken the book. Valinov had openly rebelled against the ordo after taking the book from the Librarium. Had Ghargatuloth been the source of all his depravities? Was Valinov laughing at them from Mimas, knowing he had already set something in motion at the Trail of St Evisser that could strike when the Imperium was at is weakest?

'You have my squad,' said Alaric. 'Valinov has caused them to mourn. Tancred was there, too. For the other squads I would recommend Justicars Genhain and Santoro, they were both in the force that hit the fortress from the sunward side.'

'You will be on your own, justicar,' said Tencendur. 'I can vouch for your command but in battle there will be no one else.'

'I trust the judgement of the Inquisition.'

Tencendur nodded at his command squad to leave with him. 'You have the *Rubicon*. It will be made ready for launch at Iapetus within twelve hours. I release you into the authority of Inquisitor Ligeia. For the Throne, justicar.'

'For the Throne, grand master,' said Alaric with a bow of the head.

Tencendur left, his boots and the boots of his squad ringing off the stone floor and echoing grandly around the Fallen Dagger Hall. Inquisitor Nyxos left in the opposite direction, followed by his silent advisors and honour guard, the servos of his body bracings sighing as he walked.

'You are psychic,' said Alaric as Ligeia gathered up the book and stood up from her chair. 'The wards react to it.'

Ligeia smiled. 'I have seen my fellow inquisitors throw lightning bolts. I am afraid I can manage nothing so grand as that. I deal in knowledge, I am a scholar. And yourself?'

'All Grey Knights have some psychic capacity. I am strong enough for it to be a part of my conditioning but not to focus it. You knew that already, inquisitor.'

'Of course. I also know you are curious and intelligent, and you have an imagination. Those are qualities I value. You are also a born leader, even if the grand masters would rather watch you earn your stripes for a decade or two. You can lead your Marines when we need to fight and defer to me when we need to learn. We will have to do both, I fear, if I am right about Ghargatuloth.'

Ligeia turned elegantly and walked away, her long ermine-trimmed dress sweeping along behind her.

She had known he would agree to lead her strike-force. She must have realised Alaric would want another go at Valinov, even if only to thwart whatever plan he had set in motion. Alaric had learned that was how inquisitors thought – people, whether Grey Knights or Imperial citizens or even other inquisitors, were weapons to be manoeuvred into position and let loose on whatever enemy it would be most expedient to destroy. He understood that was the only way the complex, monolithic Imperium could be manipulated into providing what an inquisitor needed to fight the enemies of humanity. But that didn't mean he had to enjoy being a part of it.

GHOLIC REN-SAR VALINOV was naked and bound, with shackles around his wrists and ankles. There was a metal collar around his neck packed with explosives that would neatly blow his head off if he left the inter-rogation cell, attempted to use psychic powers (although Valinov had never shown any measurable psychic capacity) or simply angered the supervising interrogator enough for the collar's detonator to be pushed. The cell around him was of plain obsidian flecked with white, smooth and unforgiving in the harsh light stabbing down from the bright lumosphere set into the ceiling. He sat on a metal chair in the middle of the otherwise unfurnished room. In spite of it all, he still looked dangerous. His body was hard-muscled, not big but strong. His skin was covered in scars too regular to be solely the result of the many wounds he had received in his career. Abstract tattoos covered the sides of his abdomen, curving up in thick dark blue bands over his back and shoulders to form a broad collar over his throat and lower chest like the clasp of a cloak, snaking over his scalp.

His face was sharp and alert. He had expressive, knowing eyes set into a thin hatchet of a face. His hair was shaved back brutally and his ears had been so full of rings that with all the decoration taken out they looked ragged and chewed.

Alaric waited from the monitoring station on the other side of the stone wall, watching images relayed from pict-stealers in the corners of the cell. The room was lit only by the light from the screens, casting a silvery light on the faces of the supervising interrogation staff. The prison on Mimas was staffed by men and women who had been totally mind-scrubbed and then given an education consisting of nothing but security protocols, interrogation techniques and utter hatred of the inmates. They were at a reduced risk of corruption because there was less of a mind to be corrupted.

The supervisor leaned over to a microphone jutting from the console in front of her. 'Confirm secure. You may begin, inquisitor.'

The stone door of the cell ground open. A servitor trundled in and placed a chair opposite Valinov, then left the room. Inquisitor Ligeia walked in and sat in the chair. Alaric saw she had toned down her clothing from her full regalia. Now she looked like a military officer in a dark and severe uniform, with just enough ornamentation to convey high rank.

Valinov looked up at her. Alaric could just detect a slight smile in his eyes. The same expression he had seen when Valinov stabbed Iatonn through the gut. Ligeia was carrying a thick file of papers and she opened it out on her lap, making a show of reading from one of the many files the Inquisition had on Valinov.

'Gholic Ren-Sar Valinov,' began Ligeia curtly, 'you are charged with heresy first class, grand treachery, daemonancy, warpcraft and association with persons identified as a moral threat. You will be aware that each of these charges is of such severity that no possibility of innocence can be accepted, and that each is punishable with death.'

'So,' said Valinov in that slick, smooth voice. 'You're going to kill me five times?'

Ligeia looked up at him. 'That was the plan, yes.'

Valinov said nothing.

'You have been away for some time, Valinov. You probably don't know the changes to our procedure. It's complicated, but ultimately, the office of executions has acquired a psyker who can keep you alive, even though you are dead. The Adeptus Astra Telepathica trained him up and they owed the ordo a favour, hence your impending five death sentences. I must confess, I find it difficult to imagine what it will be like for you to remain conscious while your body begins to rot.' This time Ligeia smiled faintly. 'But then I suppose you have a better imagination than I.'

At first, Ligeia was nothing but official. She stated simply the particulars of Valinov's various crimes and the authority by which he was condemned. Alaric knew them all already – the Conclave of the Ordo Malleus on Enceladus had already decided what Valinov was guilty of and what would be done to him. Every now and then Ligeia would try to flatter Valinov, such as pretending to be surprised at the speed with which he organised the cultists on the Gaolven Belt. Other times she would try to goad him into boasting about what he had done, by expressing ill-disguised disgust at his ability to kill from a distance without remorse. Valinov saw past these ruses easily – but Alaric imagined that was the point. It was a game. Valinov had played with all his interrogators, and Ligeia was playing along in the hope that Valinov would get comfortable enough running rings around her to let something important slip.

Ligeia was good, Alaric thought. But he still suspected that Valinov was better.

'I remember you,' said Valinov suddenly in a low, dangerous voice, cutting off Ligeia in mid-sentence. Alaric saw the interrogator nodding slightly to one of her underlings, whose finger hovered over the collar detonator.

'They brought you over from the Ordo Hereticus,' continued Valinov. 'That doesn't happen very often. They must have thought you had some steel in you, but it looks like they were short-changed. Do these threats work on petty witches and governors who don't pay up? Do you think an inquisitor of the Ordo Malleus will break so easily? I have seen Chaos, little girl, from both sides. You can do nothing to me.'

Ligeia didn't waver. 'Perhaps I have not made myself clear. We will make you suffer, Valinov. You have never had access to the most sensitive of the ordo's procedures. If you resist we can show you if you wish.'

'And what do you want in return for giving me a single death?' Valinov's tone was mocking. 'Information?'

'I am glad we understand one another.'

'There is not enough room in your head to understand what I could tell you. I have seen the forces that really hold this universe together, and it isn't your Emperor. All you Imperial vermin devote your lives to crushing the spirits of mankind until not one man or woman could survive knowing the truth.' Valinov sat back. 'You don't know, do you? They haven't told you. You're a messenger, Ligeia. A lackey. You think you have a future because you can do more than just smash a daemon's skull with a force hammer but you're the most pathetic of them all. They're lying to you. The ones who know, they lie.'

Ligeia leafed through the files in the folder again, as if Valinov's words just slid off her. 'While in the employ of Inquisitor Barbillus you had access to the Librarium...'

'The purpose of the Inquisition,' said Valinov suddenly, 'is to ensure that the Adeptus Terra retains power. It does this by covering up the truth with tales of your dead Emperor and fictions you call histories. Chaos is the essence of existence. It is power given form. It can be shaped, it can be used. Chaos could free mankind. Do you know what freedom is? I mean real freedom, releasing the shackles of your mind.'

'Your impending deaths,' said Ligeia levelly, 'now number six.'

'Have you ever killed a world, Ligeia? I mean, killed every single person on a planet, wiped out everything they are and everything they will ever be.'

'You did. You killed V'Run.'

'V'Run is a free world now. But I have destroyed worlds before. Under Barbillus I did everything except press the button. Whole civilisations, dead in hours.

Do you know what he did to Jurn? They had to bring in freighters full of refugees to repopulate it. They're still finding unexploded virus torpedoes in the under-hive to this day.' Valinov's eyes were alive. 'You have to be there, not just see it. I'm not a psyker, but I could feel them dying. I always told myself that I was doing the right thing, but when I finally began to understand and I made sure Barbillus couldn't get off Agnarsson's Hold, that was truly right. He burned, just like the billions he had burned. That's when I understood.

'The things the Imperium does to itself to crush the freedoms it calls heresy – that is the true heresy. You know nothing of the true glory of Chaos. If you did, you would see that the freedom and power it gives would be a better fate for the galaxy than the suffering the Imperium must dole out to keep that truth from existing.'

'Chaos is suffering,' said Ligeia. 'I have seen as much of that as you have.'

Valinov shook his head. 'Perspective, inquisitor. Some must always suffer. But Chaos gives so much more to those who do not. Under the Imperium, everyone suffers.'

'You have one chance,' said Ligeia. 'It is more than you ever gave anyone. Tell us about Ghargatuloth and the Trail of St Evisser. What were you going to do to raise him? Who did you instruct to carry on your work?'

Valinov sat back and sighed. 'You almost had me worried, inquisitor. For a moment it looked like you really knew something.'

Ligeia shut the file and stood up. She gave Valinov the kind of superior, officious look she did so well. Valinov's eyes glinted as if he were hiding a smirk.

Beside Alaric, the interrogator staff worked the cell commands and the door ground open again. Ligeia walked smartly out, the servitor removed the chair and the door shut again.

The lights in the cell went out, leaving Valinov in pitch blackness. Alaric could hear the rogue inquisitor's breathing. He knew from the interrogator's previous reports that he wouldn't break by conventional means – Ligeia had been the last realistic chance they had of cracking Valinov open.

Ligeia's voice came over Alaric's vox-receiver. 'Justicar, we have done all we can here. Assemble your force on the *Rubicon*, we are running out of time.'

FOUR
THE TRAIL OF
ST EVISSER

THE TRAIL OF St Evisser was a grimy little skein of space towards the galactic west, on the edge of the Segmentum Solar near the Ecclesiarchy heartland around Gathalamor and Chiros. The Trail consisted of a couple of dozen settled worlds forming a long, gruelling journey that twisted around nebulae and asteroid fields to describe the lengthy pilgrimage of St Evisser himself.

Ligeia had acquired reference works on the Trail before embarking and Alaric spent some of the journey reading up on it. The Trail, it seemed, had once been a centrepiece of the Imperial cult. It was a shining example of piety, with cathedrals and shrines dotting every settled world, a rich vein of charismatic senior clergy and a brand of lavish exultation that covered cathedral spires in gold. Each world competed in works of devotion until the festivals of the Adeptus

Ministorum became week-long celebrations with processions that snaked around continents. It rivalled the relic-trail of Sebastian Thor for ostentatious piety and material celebration of the Emperor.

But that had been some centuries ago. The Imperium was a vast and constantly changing place and cycles of poverty and wealth, fame and obscurity, churned between the stars. The Trail of St Evisser was all but forgotten now, just another band of worlds where billions of Imperial citizens lived out their lives. The population, Alaric saw, had fallen to about a quarter of its high point. The hive world of Volcanis Ultor was half-empty and whole agri-worlds were lying fallow. It seemed that religious fervour had at last waned and allowed warp routes to be forged that bypassed the Trail entirely. Shipping through the Trail was a fraction of what it had once been and St Evisser himself was little more than a name.

The Grey Knights strike cruiser *Rubicon* was a fast ship. Even so, it would take weeks to reach the Trail. Ligeia had sent an astropathic message to the Inquisition fortress which had jurisdiction over the Trail, but for now there was little to do but pray, train, and wait.

ALARIC AND LIGEIA met regularly in the *Rubicon's* state rooms, a complex of lavish hardwood panelled suites that could have come from inside a governor's mansion were it not for the lack of windows and the constant deep thrum of the strike cruiser's warp engines.

'What do you remember,' asked Ligeia one evening after Alaric had seen to the Grey Knights' training rites, 'of what you were before?'

Alaric, his armour removed, sat opposite Ligeia wearing his dark grey habit. Ligeia had set out her customary evening meal of exotic delicacies from worlds on the other side of the Imperium, but Alaric as usual ate little. 'Nothing,' he said.

'Nothing?' Ligeia raised an eyebrow. 'I find that difficult to believe. It is what I did before I ever heard of the Inquisition that made me the inquisitor I am now.'

'A Grey Knight must have a core of faith that cannot be broken.' Alaric picked at the daemonfish fillets on the silver plate in front of him – truth be told, he was uncomfortable amongst the luxury with which Ligeia surrounded herself. 'Like a rock in an ocean. That's the first thing we learn, although none of us remember learning it. You understand, we cannot know what it is like not to have that shield of faith. If we could remember it, that core would be flawed. There would be a way in. There is no room to remember for us.'

Ligeia leaned forward, a faint smile on her face. She looked almost girlish, like a child swapping secrets with a friend. 'But you used to be someone else, Alaric. Do you know who?'

Alaric shook his head. 'That was a different person. The Ordo Malleus has the most advanced psycho-doctrination in the Imperium. It leaves nothing behind. I could have been a hive ganger or some tribal hunter, or anything else. The Chapter recruits from hundreds of planets of all kinds. Whoever I was, I was taken before adolescence and made into someone else.'

Ligeia took a sip of wine. 'It sounds like a high price to pay.'

Alaric looked at her. He knew she was playing with him. She had an insatiable curiosity and the Grey Knights were one more area of study. 'There is no price too high,' he said. 'If we don't do it, then no one will. Chaos is always a hair's breadth away from swallowing us all and losing a flawed mind is no hardship compared to the consequences if we fail.'

'I must confess,' said Ligeia, 'we fight in very different ways.'

'I understand you were not originally recruited by the Ordo Malleus,' said Alaric, satisfying some of his own curiosity. 'From what I know of the Inquisition, that is not common.'

'I was recruited into the staff of the Ordo Hereticus fortress on Gathalamor.' Ligeia dissected her own daemonfish expertly as she spoke, and Alaric imagined the education she must have received to make it such a reflex. He was mildly surprised that such a free-minded woman could emerge from the stifling nobility of Gathalamor. 'I was more useful than they realised. As a psyker I can discern information in whatever form it is written. The Ordo Malleus… made me an offer, and I accepted. There was some resistance, but the Malleus has its ways.' She gave him an odd, sideways smile.

'Resistance? I know even less about the Inquisition than I suspected.'

'Probably deliberately, justicar. Our politics can be very complicated and you are not a politician, you are a weapon. You don't need to know about our various factions and infighting – they are all mostly matters of pride and dogma, but believe me that men like Valinov are more common than any of us would admit.'

'You are very open,' said Alaric. Out of politeness he swallowed a slice of the daemonfish – it tasted rich and spicy, a world away from the balanced but tasteless sludge synthesised for the Grey Knights on Titan. He didn't like it. Eating like this was an affectation, a show of pride. Enough Space Marines had fallen to pride for Alaric to find the whole idea distasteful.

'I trust you, justicar,' Ligeia replied. 'We rely on one another. You cannot negotiate an investigation and I certainly cannot fight, so what can we do but trust each other?'

Ligeia had brought her death cultist bodyguards with her – they stood there now, in the shadowy corners of Ligeia's suite, wearing shiny black bodygloves and masks and carrying dozens of blades between them. They were highly-trained and bound somehow to Ligeia personally; with their help Alaric doubted very much that Ligeia could not hold her own when the bullets started to fly.

A chime sounded over the *Rubicon*'s vox-casters, indicating the arrival of an astropathic message. The astropaths used by the Grey Knights were little more than ciphers, men and women mind-wiped after each mission so they could recall no sensitive information. The voice that spoke was dim and grey.

'Astropathic duct established. Inquisition fortress Trepytos asserts jurisdiction, requests itinerary, manifest and mission.'

Ligeia stood up, smoothed her long dark blue dress and snapped her fingers, calling a trundling valet-servitor forward to clean away the remains of the feast. She wiped her fingers clean on a napkin, another affectation since she had used only silver cutlery. 'We have almost arrived. I'm afraid some of those politics I mentioned come into play now, justicar. The Ordo Hereticus inquisitors watching over the Trail of St Evisser are based at the fortress on Trepytos and there are protocols to be followed if I am to act freely within their jurisdiction.'

'I will tell my men we will arrive shortly.'

'Good. Have them spick and span, justicar, a force of gleaming Grey Knights will do no harm in getting us a free reign here.'

Alaric gave her a look. 'My Marines observe their wargear rites constantly, inquisitor.'

Ligeia smiled back at him. 'Of course. Now if you will excuse me, they will need me on the bridge.'

Another snap of the fingers, and Ligeia's death cultists prowled out of the shadows to follow her as an honour guard, six black-clad assassins who moved with feline precision and always had one hand on the pommel of a blade. Their faces were covered with masks, featureless except for eyeholes. Alaric could appreciate the intimidating effect they could have. Not for the first time he wondered where Ligeia had got them – they were hardly the affectation of an aristocratic lady.

For the briefest moment, Alaric found himself wondering who he had once been. There had been a child once, who had been taken away by a chaplain of the Grey Knights or a Black Ship of the Inquisition, and who was erased from existence by endless sessions of psycho-doctrination. What could he have been, if not a Grey Knight?

He would have been nothing compared to Alaric now. That was what he had been told, and what he had always believed. He chased the thought from his mind and headed back to the training decks to muster his battle-brothers.

THE RUBICON WAS the finest ship to dock at the planet Trepytos for several hundred years. It was a shining gunmetal grey with protective prayers wrought into the hull in gold. It was a heavily modified version of the strike cruisers used by the Space Marines of the Adeptus Astartes, with an enlarged drop-pod bay, heavily reinforced quarters for Inquisition personnel and a comprehensive hexagrammic ward network built into every strut and bulkhead.

The fortress on Trepytos, on the other hand, had seen far better days. It was an impressive dark granite castle, with its fearsome battlements concealing planetary defence lasers and orbital missile bays. Beneath it was the Inquisition stronghold from which the Ordo Hereticus watched over the Trail of St Evisser. Around it were massed the decaying suburbs of what had once been the wealthy and exclusive fortress city from which the aristocracy of the Trail had watched over the officer classes of the guard and navy and the ranks of the Ecclesiarchy.

Trepytos had been the seat of authority for much of the Trail, but now it was in decay. The decline of St Evisser's worship had hit the planet worse than most. Elegant countryside, preserved for the benefit of noble houses who liked to hunt and adventure, now ran wild and encroached on the rotting cities. The population survived in enclaves, and the Ordo Hereticus presence was like a ghost in the lofty, half-abandoned fortress.

The *Rubicon* dropped into low orbit where the fortress's docking spire punched through the planet's grimy grey clouds. Docking clamps sealed and, as the cruiser refuelled, Inquisitor Ligeia, her bodyguards, and Justicar Alaric descended by dignitary shuttle to see what state the Trail of St Evisser was in after hundreds of years of decay.

* * *

INQUISITOR LAMERRIAN KLAES waited for them in the draughty, cavernous assembly hall in the heart of the Trepytos fortress. The hall had once seated audiences of hundreds in banks of seats but there was no one else there now. A giant pict-screen was folded up against the ceiling, wrapped in black fabric and gathering dust. Once the hall had been used to assemble the elite of the Trail to hear their concerns or issue Inquisitorial edicts – now it was so frequently quiet and empty that it was as good a place as any in the fortress to discuss sensitive matters. The only part of the hall that was lit was the very centre, where a semicircle of databanks and cogitators stood shedding a pale greenish light. This was where Inquisitor Klaes worked, and in spite of the small staff and garrison that ran the fortress he effectively worked alone.

Klaes was a thin, angular, harried man who looked more like an Administratum adept than an inquisitor. Were it not for the engraved power sword at his waist and the Inquisition seal around his neck, he could have been just another one of the billions of pen pushers that kept the Imperium wrapped up in red tape.

Alaric and Ligeia were led in by the Hereticus storm troopers of the fortress's garrison. Klaes, surrounded by monitor screens and reams of printouts in the centre of the hall, looked up in annoyance at their entrance. When he saw Alaric, he straightened in surprise. Ligeia had been right, of course – Alaric, nearly three metres tall in his massive polished power armour, was a usefully impressive sight.

'Inquisitor Ligeia,' he said in a sharp and surprisingly strong voice, standing to greet her. 'I have been expecting you.' He nodded at Alaric, 'Justicar.' Alaric nodded back. Klaes had not been expecting the Grey Knights.

'I fear we have arrived at a time when you are over-whelmed.' Ligeia indicated the screens and the printouts. The screens were displaying pict-stealer recordings, columns of statistics, and reams of texts. The printouts were spooling onto the floor.

'Information is our lifeblood, inquisitor,' said Klaes. 'Even these days the Trail of St Evisser creates a lot of it. I am the only one here with the authority to do anything about what he sees, so I have to see it all.'

'Then we will need to work closely, Inquisitor Klaes,' said Ligeia. She walked over to Klaes's nest of screens and cogitators and ran one of the spooling printouts through her fingers. 'We have reason to believe there is a daemonic threat emerging or due to emerge somewhere on the Trail. It is my job to find it and, with the help of Justicar Alaric and his men, to destroy it.'

Klaes walked up to Alaric. Alaric saw a heraldic crest on Klaes's sword and wondered which noble house had owed Klaes so much they had given him one of their heirlooms.

Klaes held out a hand to shake, and Alaric took it. 'Justicar, a rare pleasure. I have heard of the Grey Knights but here in the Hereticus details are scarce. Welcome to the Trail of St Evisser, for what that is worth.'

'There isn't much to tell, inquisitor,' said Alaric, slightly uncomfortable with diplomacy. 'Our purpose is simple. We are soldiers, and we need support just like any soldier.'

'Of course. But you understand...' here Klaes turned to Ligeia, 'the Trail has fallen a very long way. I am the sole permanent Inquisitorial presence for the whole of the Trail and the resources of this fortress are limited. I can call upon the Adeptus Arbites, who are far more numerous than the Hereticus troops, but they are quite embattled themselves. They effectively rule several of the planets after the nobility took flight. There are no Space Marines who would answer my call when Abaddon is killing his way through the Cadian Gate. I will give you what help I can, but the Trail is very much on the wane and if it is to rise again, I fear you will have to wait a very long time.'

'Time is exactly what we don't have,' said Ligeia. 'I will need access to all your reports of cult or otherwise suspect activity. I need details. Interviews with the investigators if possible. I am afraid I need complete access, too. Total jurisdiction.'

'Many of my interrogators are in deep cover and I cannot withdraw them at such short notice. Most of the rest I could make available but I will be undoing many Hereticus protocols and I will have to answer to the sector Conclave. I would need to know what threat you are investigating.'

'Hmm,' Ligeia thought for a moment. 'If you are willing to ignore protocol then so am I. The creature we are hunting is known to some as Ghargatuloth. Justicar Alaric will be able to tell the story better than I. Justicar, if you will?'

Alaric was not expecting to turn storyteller. But he supposed Ligeia was right – to the Grey Knights the story of Grand Master Mandulis and the Prince of a Thousand Faces was almost a religious parable, an exemplar of the Grey Knights' sacrifice and the supernatural evil they were sworn to face.

Alaric told Inquisitor Klaes the story of the death of Mandulis and the banishment of Ghargatuloth, telling it the same way the chaplains had told it to him when he was a novice still in awe of what he would become.

When he had finished, Inquisitor Klaes sat down in front of his screen and watched them for a few moments, columns of figures streaming past his eyes.

'Our records are in a sorry state,' he began. 'The Adeptus Mechanicus withdrew lexmechanic support two hundred years ago. I have had interrogators try to disentangle it but we have only made limited headway.'

'If you'd had me, inquisitor, there would not have been a problem. Information is my speciality.'

'Good, then you will know everything we know. I will put you in touch with Provost Marechal, he's the highest level Arbites contact. He won't thank me for making him available to you but make sure he understands the authority you carry and he'll give you all the help he can. I can offer you berthings for your ship here and anywhere else on the Trail with the facilities to handle a strike cruiser, not that there are many. I'll have the fortress staff prepare rooms for you, and the justicar can have access to the barracks, they're half empty anyway.'

Ligeia smiled graciously, something Alaric saw she was good at. 'I am glad you understand the importance of our mission here, inquisitor. I shall need to begin immediately, I shall bring my staff down from the *Rubicon* and start work in your records.'

'I'll assign you a guide,' said Klaes. 'I'm afraid, given the state of the fortress, you'll need it.'

INQUISITOR KLAES HAD two hundred staff at the fortress, mostly drawn from the Administratum and the Adeptus Arbites, as well as the three hundred Hereticus storm troopers in the garrison. The fortress archives were administered by a small cadre of ex-Administratum archivists and researchers, whose skill with the immensely complex bureaucracy of the Imperium meant they were better than most at dealing with the vast collection of information the Trail had generated.

Inquisitor Ligeia saw the archives were in severe disrepair. The dwindling staff had been unable to store all the ledgers, data-slates and written reports properly and many of them were uncatalogued, filling sagging, rotting shelves that in turn filled the dank vaulted catacombs beneath the draughty fortress. Each mottled yellow lumoglobe offered little more light than a candle, and the peeling gilded spines of thousands of books glinted weakly.

'The Adeptus Mechanicus maintained it at first,' the archivist was saying. She was a young, harried-looking woman with skin pale from too little sunlight and a drab Administratum uniform. 'But without their lexmechanics it was impossible to collate it all properly. We have Arbites' reports, astropathic monitoring, interrogation transcripts, everything from the Trail. We try to sort out the important information from the rest and archive it properly, but so much slips through that might be important and as you know, inquisitor...'

'...our work lies in the details,' said Ligeia. 'How many rooms like this are there?' Ligeia indicated the vault they were standing in, where dozens of ceiling-high bookshelves exuded the musty smell of decaying paper.

'Seventeen,' said the archivist. 'We think. The intact ones go back to the prime of the Trail. There are some vaults that were lost to flooding and twenty years ago a nest of rats ate their way through hundreds of books. And we're always finding new places where records were kept because the archive rooms became too full.'

'I shall need to look at your organised records,' said Ligeia, removing her velvet gloves and feeling the word-heavy air tingling against her skin. 'I shall require any information you have on active or defunct heretic cults. Give particular priority to apocalyptic sects. Find out if there are any survivors imprisoned on the Trail. I shall start here.'

'Of course, inquisitor,' said the archivist, unable to completely hide the bemusement from her voice.

Ligeia held out her hands as the archivist left. She could feel the weight of meaning in the vault, most of it stodgy and grey with irrelevance. But there were seams of violence and heresy running through it like veins in marble. The faint echo of the Trail's fallen splendour reached her – though the Trail was still home to billions of Imperial citizens it had in truth been dying for some time, and it mourned the loss of its celebrated piety and wealth. War had touched the Trail where nations or planets tried to gain independence from the Imperial yoke, and when legions of men and women had left to fight in the wars that constantly raged around the Imperium.

She started with the world she stood on, its details illuminated by the inventories and maintenance records of the fortress itself – she let the information flow into her. She could see that Trepytos's society had been almost laid bare, leaving only the cold, diamond-hard core of the Inquisition, dwindling smaller and smaller but still desperately trying to hold the Trail together.

She let Trepytos slip out of her mind and moved on to the Trail's most important world. Volcanis Ultor was a slow, irascible old world, now decrepit but still with potential for one last fight. Some of its hives were all but empty, others were full to their considerable capacity as if citizens were huddling together for safety. The handsome velvet sheen of the Ecclesiarchy lay over Volcanis Ultor – the authority the cardinals had over the planet was a relic of the Trail's religious prominence.

The forge world of Magnos Omicron throbbed with factories churning out weapons for the armies now heading for the Eye of Terror, but the Adeptus Mechanicus were insular in the extreme and the cargo ships that visited the world brought no benefit to the rest of the Trail. The planet was cloaked and dark to Ligeia, only the odd flashes of technical information – new marks of tanks or lasgun pouring out of the forges, abortive diplomatic moves to bring Magnos Omicron into the fold of the Trail's authorities. The Mechanicus had kept their world insulated from the workings of the Trail and, as far as Ligeia could tell, it was one of the few places on the Trail not trapped in a spiral of decay and obscurity.

Half-settled or depopulated worlds cast shadows of ignorance where the information stopped flowing. The garden world of Farfallen was a small bright spark, too underpopulated to ever be important but famed for its beauty. The drab grey canvases of agri-worlds spoke only of production quotas and tithing rates. A few mechanical glints betrayed the presence of monitoring stations on the outskirts of more important systems, their existence composed solely of blind numbers spooling from various sensors.

Ligeia's psychic power let her draw meaning from any medium. The whole of the Trail was there beneath the fortress at Trepytos. She could see the planets hanging in space and feel the currents of their histories

churning through her. The cults she saw were dark
wells of malice and debauchery. The Imperium's
responses were sharp wounds that bled recrimination.
But it was not enough – she needed details.

Ligeia walked up to the closest shelf, the hem of her
travelling dress becoming grimy with the thick gathering of dust. She pulled one volume off the shelf – it
was a collection of annual reports from the Officio
Medicae on the agri-world Villendion on the edge of
the Trail, going back thirty years. Disease and antiseptic desperation bled from its pages.

Ligeia placed her hands on the cover, letting the
knowledge seep into her mind.

Silently, using the skills that had so scandalised the
noble circles in which she had been brought up, Ligeia
began.

ALARIC ROSE UP almost onto his toes, his hands moving
slightly from side to side as he tensed up, ready to
strike at any moment. He moved as he had been
taught, ready with every enhanced muscle to go in any
direction at split-second notice, to dodge or parry or
strike.

Tancred was taller and so he ducked down lower,
ready to use his greater reach. All Marines were tall,
Grey Knights no exception, and Tancred was especially
huge – not just tall but broad, with huge slab-like pec-
torals lying beneath the implanted black carapace and
wide hands reaching to grab and throw. Tancred's head
was a battered knot of scars and around his neck hung
the Crux Terminatus on a silver chain.

Alaric ducked forward and kicked out at Tancred's
knee. Tancred saw it coming and did what Alaric
hoped he would – he turned to one side and half-

stepped away from Alaric's kick. Alaric swung behind Tancred and drove an elbow into his back, knocking him forward off-balance.

Alaric pounced, throwing his body weight onto the bigger man. Tancred fell forward but turned as he did so with dexterity that was always so alarming in such a huge man, bringing a foot up into Alaric's stomach. Tancred slammed into the riveted steel floor and kicked out, throwing Alaric solidly over his head to land hard.

Alaric turned over as quickly as he could, ready to dive forward and pin Tancred down. Suddenly there was a weight on the back of his neck – Tancred's foot pressed down on him. Like a hunter with a kill, Tancred stood over him.

'You're dead, justicar,' said Tancred in his customary growl.

Tancred took his foot off Alaric's neck, and the smaller man pulled himself to his feet. The sparring had left him breathless but Tancred seemed to be barely breaking a sweat.

'Good,' continued Tancred. 'What have you learned?'

'Not to try to beat you on the ground.'

'Apart from that.' Tancred was a true veteran, with an extraordinary panoply of scars and a place amongst the Terminator-armoured assault troops to prove it. He was older than Alaric and he had fought for longer – there was little he couldn't teach about combat of the up close and personal kind.

'Not to face a stronger opponent on his terms.'

'Wrong.' Tancred walked towards the edge of the training circle where an age-blackened steel arch led through to the cells. The *Rubicon* had been built with a deck set aside for the monastic cells in which the battle-brothers slept and spent their few moments of spare time, along with training areas, a chapel, an armaments workshop, a scaled-down apothecarion and all the facilities they needed to keep healthy in body and mind. The Grey Knights were segregated from the rest of the *Rubicon*'s crew, which consisted of well-drilled engine and weapon gangs wholly owned by the Ordo Malleus.

'The lesson,' continued Tancred as the two Marines walked through the shadowy corridors of the ship, 'is to play to your strengths. I am stronger and heavier. You are smaller and quicker. I used what advantage I had and you did not use yours.'

Alaric shook his head. 'Have you ever lost?' he asked.

'To Brother-Captain Stern,' replied Tancred. 'He did me the honour of breaking my nose.'

Brother-Captain Stern was one of the most respected warriors the Grey Knights possessed. Alaric was not surprised that it had taken such a man to best Tancred.

'What are your men saying?' asked Alaric. Tancred was not considered a leader with Alaric's potential, which meant he had stayed a justicar for far longer than most and had forged a bond with his Terminator squad that meant he was well worth listening to when it came to the morale of his men.

'I feel they would rather be at the Eye,' said Tancred, almost sadly. 'They have said nothing, but I can feel their doubt. They do not think Ligeia is a warrior.'

'She is not,' said Alaric. 'She does not pretend to be. And I trust her.'

'Then so will they. But it will not be helped if we are kept here without acting against the Enemy.' Tancred did not speak the name of Ghargatuloth. It was out of

habit rather than Alaric's orders – the very names of
daemons were unclean.

'We don't even know if he's on the Trail. Even if he is
not, this place has been spared the Emperor's gaze for
too long. I feel we will be called upon soon.'

They reached Tancred's cell, a simple, small room
with texts from the *Liber Daemonicum* pinned to the
walls. The stern words of the Rites of Detestation were
the first thing Tancred saw when he woke and the last
thing he saw before he entered half-sleep. Tancred's
Terminator armour was laid out in one corner, the
baroque polished armour plates shining dully in the
dim light. The shield-shaped plaque of the Insignium
Valoris mounted on one shoulder bore Tancred's personal heraldry – one half was glossy black representing
space and the other was red with a field of white starbursts. One star for each boarding action.

'Take your men through the Catechisms of Intolerance,' said Alaric. 'I think it is an appropriate prayer for
the Trail. I will lead Squad Santoro's firing rites, we will
need them when the time comes.'

'Santoro is a good man,' said Tancred as he entered
his cell and took his copy of the *Liber Daemonicum*
from where it lay beside his armour. 'Tough. And Genhain lost a battle-brother at the Gaolven Belt, he will
want revenge, too. I think you have chosen your justicars well.'

'This isn't about revenge, Tancred. This is about stopping Ghargatuloth.'

'Maybe,' Tancred leafed through the pages of the
Liber Daemonicum until he found the well-thumbed
page with the Catechisms of Intolerance. 'But revenge
helps.'

* * *

INTERROGATION CHAMBER IX was stained black with blood.

The Ordo Malleus possessed the best interrogation personnel and equipment in the Imperium, and each interrogation chamber had seen generations of psychological theories turned into practice.

Psychic surgery that placed a new, compliant personality inside a prisoner's head. Complex stress cascade scenarios that could convince a man the universe had ended and that his interrogators were gods. Total personality destruction that removed every facet of a person's mind except for the part that contained whatever the Malleus wanted to know.

Usually, the interrogators started with some of the more old-fashioned techniques. Which accounted for the blood.

All the conventional techniques had been tried on Gholic Ren-Sar Valinov in Interrogation Chamber IX. He had been worked on for weeks, but he had not broken. Careful examination of his body would reveal near-invisible surgical scars where the damage done to him had been repaired, because the Ordo Malleus did not do anything so crude as to cripple their enemies out of spite.

It was almost a matter of procedure when dealing with a man like Valinov. As an inquisitor his training, indoctrination and hard-won experience would all but ensure he would not break under conventional measures. The staff on Mimas had gone through the motions with grim efficiency, pausing only to ask the questions. Who was Valinov working for? What was his connection to Ghargatuloth? Why had he been in possession of the *Codicium Aeternum*?

The time came, eventually and inevitably, to move to the next stages, for which the lord inquisitors themselves had to give permission.

Explicator Riggensen was one of a small staff of psykers apprenticed to Ordo Malleus inquisitors whose minds had proven strong enough to allow for their powers to be developed and expanded. Riggensen was a telepath who had studied under Lord Inquisitor Coteaz and had learned to use his power to lever open recalcitrant minds. Riggensen and a handful of men and women like him were permanently seconded to Mimas, to eke vital information from the minds of the toughest prisoners the Malleus brought in.

The interrogation chamber was monitored from a tiny adjoining room. A large window looked in on Valinov sitting naked in the corner of the unfurnished chamber. Screens on the walls showed the same image in various wavelengths, and several monitors displayed Valinov's life signs. Psychic and anti-daemonic wards hung on the walls of the monitoring room in the forms of devotional texts and purity seals. Gun servitors flanked Riggensen as he sat watching his latest charge, because more than one such explicator had been compromised by a psychic prisoner.

Two of the interrogation staff watched Valinov's life signs and provided communications with staff headquarters and the Inquisitorial fortress on Encaladus. The Ordo Malleus's brightest lights were mostly on their way to the Eye of Terror or were already behind enemy lines, but there was still a heady wealth of authority on Encaladus and many inquisitors were listening in.

'Wards down,' said Riggensen, as the interrogator beside him deactivated the psychic wards woven into the walls of the chamber. Riggensen closed his eyes and reached out with his mind. The chamber was dull and throbbing with the pain that had been inflicted there and the blood that covered its walls. Valinov was a complex knot of life in the corner, a tiny diamond-hard centre of resolve behind his eyes. Riggensen had felt the iron will of an inquisitor before; he had always known that one day he would have to try to crack one open. He was also certain that he would fail. But every attempt had to be made to find out as much information as possible before Valinov was executed, and Riggensen was probably the last chance the Malleus had of breaking Valinov.

'Open it up,' said Riggensen, standing up.

The front wall of the monitoring room ground slowly open, and Riggensen walked through into the chamber. The smoothed layers of dried blood were like slick stone beneath his feet. The chamber stank of stale sweat.

Valinov looked up at him. The rogue inquisitor had been deprived of sleep and food but he seemed to take pride in not letting his health degenerate.

'Explicator? Then you are finally getting desperate. I was wondering how long it would take.'

'This does not have to happen, inquisitor,' said Riggensen.

'Yes it does. That's the way it works, isn't it? You do everything you can to bleed me dry and then you kill me. So get it over and done with.'

Riggensen held out his hand in front of Valinov's face, focusing his energy through it so that it poured out and flowed through Valinov's mind.

Valinov resisted, and he was strong. Riggensen could feel landscapes of hatred in the man's mind, a seething storm of arrogance. He was driven by the same conviction that drove every inquisitor, an absolute faith that could not be broken. But Valinov's faith was in darkness. The stink of Chaos filled him. The names of gods that Riggensen had been forbidden to speak echoed through the parts of Valinov's memory that the rogue inquisitor let the explicator feel.

Valinov was taunting him. Riggensen had never felt such strength of mind. Valinov couldn't hide his corruption but he could pick and choose which details Riggensen pried out of him, and he wasn't giving anything away. That diamond core of willpower shielded everything – there were no records that suggested Valinov was psychic, but his sheer resolve was superhuman.

Without warning, Valinov pushed back. Psychic feedback flooded into Riggensen's mind and he was hurled across the chamber, crashing through into the monitoring room. The two interrogator staff were thrown to the ground and the gun-servitors whirred angrily as they trained their guns on both Riggensen and Valinov.

Riggensen pulled back from Valinov's mind before the feedback knocked him unconscious. The wrecked monitoring room swam back into view, with shattered machines sparking.

'Abort!' yelled one of the interrogators, reaching for the control that would send the psychic wards leaping up around the chamber again.

'No,' said Riggensen, grabbing the man's wrist.

Valinov stood up and walked slowly across the chamber. 'I kill millions of vermin in the plain sight of your Inquisition, and they send me a boy,' he sneered. 'This mind will never crack. Don't you see? There is nothing left for me to fear.'

Riggensen sent a white-hot psychic spike into Valinov's mind, visibly leaping from the monitoring room into the chamber and spearing into Valinov's forehead. Valinov spasmed as the motor control portions of his brain were overloaded but the spike shattered like a glass arrow against the core of his resolve.

Riggensen's mind flowed around Valinov's psyche, finding only deserts of boiling hatred. Valinov spat wordless filth back at him. *Traitor*, he called him. *Scum. Failure. Child. Less than nothing.*

Riggensen screamed prayers straight into Valinov's mind. Words that would draw tears from daemons scoured through storms of anger. Valinov grabbed hold of Riggensen's psychic probe and the two men wrestled, Valinov's willpower against Riggensen's psychic strength. Valinov was on his knees and grinning wildly through bloodied teeth, but his mind was undamaged.

'Life signs fluctuating,' said one of the interrogators at the edge of Riggensen's perception. He could just hear the screams of the medical cogitator as it told him that Valinov was going into cardiac and respiratory arrest. But Valinov kept fighting.

Sharp flashes of pain washed through the mental battleground as Valinov's body reached the edge of its limits. Riggensen could taste Valinov's heart as it beat wildly out of time and the agonising grind of his lungs as they tried to draw breath.

Riggensen limped into the chamber, staggering against Valinov's resistance like a man walking against a hurricane. Valinov lashed out with a bolt of sheer malice and Riggensen was thrown against one of the chamber's walls, then yanked the other way and slammed against the opposite wall. Riggensen kept hold of Valinov's mind, clinging on grimly as the most powerful psyche he had ever faced clawed at him like a wild animal.

'Signs critical! Get the apothecarion crew in here!' someone shouted. Riggensen didn't listen. Everything he despised was staring at him like a single huge burning eye of hate. Corruption. Treachery. Surrender to the great Enemy. Valinov had hatred, but so did Riggensen.

Riggensen reached out with the last ounce of his willpower and wrapped a mental fist around the diamond at the heart of Valinov's mind. As his sight greyed out he put more willpower that he knew he had into crushing that diamond.

The dried blood was flaking off the walls. The white tiles beneath were cracking, falling like sharp flurries of snow. Klaxons were blaring on the gun-servitors that were demanding the order to fire. Life sign indicators were bleating that Valinov was about to die. The interrogators were shouting orders. The cacophony grew louder and louder, merging with the din spouting from Valinov's mind.

As the storm rose to a crescendo and Riggensen knew he was about to black out, Valinov cracked.

The diamond of resolve shattered and the shards ripped through Valinov's mind. Valinov himself was thrown backwards to land flat on his back, blood pumping from his ears and nose, his breath gasping hopelessly through a blood-flecked grimace.

'Speak,' said Riggensen breathlessly.

Valinov's mind was blown wide open. Riggensen could see atrocity and corruption in hideous vistas of memory. Faces screamed. Blood flowed. Whole worlds died before Riggensen's psychic eye.

'The Prince will rise,' said Valinov weakly. 'The Thousand Faces will look on the galaxy and make it ours. The Prince will give mankind to the Lord of Change and the galaxy will turn to Chaos under his eye.'

'More.'

'The… the tides of fate are his to control, the ways of men are weapons in his hands, the course of time runs as he wishes, everything that makes you and decides your fate is the tool he uses to rule…'

'More. Tell me everything. Everything.'

Valinov coughed and thick blood flowed down his chin. 'My Prince Ghargatuloth will never die. Only the lightning bolt will cleanse this reality of Ghargatuloth's presence, and the bolt is buried so deep… there is no time, no space, no fate, no will, there is only Chaos… for the bolt is buried so deep…'

Valinov convulsed and couldn't speak further. Riggensen felt blind horror emanating from Valinov's mind, and he knew that the man had spoken the truth. He was horrified that he had broken, that he had given away so much. That meant his words represented a great and terrible secret he had sworn to keep.

Riggensen turned to the interrogators in the monitoring station behind him. They were covered in cuts from shattered monitor screens, but they were still at their stations.

'Did Enceladus get that?' said Riggensen.

'Everything,' replied one of the interrogators. 'Recorded and sent. Comms never went down.'

'Good. We'll need to get a transcript to the astropaths for transmission to Inquisitor Ligeia.' Riggensen looked down at Valinov, who barely had the strength left to breath. 'And get the apothecary crew in here. We want him healthy for his execution.'

FIVE
VICTRIX SONORA

THE DIRTY TURQUOISE sky of Victrix Sonora was darkening as late evening rolled by and the siege entered its eighth hour. A cordon of steel had been thrown around the Administratum complex in the heart of Theograd, the second-largest of the agri-world's settlements, where barricades of spiked steel had been set up covering every angle of fire and rows of Arbites riot-control APCs sheltered assault groups as they edged towards the sinister black-windowed building.

Several of the windows were broken. Here and there bodies lay broken on the paving outside the building where they had been thrown from the upper floors or gunned down as they ran. The remains of Squad 12, the Adeptus Arbites unit that had tried to force entry to the building, were piled around the door where high-powered las-weapons and sniper-fitted autorifles had cut them down from within the expansive entrance lobby.

Arbites officers had been called in from all over Victrix Sonora, and some from off-planet. The Arbites were the ultimate law enforcement of the Imperium – they answered not to local authority but to their own higher echelons, forming a galaxy-wide body that enforced Imperial law. Arbites officers had commandeered the best riot and assault troopers from law enforcement throughout the Victrix system, armed them with their best equipment, and organised them into units for the operation against Theograd's Administratum complex. When the darkness was this deep it had to be the Emperor's Justice that was served, and the Arbites were the instruments of that justice.

Whatever heresy and treachery festered within the Theograd Administratum complex, it had finally shown its hand and there was no reason left not to take the building by force and enact justice upon anything they found. Squad 12 had been prepared to do things with civility, to serve notice of the inquiry in extremis – Provost Marechal himself had put his name to this action. But the heretics had been waiting and had cut down Squad 12 where they stood, eight officers compelled to give their lives in service to the Imperial law, and so every Arbites on the planet had been brought in to ensure justice was done.

Provost Marechal himself arrived in the sixth hour of the siege, shuttled down from visiting Victrix Sonora's orbital dockyards. By the time he arrived at the mobile command post the officers surrounding the buildings had been fired at several times from the building's upper floors. Arbites sharpshooters trained their long-las rifles on the blacked-out windows but still the information about the hostiles was sketchy in the extreme. The heretics were numerous and well-armed.

They knew the complex and they were well-led and organised. The two survivors of Squad 12 reported men and women masked in scarlet, yelling horrible high-pitched war cries. They were wearing the floor-length black greatcoats typical of Administratum dress uniforms. Other than that, the Arbites were working blind.

No one knew if the heretics had hostages. They probably did, but hostages were not a priority for the Arbites. Something foul had taken root in Theograd, and justice must be done.

Shortly after Provost Marechal took over on the ground, local defence monitoring reported with shock the two Thunderhawk gunships descending from close orbit towards Theograd. At the same time a strike cruiser made itself known to the small planetary defence installation orbiting Victrix Sonora, identifying itself as the *Rubicon*.

ALARIC COULD SEE the weight of duty etched on the faces of the officers around him. They had known they would have to assault the Administratum building eventually, and that some of them would end up like Squad 12. The fact that they had been joined by Space Marines – half-mythical warriors from children's stories and preachers' parables – had shaken them up even more. The Adeptus Astartes had not been deployed in the Trail for eight hundred years, and the fact that thirty of them were here, now, meant that the enemy they faced must be far fouler than they had suspected.

Some of them were more scared of the Space Marines than they were of the coming assault, Alaric guessed. They would not speak when they were within earshot of the Marines, whispering to one another as though in reverence. They didn't understand why Marines were here – it was bad enough that the Arbites had come down and taken over command of the assault, but Marines! That was unheard of. Even the Arbites who led the squads were shocked by their presence, radioing in to the command post to get sketchy explanations from Marechal's staff.

Alaric hoped the officers would not be put off by the giants fighting beside them. But everything Ligeia had told him suggested that Theograd's cult was more than an isolated Chaos sect. He didn't know how she had managed to absorb and quantify the astounding amounts of information on Trepytos, but she had collated details of thousands of the Trail's cults and found that some of them had things in common. The debasement of sacred objects, the worship of a being who had many forms, the idea of playing a part in an immense plan far too vast for human minds to understand. They were nihilistic cults who believed they were nothing compared to their half-glimpsed masters, mere vermin to be used and crushed at the unknowable whims of Chaos. They wanted to serve. They wanted to die. The Trail's overstretched Adeptus Arbites had shown admirable dedication in ensuring the latter wish came true.

'Santoro in position,' came Justicar Santoro's voice over the vox. Santoro's squad were best up close, right in the thick of the action where Santoro's own Nemesis mace would extract a toll of blood from anyone who got too close. Tancred's Terminators and Genhain's retributor squad were on the other side of the plaza, moving into position with the Arbites tasked with storming the service entrances at the building's rear.

'Brother Arbites, officers of the law,' came Provost Marechal's grim tones on the Arbites vox-channel. 'The time has come for this heresy to end. We all knew it would come to this. Something foul has taken root on this world, for most of you your own world, and we are the only force for justice on Victrix Sonora. Battle-brothers from the Adeptus Astartes, the Space Marines themselves, are with us. That alone should tell you what is at stake.'

Provost Marechal had heard there was a Space Marine force under Inquisitorial auspices on the Trail. If he had been unnerved at Alaric's sudden appearance, or offended that they were going to spearhead an assault that belonged to his Arbites, he had not shown it. Alaric had been impressed by the Provost who now sat in the mobile command APC coordinating the two hundred officers and Arbites arranged around the plaza. He was a huge man with skin the colour of old leather, wearing full ceremonial armour and carrying a power maul in one hand. He had been professional and curt – Alaric and Santoro were to take their place in the charge into the lobby, through the fire fields that had cut Squad 12 to pieces. Tancred's peerless assault troops were to batter their way into the back of the building where a nightmarish warren of offices, corridors and labyrinthine networks of chapels and workshops would reward sheer up-front momentum. Genhain would form a fire base duelling with the heretics who would be sure to use the large loading yards to the building's rear as a killing zone.

The Arbites would be with them. Fifty officers were behind the same barricade as Alaric, glancing with disguised awe at the giant silver-armoured warriors who had joined them without warning. They were armed with shotguns and autoguns, with the Arbites to the front wielding power mauls and riot shields. In total the law enforcement troops and Arbites numbered more than two hundred, representing the whole squad strength of Victrix Sonora. The assault was the culmination of an effort against the planet's cult that had cost them much in manpower and resources. If they failed here, the whole Trail would suffer.

'In position, lord provost,' voxed Alaric. Santoro, Genhain and Tancred sounded off in similar fashion. Alaric glanced back at his Marines, who were sheltering behind the massive sloping plasteel barricade. 'Lykkos, stay with me. Dvorn, you're up front. Break the doors down if you have to.' Dvorn nodded. Of all Alaric's squad he had the highest muscle mass and raw physical strength – his Nemesis weapon was a hammer, a rare form that had almost died out amongst the Chapter artificers but was perfectly suited to Dvorn. 'The rest of you, keep firing and keep moving. The Arbites will do the fighting, we must get into the heart of the place and crack open whatever lies in the centre. Tancred will be doing the same. Remember, we do not know what the enemy is capable of. We cannot guarantee that we can hold our own if we get bogged down. We have lost too many brothers to the Prince's followers already.'

Lykkos gripped the psycannon. Dvorn, Vien, Haulvarn and Clostus placed hands to the compartment in their breastplates that held their copies of the *Liber Daemonicum*, letting its sacred knowledge guide their hands.

'I am the hammer,' began Alaric.

'I am the hammer,' replied his squad. 'I am the hate. I am the woes of daemonkind…'

It was an old pre-battle prayer, one of the oldest. One of Alaric's roles as justicar was to prepare the minds of his men before battle, just as they prepared their bodies and their battle-gear. Over the vox he could hear Tancred leading his squad in a similar prayer, as Santoro joined in with Alaric. The officers nearby watched them warily, intimidated by having to witness this ancient battle-rite.

'...from the frenzy, temptation, corruption and deceit, deliver us, our Emperor, that the enemy might face us in Your wrath...'

'Marechal to all units,' came the provost's strident voice. 'Assault plan primary! All units advance!'

The front plates of the barricade were rammed outward, and the plaza opened up before Alaric. Almost instantly bright streaks of fire spattered down from the upper floors of the ugly, black-windowed Administratum building. Return fire from Arbites sharpshooters coughed up in reply, kicking showers of broken glass from the sides of the building.

The riot-equipped Arbites were in front, their shields held up to protect the officers behind them. Alaric refused such protection and strode out in front of Arbites as the line broke into a jog, Dvorn ahead of him. Alaric could see Santoro doing the same, leading his Marines at a run. They would hit the doors first, charging onto one side of the cavernous lobby while Alaric took the other side – the side where the men of Squad 12 had died.

Shots punched into the smooth ferrocrete of the plaza. Muffled cries marked where officers were hit and wounded, metallic thuds where shots impacted on riot shields. An autogun shot spanged off Vien's shoulder pad, and another hit Alaric's foot. The age-old power armour turned both shots aside easily.

'Clostus, give me range!' called Alaric as the building loomed closer – he could see where upper windows had been blown out, where the shapes of heretics could just be seen taking up firing position. Clostus, the best shot in Alaric's squad, fired a roaring volley of shots from his wrist-mounted storm bolter, firing at a run when the recoil of the bolter might break the arm of a normal man. Explosive shells ripped around the frame of one of the windows – the heretic sheltering there broke cover and ran, only to jerk suddenly as a sharpshooter's long-las round punched through his throat.

'Haulvarn, Vien, keep their heads down!' called Alaric and bolter fire ripped up from his squad, slamming into the building. The fire coming down at them in return was thicker now – they had a rapid-firing lasweapon, probably a multilaser, that stitched glowing red spears of fire through the advancing officers. Men tumbled to the floor. Haulvarn stumbled as lasshots spattered up one leg, leaving glowing dents in his armour.

Santoro was at the door. He had kicked in one door and brother Mykros was pouring a gout of flame from his incinerator into the lobby.

'Dvorn!' called Alaric. 'Take the doors!'

The squad broke into a headlong run as heavier fire spattered down from above. Dvorn reached the doors and without breaking stride swung his Nemesis hammer in a wide arc, shattering the flak-glass of the doors in a shimmering crescent of shards.

Alaric was next in. His auto-senses adjusted instantly to the shadowy interior of the lobby and in a heartbeat he took in his surroundings – several floors rose around him, hung with banners bearing litanies of obedience and diligence, the mantras of the Administratum. A fountain in the form of a statue of the current High Lord of the Administratum dominated the lobby, its hands sheared off and its stone eyes gouged out. The water was black and foul, pouring from the base of the statue into a fountain pool choked with bodies. Gunfire ripped down from the first and second floors – Alaric saw faces wrapped in scarlet, Administratum uniforms worn like a badge of treachery. The bodies were Administratum, too, workers in drab fatigues or foremen's greatcoats, except for the black-armoured bodies of officers by the doors.

Alaric opened fire, bolter rounds streaking upwards. The fire blew the arm off one heretic and he tumbled raggedly over the railing around the first floor, but there were still dozens more of them up there. They had upturned desks to use as cover and, though they would offer scant protection against storm bolters, the Grey Knights could not fight it out here; enough fire could be brought to bear to pin them down.

Santoro was already moving into the building, vaulting over the scattered furniture of the lobby into the networks of offices.

Alaric made a sharp, stabbing hand signal to the chapel entrance leading off from the lobby's near side as the rest of his squad charged in through the broken doors and heavy fire suddenly stitched down from above. Chunks of marble were ripped from the floor and stray shots blew half the head off the stone High Lord.

'They've got an autocannon up there!' voxed Dvorn.

'Suppress fire and move!' shouted Alaric. An autocannon was a loud, inefficient, old-fashioned weapon that fired shells of sufficient size to crack even power armour. Alaric's squad fired streaks of rapid storm bolter fire up at the source of the autocannon fire as they ran through the arch leading to the chapel.

The chapel was a long narrow room of black marble crowded with pews, with an altarpiece depicting diligent Imperial citizens locked in lives of holy obedience. The body of an Administratum under-consul lay draped over the lectern, where he had apparently been killed while lecturing the adepts.

Alaric knew they were in here – it was little more than an instinct, a sound, a flicker of movement. Even as he turned they screamed and charged out from between the pews, a dozen cultists, tattered blood-stained cloth covering their whole faces except for their hate-filled eyes.

One of them dived onto Alaric, a knife flashing down. Alaric threw the man aside and heard him slam into the wall, ribs crumpling. Alaric's Nemesis halberd flashed out and beheaded another before he stabbed the butt-end of the halberd into the stomach of yet another, pitched him into the air, and brought him smashing down through a pew that splintered under the impact. Storm bolter fire streaked past Alaric, punching through the wood of the pews and through the bodies of the cultists trying to shelter there. They screamed as they died, not with pain but with hate.

Laspistol fire rattled up from the survivors – Alaric grabbed the nearest and fired the storm bolter mounted on his wrist, blasting the cultist out of his hand to spatter against the far wall. Dvorn charged right through the pews and knocked two more flying with a single swipe of his hammer while Haulvarn impaled another with his sword.

The squad ran forward to secure the chapel, sweeping the shadows between the pews with the barrels of their guns. Alaric bent down and turned over the closest body. The scarlet cloth wrapped around the cultist's head fell away and Alaric saw the face of a young adept, the same as billions of men and women who ran the endless bureaucracy of the Imperium. But this man's skin was altered. Scales, like scabs over burnt skin, surrounded the dead staring eyes and ran under the cultist's throat down into the redolent remains of his adept's uniform. Those truly marked by Chaos carried a mark on their bodies as well as on their soul, and the cult on Victrix Sonora had sunk deep indeed.

Gunfire rattled from the lobby where the Arbites and officers were swapping volleys of fire with the cultists. Alaric knew that if the momentum of the assault was lost, the Arbites could be surrounded and massacred. The Grey Knights had to keep moving.

'Dvorn!' said Alaric nodding to the closest wall of the chapel. 'Get us moving.'

Dvorn nodded and sprinted at the stone of the wall, hitting it with all his running strength. The thin covering of marble shattered and Dvorn's armoured body ripped through further into the building, crashing through wood and plaster.

Haulvarn followed, sword flashing. Alaric went next, charging through the ragged hole. He saw rows of glowstrips up above, networks of workdesks in front of him in a wide, low-ceilinged room. Cogitators were surrounded by reams of paper. Supervisors' pulpits broke the sea of partitioned workstations like columns, and above them slogans of obedience looked down sternly from the beams of the ceiling. 'Diligence is salvation', read one. 'The Emperor's eye is upon you.'

Las-fire spattered out at Alaric even as his eyes took all this in. He dropped low, behind the flimsy partition of the closest workstation, as lasblasts rang off his armour. Cultists were shouting and Dvorn was bellowing as he charged through the workstations to get to grips with the closest cultists. Dvorn understood very well one of the tenets of any Space Marine – when you fight, fight up close, where your strengths count for so much more.

Alaric ran forward, using the workstations for what little cover they provided. He could see the cultists sheltering behind the wooden partitions as they fired – two of them died as Haulvarn's return fire chewed up their flimsy cover and ripped through their bodies. Dvorn was at the centre of a storm of splintered wood as he charged into the closest knot of cultists, hammer swinging, storm bolter blazing at point blank range. More fire streaked past as the rest of the squad entered.

Alaric heard the voice as clearly as if it were in his own head. It cut through his auto-senses and right into his very soul. It was a language Alaric had heard before on a benighted forest world where Chaotic witch-cults haunted the woods, a language taught to the cultists through communion with the dark power they had sworn themselves to. It was understood only by high priests and champions of Chaos, and what Alaric knew of it told him the speaker was ordering his men to charge.

Dozens of men and women charged in a storm of las-fire. They had been waiting in the offices of the Administratum building, waiting for the first assault to break through so they could counter-attack. They were adepts and menials, supervisors and even one in the uniform of an under-consul, armed with lasguns and

autoguns looted from Departmento Munitorum ship-
ments. They had bayonets and swords, pistols and bare
hands, and as they charged they screamed foul curses
in the tongues of Chaos.

'Hold!' yelled Alaric and, in the seconds it took for
the charge to hit, his squad gathered around him,
Nemesis weapons ready to receive the weight of the
assault, las-blasts spattering against their armour and
shredding the air around them. Alaric could feel the
faint hum in the back of his head as the anti-daemonic
wards woven into his armour overlapped, their feedback echoing in his psychic perception.

He could feel the hatred, too, pouring off the cultists
like a stink.

The wave of forty or fifty cultists broke against the
Grey Knights. Their priest kept yelling his orders as
Alaric and his battle-brothers slashed and bludgeoned
around them, every stroke severing a limb or a head.
Dvorn's hammer carved great red crescents from the
throng. Alaric saw mad eyes rolling between folds of
red cloth, men and women, old and young. The din
was appalling as the living howled curses and the
dying screamed in pain.

Alaric reached forward and hauled himself out of the
mass of bodies, throwing attackers aside. The priest
was on the far side of the workroom – it was an under-
consul, the highest Adept rank likely to be found on a
world like Victrix Sonora, resplendent in a black great-
coat trimmed with silver braids and the golden sash of
his office. His face was covered in layers of scabby
scales, so thick that his features were just ugly lumps.

He held out a hand as Alaric clambered over the
workstations towards him. A lance of lightning spat
out and a blue-white flash burst around Alaric, but his

wards kept his body safe and the rock-solid wall of faith shielded his mind. Alaric's storm bolter barked out a dozen rounds but they shattered in purple starbursts in the air just in front of the priest.

The sorcerer turned and ran, and Alaric followed. From the noise of the fight behind him he knew his squad were wading through the cultists to follow him but Alaric had to give chase. The sorcerer ran through the workstations and through a narrow exit deeper into the building. Alaric charged through the wooden partitions and smashed through the narrow doorway, his auto-senses adjusting to the darkness beyond it.

At one time the main Administratum workhouse had filled the centre of the building, where the most menial adepts slaved at long wooden benches, stamping forms and marking timesheets in their hundreds. They had been surrounded by icons of diligence and berated by the building's under-consuls, who constantly sermonised them on the meaninglessness of any labour save that in the Emperor's name.

The workhouse was gone now. The floor and ceiling had been ripped away to form a cavernous space filling most of the inside of the building. Below was a tangled mess of smouldering wreckage. From the bared rafters above hung scores of banners, foul symbols and heretic words daubed in blood and filth.

In the centre of the room, three storeys high, was a monstrous cogitator. Like a massive mechanical church organ, teetering stacks of datacores jutted from the top and fumes belched from the grotesque furnace-like body. Every working cogitator from the workhouse must have been combined into one huge calculating engine, and the whole mass sat in a nest of printouts. Its tarnished black surface writhed with dull red runes and it groaned menacingly as it worked, valves and armatures chattering like a swarm of insects.

The sorcerer was running in the air above the mass of wreckage, sorcerous energy crackling around his feet. He turned, saw Alaric following him, and began to wail a hideous high-pitched chant as he flew towards the monstrous cogitator.

Flashes of blackness began to burst around the cogitator and it rumbled hungrily. Alaric's wards flared hot as the wall between realities was pulled thin and began to fracture. Horrible cackling laughter echoed around the chamber. Leering faces and gnarled limbs reached from the black gashes in the air.

'Daemons!' yelled Alaric over the vox. 'Squad Alaric, Squad Santoro, to me now!'

Daemons were Chaotic will made flesh, at once a part of the dark gods and their servants. They were the tempters of foolish humans and the foot soldiers in the armies of darkness. Daemons were a threat both moral and physical, capable of corrupting the human armies sent against them. That was why the Grey Knights had been created. To them, the words of daemons were not temptations but just another sign of their evil.

It looked like Ligeia was right, thought Alaric as he leapt into the pit. He could hear his squad close behind him. Alaric landed on his feet and carried on running as the shimmering, reaching shapes coalesced from the darkness.

He reached the closest daemons at a sprint and he could feel them recoil from the shield of faith around his soul – a dozen of them formed a wall of iridescent flesh around him and Alaric used their revulsion to get in the first blow. He carved through one with a stroke of his halberd, but suddenly he was surrounded by them. The sorcerer must have been more powerful than even Ligeia had suspected, because he was pulling a veritable horde of daemons from the warp.

Alaric stabbed and hacked at the unbroken mass of daemon's flesh around him. Deformed hands grabbed at him, howling mouths vomited flame over his armour, mad eyes spat hate. Alaric's battle-brothers were trying to pull the daemons off him as storm bolter fire ripped overhead from squad Santoro, arriving at the edge of the pit.

Alaric plunged both hands into the mass, dragged a daemon above his head and ripped it in two. He forged through the gap, storm bolter ripping shells into the daemons behind him. Over him loomed the cogitator, deep red fires burning inside and steam billowing from malignant vents. Alaric saw that there was a ring of crude wooden statues surrounding the machine's base, and black lightning was playing around them. The sorcerer himself was standing on top of the machine, lit by the silver fire surrounding his hands. Alaric took aim, hoping to knock him off-balance and prevent him from completing the sorcery he was working. The Grey Knights were proof against direct attack from sorcery or psychic powers, but that did not mean the sorcerer could not summon yet more daemons or collapse the building around them.

'I am the hammer!' yelled a voice over the vox, and Alaric saw the enormous form of Justicar Tancred clamber up beside the sorcerer. The sorcerer turned and silver fire streamed from his hands over Tancred, framing the Terminator armour with a blazing halo. Tancred swung his Nemesis sword and, with a single stroke, carved through the sorcerer's body, the blade passing into the heretic's shoulder and slicing down through his body to come out at his waist. The upper half tumbled off down the casing of the monstrous cogitator and silver fire sprayed from the lower half, which blazed and guttered as it disintegrated with the force of the power released.

There was a terrible, high-pitched scream as the sorcerer's soul was immolated in the power gushing out of his ruptured body. The runes on the giant cogitator flared white as if they were drinking the energies of the sorcerer's death, before the two halves of the corpse thudded wetly to the floor and the runes faded.

'Well met, Brother Tancred!' voxed Alaric. 'You made good time.'

'Had to go through a few of them to get here,' replied Tancred as his fellow Terminator Marines took up firing positions on the machine beside him.

A scream went up from the daemons. Justicar Santoro directed his Marines to fire a savage volley of fire through their ranks, and squad Genhain on the far lip of the pit did the same. Daemon flesh dissolved in the crossfire. Tancred led his men down the side of the cogitator, charging past Alaric and into the broken mass of daemons. The screams as the daemons discorporated were hideous and they rose higher as Tancred's Marines trampled their bodies and impaled them on their Nemesis weapons. Alaric saw Brother Locath strike off a head, Brother deVarne cut one in two. Alaric's squad helped them and Dvorn drove another daemon into the ground with his hammer. In a few moments, all the daemons had dissolved into gory stains of many-coloured blood, leaving only the echoes of their dying screams.

Squads of officers were starting to emerge around the pit, and shotgun blasts echoed from elsewhere in the building as the rest of the heretics were hunted and cut down. Provost Marechal's voice was barking orders over the Arbites vox, organising squads to dissect the Administratum building and cut their heretic defence into pieces, using the pandemonium wrought by the Grey Knights to press home the attack. Arbites were leading the officers in kill-sweeps, partitioning the building into zones where each squad killed anything that moved. The Victrix Sonora cult was dying, with their under-consul leader dead and the cogitator at the heart of their worship in Imperial hands.

Alaric walked through the wreckage and picked up one of the looping strips of paper that spooled from the cogitator. The giant machine was still billowing smoke but its rumbling was becoming quieter.

'...and when the Prince rises, so shall the galaxy become His plaything, and mankind will become His lieutenants in the ways of the Change just as shall the stars themselves be blotted out by the Alterer of Ways with the Prince of a Thousand Faces at His right hand...'

Rantings covered every sheet of paper. The cogitator had evidently been the means by which Ghargatuloth communicated with the cult. The fires in the heart of the machine were dying now and, without the cult leader's magic to keep it going, ugly grinding noises came from within as its workings tore apart.

Alaric dropped the paper and walked to one of the statues that surrounded the machine. It was a crude wooden figure hacked from the trunk of a tree, the dark wood charred black. The figure was vaguely humanoid but it had dozens of hands and a face covered with eyes, staring out from around a wide leering mouth. The statue was carved in a harsh, angular fashion that made it even more grotesque.

'Alaric to Marechal,' voxed Alaric, 'We're done here. We'll take what we need and leave the rest to you. I suggest you burn everything here.'

'Understood,' replied Marechal. 'I hear what you have found there. Is it true?'

'Too true, lord provost. Do not let your men tarry here. Destroy it all.'

'Of course, justicar... my men are honoured that they could fight alongside you. I do not think any of them thought they would see they day when the Astartes joined them.'

Marechal was just like the officers in a way – he had been shocked by the Space Marines, and he couldn't entirely keep it out of his voice. 'We all have the same enemies, lord provost,' said Alaric. 'Your Arbites led well here. Just be sure to finish the job and make sure nothing of this cult remains.'

'Of course, Emperor be with you, commander.'

'Emperor be with you, lord provost.'

Alaric picked up the statue and a handful of the printouts. The statue was heavier than it should be, as if it didn't want to be picked up. 'Alaric to all squads, get back to the Thunderhawks. We have what we need. Santoro, cover us over the front plaza. Genhain, we'll meet you at the landing zone. Tancred, with me.'

Alaric waved his squad back through the wreckage of the pit. They passed back through the body-strewn offices and chapel, and through the lobby where a massive firefight had erupted between the Arbites and the heretics on the upper levels. The Arbites were counting the dead and helping their wounded, and the floor was smeared maroon with blood.

The Grey Knights crossed the bullet-scarred plaza back towards where their Thunderhawks were waiting.

Alaric glanced back and saw smoke billowing from the top floors. Marechal had followed his advice. Already, the Administratum building was starting to burn.

SIX
RUBICON

THE CULT ON Victrix Sonora had found itself an excellent hiding place. The Administratum, as the largest and most notoriously hidebound Imperial organisation, could have deflected less urgent enquiries indefinitely. It took Provost Marechal himself to cut through the red tape and authorise an intervention from the Arbites.

No one knew how long the cult had been there. Victrix Sonora had been a prosperous agri-world with several large cities in the Trail's heyday, but with the decline of St Evisser's worship those cities had kept their populations and lost their income. Crime became one of the most viable routes to survival. The planet's law enforcement had left Victrix Sonora to its own devices since the decline of the Trail, maintaining order around the properties of the Imperium and leaving the rest of the world to rot. They hadn't possessed the resources to police the rest of the planet and no leadership emerged from the civilian population to restore any form of order. There was no telling what had festered in the slums of Victrix Sonora before the cult came to Theograd and found its way into the Administratum.

Perhaps it had even started with the under-consul. The possibility was frightening but very real.

The cult's activities were mostly hidden but from the scattered reports in the archives of Trepytos, Ligeia had built them up into a vivid picture. What few holy places there were on Victrix Sonora had been systematically raided for the past fifty years and relics were stolen. A cargo freighter was intercepted twenty years before and an illegal cargo of looted relics stolen. It was assumed to have been little more than cutthroat smugglers feuding, but now it seemed the cult had wanted the relics and had used its influence in Victrix Sonora's criminal world to get them.

There were killings, for there were few cults that did not vent their rage or exalt their masters with violence. The cult slew apparently random victims all across Victrix Sonora, always taking body parts back with them. All these individual crimes had meant little in the planet's decaying cities, but each one had shone like a jewel in Ligeia's perception. She had known the cult that the Arbites had traced to the Administratum building was the same cult that had been doing the work of Ghargatuloth for decades, just as she had known that Ghargatuloth was somewhere on the Trail, pulling the strings that would bring it back into real space.

The Prince of a Thousand Faces, in its reign before Mandulis banished it, had directed cults in long-term plots that they themselves rarely understood. The cult on Victrix Sonora was engaged in the same sort of inscrutable, slow-burning plan Ghargatuloth favoured. To most it would be a tenuous link, but to Ligeia it was the mark of certainty. That was why she had been recruited by the Inquisition, and why the Ordo Malleus had worked so hard to take her from the Hereticus. She could be certain when others could not – she could sift meaning from the most disparate of facts. Ghargatuloth was on the Trail, Victrix Sonora had been tainted by his will, and the evidence Alaric had brought back from the planet had confirmed it.

LIGEIA HAD SET the staff at Trepytos to furnishing her a set of quarters fit for a lady. They had been busy in the three weeks since she had begun her hunt for meaning. Her suite of rooms was lavish, panelled with dark hardwood and hung with tapestries. A large fire burned in an open hearth and antique furniture salvaged from the derelict portions of the fortress was now gleaming and restored. Mouldering rugs had been cleaned up and now lay on the polished wood floor. Pict-screens set into burnished gold frames hung on the walls and a vox array was set into a wide hardwood desk in one corner. An intricate crystal chandelier hung from the ceiling. One of Ligeia's death cultists stood in the corner of each room, silent and immobile, all but invisible against the finery that Ligeia affected everywhere she went.

Ligeia knew that the Grey Knights would not approve. They slept on hard beds in monastic cells free of luxury. Ligeia had detected slight unease in Justicar Alaric when he was forced to confront the finery Ligeia brought with her – it was almost amusing to

see. Probably he saw lavish expense as one of the fore-
runners of weak-mindedness and corruption. For
Ligeia, it was a way to cloak herself in the image of a
noblewoman, so her real talents would be hidden.

Against this backdrop, then, the statue in the middle
of the room was incongruously horrible. Ligeia didn't
want to guess what it was supposed to depict, but that
was her job. It was something daemonic, certainly. Its
every angle screamed insanity. Ligeia felt it hurting the
psychic corners of her mind just looking at it. Unbid-
den, hints of its meaning filtered into her
consciousness – it was a celebration of something foul,
an imperfect rendition of something the sculptor had
seen and wanted to emulate in his art.

Ligeia flicked a switch on her vox-array and the
device began recording her voice onto a data-slate.
Many inquisitors travelled with a savant or a lexmechanic to keep their records and collate findings, but
Ligeia preferred to do her own bookkeeping, accompanied only by her silent death cultists. 'The… item,'
began Ligeia, unwilling to assign the repulsive sculpture a name, 'is of hardwood not native to Victrix
Sonora. It must have been made off-world and
imported by the cult, which means it is of ritual sig-
nificance.' She paused. Half the thing's many eyes
seemed to be staring at her through hard wooden
pupils, the rest of them scanning the room as if looking for a way out.

'The texts recovered from the cult's cogitator, coupled with the obvious heretical references in the
carving's shape, suggest that the sculpture depicts one
of the Thousand Faces of Ghargatuloth.'

Ligeia stared at the sculpture for a good few minutes.
She reached out gingerly with her psychic perception,

feeling oceans of meaning wrapped up in the carvings which might be too much for her consciousness to cope with. She tasted metal in her mouth and heard something laughing, or perhaps screaming, far away.

She could hear a name – very, very faint, too distant for her to make out. She listened harder, reached closer. The eyes were windows onto a perfect galaxy, a place devoted to the architecture of Chaos. The leering mouth spoke the unending spell that would remake the universe for the Lord of Change. The grain of the wood was the swirling pattern of fate that wrapped around everything, dragging it inexorably towards the final end – ultimate Chaos, the totality of the Change, the unending magnificence and pure horror of which Ghargatuloth was the herald.

Ligeia saw the galaxy, saturated with the power of the Change. She saw stars weeping and dying. She saw worlds crushed into crystal shards of hate. She saw the galaxy uncoiling and spilling all creation out into nothingness, down the throat of the ringmaster of Chaos, Ghargatuloth's master, the Change God Tzeentch.

Ligeia snapped her mind away just in time. She was on her knees, gasping, sweating. A lock of her carefully dressed hair lay lank across her face. She brushed it away with a shaking hand.

The death cultist in the corner, Taici, inclined his head almost imperceptibly forward. The subtle, silent code Ligeia and her bodyguards used was clear – did she need help? Medical assistance?

Ligeia shook her head, clambered shakily to her feet and tottered over to a table, where there were several crystal glasses and a decanter of syrupy, vintage amasec. She poured herself a good bolt and swallowed it down – she knew it did her no good but her mind told her differently, relaxing its grip on her and shedding some of the after-image of a galaxy gone mad.

'The… the item,' she continued, 'is now under absolute quarantine, with access available only to myself. Should I be lost, access shall be granted only on the permission of the Conclave of the High Lords of the Ordo Malleus.' She opened a draw of the desk and took out a slim wooden case, flipped it open, and withdrew a surgeon's scalpel. Carefully she sliced a sliver of wood off the sculpture, placing the sliver in a specimen bottle. 'A sample from the item is to be tested under my authority as soon as possible.'

Ligeia took another bolt of amasec and composed herself. If she had needed proof, it was here. That only she could see it – her power was extremely rare and she had never heard of another inquisitor possessing it – was frustrating. She would probably have to provide proof eventually that did not rely on her ability to draw meaning from any form of communication. But for her, this was enough. She could still taste in her mind the after-image of Ghargatuloth draped across the stars, an endless ocean of seething Change. A lesser mind, untrained by the rigours of an interrogator's apprenticeship and the demands of the inquisitor lords, might have snapped. If that madness came out from the warp back to real space, how many minds would be lost?

ALARIC WAS CLEAN at last. Twelve hours of prayers, seeking deliverance from the corruption he had come so close to, had scoured his soul of the sorcery that had blasted against it. Ritual decontamination had left his skin raw and tingling beneath armour gleaming from a ceremonial bath of mild acids and incense. The *Rubicon* echoed to the rituals that followed battle, slower and more reflective, as the battle-brothers sought to understand what they had experienced without letting it corrupt them. Alaric had seen terrible things before, from the sky turning red and bleeding over Soligor IV to the legions of the Lust God marching across the plains of Alazon. Each of them had left its mark, but observance of the prayers and rituals of the Grey Knights had washed those marks away. Other men were driven mad, but a Grey Knight was made clean and became stronger.

In the dim light of his cell, Alaric read from his copy of the *Liber Daemonicum*. The Rituals of Conclusion told of the soul being wrapped in faith like a planet is wrapped in an atmosphere, like a warrior is clothed in armour. Faith is a shield, a badge of the righteous, and is required for the very survival of the Emperor's soldiers. They were words Alaric had read thousands of times, but each time it gave him comfort as it did now. He was not alone. If the Emperor was not watching, then faith would mean nothing – but Alaric's soul was intact, and so faith must be a shield against corruption, and so the Emperor must have His eyes upon the Grey Knights.

In the infinite, cold, hostile universe, where the futures of so many trillions hung by the slimmest of threads and the tendrils of Chaos reached everywhere, it was only the Emperor who could show the way. To know He was there gave Alaric all the strength he needed.

The rituals were done. Alaric was safe from the depredations of the enemy until the next battle. But he knew, as always, that would not be very long.

Alaric put on his armour in time for Justicar Santoro's arrival. Santoro was a quiet and intense man
who rarely let any emotion surface. That did not mean
he had no presence, however, because his men followed him as if his every word was that of the
Emperor. If he further proved his prowess as a justicar,
Santoro would have a place in the chaplain's seminary
under Durendin if he wanted it, and Alaric knew he
would take it.

Santoro stood outside Alaric's cell. He was in full
armour – as a justicar he could display his own heraldry on the stylised shield attached to one shoulder.
Santoro's heraldry consisted of a single white starburst
on a black field – the light in the darkness, the cleans-
ing flame of the Emperor, the wrath of the Knights
piercing the black heart of the enemy.

'Justicar,' said Alaric. 'How are your men?'

'The rites are done,' replied Santoro. 'Jaeknos suffered a lasgun shot to the back of the knee but it will
be healed in a day or two. Their spirits are good, but
they do not feel they know enough about our enemy
here.'

'Have they told you this?'

'It is what I feel. My men always feel the same.'

'It cannot be helped. Knowing too much is as dangerous as knowing nothing when it comes to the
Enemy.'

'Too true. But that was not why I needed to speak
with you. Inquisitor Ligeia contacted the bridge a few
minutes ago with new orders. She needs us to go to a
world named Sophano Secundus.'

Alaric though for a moment, then went back into the
cell and found the data-slate onto which he had down-
loaded the basic information about the Trail. Sophano

Secundus, he read, was a backwater, a feudal world that hadn't yet reached blackpowder-level technology, where the sole Imperial authority was a preacher of the Missonaria Galaxia. The world had been bypassed by the Trail's prosperity because it had no resources of any note and had been lost in the bureaucracy surrounding the settling and development of new worlds.

'It does not sound promising,' said Alaric. 'The population would normally be too small to hide a cult of any size.'

'The inquisitor believes the statue you recovered from Victrix Sonora originated from there,' continued Santoro. 'She thinks there could be a link between the cults of the Trail and that she could find it on Sophano Secundus. We are to remain in orbit and back her up. She does not seem to think it would be wise for us to accompany her.'

'And you disagree?'

'The inquisitor is in command of this mission. There is nothing to disagree with.'

Alaric knew the men under his command. Santoro was not so inscrutable that he could hide his lack of enthusiasm. 'Inquisitor Ligeia will have a lot in common with the nobles she will need to deal with,' said Alaric. 'It would hardly help her cause if she had to go everywhere surrounded by armoured superhumans. She's better off on her own in this case.'

'Of course. I will tell my squad.'

'Let Genhain and Tancred know, too,' said Alaric. 'I need to read up on our destination.'

As Santoro left, Alaric began to search the *Rubicon*'s databanks for information on Sophano Secundus, using the data-slate terminal in his cell. He had certainly not expected to end up on an undeveloped backwater of the Trail when there were still so many population centres where, he knew from experience, a cunning leader could hide whole armies of cultists. The Missionaria Galaxia, the organisation through which the Adeptus Ministorum sent preachers and confessors to benighted worlds throughout the galaxy, was notoriously quick to call in the Sisters of Battle or even the Ordo Hereticus when they suspected something evil had taken root in their flock. If there really was a connection to Ghargatuloth on Sophano Secundus, it would have to be subtle. And subtle, Alaric suspected, was something Ligeia did well.

Once again, however, he had to trust her. All the prowess of the Grey Knights would mean nothing if Inquisitor Ligeia's hunches proved wrong. She was a psyker, yes, a powerful one, and a determined woman devoted to the eradication of the Enemy – but she was still human, and even her most precise divinations were ultimately guesswork.

Alaric had learned long ago to put his trust in the Emperor, for he was engaged in a fight against such odds that only through the Emperor could he prevail. But he was still not completely certain that he should have the same level of trust in Inquisitor Ligeia.

SOPHANO SECUNDUS HAD been discovered so long ago that it was all but impossible to trace its whole history under nominal Imperial rule. In the latter years of the Great Crusade, when the Emperor was already worshipped as a god, missionaries from his fledgling church had sent one of their number to Sophano Secundus to preach the word. They found a world mostly barren and drab with only one habitable continent that could only support a handful of feudal kingdoms around a few cities. Such rediscovered worlds were common, because the scattered human worlds had been torn apart in the Age of Strife and during the Crusade many were found that had been forgotten since the first waves of colonisation.

The Missionaria Galaxia maintained a presence on Sophano Secundus, which was why there were any records of it at all. The first missionary to be named in the records, Crucien, described primitive but broadly harmless kingdoms that bowed before an Allking and occasionally settled disputes with pitched battles. At some point the planet was forgotten by the Administratum and so a formal settlement order was never drawn up for Sophano Secundus – it became, by default, the responsibility of the Adeptus Ministorum, who were unwilling to waste any more resources on the backwater than the personnel required to keep a mission on the planet.

There were many such planets in the Imperium, most of them on the outer reaches of settled space or scattered through the Halo Zone, but more than a few surrounded by more developed systems. The Imperium's official policy was to 'civilise' such worlds and open them up for settlement, but even at the best of times there were more than enough wars and rebellions to keep Imperial efforts elsewhere. And times were never the best.

Sophano Secundus, according to the reports that had filtered back to the Trail authorities from the missionaries, was almost deliberately bad at accepting new technology and ideas. In any case, the Ecclesiarchy knew better than to cause a perfectly good Imperial flock to decimate itself by giving them lasguns. The Allking had therefore ruled over a feudal nation for as long as the

records stretched back, knowing nothing of the
Imperium other than that the missionary was holy and
untouchable and that fire would rain from the sky if
heresy ever showed its head. The missionaries considered the population's faith to be relatively stable, albeit
prone to the sorts of misunderstandings inevitable
when existing beliefs came into contact with the Imperial faith. There was no suggestion that the Ecclesiarchy
had been forced to quell any rebellions or cult activity
(although the Ecclesiarchy kept such things to itself)
and other Imperial authorities seemed not to have even
visited the world for several thousand years. Aside from
the missionaries and perhaps a few curious wealthy vis-
itors keen to observe how humans survived outside the
hive cities, Inquisitor Ligeia would be the first 'outsider'
to set foot on Sophano Secundus for all that time.

Alaric reviewed this information on a data-slate as
he waited on the bridge of the *Rubicon* for Ligeia's shuttle to drop out of orbit and start its descent. He tapped
the slate mounted on the rail around the captain's pulpit, trying to work out why Ghargatuloth might want
to make his presence felt on such a world. He had certainly inspired cults on feudal and feral worlds before
his banishment – Khorion IX itself was such a backwater. But was there any real benefit for him in doing
so, or was it just another feint? Alaric knew that the
Prince of a Thousand Faces would not let anything
lead the Grey Knights to him as directly as the statue
on Victrix Sonora, but perhaps there would be a link
somewhere on the planet below them, and perhaps
Ligeia would be able to find it. Much would lie in how
she negotiated with the current Allking Rashemha the
Stout, and with the current missionary, a hardy confessor named Polonias.

The bridge was a huge space, all highly polished metal wrought into elaborate scrollwork on every surface, swirling and organic, forming a grand series of murals around the huge viewscreen on the sloping ceiling like an ornate frame around a picture. Command pulpits stood around the walls, each with a grim, silent Ordo Hereticus crew member manning the controls. The Hereticus raised its own fleets and provided most of the crews for the Grey Knights – each had a complex psycho-trigger, built into their minds by sleep-doctrination, that would wipe out their higher brain functions if the order was given from a Grey Knight. That way, if the taint of Chaos ever touched the crew they could all be reduced to drooling idiots before they took control of the *Rubicon*. The crew knew it, too, and they were generally a grim and humourless lot. They never associated with the Grey Knights, and were replaced regularly. The *Rubicon* itself, a heavily modified Space Marine strike cruiser, was a fine enough ship to fight above its weight even with such a fatalistic crew.

The viewscreen was showing an image of Sophano Secundus, half-lit by its sun. Most of it was grey-brown slabs of land rearing up from dark blue oceans, but towards the equator one continent bloomed with life, a burst of green against the drabness. Somewhere in the middle of it was Hadjisheim, named after a legendary Allking, the capital of Sophano Secundus. It contained the Allking's palace and the temple built around Crucien's original mission, and it was where Inquisitor Ligeia was headed.

Alaric wished he could be down there. Though he had not heard anything so vulgar as a complaint from his Marines, he knew that they would rather know where the enemy was and have the chance to fight it than wait in orbit while Ligeia navigated through unfamiliar politics a Grey Knight had no time for. Tancred, in particular, was bristling – the old warhorse was most at home in the thick of the fight, and he must have felt like every moment out of it was a moment of unforgivable dereliction of duty. Alaric had felt that same impatience himself, many times, when the forces of Chaos had run rings around Imperial intelligence and forced the Grey Knights to wait for the next atrocity to happen. As a justicar and as the leading military officer on this mission, though, he knew how such distractions could take the edge off a fighter's instincts. The Grey Knights were some of the most dangerous troops in the Imperium, but that did not mean they could afford to lose their edge. He hoped he could keep his Marines sharp enough to face Ghargatuloth, because he still had to keep faith that Ligeia would lead them to it.

'Seventh stage,' came the flat, monotonous voice of the crewman at the shuttle control pulpit. 'Atmospheric controls on-line.'

'Descending,' said the shuttle pilot in reply, voice crackling over the vox. Ligeia's shuttle pierced the atmospheric envelope around Sophano Secundus.

'Wish me luck, justicar,' said Ligeia cheerfully over the bridge's vox-casters.

'You don't need it, inquisitor,' replied Alaric. 'Just find out what they're hiding down there.'

An inset image showed the faint orange streak as the shuttle entered the atmosphere, and then it was gone. It was time, thought Alaric, for Ligeia to do with words what the Grey Knights could not do with strength.

* * *

THE FIRST TASTE Inquisitor Ligeia had of Sophano Secundus was from the warm, slightly damp air that filled the passenger cabin of the shuttle as the rear ramp slid down. It was faintly spicy, faintly dusty, with a slight taste of the forests that rolled out across the continent. The light that streamed in was bright and yellowish, a stark contrast to the cool harsh lumostrips of the *Rubicon* and the feeble illumination in the archives of Trepytos.

She hoped the change would do her good. She had been suffering headaches and painful joints, and she had been woken by sudden sharp nightmares where invisible hands clawed at her while she slept. She had rarely used her powers as intensively as she had done scouring the Trepytos archives for information on primitive sculpture and the trade in artwork through the Trail, and it had taken its toll. She was reminded that she was not a young woman any more.

'Taici,' she said to the leader of her death cultists, who surrounded her in a silent, sinister honour guard. 'Follow.' The death cultists slunk out of their grav-couch restraints to surround her. Xiang, a deceptively slightly-built young woman whose death cult mask showed only a pair of exotically-shaped eyes, carried a plain black case containing Ligeia's effects.

Ligeia left the Hereticus crew on the shuttle and walked elegantly down the ramp to see what she had to work with.

The buildings of Hadjisheim were of pale stone and plaster, with marble tiled roofs that shone in the strong light. The roads were paved light grey. Brightly coloured curtains, banners and signs hung everywhere in contrast to the pale tones of the buildings, announcing shopfronts and street names in a language that used elaborate loops and whorls as an alphabet. Ligeia's shuttle, on advice from Polonias's Mission, had landed in a broad round space at the head of Hadjisheim's longest road, the broad avenue leading up to the Allking's palace.

It was along this road that the reception had been set. Ligeia had let Polonias know of her visit in time for the Allking to receive her as befitted a visiting dignitary, and he had not disappointed her. The road was lined with ranks of soldiers, men in polished armour over bright crimson uniforms, all carrying spears and shields with the twin crescent design of Allking Rashemha. Behind them, thousands of chattering men, women and children had gathered to watch – word had evidently spread, probably against Polonias's wishes, that a stranger from the sky was coming to visit, and they all wanted to see her. Ligeia saw the people of Sophano Secundus had an odd blend of dark skin and pale hair, giving them a faintly unearthly look when coupled with the bright colours they seemed to wear habitually.

The soldier-lined avenue ran up toward the Allking's palace, a creation of massive white stone that reared up to overlook Hadjisheim from a rise in the centre of the city, festooned with banners and pennants in dozens of colours.

The honour guard were riding from the direction of the palace. A hundred of the Allking's own cavalry, ribbons fluttering from their lances and the powerful sunlight gleaming off their highly polished armour, trotted towards Ligeia. As they came closer, Ligeia saw that most of them were riding tharr rather than horses – tharr were odd hunched creatures with dark, scabbed scaly skin and powerful hind legs that, according to the sketchy histories of Sophano Secundus, could be ridden into fearsome cavalry charges. A few of the officers in the front, their ranks denoted by golden trims to their armour, rode more familiar Terran-style horses, a symbol of prestige since so few breeding animals were ever brought to the planet.

A single rider galloped out of the cavalry ranks. Ligeia sensed her death cultists tensing slightly, their hands ready to fly to the hilts of their swords or throwing knives, but with a motion of her finger Ligeia had them stand down. The rider carried a long curved horn instead of a lance and pulled up suddenly a short distance away, blowing a long rasping blast from his horn. The riders behind him halted at the sound.

'In the nineteenth year of the reign of Allking Rashemha,' he called out in strongly-accented Low Gothic. 'His overhighness made it be known that his home is home to the representative of the realms above, that his soldiers are hers to protect her and that his people are her people to exalt her. In the name of the Emperor and of the kings long dead! So has the Allking decreed!'

There was another blast of the horn and the herald rode back into the ranks of the Allking's cavalry, which trotted forward to surround Ligeia and escort her to the palace. A squire rode forward on a tharr to offer her a Terran horse and, with a nod of appreciation, she mounted it sidesaddle. She had ridden once or twice in her youth but she thought it wisest to let the squire take the reins as the cavalry clattered their way back towards the palace.

The death cultists walked alongside, barely breaking into a jog to keep up with the brisk pace of the escort. Ligeia glanced at the people behind the soldiers lining the road, and the death cultists drew rather more attention than she did. Sophano Secundus had probably never seen anything like them – half a dozen perfectly muscled men and women in skin-tight black bodygloves, three or four weapons apiece, moving with such elegance and grace it was hard to believe they were human. Their sinister, near-featureless masks enhanced the impression that there were not normal faces underneath.

Allking Rashemha met Ligeia at the gates to his palace grounds, a broad belt of lavish lawns, flower beds and stands of exotic trees that surrounded the imposing white walls. Rashemha was a huge man with nut-coloured skin and shockingly pale blond hair and beard, wearing layers of bright flowing silks. Behind him stood a small army of courtiers and advisors, all competing in the brightness and elaboration of their dress but all dwarfed by the presence of their Allking. A small delegation of plainly-dressed young men and women, representing Polonias's mission, stood to one side.

Ligeia rode up to the Alking and dismounted. The Allking strode forward with a practiced beaming smile of welcome and grabbed Ligeia's hand in his two massive paws.

'Our people are your people,' he rumbled impressively. 'Greetings.'

Ligeia smiled back. The Allking smelled strongly of spices. 'Greetings from the Imperium, your overhighness. I am glad you have received me so readily, I have urgent business with Missionary Polonias.'

'Of course. Come inside, Outworlder Ligeia. I would not have the kingdoms of the sky believe the Allking's hospitality is lacking.'

The delegation headed across the grounds towards the palace. Ligeia saw that the representatives from the mission had a sickly greyish cast to their skin, and she imagined that endless hours of prayer inside the mission temple meant they rarely saw the sun. They wore simple habits of undyed cloth, evidently to show their humility before the Emperor – they would probably be most alarmed to see the extravagance of the Ecclesiarchy in the Imperium proper.

'Our lands are fertile and broad,' the Allking was rumbling, to be echoed by the agreements of his courtiers. 'Our people adore their king and the spirits of the kings long dead. They do well in the worship of your Emperor.'

Ligeia wasn't really listening. She knew that the centre of Hadjisheim was impressive but that the rest of the city, and the rest of the Allking's domain, was poor and backwards, and the underkings and barons had little ability to properly monitor the population. The Allking's blustering was less interesting than the palace itself – inside, shaded from the unforgiving sun, the cavernous spaces were cool and the inlaid marble floors formed complicated murals of the deeds of past Allkings. The double eagle of the Imperium crowned every pillar and devotional High Gothic texts were inscribed alongside prayers to the long-dead kings of Sophano Secundus. Gaggles of courtiers gathered around the columns, watching the Allking and his dignitaries as they passed, occasionally applauding as he expounded the glories of his world.

Ligeia saw how fragile Sophano Secundus was in those few minutes. The Allking held his underkings and barons together by the force of his personality. His household troops numbered a few hundred tharrback cavalry, never enough to properly rule even Sophano Secundus's single continent. A rebel underking could forge havoc, and Ligeia knew this had happened in the past. The Allking's rule was personal, not by strength but by unspoken agreement. It was weak. It was the way mankind had once ruled itself before the Age of Strife had shown how dangerous it was to rule by anything other than strength and vigilance.

Polonias was waiting in a side chapel, which had been decorated with dark marble and a plethora of incense burners more typical of Imperial architecture. Ligeia made her excuses to the Allking, promised to join him in an extravagant feast that evening, and took her death cultists into the chapel. The courtiers followed their Allking into the heart of the palace, towards the audience chamber where Rashemha the Stout would continue the long task of holding his planet together.

Polonias was an old, old man, stooped and gnarled. His long robes hid a body that moved achingly slowly through the incense-drenched interior of the chapel like a ghost. His head was covered by the heavy cowl of his habit and a golden double eagle hung from around his neck, giving the impression that he was bending under its weight.

Ligeia waved her death cultists back to a respectable distance. Polonias was surrounded by piles of papers and books, spread across the stone floor or lying on the front pews.

'Missionary,' said Ligeia. 'I bear the authority of the Emperor's Inquisition, and I require your co-operation.'

Polonias smiled, and the visible lower half of his face creased up unpleasantly. 'Inquisitor Ligeia. I trust the Allking gave you an appropriate welcome.'

'He made sure I was thoroughly impressed. I was more concerned with what you might tell me.' Ligeia walked to the front of the chapel and sat down on the front pew, surrounded by Polonias's books.

'As you can see,' said Polonias, waving a liver-spotted hand to indicate the spilled parchment and piled books, 'I have been preparing for your visit. There is only one reason why the Ordo Malleus would visit my world. You think I have not been thorough enough in preparing the minds of the people for the inevitable designs of the Enemy.'

'I am not here to accuse,' replied Ligeia calmly, picking up the closest book and turning it over in her hands. 'I am here to investigate. Someone or something on Sophano Secundus is connected to the imminent rebirth of a very powerful daemon.'

Polonias looked up at her and for the first time Ligeia saw his eyes – large and pale like the eyes of a sea creature. 'Daemons? The throne preserve us.'

'The inquisitors responsible for the Trail have very little information on Sophano Secundus, and that makes you my best source.' Ligeia spoke almost conversationally, inspecting the cover of the book as she did so. It was heavy and old, sealed with an elaborate brass lock mechanism. 'I am looking for any signs of cult activity on your world.'

Polonias shook his head. 'The people here are devout in their worship. There are few rivals to the Imperial cult, just a few ancestor-worshipping sects. I have felt no trace of the Enemy amongst them and I would have let the cardinals know if I had. Of course, there are tribes scattered through the forests that the Allking can do little about, but they are bandits, not fanatics.'

Ligeia snapped her fingers and Xiang strode forward lithely, holding Ligeia's case. The death cultist snapped the clasps and the case opened. Ligeia took out the ugly wood sculpture from Victrix Sonora. 'What can you tell me about this?'

Polonias shuffled forward and bent over to peer at the sculpture. Ligeia noted that he smelled strongly of incense and chemicals, as if he was pumped full of preservatives to keep his ancient body from deteriorating. 'A hideous thing. Degenerates of the nobility used to collect such things, I believe, back when St Evisser's worship was at its height. Traders would come to buy them off the forest peoples. There has been no such trade for many years. This planet's art is a curiosity now, nothing more.'

'When were the last ones taken off-planet?'

Polonias shrugged. 'Fifty years. Seventy. The Allking will have some historical advisor who could tell you. I think such heathen images are hideous, myself. I preach against such things.' Polonias straightened and Ligeia placed the statue back in the case – gratefully, because she could feel it squirming in her hands. 'My world has many problems,' continued Polonias, 'but the grasp of the Enemy is not one of them. The people are poor and benighted and the land provides little, but there is no corruption here. I have preached from Hadjisheim to the Callianan Flow on the northern coast and all the wickedness I have seen is wrought by human hands.'

'I am glad to hear it,' said Ligeia. 'But that makes my work here rather less promising.'

'I am sorry I could not help you more. The Emperor's Inquisition will have to look elsewhere for its ghosts and its heretics.' Ligeia thought Polonias was smiling as he spoke, but she could not be sure.

'Well, then, it seems I have little more to do here.' Ligeia stood, straightening her long skirts. 'I will go through the motions, see what I can get from the Allking and his advisors, but I doubt they know anything meaningful that you do not. You are well-read,' she added, holding up the book she had found. 'I haven't seen a volume of Myrmandos's *Lamentations* for a long time.'

'My predecessor left it for me,' said Polonias. 'I have always felt Myrmandos lacking, but his parables are simple enough to use in my sermons.'

'The cardinals on the Trail have made it a standard text for seminary study,' said Ligeia. 'They would be disappointed to hear your lack of appreciation.'

'Well, the cardinals are entitled to disagree with a crude old missionary,' said Polonias.

'The *Lamentations*,' said Ligeia simply, 'have been lost for twelve hundred years. No member of the Ecclesiarchy would have a copy unless they had been alive since then, not even the cardinals.'

The death cultists strode forward from the back of the chapel, swords and throwing blades in their hands. Ligeia's hand was held flat on the cover of the *Lamentations*, absorbing the flow of information confirming the book was the same volume believed lost by all the authorities she knew, including Trepytos.

'I do not believe you are Polonias,' continued Ligeia. 'By the authority of the Holy Orders of the Emperor's Inquisition I demand you submit yourself to moral examination. You will accept all grades of interrogation and your every word will be true at the expense of your life and your soul.' Her voice was suddenly cold, and the muscles of her death cultists were so taut she could almost hear them humming.

'Stupid girl,' spat the missionary. 'Stupid, stubborn, weak little girl!' Something flared under his cowl and his eyes were suddenly burning with violet fire, illuminating a face so hollow and aged that no human could have naturally lived all the years that weighed down on it.

The air turned thick as Missionary Crucien, his identity revealed for the first time in millennia, was suddenly ablaze with sorcerous fire.

A HANDFUL OF seconds later, the *Rubicon* lost all contact with the surface of Sophano Secundus.

SEVEN
SOPHANO SECUNDUS

'NOTHING,' SAID THE crewman at the comms helm. 'We've lost it all. Life signs, the shuttle beacon, everything.'

Alaric jumped down from the command pulpit. 'How?'

'I'm not…'

'On screen!'

The image of Sophano Secundus on the viewscreen disappeared to be replaced with shifting static. The crewmen in the sensor pit in the floor of the bridge, surrounded by monitors and chattering cogitator banks, scrambled to find some meaningful signal from the surface. There was a flash as something shorted and sparked.

'Tancred, Genhain, get your squads onto your Thunderhawk and launch, await landing coordinates. Santoro, wait for me. I'll be there as soon as I know more.'

'Trouble, justicar?' came Tancred's gruff voice.

'Nothing but,' replied Alaric, as something appeared on the viewscreen.

The image was of the hinterland of Hadjisheim, dominated by a steep valley surrounded by rolling forests. Where Hadjisheim itself should have been was a purple-black circle of interference, boiling evilly.

'Are they jamming us?'

'If they are it's nothing we've seen before,' shouted someone from the sensor pit.

Alaric paused, looking at the horrible stormy blot on the surface of Sophano Secundus. 'I think they've seen plenty of it,' replied Alaric. 'That's sorcery.'

Even from orbit he could feel it, fingers of magic spattering against his armoured soul like cold rain.

There was no time for the wargear rites or for the ritual purification of the soul that a Grey Knight should undergo before battle. Ligeia was down there, and if she was not dead already then she very soon would be. The Grey Knights were her only chance.

'Navigation, take the pulpit!' called Alaric as he ran towards the doors leading out of the bridge. 'Get us into a launch position. Flight control, get me a landing course before I get to the flight decks!'

Alaric mumbled quickly through the Seven Prayers of Detestation as he ran through the decks towards the *Rubicon's* flight hangar, the ship's engines rumbling angrily somewhere below him. Ordo Malleus crewmen and servitors hurried through the corridors around him and the ship lurched suddenly as it made a sharp turn to bring its flight doors around to face the planet's surface.

'... and fill my soul with righteous hate to steel my arm the stronger...'

'The astropaths are reporting something in the warp,' came a voice from the bridge, cutting through the vox-traffic. 'They say it's screaming.'

Alaric wrenched open the bulkhead leading to the flight deck. Two of the *Rubicon*'s three Thunderhawks were fuelled up and ready for flight, the deck servitors even now unhooking the promethium lines from the hulls. Tancred and Genhain's gunship was ready for takeoff, while Alaric and Santoro's still had its ramp down. The rest of Alaric's squad were already waiting for him.

'… and guide my aim, bless my gun, make my hate your hate and through me let it scorch the flesh of the Great Enemy…'

'We've got a signal!' came a vox from the comms helm.

'Ligeia?'

'Taici.'

'Good enough. What does he say?'

'It's just a string of coordinates. But it's definitely him.'

'Where?'

'The valley outside the city, just beyond the zone of interference.'

'Then that's our landing spot.' Alaric ran up the ramp into the passenger compartment of the Thunderhawk, the familiar faces of his squad nodding in silent salute at him before they put on their helmets and fixed their grav-restraints. 'Nav helm?'

'Landing solutions already loaded.'

The exit ramp slid up into place behind Alaric. 'Then open the hangar doors and launch.'

The pitch of the Thunderhawk engines kicked in and rose as the pre-launch countdown flicked the gunship's systems on. The air in the hangar boomed out as the doors ground open and there was a lurch as the ship bolted forwards on its primary thrust engines, jamming the occupants back into their grav-couches. Alaric glanced out of the gunship's porthole as it roared out of the *Rubicon* – the strike cruiser's hull ripped past and the glowing crescent of Sophano Secundus slid into view, barren and grim, the sole streak of fertile green now blackening purple.

Alaric could taste the sorcery, dark and mocking. But sorcery was what the Grey Knights had been trained to fight.

THE FORESTS STREAKED by beneath a darkening sky slashed with purple lightning, the valleys deep in shadows like rivers of ink, the distant barren mountains like broken teeth around the horizon. The Thunderhawk engines screamed as the deceleration thrusters resisted the pull of gravity on the falling gunship.

The valley yawned blackly below the Thunderhawk as it dipped into its approach. The Thunderhawk's sensors were barely functioning thanks to the interference flowing from Hadjisheim and the Malleus pilots in the cockpit were flying mostly by eye. The dark grassy sides of the valley swept upwards and the Thunderhawk slewed into a wide crescent, landing gear grinding down from the hull. With a jolt the runners hit the ground and the main engines cut out.

The valley was deep and shadowy. The forest that rolled up to the crests on either side was deep and very dark, the greenery like a solid mass. The valley was covered in coarse grasses and shrubs. In the distance, some way along the valley, the sorcery could be seen like a solid blackish dome. The sky above was almost the same colour as the sorcery – black streaked with purple, the stars like silver dust. The runners of the Thunderhawks carved deep furrows in the thick earth as they came to a halt.

'Deploy!' called Alaric and, as the ramp descended, Squad Alaric and Squad Santoro were out of the gunship in seconds, storm bolters raised. Alaric hit the ground and at once felt the echoes the astropaths had reported – a seething in the warp, an agitation just beyond the veil of reality.

Alaric's auto-senses cut through the gloom. The vegetation of Sophano Secundus was dark and wretched, clinging feebly to the banks of the valley until it became a thick tangled row of trees at the crest. 'Tancred?' voxed Alaric on the all-squad channel.

'Coming down now. Do you have him?'

'Negative. We're searching.'

Tancred's Thunderhawk curved around, its landing thrusters leaving glowing blue streaks in the air, to settle behind Alaric's. The ramp was down and Tancred's squad was out before the thrusters cut out, massive Terminator-armoured bodies dropping to thump onto the damp grass.

'Got something,' came a sudden vox from Brother Marl, one of Santoro's Marines. 'I think it's him.'

Santoro waved his squad forward in the direction Marl was indicating. 'Squad, get their back,' said Alaric, and his own Marines turned to keep an eye on the perimeter.

'Confirmed,' voxed Santoro. 'It's one of hers.'

'Taici?'

'It's hard to tell.'

'Squad, hold,' voxed Alaric to his squad and hurried over to where Santoro was standing over a dark shape sprawled on the ground.

It was one of Ligeia's death cultists, that was certain, wearing a glossy black bodysuit now torn and shredded. The hood had been torn off and Alaric realised it was the first time he had seen the face of one of Ligeia's cultists.

He recognised the sword still held in the man's hand as belonging to Taici – if the death cultists had a leader other than Ligeia, it was Taici. And if there was anyone she would send to summon the Grey Knights to a safe landing site, it was him.

Alaric knelt down beside Taici. He was still breathing, but he had taken a severe beating. His skin was torn and tattered. One leg was clearly broken and his chest was lopsided so much that Alaric was surprised he could manage even the shallow breaths he was taking. A sleek, handsome face was now bloody and broken, glossy black hair, bloodied golden skin, the jaw now broken and shattered. Slivers of teeth were mixed in with the blood running down his chin.

'He's alive,' said Alaric. 'Can you speak?'

Taici's eyes opened. But they were not eyes.

Like fat, pink worms, two tendrils poked from Taici's eye sockets, writhing obscenely like pointing fingers, tiny ravenous maws opening in the tips. Taici's face disintegrated and a nest of worms gnawed out through the bones, chewing the death cultist's head into a foul mess of bubbling gore.

'Mykros!' called Santoro, and his squad's flamer bearer stepped up. Alaric stood back and Mykros immolated the writhing mess with a heavy gout of blessed flame. Harsh, spicy incense mixed with the stink of charred flesh and soon the corpse was gone.

'That was–' began Santoro.

'Tancred, Genhain,' voxed Alaric, and he saw that both squads were now on the ground. 'Taici was being controlled. They've got her. Give me a...'

Tancred saw them first and Alaric knew something was wrong by the way his squad's aim suddenly snapped upwards, to the ridge along the top of the valley slope. Alaric followed their gaze and saw the ridge bristling, as if the forest itself were marching down towards them. There were suddenly spearpoints and banners, the bright colours of the Allking's barons muted in the gathering gloom, the jangling of armour and the grunt of the tharr filtering down over the sound of the cold wind through the trees.

Alaric looked around. There were men on both sides of the valleys, probably thousands of them. Waiting for the Grey Knights. The creature in Taici's head had controlled him, tricking him into leading the Grey Knights into the trap.

'Soldiers from the sky,' called down a herald's voice from the Allking's men. 'Our Emperor abhors the heretics who hunt His people. The spirits of the kings long dead spit on infidel invaders who befoul the Allking's lands. The Emperor, the Lord of Change, and the Prince of a Thousand Faces rot your hearts. Your deaths are our lives.'

'Close up,' voxed Alaric, and the Grey Knights gathered in a tight circle between the Thunderhawks. Then to his own squad, 'They'll charge. Vien, Clostus, in the front with me. Lykkos, in the centre with Squad Glaivan. Let them come to us. Cleanse your souls and have faith.'

A hunting horn brayed above and the army's leaders yelled a final order in the language of their dead kings. As one, in a spiky black mass, the tharr cavalry charged forward and the valley thundered. Alaric saw the massively muscled legs of the tharr powering them forward, the flashing armour of the knights on top and the streaming coloured pennants of a dozen feudal barons.

Justicar Genhain, in the centre of the Grey Knights, bellowed an order and storm bolter fire streaked out. Every Grey Knight's gun spat bright white streaks into the charging mass of soldiers, kicking up bursts of blood. Bodies wheeled as tharr hit the ground and threw their riders. Men were blasted backwards in flailing broken bursts of blood. But more came, trampling the bodies of their dead and, as the killing zone around the Grey Knights was piled deeper with the dead, the rear ranks of the cavalry galloped over the heaps of corpses and bore down on Alaric's Marines. The too-familiar stink of death flooded forward as the charge slammed home.

The first of them hit. Alaric saw gritted teeth beneath the noseguard, banded armour over bright flowing cloth, dark skin and white hair. Alaric turned the lance aimed at his head with the blade of his Nemesis halberd and punched his other hand into the grisly maw of the tharr beneath the rider. His fist smashed through ranks of teeth and Alaric squeezed the firing stud, sending a volley of bolt shells from the wrist-mounted storm bolter ripping through the beast.

Alaric impaled the rider on his halberd and, without throwing the body off his blade, hacked clean through the rider behind him. Beside Alaric, Brother Vien had sheared the head off a tharr and clambered over its fallen body, swinging his halberd like a mace and knocking men aside. Haulvarn reached over Alaric's shoulder and plunged his sword through yet another rider while Dvorn waded in, his hammer sweeping the squad's flank clear to leave a wide semicircle of shattered bodies.

Alaric felt, more than heard, the charge hit Tancred's squad, and saw a tharr sailing through the air no doubt flung by one of Tancred's Terminators. He heard Santoro's voice yelling a prayer of steadfastness as the ringing of steel showed Santoro's Marines were already duelling with the swordsmen on foot.

Under the guns and blades of the Grey Knights the charge had been reduced to bloody tatters but the mass of the Allking's army was on foot, swordsmen and spearmen swarming forward. This was how the Grey Knights could be lost – swamped and smothered, trapped between a mountain of men where, eventually, their power armour would fail them, their bolters would run out of shells, their sword arms would be pinned and they would die.

Alaric spotted the Thunderhawks swarming with men who were clambering over them, trying to lever the hatches open and smash the windows. He caught sight of movement inside one cockpit where the Malleus pilots were evidently fighting soldiers who had got inside. They would fight to the death, but die they would. The Thunderhawks wouldn't survive, either.

The mass of men pressed home. Swords stabbed out at Alaric, clanging off his armour, a wall of steel in front of a sea of hate-filled faces. One of them ducked Dvorn's hammer and leapt on the Marine, knocking him back a step to be followed by a dozen more who dragged Dvorn to the ground. Clostus cut one swordsman from throat to groin and threw off another, but they were pouring in through the breach, fearless, fanatical.

'Tancred! Break us out, there are too many!' voxed Alaric. He spotted Santoro clambering over the sea of soldiers, striking left and right with his Nemesis mace. Storm bolter fire was still streaking from Genhain's squad, and Lykkos's psycannon threw shining blasts into the rear ranks, but there were too many to thin out.

Tancred, Alaric knew, was probably their only way out.

'Brothers!' Tancred was yelling. 'For vengeance! For purity! In hatred be strong, in valour be sure!'

'In vengeance be foremost!' echoed his men, and Alaric could feel the buzzing in that part of his mind that possessed enough psychic talent to accept the training of a Grey Knight.

'In suffering! In glory!' lead Tancred, slicing two men in half with a sweep of his Nemesis sword as the crescendo rose, a deafening choir, and white blades of light flickered around Squad Tancred.

Finally, like a bomb detonating, like a meteor hitting, a titanic burst of light ripped through the surging throng in front of Tancred, sending a shockwave tearing through the Allking's ranks. In the flash Alaric saw men blasted clean of their flesh, tharr disintegrating, a wide space scoured of the enemy who were sent flying through the air and thrown backwards onto the men behind them.

The inquisitors of the Ordo Malleus had nicknamed it the holocaust, but it was something far more complicated than that. Only those of the Grey Knights with the strongest psychic signature could do it, and even then not alone – it took a full squad, led by a psyker, to channel the hatred placed in them by years of training and prayer into a devastating physical form.

The holocaust had blasted a space clear in front of Tancred, the earth scoured white. With a roar Tancred charged into the broken ranks and Squad Genhain followed, spraying gunfire into the mass. Tancred's Terminators excelled on the offensive and they carved through the Secundan swordsmen, Nemesis weapons flashing, gunfire blazing.

Alaric and Santoro followed, hacking all around them to keep back the press, following the trail of carnage that Tancred bored into the army. The ranks were fleeing now, dropping their weapons and running back up the side of the valley as Tancred chased them. The battle had turned into a rout and more and more swordsmen followed. Officers, noblemen on tharrback or even on horses, yelled at their men to keep fighting, but the banners of the barons were down now.

That was how to break an army. Show them what the Grey Knights could do, make sure every man saw it, and convince them that if they stayed then they would be next.

Alaric checked the runes projected by his auto-senses back onto his retina. Dvorn's rune was flickering, he must be wounded. 'Any men lost?' voxed Alaric.

'Caanos is dead,' said Santoro simply. 'Mykros is carrying him.'

Alaric felt a flare of anger. Sophano Secundus had betrayed the Grey Knights and now it had taken the life of a Marine. Alaric remembered a Marine in Santoro's own mould, quiet, devout, devoted. Now Caanos would never pray for anything again.

It was the worst of omens to leave a Grey Knight's body on the battlefield. The gene-seed that regulated Caanos's metabolism and his vat-grown organs would be removed and taken back to Titan, so they could be implanted in a novice just beginning the path of the Grey Knight. But that would only happen if any of them got off Sophano Secundus.

'Take cover in the treeline and keep moving,' voxed Alaric. 'They'll have men following us.' He switched to squad frequency. 'Dvorn?'

'Broken arm,' said Dvorn. It was all the answer Alaric needed – a Marine's metabolism would quickly heal a broken bone, but Dvorn would be fighting below his best until then.

The Allking's army was disintegrating below the Grey Knights. Nobles tried to organise the swarming mob to pursue the Grey Knights but it was bedlam down there, all order lost. Tancred was already in the forest, his Marines snapping storm bolter shots off at the few men trying to follow them.

Alaric glanced down and saw orange flames burning in the engines of the two Thunderhawk gunships where the Allking's men – either with great prescience or, more likely, under orders – had cut the fuel lines and set the promethium alight. If the Grey Knights were going to escape Sophano Secundus, it would not be by gunship.

IN THE MIDDLE of the night, in the heart of the forest, they buried Caanos. Stripped of his armour, the gene-seed organ in his throat cut out by Justicar Santoro, Brother Caanos was lowered into the makeshift grave.

Santoro made a short speech about duty and sacrifice and an honourable death before the gaze of the Emperor, the sort of thing Caanos might have said himself.

Alaric understood, as he heard again the same words he had listened to in every sermon and hero's funeral he had ever heard, why Ligeia had wanted him to lead. He could think outside the constraints that bound most Grey Knights, but at the same time, he was strong enough to always remember the truly important things – strength against the corruption of the Enemy, devotion to a fight that could not be won, faith in the strength the Emperor had given him.

Santoro could not lead, not really. Not when he understood his place in the universe as rigid and unchangeable. Neither could Genhain or Tancred, good men though they were. They were the soldiers that could hold back the darkness, but to lead them, they needed men like Alaric. He would be able to change the rules they lived by when the Enemy's designs meant they had to adapt. That was why Durendin had shown such faith in him, and why Ligeia had seen something in him that even grand masters did not possess.

Alaric was not sure if he was grateful. It would be so much easier just to fight and to obey. Leadership over men like the Grey Knights needed so much more than he could offer now, he had so much to learn and so many trials to endure before he could prove he was worthy.

Santoro had finished. Caanos's battle-brothers were heaping earth into the shallow grave. Alaric noted down the grave's coordinates on his data-slate to make sure that, if possible, Malleus interrogators could return and recover Caanos's body for burial in the vaults of Titan. They would recover Caanos's armour and weapons, too, which had been buried at his feet once Santoro's squad had shared out his ammunition. Alaric realised that, if they were trapped on the planet without support, they might find themselves running low.

Before they moved off Alaric sent a secure communication to the *Rubicon* telling the Malleus crew that the Thunderhawks were lost, but that shuttles could not come down to the planet. He ordered the crew not to accept any communication from anyone but him, even Ligeia herself, and told them he would contact them if those orders changed.

He received a terse acknowledgement code in reply.

Justicar Genhain walked over from Caanos's grave. 'Justicar?' he said, his bionic eye glinting in the faint moonlight. 'Where next?'

'Where else is there?' said Alaric, putting away his data-slate and unholstering his Nemesis halberd. 'Hadjisheim.'

THE ALLKING'S PALACE was a huge labyrinth, extending underground where the huge vaulted chambers became long, low galleries, plunging white stone staircases, complexes of rooms and narrow hallways, all covered in holy texts chiselled into the stone. The deeper the palace went, the more the Imperial prayers were replaced by profane texts glorifying the Secundan people's service to the Lord of Change and to a many-faced servant god that could only be Ghargatuloth. The air was close and smelled of burned flesh, the lanterns guttered and whole floors were plunged into darkness at random. The sound of angry men filtered down from every direction at once, and the whole place was like the stone warren of a hunted animal.

That animal was Inquisitor Ligeia. Five of her death cultists still lived – Taici had given his life so the rest could escape down the staircase from the grand ground floor – but there were scores of men closing in on her. She could hear prayers and curses, soldier's songs, orders yelled, the clank of armoured feet on stone, the hiss of swords unsheathed.

'Xiang, Shan, go ahead. We have to go deeper,' said Ligeia as she hurried along a long, low corridor lined with statues. Each statue's face had been eaten away as if by acid. The two death cultists loped ahead in long, graceful strides, slipped around the corner like ghosts. The others stuck close by their mistress – Ligeia could smell the spices of the artificial hormones now coursing through their veins.

The death cultists owed Ligeia lifelong fealty, even to the death, and they were literally bred to kill. The cult was a curious offshoot of the Imperial church, developing away from the monitoring of the Ecclesiarchy. It offered the deaths of their enemies as a sacrifice to the Emperor. The cultists offered their services to anyone who did the Emperor's work, and since Ligeia had saved the cult from a parasitic daemon in their midst the cult had given six of its best to guard Ligeia permanently. Each one had a complement of artificial tendons, neuro-activated hormone injectors, muscular enhancements, and digestive alterations to allow them to live off the blood they drew from their victims.

Now, they were down to five. And Ligeia knew the Allking's forces were too many for even her death cultists to face on their own. She would be trapped down beneath the palace and killed, and there was nothing she could do except fight her best and put off the inevitable.

Torch lights danced from around the corner behind Ligeia. 'Lo! Gao!' she called, but the two cultists were already sprinting back down the gallery.

Gao jumped and planted a foot on the head of the closest statue, pushing off to somersault across the corridors. A blade flashed down and the head of the first attacker to round the corner was sheared clean off. Lo dived along the floor, twin daggers flashing upwards to gut the next attacker. The attackers were members of the Allking's own guard, the same men that had escorted Ligeia to the palace on tharrback – their heads were hidden by helms with a dozen eyeholes cut into each, and they carried swords of what looked like pale bone.

Something screamed as the men hit the ground, something just beyond the wall of reality between real space and the warp. Ligeia held out a hand and let the meaning of the inscriptions on the wall bleed into her – somewhere she had passed a barrier and headed into a place where the creatures of the 'Emperor' – the Lord of Change, the Prince of a Thousand Faces, the horrible mingling of Imperial and Chaotic religion the Secundans worshipped – could walk freely. Ligeia could feel the walls of reality wearing thin.

Ligeia reached the next corner. Shan was crouched beside it, pointing forward to indicate the way was safe. 'The Enemy holds sway here,' said Ligeia to her death cultists as Gao and Lo sprinted back towards her. 'This is their territory, I can feel it. Your strength may not be enough here. I do not think we will survive, so you should know that you have always served me well, my brothers and sisters.'

The death cultists did not answer – they never spoke. But Ligeia knew they understood her.

Gao flipped out of the way as a shower of arrows broke against the wall. Someone was yelling back there – Ligeia let the meaning of the words through into her mind and she translated hatred and the joy of the hunt.

Ligeia ran on. She heard blades clashing ahead and by the time she reached the next junction, Xiang was standing between four dismembered bodies, knives slick with blood.

'They are closing in?'

Xiang nodded. Ligeia looked down at the bodies. One corpse sported three arms, and the dislodged helmet revealed a third eye in the middle of its forehead, blood-red and staring. Mutants. The touch of Chaos was hidden even in the Allking's own guard. Emperor alone knew how far the Allking himself had fallen.

Ligeia could feel hate seeping from the walls, the ceiling, the floor. With a yell, more attackers flooded forward – Ligeia saw tentacles reaching and a horribly distended jaw bristling with teeth as a score of men attacked from three directions.

Xiang ran up the wall and along the ceiling, cutting through two men's necks before she hit the ground. Lo dived headfirst, spinning, into a mass of men, daggers rotating with her, slicing limbs from bodies. Three attackers clambered over Lo and charged towards Ligeia herself – she pointed and willed the neuro-receptor in her large amethyst ring to fire. The digital weapon, rare xenos tech that had cost more than her father's palace, spat a blue-hot lance of laser through a man's throat and killed the charge before Xiahou flipped over her and killed the other two as they stumbled.

Ligeia felt the power before it was unleashed, a deep roar just below the range of hearing, building up to a psychic crescendo as a bolt of black fire ripped down one corridor. Darkness flooded the area and pincer-strong hands grabbed Ligeia from behind, throwing her across the corridor and hard into the wall. Light washed back and Ligeia saw Gao, the cultist who had saved her, blasted to bits by the psychic explosion. Gao's blood spattered over her and so loaded with hormones and stimulants was it that it burned her eyes.

The burning chunks of Gao's body thumped into the walls and floor. Ligeia shook the gore form her eyes and through her tears she saw the sorcerer, naked to the waist, his legs wrapped in a kilt made of dozens of pieces of brightly coloured cloth, the symbols of the Change God cut deep into his scrawny torso. The blood that ran from the wounds was deep blue. His face was completely featureless, a smooth globe of pale skin, but his shoulders and upper chest were covered in eyes. Black fire rippled around his hands and he launched another blast at where Xiang was holding off six swordsmen. Xiang jumped out of the way but was thrown hard against the ceiling by the force of the blast.

With each explosion the voices from the warp gibbered louder. Ligeia knew they were close to the source of the corruption that saturated Sophano Secundus.

Xiang and Shan grabbed Ligeia and dragged her through the smoke-choked corridor, away from the sorcerer and the soldiers charging past him.

Ligeia tried to read the very stones around her, divine the intricate pattern of the palace's sub-levels. She could taste the tangled knot of corridors and anterooms around her, and feel them radiating from a dark central heart.

'This way,' she gasped, indicating where the corridor turned sharply. Lo and Xaihou ran ahead while Xiang and Shan carried her as they ran, darkness swarming around her and black flames flickering.

There was a large wooden door stained dark red up ahead. Xaihou kicked it open and it splintered, red light and unearthly screams flooding out.

Ligeia was bundled inside. The room was blood-warm, the stone floor buzzing. It had many sides, but Ligeia couldn't count them; every time she looked the angles altered and the room changed size, the dimensions squirming before her eyes.

The wall hangings were covered with writing in the flowing Secundan language, the letters wriggling like worms. Piles of books and scrolls choked the edges of the room and in the centre was a shallow pit blackened by fire and redolent with burnt spices and flesh. The symbols of Chaos were everywhere, the eight-pointed star and the arcane stylised comet of the Lord of Change, fleeing from Ligeia's vision as if they were afraid to be read. The walls pulsed with power, and a blood-red glow oozed from them.

There were three doors. The shattered door behind her was already breached, Xaihou's sword flashing out to sever the sword-arms reaching through. The other two burst open and through one stormed a swarm of the Allking's soldiers. There was no doubt about their allegiance now – every one sported grotesque mutations, claws and insectoid limbs, multifaceted eyes rolling in their chests, mouths screaming from their stomachs. Some had dropped their swords to fight with spines and pincers.

Through the other door came the sorcerer. He was powerful, Ligeia could taste it. He burned his way through the door with the black fire that covered the upper half of his body. Ligeia could see his skeleton through his burning skin, glowing with power, his dozens of eyes like bright pearls jutting from his body.

'Don't touch him!' yelled Ligeia over the noise in her head. She knew that the very presence of the sorcerer was toxic – without their minds shielded, the death cultists could be killed just by touching the sorcerer. Ligeia could not move as quickly or kill as cleanly as they could, but as a Malleus-trained psyker her mind was stronger than their bodies.

Shan was sprinting around the walls, hurling knives as fast as bullets, the blades thunking into throats and stomachs. Xiang was surrounded and holding a dozen men at bay on her own, twin daggers ripping mutants open and spilling ropy entrails onto the ground. Xiahou and Lo were by Ligeia, lashing out with their swords against anyone who approached, but there were just too many of them to kill and they were getting closer.

The sorcerer stepped into the air. The room – the temple, for that was what it must be – elongated around him and suddenly he had space to rise into the air, black lightning fountaining off him. Ligeia could hear the crescendo rising again. For her and her death cultists the room was shrinking, too small to contain the psychic blast that was coming – it would incinerate everyone in the temple.

She was dead. She could not match that power in combat. Her power was to do with meaning, not destruction. But the meaning in the temple, the corruption, the hate...

Ligeia opened up her mind and it flooded in, words of hatred that covered the pages of the books, prayers of corruption from the hangings on the wall, suffering and death from the very stones beneath her feet. She rose into the air with the power of it all, she could feel it filling her. She had never felt that magnitude of hatred before, not with the Hereticus or the Malleus. It was like a living thing inside her, welling up and taking form, hot and angry, too huge for her to contain.

The Prince of a Thousand faces would rise. The Lord of Change would follow in the path Ghargatuloth carved through the stars. Chaos was the natural state of all things, and the feeble resistance of the blind would fall before the rising tide. Tzeentch would rule, and there would be no law but Chaos.

Ligeia crushed all those thoughts and images into a tiny hard ball of hate in the pit of her stomach, every word, every syllable. With a scream she tore them out of her mind and spat them out into the outside world.

A white-hot stream of pure hatred tore out of her open mouth and punched right through the chest of the sorcerer. Its power filled him up and he burst in a shower of white flame, black lightning, charred bones and shattered jewel-hard eyes. The flame coursed around the temple like a whirlpool; her death cultists somersaulted into the air over the tide of hatred as it smothered the Allking's men and stripped their deformed bodies to the bone.

The books and hangings were untouched. This was hatred so pure it could only touch living things. Then the last of it was gone and Ligeia was exhausted. Her body spasmed and fell – one of her death cultists darted forwards and caught her before she hit the hard stone floor.

She was gasping for air. She had never felt that magnitude of power before, never. She had never understood that she could contain such sheer strength of emotion – the Hereticus had never trained her to her full potential, and the Malleus after them had only wanted to ensure that her kind was proof against the Enemy. By the Throne, she could be magnificent.

Shan helped Ligeia to her feet. The death cultist inclined her head very slightly – a question. What now? Where do we go?

Ligeia looked around her. The charred bones of the Allking's men lay mingled with the books and papers piled up against the walls. She could hear no more orders yelled or feet ringing on the stone floor. She had incinerated the whole of the force sent down to corner her.

'We go back up,' said Ligeia.

EIGHT
THE MISSION

THE GREY KNIGHTS' attack came just before dawn. The storm surrounding the city formed a dome that began beyond the city walls and curved right overhead in a shield of near-opaque dark cloud and lightning, so the sun's light barely pushed through. The storm cut out all communications, electronic or psychic, but a man could walk right through it to reach the edge of the forest just beyond the high walls.

The walls were of hardwood with stone foundations and watchtowers. The Allking had put the city on a war footing – his household cavalry were in the palace, hunting down Ligeia and her death cultists, but the rest of Hadjisheim's standing army was on the walls. There were thousands of them patrolling the battlements and manning the gates that led into courtyards which would be turned into killing zones by archers and spearmen. Beyond that the lower city of Hadjisheim was a warren of poor crumbling houses, where a small body of men could mount a defence that might last for weeks. The upper city, surrounding the Allking's palace and the imposing black marble temple of the mission, was more open ground where the streets would funnel attackers into crossfires from archers on the roofs.

The Allking, however, had only ever had to fend off attacks from jealous barons or forest bandits. He didn't even know that such men as Space Marines existed.

Squad Genhain led the attack, shredding the wooden battlements and men behind them before Tancred's Terminators charged straight through the wall, splintering through into the cavity at the centre of the wall before tearing through into the city itself. Alaric and Santoro followed him through the breach, stitching storm bolter fire through the men pouring down off the walls to stop them.

Tancred kept going. The flimsy mud brick walls collapsed into powder under the boots of his Terminator armour. Townspeople fled in terror as Tancred led the charge deeper and deeper, Alaric and Santoro keeping counter-attacks off him. The Allking's soldiers were not fanatics like the household troops and they found themselves hopelessly tangled in the same streets that were supposed to fox invading enemies. When they saw the eight-foot armour-clad monsters that battered their way through the city, most of them fled. Those that fought on died beneath the guns and Nemesis blades of Alaric and Santoro.

The first archers to sight the spearhead gathered hastily on the rooftops of the upper city where the Allking's nobles cowered in the cellars below. They loosed volleys of arrows at the invaders, but every shot bounced off their armour. They set rivers of burning oil running down into the old city, but the attackers just charged straight through as if they couldn't feel pain at all.

Sprays of bolter fire sent archers fleeing from the rooftops. By the time the Grey Knights reached the avenue that led to the Allking's palace, black swarms of arrows lashed down at them like rain. Tharr were corralled into the road and lashed until they charged madly at the attackers, only to be hacked apart by the Grey Knights' blades. Squad Tancred crushed hastily-erected barricades beneath their feet, ripped apart a formation of pikemen stretched across the avenue, and pressed onwards. Squad Genhain in the rearguard sent volley after volley of bolts into the swordsmen and spearmen trying to surround the spearhead, until their weapons were dry and they had to share ammunition from Alaric and Santoro.

More and more men were drawn into the carnage. Barons eager to earn the Allking's favour charged their contingents into the upper city, forming huge swelling crowds of men who were herded like cattle into Genhain's fire zones. Dozens were trampled and crushed as they tried to flee. Archers ducked rattling volleys of bolter fire and ran when they saw the slaughter the Grey Knights wreaked on their fellow soldiers.

The last hundred men of the Allking's household army massed in the grand entrance to the palace, ready to meet the Grey Knights with claws and tentacles, the banner of the Lord of Change above them. The Allking stood ready to face the invaders personally, and his retainers were ready to collapse the roof of the entrance hall on the invaders if they broke the line.

But the Grey Knights didn't attack the palace. Tancred led them through the villa of a baron in the shadow of the palace, bypassing the palace defences. Alaric and Santoro fended off a frenzied charge from the Allking's men while Tancred bashed through the stone walls and crunched through carved black wood furniture.

The Grey Knights went out through the back wall and their objective became clear. Alaric had ordered his Marines to head for the most likely source of the darkness on Sophano Secundus: the mission temple.

TANCRED TORE THE tall black-stained wooden doors off the front of the mission, his gauntleted hands splintering through the wood. Tancred was covered in dust from pulverised mud brick houses and battered from where he had charged straight through solid marble walls, but there was no sign of his slowing down. His Terminators charged in through the breach with him, their massive frames splintering the stone steps that led up to the doorway.

'Genhain, cover us!' voxed Alaric. 'Santoro, with me!' Alaric led his squad and Santoro's in the wake of Squad Tancred. Arrows were lancing down from the nearby palace and Alaric could hear the chattering of Squad Genhain's storm bolters as they returned fire. Genhain would be responsible for keeping the battle for Hadjisheim outside the entrance to the mission, allowing the rest of the Grey Knights to deal with whatever they found inside.

Thick, heavy air rolled out as Alaric followed Tancred through the doorway: incense and burnt flesh stank. A hoarse, dim roaring, like a distant hurricane, keened from the heart of the temple.

Alaric's auto-senses automatically yanked his pupils open in response to the dark but still it was like charging into a sandstorm. Heavy, solid darkness crowded Alaric. He could just see the shadowy shapes of the Terminators ahead, muted muzzle flashes marking the gunfire they were sending ripping through the interior of the temple.

Static flooded the vox. 'Santoro, back us up!' yelled Alaric above the roar, and plunged into the darkness after Tancred.

The screams of daemons rang out like a peal of bells, discordant and terrible, flooding Alaric's senses. For a moment he thought he would black out – and then he saw the pink and blue flames billowing up from the marble floor, bright in the shadows, reaching up like fingers to surround Squad Tancred.

A blast of light burned straight up from the floor like a spotlight, illuminating the ceiling of the temple. Alaric saw it was impossibly high – the dimensions of the Mission had warped horribly, far too large to be contained within the building itself. This was a place not fully within real space – it was saturated by the warp, taking on the strange properties of the immaterium. The ceiling was like an unnatural sky far above, ugly bulbous shapes of stone looming down from the distant walls. It was like being inside the belly of a titanic stone creature, and the mission's structure flexed and bowed as if that creature were taking breath. Lightning crackled far overhead. The walls groaned.

Daemons were boiling up through the glowing floor, long-limbed, shining, flame-spewing creatures. Alaric dived into the fray to cut through the circle of daemons surrounding Tancred.

The daemons screamed as they touched the sacred wards woven into the Grey Knights' armour. Tancred beheaded one, spilling globules of glowing blood that fell upwards towards the distant ceiling. Alaric glimpsed surreal, individual combats through the darkness, illuminated in shafts of light from below. He saw Justicar Tancred slashing at the daemons, Brother Locath fending off reaching hands that grabbed at him with charred fingers, Brother Karlin aiming his incinerator into the monsters rising around his feet and pumping a gout of flame straight downwards until it looked like he was standing in a volcano.

Alaric cut downwards and felt daemon's flesh coming apart under the blade of his halberd. A crack rang out as Dvorn, at Alaric's side, drove the head of his Nemesis hammer down into the body of a gibbering daemon. Alaric saw that Tancred was surrounded – the Grey Knights were trained and equipped to fight the daemonic, but there was a prodigious tide of them erupting now, just like on Victrix Sonora, just like on Khorion IX a thousand years before.

A shrill scream cut through the din of battle and shapes speared down, flying creatures with bladed wings that swooped low and tore through Squad Tancred. Alaric jabbed upwards and gouged off the wing of one screamer, sending it cartwheeling away, spraying burning blood. Alaric saw Brother Krae, one of Tancred's oldest battle-brothers, beheaded by a swooping daemon that caught fire as it touched him. Krae's Terminator-armoured body fell to the ground and his body sunk into the deeper darkness that opened beneath him.

'Krae!' bellowed Tancred. He grabbed one of the swooping daemons with his bolter hand, dragging it downwards and slicing it clean in half with his sword. But there were more of them, whole squadrons of them dropping from far above to shriek through the shadows. Brother Vien, just behind Alaric, brought one screamer down with a volley of bolt shells, and Haulvarn spitted another on the point of his sword.

But Squad Tancred were in the centre of it all. Tancred himself almost lost an arm to one that ripped its blades deep into his shoulder pad. Alaric plunged deeper into the fray and the daemons below parted as he waded through them, his wards burning bright-hot, reflected in the burns that covered the daemons' skin. But there were so many of them.

A white light shone down suddenly as they fended off the daemons around them, and Alaric saw that someone was rising from the flood in the middle of Squad Tancred, directing the screamers – a bent and wizened figure dressed in a long flowing cloak, a mockery of Ecclesiarchical robes. The hood fell back and Alaric saw an emaciated face, thin as a corpse's, with huge, white, pupilless eyes that dripped purple lightning.

Polonias, the missionary – but Alaric felt such age and malice emanating from the figure that it must be someone far older than Polonias was supposed to be, perhaps even the first missionary, Crucien. If that was the case then Ghargatuloth had planted his plan on Sophano Secundus even before he was first banished by Mandulis.

Tancred strode towards the elevated figure but the missionary drew a long, gnarled wooden club from thin air and met Tancred's Nemesis sword in a flash of sparks. The missionary struck back with inhuman speed and Tancred only just parried the blow, forced onto the back foot.

Alaric tried to close with Tancred and the missionary but the hands reaching up from the floor slowed him down, and for every one he and his squad severed three more seemed to reach up in their place. Tancred fought on, cutting deep into the missionary's body only for the wound to heal up with a ripple of purple fire.

Tancred was almost on his knees, the missionary's staff striking again and again, the storm bolter fire from his Terminators spattering against a shield of purple-black lightning that the missionary span around himself. Tancred was as physically strong a man as Alaric had ever fought with, but the missionary was a fearsome champion of Chaos and his blows kept raining down.

There was a flash of light from a discharging Nemesis blade and the head of a halberd punched out through the front of the missionary's chest. Behind the missionary, Alaric saw Justicar Santoro flanked by his squad, covered from head to feet in smoking daemon's blood, determination behind the glinting glass of his helmet's eyepieces. Santoro twisted the blade of his halberd and opened up the missionary's torso, spilling burning organs onto the floor. Tancred rose to his knees and sliced off one of the missionary's arms, then as Santoro held the missionary wriggling like a worm on a hook Tancred cut down with his sword and clove the missionary's head clean in two down to the collar bone.

Pink fire blossomed up from the missionary's ruined skull and spurted from his massive chest wound. The screaming of daemons rose higher and with a thunderclap the missionary exploded, throwing Terminators and power-armoured Grey Knights to the floor. Chunks of flaming flesh flew everywhere.

The discharge of sorcerous energy rippled through the stones and Alaric felt them shift beneath his feet. Not trusting the vox, he ripped off his helmet and took in a searing breath of hot incense, blood, and flamer chemicals.

'Out! Everyone, now!' he yelled at the top of his voice as the floor pitched suddenly, huge chunks of black marble falling. A pillar gave way and crashed to the ground like a falling tree. Falling sheets of crumbling marble reduced the visibility even more, and even through his auto-senses Alaric felt as if he were blundering through pitch darkness.

The shards of fire that leapt past him were bolts of covering fire from Squad Genhain, and Alaric knew he was heading the right way. He stumbled, but Brother Clostus grabbed his shoulder pad and dragged him forward, through the doorway and into the comparative brightness outside.

Alaric saw the steps up to the mission temple were littered with bodies, many of them mutants in the livery of the Allking's household troops. Squad Genhain had held off a spirited counter-attack on the steps, and by the wounds on the bodies had used hand-to-hand combat when their ammunition ran low.

'Good work, justicar,' said Alaric, his helmet still off.

'What was in there?' asked Genhain.

'The missionary. He's dead but the whole place is coming down. Get us into cover.'

Genhain nodded and pointed towards a single-storey complex, the villa of some feudal lord a short sprint away from the temple. Tharn and Horst, Genhain's two psycannon Marines, led the way, hunting for targets as they ran towards the building. Alaric ordered his squad to follow and hung back to see

Santoro lead Squad Tancred out. Both squads were badly beaten up, their armour covered in claw marks and spattered with smouldering gore. The smell was appalling. Brother Mykros and Brother Marl from Squad Santoro carried Brother Krae's massive body between them, Tancred himself close behind with his Terminators.

Alaric jammed his helmet back on his head in time for Brother Tharn's vox. 'We've got hostiles at the palace's rear gates,' he said.

'Heading this way?' asked Alaric, looking towards the imposing rear wall of the palace where an ornate archway led into the Allking's gardens.

'I don't think so. Looks like they're fleeing... one's huge, a mutant maybe...'

Alaric saw Allking Rashemha the Stout storm through the archway leading from the white stone palace, a ragged band of his retainers and courtiers around him. The Allking carried a huge mace and was swinging it indiscriminately, knocking his own troops off their feet to keep some unseen enemy away from him. He was yelling orders and curses, and blood streamed down his face.

Alaric hadn't seen the Allking before but the man's massive girth and authority over the hapless stragglers around him left him in little doubt.

Dark shapes flitted around him. One of them stopped for a split-second, spinning in the air, and Alaric recognised it as one of Ligeia's death cultists. Twin swords flashed and two retainers fell dead, their heads neatly removed. Another death cultist ran up the inside of the arch, flipped over, and took off the Allking's hand. His hand and mace clattered to the ground and the Allking roared as thick, writhing worms spurted from the stump of his wrist instead of blood.

Both death cultists slashed at the Allking, opening up dozens of wounds that all bled fountains of hideous worms. With a final bellow of defiance the Allking's body disintegrated into a foul squirming heap of wriggling vermin.

The death cultists landed and gave the heap a wide berth, neatly despatching the few surviving courtiers as they skirted around it. Then, two more death cultists stepped through the arch and around the bubbling mess – these two were carrying Inquisitor Ligeia between them, who somehow managed to look stately and unflustered as the death cultists placed her back on the ground.

The death cultists and Ligeia hurried towards Alaric, the cultists swatting away the few arrows that were still being fired their way from the upper levels of the palace. Ligeia's face was stained with smoke and blood and her hair was messy and singed, but she didn't seem hurt. In fact, to Alaric she looked rather more dangerous than he had seen her before.

'Justicar,' said Ligeia as her death cultists accompanied her to the threshold of the mansion Genhain had indicated. 'I am glad you could join us.' She glanced back at the mission – the roof had just fallen in and a cloud of noisome black dust spewed from the open entrance. 'I think we have found ample evidence of Ghargatuloth here.' Alaric saw that both Ligeia and the two death cultists who had carried her were also carrying several large leatherbound books and rolled-up scrolls and banners.

'The missionary is dead,' said Alaric. 'We have lost two men and several injured.'

'The missionary was Crucien,' said Ligeia. 'Ghargatuloth has had this planet marked since before the Imperium discovered it.'

'It must be important to it,' said Alaric, leading Ligeia into the shelter of the mansion. It was all white marble and hanging tapestries, relatively untouched by the fighting. 'Crucien had daemons and sorcery at his command. He almost overwhelmed us. It takes a very powerful man to do that and Ghargatuloth must have taken a great risk to give him such power.'

Ligeia indicated the books she was carrying. 'Perhaps there is something here that will tell us why. We need to get back to the *Rubicon*.'

'We lost the Thunderhawks,' said Alaric, 'but I can get a message to the *Rubicon* once we're out of the city and they can send shuttles down for us.'

'Good. Once we're out of here we can drop a few torpedoes on this place. What do you think?'

Alaric nodded. 'It would be my pleasure.'

Ligeia smiled. The expression was stark contrast to the blood on her face. 'We'd better get moving, then.'

NINE
THALASSOCRES

Two thousand years before the outpost on Sophano Secundus was lost, a great compact was signed.

The Prince of a Thousand faces withdrew from his real space lair on Khorion IX into the warp, where the Lord of Change himself had cried out – a terrible keening loaded with unholy knowledge, the tolling of a great bell at the heart of the warp. The other powers of the warp – sometimes allies, usually accursed – shrunk away, the daemons said, cowering from the incandescent might of Tzeentch. The god himself sent ripples through the warp, calling his servants to him.

The Prince heeded the call. The Prince could do this because he was much, much more than his daemonic body – he was knowledge, pure information, revelations of darkness hidden in the hearts of millions of men. He could be in real space and the warp at the same time, pulling puppet strings in both universes, doing the work of the Change. For the Prince of a Thousand Faces was one of the most powerful of its kind.

The Conclave gathered at Thalassocres, a benighted world trapped screaming in the warp like a madman in a cell. Every hour its continents changed, melting into the seas of liquid nitrogen and spewing great mountains into the sky. The Change God's faithful gathered and soon those awestruck by their fellow daemons fled in terror, leaving only the most powerful sons of Tzeentch.

Their followers ran out across the melting plains of Thalassocres, settling old scores and marking up new ones in idle battle while their masters brooded. The Princes competed in the might of their armies and the magnificence of their displays. Tzeentch ignored the best and awarded the least with gifts that, in centuries to come, would rot their souls and lead to their downfall, for this was the favoured vengeance of the Lord of Change.

Ghargatuloth was in the foremost group, along with Bokor the Wildsman who turned whole species to the cause of the Change, and Maleficos of the Burning Hands who struck like a thunderbolt to plunge star systems into war. Master Darkeye, who hid amongst mankind and tormented it invisibly, and Themiscyron the Star-Dragon held court on Thalassocres, too, magnificent and savage. A hundred other Lords of the Change took their places on the melting plains, and courts of daemons cavorted around them, gibbering and monstrous, until the whole planet rang with the praises of the Change.

Thalassocres was a great beacon of worship, a lynchpin of the Change, and the Conclave caused much mayhem in the minds of humankind. Although mankind's sages searched long for the reasons behind rashes of madness throughout their galaxy, to them Thalassocres remained hidden.

When Tzeentch spoke, the planet shook. Its crust and mantle were torn off and to this day, they say, Thalassocres is not one planet but a shoal of drifting continents surrounding a single core. Those not strong enough to hear the words of Tzeentch were thrown off into the warp, but the strongest stayed, their courts remaining glorious on the floating shelves of melting stone.

Tzeentch spoke to them of impossible things, of the tangled threads of fate that ran through the universe like threads of a tapestry, of the immense shifting components of reality – time, space, the massed minds of humanity and the dozens of alien species that had yet to play their parts, the mindless hordes of predators teeming in the warp, the powers of Chaos themselves. The greatest of Tzeentch's followers could divine meaning from the stream of concepts the voice of Tzeentch conveyed. Some found intricate plots for them to enact on reality. Others saw glimpses of a future they could alter, or bring to pass. Some saw only desolation and hatred, and revelled in it, for they were the most savage agents of the Change.

Some were destroyed, unable to comprehend the majesty of the Change God's vision.

Ghargatuloth was not destroyed. Nor did he skim some plan from the surface of Tzeentch's words. Instead, the Prince of a Thousand Faces immersed himself in his god's message. Knowledge streamed around him, and straight through him until he was wallowing in a raging torrent of information like a white river of flame that coursed through the broken heart of Thallasocres.

For days on end, measured in the strange timescale of the warp, Ghargatuloth received the revelation of Tzeentch. The other daemon princes looked on in awe, hatred and jealousy. Some were certain that Ghargatuloth would be destroyed. The daemons at his feet were swept aside by the tide of revelations. The substance of Thalassocres was further fractured by the sheer power of Tzeentch. There was a permanent scar left on the warp, a dark barren shadow, but Ghargatuloth remained.

In real space, Ghargatuloth's daemonic body shuddered with the effort of receiving the revelation. Some say this caused the sages of mankind to first realise that the Prince of a Thousand Faces was in their midst. The indigenous life of Khorion IX was extinguished, and space was tormented for light years around.

Then, at last, it was over. The white river of knowledge stopped. Thalassocres fell silent.

And when Ghargatuloth arose again, a thousand new faces looked out upon the warp.

LIGEIA SNAPPED HER head back in her seat, trying to shake out the images that filled it. She pulled her hands away from the book on her writing desk, the skin on her fingers and palms burning with the unholiness of the knowledge covering the pages.

The dark wood panelling and lustrous furnishings of her quarters filtered back into view. She was back on Trepytos, in the quarters Inquisitor Klaes's staff had supplied – but the images in her head were still ghosted over her vision. Ghargatuloth, a formless chaotic monster, bowing beneath a raging river of obscene knowledge. The words of Tzeentch – the god of change, trickery and sorcery, one of the foremost of the Chaos powers – echoing around the warp and shattering a world with their power.

The contents of the book were even more invasive than the brief flashes of blasphemy she had received from the wooden sculpture. The passage she had just experienced – pulled directly from the pages by her psychic sight – was just a tiny fragment of the revelations the book contained. The meaning was so pure and undiluted that it had to have been dictated directly to the author by Ghargatuloth himself, and Ligeia was sure she could taste the old human malice of Crucien behind the words.

Dictated by a daemon prince, written down by a thousand-year-old Chaos sorcerer; Ligeia was shocked at their sheer intensity.

The book in front of her was just one of more than a dozen recovered from the temple beneath the Allking's palace. In addition there were more than thirty scrolls, each one holding a complex prayer or spell, and the banners from the walls. Many of them were written in the Secundan language which Ligeia was having to learn very quickly from the sketchiest of references, and most referred to 'the Emperor' as a euphemism for the Prince of a Thousand Faces. Without Ligeia's powers, they would take years to translate. Ligeia wished that she had years to do it in, instead of receiving the concentrated meaning straight into the centre of her mind.

She closed the book and placed it on the floor of her chambers. Even wearing her nightdress she was sweating with the effort of understanding, and straggles of her hair were clinging to her cold, damp face.

She heard footsteps on the carpet behind her. When not actively defending her, the death cultists were courteous enough to make some noise when they moved around so she knew where they were.

Ligeia turned to see Xiang standing behind her. The death cultist's quizzical stance reminded Ligeia that she had summoned the death cultists – Xiang had probably been standing there some time before letting Ligeia know she was there.

'Ah. Xiang, yes. Please excuse me.' Ligeia managed a faltering smile. 'I need you to perform an errand for me. It is rather menial but I need to know it will be done. Here.'

Ligeia took a folded piece of parchment from her desk, on which she had written her orders in her elegant, sloping hand. Xiang plucked it from her hand, and read it.

'I know,' said Ligeia. 'One of the justicars would probably be more efficient. But... you are mine, you four. They do not belong to me like you do. I have arranged for Inquisitor Klaes to supply a ship – it is small and lightly armed but it is very fast. You should be there within two weeks, if you leave immediately.'

Xiang bowed her head and, without turning around, backed swiftly out of the room. Ligeia had never worked out how the death cultists communicated with one another – she could sense the meanings of their conversations without seeing any movement or hearing any sound – but Xiang would be going to tell her fellow death cultists what Ligeia wanted of them.

There were only four left now. Death cultists, almost by definition, did not grieve – death was a welcome end for them, as long as it came in such a way that their own lives were offered to the Emperor in sacred combat. But they had lost two of their number on Sophano Secundus, and Ligeia was saddened to see two such highly trained and devoted servants of the Emperor lose their lives. They protected Ligeia but, even more, Ligeia was responsible for them. She owned them, and she was their reason to exist. Their deaths were echoes of her own death.

There had been no funeral rites – they had left Taici and Gao on Sophano Secundus. Their deaths alone were sacred, and what happened to the bodies was irrelevant. Ligeia found their lack of pretensions quite refreshing but she would still not want to be left, decaying and forgotten where she had died. She hoped that someone would feel responsible for her when the time came.

Ligeia poured herself another glass of amasec, letting its strong fruity smell chase some of the horrors out of her head before taking a swallow to calm her shaking hands.

Then, she took one of the other books from the floor, put it on the desk, and placed her hands on the cover. She took a deep breath, and dived back into the revelations of Ghargatuloth.

JUSTICAR GENHAIN TOOK careful aim and waited for a moment, as the lenses of his bionic eye snapped into focus. Then he fired a single bolt through the forehead of the human-shaped target at the far end of the gallery.

The shooting gallery on the *Rubicon* was a long, low room, windowless like an underground chamber, with walls carved deeply with scenes of battle and victory intended to focus the mind on diligence and improvement. The columns separating the firing positions were carved into the likenesses of Imperial saints – Genhain at that moment was flanked by a glowering Saint Praxides and Saint Jason of Huale, who were both trampling hapless heretics beneath their feet. Several servitors patrolled the shooters' area, waiting for the Grey Knight to require more ammunition, while the firing range itself was empty save for targets hanging from the ceiling as they trundled along.

'Good?' asked Alaric, standing just behind Genhain.

'Doesn't feel right,' replied Genhain, lowering Alaric's storm bolter. 'Leave it with me for a few hours. I'll have it better than new.'

Genhain had a feel for guns that rivalled any Grey Knight in the Chapter. He was one of the best shots the Grey Knights could field and, even with the existing wargear rites, many of the Grey Knights who knew him would ask him to check their guns for flaws they could not detect. A storm bolter might be working perfectly as far as other Marines were concerned, but Genhain would know if it was too likely to jam, to buck in the hand on full auto, to lose its accuracy in certain conditions.

'Do not neglect your own men on my account,' said Alaric.

'My squad are doing well,' said Genhain. 'They are observant and in good spirits. I'd rather not lead them too closely when it comes to prayers and suchlike. It always feels better to lead yourself in such things.'

'And their guns?'

Genhain smiled and took aim at the same target again. 'Their guns are good.' He fired again, the bullet hole appearing just above the first.

'They fought well on Sophano Secundus.'

'They did. I am proud.' Another shot, this one wide. Genhain bit down a curse and began to inspect the bolter's firing mechanism. 'I was worried about the inquisitor.'

'Ligeia?'

'I don't think she is a fighter. She looked rattled.'

'Ligeia is a strong woman, justicar. You're right though, she'd rather leave all the fighting to us.' Alaric thought for a moment. Genhain led his men very differently from Santoro or Tancred, and Alaric knew Genhain's judgement was sound. 'What do you think of her?'

Genhain looked up from Alaric's bolter. 'Me? I think she is very good at her job, just not as good at ours.'

'Well, she won't be fighting any time soon. They broke Valinov back on Mimas and he let slip that Ghargatuloth can only be killed by a "lightning bolt". The Nemesis sword Mandulis used was fashioned into a lightning bolt, so Ligeia has sent her death cultists to get it from the catacombs on Titan.'

'They could have trouble,' said Genhain. 'It is difficult even for inquisitors to get into Titan, let alone have one of the grand masters disinterred.' Genhain tightened the firing mechanism and took aim again. 'But at least it shows Ligeia understands us.'

'How so?'

'She asks us only to fight and doesn't expect anything else. She could have sent you to Titan, and you could have retrieved Mandulis's sword far more effectively, but she didn't. She respects us. Some of the Ordo Malleus think the Grey Knights were created to serve them, but we are a sovereign and independent Chapter, as much as the Space Wolves or Dark Angels or anyone else.'

Genhain had deliberately named two of the more unpredictable Space Marine Chapters. 'Few Grey Knights would speak that way,' said Alaric.

'It is only the truth.' Genhain fired again, this time on full auto, and a cluster of holes blossomed in the centre of the target's head. 'If the Grey Knights did not think for themselves, they would be far weaker soldiers. That is the core of what a Space Marine is. We work with the Ordo Malleus because it is the most effective way to do what we have to do, but we were not founded for their benefit. We were founded to do the will of the Emperor, just like the Inquisition. I think Ligeia understands that.'

'I am glad you trust me well enough to tell me this,' said Alaric. Many of the more traditionally-minded Grey Knights would think that Genhain had strayed dangerously close to insubordination. Alaric, on the other hand, was quite glad that the Marines he had chosen to accompany him on this mission were able to think for themselves. If there was one danger in the way Grey Knights were trained and indoctrinated, it was that their own spirits would be so crushed beneath the weight of dogma and duty and they would not be able to form their own judgement.

'If I cannot trust my commander, Alaric,' replied Genhain, handing Alaric his bolter, 'then who can I trust? This gun could have lost accuracy in a protracted firefight, but its machine-spirit has been persuaded to be more co-operative.'

Alaric took the gun and fitted it back onto his gauntlet. It felt subtly different, as if it belonged there. 'Thank you, justicar. It always helps to shoot straighter.'

'You have to trust your gun,' said Genhain with a smile. 'Otherwise, where would we be?'

WHEN SOPHANO SECUNDUS fell, a silent call went out across the Trail.

On Volcanis Ultor, a sect hidden deep in the under-hive of Hive Tertius overloaded the city's geothermal heatsinks and caused several layers of hive city to be swallowed up in nuclear fire.

Even as ships sent by Inquisitor Klaes pounded Had-jisheim into smouldering ash from orbit, a mutiny in the small sector battlefleet caused three cruisers to be scuttled with all hands.

A prophet appeared on the forge world Magnos Omicron preaching the new word of the Machine God, demanding innovation and creativity over the worship of the Omnissiah and the endless search for perfection. Before he was found and killed, he had rallied three forge cities to his cause and it took a minor civil war amongst the tech-guard to stop his crusade.

Provost Marechal lost thousands of Arbites as he shuttled them from world to world to douse the flash-points where heretics suddenly played their hands. From an orbital command station around Victrix Sonora, Marechal co-ordinated hundreds of Precincts as they battled riots and rebellion across the Trail.

On the garden world of Farfallen, once a playground for the Trail's rich, a previously unknown tribe of feral humans crept out of the overgrown botanical gardens to slaughter the planet's isolated Imperial communities.

The governor's villa on Solshen XIX, an agri-world whose wide oceans teemed with fish that fed the Trail's hives, was transformed overnight into a charnel house overrun with daemons. A cult led by the governor's own son had summoned creatures of the warp in response to visions from the Prince of a Thousand Faces, and the governor had been hanged in a noose of his own skin from the cliffs surrounding his villa.

Many thousands on the Trail's downtrodden hive worlds would starve with the planet lost to Chaos and anarchy.

A hundred cults broke their cover and engaged in wanton, apparently purposeless destruction. Places of worship were looted, hundreds in one night in a seemingly co-ordinated strike against the Ecclesiarchy and the Imperial Church.

It could not last long. The cults could only do so much before the combined efforts of the Arbites, the Imperial Navy and the horrified population stamped them out. And in a way, that was the worst thing about the uprisings on the Trail of St Evisser – they had all the hallmarks of an endgame. It was the final setting of the stage for something vast and terrible, where cults hidden for centuries gave their lives away to enact plots dictated to them by sinister voices in their heads.

The Ecclesiarchy responded with uncharacteristic speed. The Order of the Bloody Rose sent a Preceptory of Sisters of Battle to be co-ordinated by Cardinal Recoba on Volcanis Ultor, and their request for additional manpower was met by the Imperial Guard, namely the Methalor 12th Scout Regiment and the Balurian Heavy Infantry. Even the Imperial Navy diverted a force of subsector battlefleet size from the long journey up to Cadia. Someone powerful in the Ecclesiarchy was clearly rattled by what was happening on the Trail – but though the Sisters and Guardsmen were deployed to guard religious sites throughout the Trail, they could do little to stop the steadily rising tide of heresy.

Ghargatuloth had spoken. And to those who knew how to listen, everything he said indicated that it would not be long now before the Trail was drowned in horror.

TEN
MIMAS

THERE WAS A place on Mimas, just outside the great crater, where the earth was torn and scarred. It had been dug up thousands of times by servitor labourers and covered over again. Here and there seismic activity had caused broken bones, even the odd grinning skull, to break the surface, only to be re-buried by roving patrol servitors. In the centre of the broken land was a single building in the High Gothic style, its every surface tooled deeply with images of punishment and retribution – sinners burning in the many indistinct hells of the Imperial cult, vengeance crashing down on the heads of the heretic, the eyes of the Emperor seeing every sin and the servants of the Emperor exacting revenge. Men were killed in scores of ways, from hanging to dismemberment to exposure in the toxic Miman atmosphere, all recorded in sculpture on the building's pillars and pediments.

Dozens of gun-servitors guarded each door. A garrison of Ordo Malleus mind-scrubbed troops stood permanently at attention in their quarters below the building, ready to react to any threat. The building itself was formed around a central chamber with many galleries looking onto it, where a single raised platform stood surrounded by seating for dignitaries, technicians and archivists, like the slab at the centre of an anatomist's theatre.

Gholic Ren-Sar Valinov was brought to the execution chamber on Mimas seven weeks after he had been broken by Explicator Riggensen. Valinov had not said one more word since that day. If anything he appeared more sullen and uncooperative than before, as if cursing himself silently for letting Riggensen's interrogation crack his mask of infallibility. And so the interrogation staff on Mimas had advised the lord inquisitors of the Ordo Malleus that Valinov was of no further intelligence value.

The Conclave of the lord inquisitors unanimously approved the execution of Valinov. It transpired that Ligeia had indeed been bluffing when she had first questioned Valinov – there would be no elaborate psychic half-death, just an old-fashioned execution. Valinov had been convicted of several capital charges but it was as punishment for grand heresy that he was brought from the prison to the execution chamber just outside Mimas's crater, and Imperial law required that the punishment for grand heresy was death by dismemberment.

IT WAS A solemn occasion. There was no sadness that Valinov was about to die – there was, however, a shame-tinged regret that a fellow inquisitor, once a greatly respected and valuable man, should have fallen so low. The Ordo Malleus had lost inquisitors before to Radicalism and worse fates, but every time it happened the wound was as deep. The Malleus was proud of what it did, and every traitor amongst them was an affront to that pride.

Explicator Riggensen was there to take down any deathbed confessions Valinov might make. He had witnessed executions before but the antiseptic smell of the execution chamber and the gleaming insectoid shape of the servitor-mangler suspended from the ceiling still made him uneasy – which was saying something, considering his occupation.

An official clerk sat at a lectern in front of Riggensen, a pale and heavily augmented woman who scritched details of the execution with quills mounted on metal armatures she had instead of arms. The clerk's head darted from side to side as she noticed who entered the darkened, circular chamber – several more clerks and archivists observing particular aspects of the execution entered, shuffling along in their long robes.

Inquisitor Nyxos entered next, wearing ceremonial crimson robes over his whirring exoskeleton. His two advisors were with him, the ancient astropath and the young tactical officer in her undecorated Naval officer's uniform.

Medical technicians were next, the chief medicae manning the controls for the servitor-mangler and the others checking the lifesign monitors attached to the table in the raised centre of the room. There had been occasions in the past where the executed criminal had not died in spite of the comprehensive nature of the servitor-mangler, and so the chief medicae would be required to assert that lifesigns had ceased.

The next individuals to enter were a surprise to Riggensen. Four death cultists walked in, lithe and athletic figures in glossy bodygloves festooned with daggers and swords. Riggensen glanced over the clerk's shoulder as she wrote down that the death cultists were representing Inquisitor Ligeia. It seemed right to Riggensen that Ligeia would want someone she trusted to witness Valinov die with their own eyes. Otherwise she might never have believed he was truly dead.

The various dignitaries and adepts filled the seats around the pedestal. The lumoglobes dimmed until only the pedestal was lit, bathed in a pool of pale unforgiving light. Then a set of mechanical security doors slid open and Valinov was brought in.

Stripped to the waist, with his hands and feet shackled, Valinov was still an imposing figure. His heavy dark tattoos gave him an almost feral look, accentuated by his sharp, intelligent face and the cords of muscle wrapped around his arms and torso. His head was high and he showed no fear – but then true heretics never did, not until their souls were removed from their body and thrust before the vengeful gaze of the Emperor.

Just by looking at the prisoner, every witness to the execution could tell the ex-inquisitor was a dangerous man. Not even the rigorous work of Mimas's interrogators and explicators had broken him, save for Riggensen's sole moment of fleeting triumph. Death, most of them would agree, was too good for Valinov – but when someone this dangerous was still alive, there could be no guarantee he was safe.

An old preacher stood in the front row, his heavy crimson and white robes dark in the dim light. He read from a battered leather prayer book, giving Valinov the

Cursed Rites that would mark his diseased soul as an enemy of the Emperor.

'Though your spirit is rotten and your deeds most heinous, we call upon the Emperor to look upon that spirit in pure and just judgement...'

The preacher's voice droned on through the familiar lines. The chief medicae made a last few checks of the mangler apparatus while his orderlies affixed various electrodes and sensors to Valinov's shaven skin. The clerk seated in front of Riggensen wrote constantly, noting every correct procedure as it was completed. The blood drains were opened in the chamber's floor. Riggensen himself was handed a data-slate and quill, so he could sign that he had witnessed Valinov's death. The servitor-mangler unfolded and each of its six bladed manipulators were tested quickly in turn as the preacher's assistants made the sign of the aquila over Valinov's chest.

The orderly carrying the organ bucket stood ready. The various parts of Valinov's body – head, torso, viscera – would be buried separately in the plain of unmarked graves around the execution building, to prevent some dark power from bringing the corpse back to life. It was a lesson that had been learned the hard way.

The death cultists observed keenly, their eyes expressionless, their bodies motionless save for the occasional twitch of their drum-taut muscles.

The preacher was finishing. The two Malleus troopers flanking Valinov manhandled the prisoner onto the pedestal, where his manacles slotted neatly into the locks at the base and above the head.

The mangler descended, the chief medicae working the controls. The clerk scribbled with greater rapidity.

The front rows would be spattered with blood, but it was worth the indignity to ensure that another foe of the Emperor was dead.

'...and so, Lord Emperor, we place this wretched soul before you and remove it from this body whose hands have committed such foulness. May there be redemption for this soul in the eyes of the God-Emperor, and when there can be no redemption, may the hatred of the God-Emperor destroy it for ever.'

There was a pause before the mangler did its work. It was traditional, like so much of the execution – the prisoner to be executed could, if there was some possibility of redemption, cry out for mercy from the Emperor. No one expected Valinov to speak.

'So it has come to this,' he said in a low, quiet voice, as if speaking to himself. 'The threads are drawing taut. This death is the death of galaxies. You may begin.'

As if in response, the hand of the chief medicae reached for the switch that would begin the dismemberment. His hand never got that far.

There was a flash of silver, like a tiny sliver of lightning arcing across the room, and suddenly a long bright blade was stuck quivering into the seat behind the medicae and his severed hand thudded onto the floor beneath him.

Riggensen saw the chief medicae look up at his attacker and stare into the unblinking, unforgiving eyes behind the mask of a death cultist.

The mind-wiped troops standing by the pedestal reacted first. The lasblasts from the hellguns they carried spattered across the room but the death cultist had read their movements perfectly and she twisted like a gymnast, the blasts ripping through the air centimetres from her skin. A split second later both troopers were dead, sliced in two across the waist by the twin curved short swords of the second cultist.

Inquisitor Nyxos bellowed and took a silver-plated plasma pistol from beneath his robes, his servos screaming as they forced his limbs to move with supernatural speed. The young tactical officer beside him hit the ground, her Naval officer's cap flying.

The two remaining death cultists leapt from their seats, one heading for Nyxos, the other for the pedestal where Valinov lay. The preacher threw his old, frail body between the cultists and the pedestal, but he didn't even slow the cultist down as he was neatly bisected by the cultist's sword.

Riggensen carried an autopistol as a sidearm, and he took it out from beneath his plain explicator's uniform as he stood up. He snapped off a shot at the cultist who had just cut off the medicae's hand, but the cultist jinked to the side faster than the bullet.

The cultist by the pedestal flashed his sword down twice, and Valinov was out of his restraints. He rolled off the pedestal and Nyxos, quickly realising that Valinov was the biggest threat in the room, fired. The cultist threw himself in front of Nyxos and the plasma pistol's blast ripped through the cultist, the power of the shot dissipating as it vaporised his midriff.

Gunfire shattered down from everywhere, from adepts' sidearms, from Nyxos, from Riggensen. The cultist whom Riggensen had so nearly killed flipped over the head of the adept in front of him. Riggensen felt sure the cold steel would slice through him but instead the cultist flipped over the heads of the audience and ran impossibly along the wall behind them, sprinting halfway round the circular room to slash her sword through the Malleus troopers.

Riggensen fired again at her but, as the autopistol kicked in his hand, he could see the cultist ducking the shots or stepping to the side, moving faster than anyone should.

Valinov was taking shelter by the slab he should have died on. He was showered in the blood of the cultist who had died for him, and his hard dark eyes were glancing back and forth as he evaluated all the many threats to his life that were unfolding. Nyxos with his plasma pistol, who would at least have to wait a few seconds while the weapon recharged. Nyxos's assistant, the tactical officer who would surely have a sidearm of her own. The mind-wiped troopers who would shoot him without hesitation if any of them survived long enough. The servitor-mangler which was still writhing lethally less than a metre over his head.

Riggensen, whose autopistol shots seemed to be moving slower than if he had thrown them.

The cultist heading for Nyxos leapt across the room, slamming into the ageing inquisitor. Mechanised limbs clattered to the ground. A blade shot out and rang against the bracing around his pistol arm. A second plasma bolt ripped out, scouring the black glossy mask off half the cultist's face.

The tactical officer leapt to her feet, plunging a glowing power knife (a beautiful weapon, something that would be awarded to an outstanding cadet at one of the Imperial Navy's finest academies) into the cultist's calf. A flick of the wrist and the cultist threw her across the room to slam into the front row of seats with a gruesome crack.

The third surviving cultist, the one who had cut up Valinov's guards, finished the job of killing the chief medicae with a thrown knife that thudded into his throat and pinned him to his seat. Riggensen fired again, three shots streaking towards the last cultist. The cultist ducked low and ran towards Riggensen – Riggensen was a well-built man, young compared to many of the aged adepts and veterans of the Ordo Malleus. He was a prime target, a definite threat.

The cultist crossed the room in a flash. A second flash and the cultist fell, the tactical officer's power knife still stuck through his ankle.

The cultist landed on top of the clerk in front of Riggensen. Riggensen flicked the shot selector and fired the whole magazine of his autopistol into the cultist's back, the cultist jerking as finally there was no more room to dodge and the bullets tore through him.

Riggensen had probably killed the clerk, too. The fact was a bleak, dark veil at the back of his mind. He couldn't let it stop him, slow him down. He would do penance later. Now, he had to survive.

One of the cultists had thrown Valinov a hellgun and he had it on full auto – a fan of glittering crimson blasts ripped across the chamber. By now everyone was in cover or firing back, yelling, screaming. Nyxos was struggling with the cultist on top of him, blades slicing into him time and time again, threatening to shut down even his multiple augmetic systems.

Riggensen pulled the power knife out of the cultist's calf. He scrambled over the mess, his eyes fixed on Valinov. Riggensen was a servant of the Emperor. Riggensen would not run. He would not cower. He had shown no fear in the interrogation room, when he faced Valinov not knowing fully what he was. He would show no fear now.

Valinov was firing at the troopers now coming in. They were returning fire, shots spattering against the pedestal. Valinov hadn't seen Riggensen.

Time was going by in slow, tortured heartbeats. Riggensen was not a trained killer like Valinov, but he was strong and capable. He just needed one good shot – Valinov was tough and had many augmetics that would help him resist injury, but he could not go through a wound from a power knife and carry on defending himself.

Valinov span round and quick as lightning he brought the butt of the hellgun slamming into Riggensen's ribs. Riggensen fell, the hard cold metal of the pedestal cracking into the side of his head.

Valinov was kneeling, looming over the sprawling Riggensen. But Riggensen was not dead yet.

He had one last weapon. Something no one else had. It was the death of Nyxos's astropath that reminded him – Riggensen felt the psychic feedback of the astropath's mind flitting out of existence, the psychic spark going out.

He had broken Valinov once. He could do it again.

Riggensen reached through the fog of pain and shock, into the part of his mind where he kept the weapon that had made him an explicator. The eye inside him opened and looked out at Valinov's mind, reaching a lance of perception into the ex-inquisitor's soul. He could crack him open again, lever open Valinov's mind, blind him, deafen him, fill his head with noise and insanity.

Riggensen let everything he had flood out of his mind to crack that diamond at the heart of Valinov's soul. He dug into his half-remembered childhood amongst the dregs of Hydraphur, the even murkier months of testing and conditioning on the Black Ship that had picked him up, the pain, the humiliation, the fear of the power that grew inside his head that might see him executed at any moment.

He found it all and compressed it into a crystal-hard mental spear. With all the strength the Malleus had taught him, he hurled it at Valinov.

There was nothing for it to hit. There was nothing, nowhere, no one.

Riggensen's mind flailed hopelessly at nothing, because Gholic Ren-Sar Valinov had no soul.

That abyss, where Valinov's soul should be, was the last thing Riggensen saw. He couldn't even see beyond it to the writhing arms of the servitor-mangler as Valinov hauled his body up into its grip and it started the quick, slippery work of cutting Explicator Riggensen apart.

WHEN GHARGATULOTH WAS young – relatively speaking, for a true daemon suffered neither birth nor death – it was said that he walked like a mortal man, sometimes striding through from the warp when there was a mind of sufficient psychic power for him to possess.

He did what so many daemons did. He gloried in the feeling of flesh wrapped around him. He danced with his new feet. He told stories with his new tongue, stories that the small-minded human beings called insanity. Everyone who met him knew that he was not human – whatever body he wore, power dripped like tears of blue fire from his eyes and he spoke in riddles that drove men mad. But Ghargatuloth was fortunate, for he made his first forays into real space in a time of unfettered destruction and war. They called it the Age of Strife and, for one of the rare times in the history of mankind, the name they gave their era was completely appropriate.

He saw whole cultures stripped away until only plains of charred bones remained. He saw madmen made kings, brutal warlords who burned whole worlds as fuel to generate their personal power. Mankind lost the means to travel the stars in the slaughter, and retreated to their planets like vermin into their burrows, to consume one another in their wars.

He saw them rediscover space flight, too, and mankind was suddenly divided into a million blood-stained factions thrust into the same melting pot. Ghargatuloth, in a series of madmen's bodies, was a hero. Billions worshipped him. He was the prince who wore a cloak of many faces, each cut from the head of a traitor. He was the woman who swam in an ocean of blood every morning, so the strength of her exsanguinated foes would leach into her. He was the pirate king who united a dozen star systems, only to set them on one another to see which one would survive.

The Age of Strife lasted for longer than human history could properly record. In those days, Ghargatuloth lived out several lifetimes of warfare, suffering and mayhem. He had striven and triumphed, he had been defeated, he had died. Every moment fed the lust for knowledge that infected every servant of Tzeentch.

But Ghargatuloth slowly came to understand the truth. He was just a child, and the Age of Strife was his playground. The more he understood mankind, the more he began to understand the will of the Chaos powers. For every victory he achieved while amusing himself with war, there was a defeat. For every empire that rose, there would be a fall.

Mankind was fundamentally weak. It was incapable of true victory – it would always fail. Always. In the warp, there were gods, beings that had gathered such power that they would be gods forever. But mankind could not emulate them. When Ghargatuloth realised this, he came to despise the species he had played with for so long.

He became bored. He would sometimes make forays into real space and cause wanton havoc, but it was empty and meaningless. There was no knowledge to be found there. No secrets to learn. Mankind was a crude and ignorant animal, incapable of gathering true, meaningful power.

Until the crusade.

A man calling himself the Emperor conquered the cradle of mankind, holy Terra, the homeworld. He led a crusade across the stars, conquering the space mankind had settled, reuniting the species into the Imperium. Every human being in the galaxy was declared an automatic citizen of the Imperium, whether they knew it or not. The crusade had never truly ended, for the Imperium throughout its entire history had striven to bring every human world into its oppressive embrace.

And suddenly, the galaxy was interesting again. For the first time mankind had secured enduring power for itself, a dominion over the known galaxy that had remained for well over ten thousand years. It had survived even the death of the Emperor himself at the hands of the Chaos-blessed Warmaster Horus, civil wars and invasions, everything the universe could throw at it. The Imperium endured, in spite of the dimness of the human intellect and the tiny scope of their minds.

And as Ghargatuloth had seen, every victory was followed by defeat. Every empire built, must fall.

Ghargatuloth's existence had meaning again. One day, the Imperium would fall. And Ghargatuloth would be there when it happened…

LIGEIA THREW HERSELF against the far wall of her bedchamber, her clothes drenched in sweat, her mouth dry and her breath hot and painful. She was shaking. On the table across the room, the book lay crackling the antique patina with its evil. It was a small, slim volume, small enough to hide in the palm of one hand, but written onto its pages were the revelations of Ghargatuloth, pure and undiluted, an unabridged tirade of madness. Ligeia had to forcibly shut down her mind to stop its meaning from seeping into her.

Her chambers were a mess. Clothes were strewn around and half-eaten meals curdled on silver plates balanced on every surface. There had been too much in Ligeia's head for her to keep up the appearance of a noblewoman – such things didn't seem to matter anymore, not when she had seen some of the full horror of the forces that were tearing at the fabric of reality.

Ghargatuloth was speaking to her. Ghargatuloth was not just a daemonic body – he was knowledge. He was all the knowledge that he had gathered in his immensely long lifetime. That was why he could not be killed, only banished – he left that knowledge in the hearts and minds of his cultists, so that even if he were banished from real space enough of him would remain written in books or madmen's minds to bring him back.

Ligeia couldn't beat him. She couldn't face something like that. The most basic understanding of

Ghargatuloth was simply too vast and complex to fit into her mind.

She wished she had her death cultists still, so she could explain to them what she felt. They never answered, of course, but even just talking helped. She could not talk to the Grey Knights, not even Alaric, not about something like this. The Malleus crew who skulked through the guts of the *Rubicon* were no better, nor was Inquisitor Klaes or the rest of the Inquisition. Ligeia was completely alone, with no one but the after-image of Ghargatuloth in her head for company.

But her death cultists were gone. They would not be coming back.

There was a loud bang from elsewhere in her chambers, as an explosive charge blew the door in. Ligeia heard someone yelling an order and armoured feet crunched through the antique furniture in the next room.

Ligeia straightened up. She still had her digital weapon disguised as a large ornate ring on her finger, and there was a needle pistol somewhere in her luggage that she could use competently. But she knew that neither of them would do any good. Tzeentch was going to swallow the galaxy. What good was any weapon?

The door to her bedchamber was kicked in. Splintered wood flew everywhere. Ligeia stepped back from the door, shaking, knowing what a pathetic figure she would cut – bedraggled, exhausted, ill, looking all her many years and more.

She recognised Justicar Santoro, the most straight-laced Grey Knight, barging his way into the room. He was just the person they would bring down from the *Rubicon* to face her. No imagination. No chance of listening to her pleas.

Santoro levelled his storm bolter at Ligeia's head. If she moved, if she spoke, he would kill her.

Somehow, she had known it would come to this. Even before she had ever heard of Ghargatuloth, as a junior investigator for the Ordo Hereticus before the Malleus had even found her, she had known she would end her days at the point of gun a held by someone who was supposed to be her ally. That was the way the Inquisition worked, how the whole Imperium worked – mankind always killed its own in the end.

Three more members of Squad Santoro moved into the room, their weapons trained at Ligeia, their huge armoured bodies filing the room. Ligeia shivered in a sudden cold.

'Clear,' said Santoro.

Inquisitor Klaes followed the Grey Knights into the room. He held a data-slate in one hand – the other hand was on the hilt of his power sword.

'Inquisitor Briseis Ligeia,' said Klaes carefully. 'We have received a communication from the Ordo Malleus Conclave on Encaladus demanding your immediate arrest. As the principal Inquisitorial authority in this area I am required to carry out that order. The rules of your situation are now very simple, Ligeia: surrender or Justicar Santoro will kill you.'

Ligeia held her shaking hands up. At a hand signal from Santoro, a Marine Ligeia recognised as Brother Traevan stepped forward, grabbed her hand and pulled the ring off her finger, grinding its precious miniaturised technology beneath his boot.

'Do you have any other weapons?' said Santoro grimly.

Ligeia shook her head.

'Restrain her.'

Traevan pulled Ligeia's arms behind her and she felt manacles being clamped around her wrists. It was only professional courtesy from Klaes, she knew, that kept her from being strip-searched and put in chains.

'Inquisitor Ligeia,' said Klaes, reading now from the data-slate, 'the orders of the Emperor's Holy Inquisition are placing you under arrest for the crimes of grand heresy, association with enemies of the Emperor, corruption of the Emperor's servants, and other charges pending a full hearing. You will be taken to the facilities on Mimas where the truth will be drawn from you and your fate decided by the Conclave of the Ordo Malleus. You will be afforded no freedom that might lead to the furtherance of your crimes. Your authority as an inquisitor is revoked.

'These charges relate to the assistance received by the condemned enemy of the Emperor, Gholic Ren-Sar Valinov, and the deaths of Imperial servants in the commission of this heresy. By the decree of the Ordo Malleus there can be no innocence of your crimes, only degrees of guilt, which shall be decided upon in due time. Until then you are no longer a citizen of the Imperium but a creature owned and disposed of by the Ordo Malleus. May the Emperor have mercy on you, for we will not.'

Klaes switched off the data-slate. Ligeia could see the sadness in his eyes. No inquisitor could enjoy persecuting one of their colleagues – it reminded them of how close they themselves were to falling. 'Tell me why, Ligeia, and I'll see that they treat you well.'

'Why?' A hot tear ran down Ligeia's face. 'What else is there? The galaxy will die. The Change will swallow everything. No matter how hard we fight, we are all lost in the end. I have seen it happen. There can be no victory against fate, inquisitor. Valinov's freedom is a part of that fate, just like my arrest, just like the fact that you will all die, and all your triumphs will crumble to dust.'

'Enough,' said Santoro. He stepped forward and hit Ligeia with a backhanded strike across the face that sent her reeling to the floor.

As unconsciousness took Ligeia, she could still see Ghargatuloth smothering the stars and the Lord of Change marching in step behind him, infecting the very fabric of the universe with the stain of Chaos.

ALARIC HAD LOST a colleague he trusted. He had also lost a friend. When Ligeia was brought onto the *Rubicon* and shut into the ship's psyker-warded brig, Alaric had seen a broken woman, not much more than a shadow of the insightful noblewoman he had come to trust.

Inquisitor Klaes, Alaric could tell from looking at his face, felt the same. To think that Ghargatuloth could rob such a woman of her reason, without her even having to come close to him, was terrifying. No one was safe. For the first time, Alaric seriously wondered if Ghargatuloth could do the same thing to a Grey Knight if one of them got near enough. Not one single Grey Knight had ever fallen to Chaos – would Alaric, or one of the men under his command, be the first? The thought all but made him sick.

Ligeia had not sent her death cultists to retrieve the sword of Mandulis. She had sent them to Mimas where, acting on her orders, they had helped Valinov escape his execution. The last anyone heard of Valinov, he was fleeing on a stolen gunship out of Saturn's rings, followed by a host of Ordo Malleus ships from Iapetus which lost him in the gas giant's outer ring.

Valinov would have been well out of the solar system by the time Ligeia was arrested. There was a possibility that one of the death cultists was still alive and accompanying him. It was treachery on a grand scale – Ligeia, who knew more than most about the many atrocities Valinov had committed against the Imperial citizenry, had conspired with him to help him escape his punishment.

Quite how Valinov had got his claws into her, Alaric couldn't be certain. But he was certain of one thing – Ghargatuloth had helped him do it. Probably it had started with the *Codicium Aeternum* itself, and with Ligeia's first interrogation of Valinov on Mimas. Alaric himself had read the pages of the *Codicium Aeternum* – had Ghargatuloth tried to lever open his mind, too, and plant his orders inside?

Ghargatuloth had acted through the statue from Victrix Sonora and the texts recovered from Sophano Secundus, maybe even the archives on Trepytos in which Ligeia had immersed herself, planting hidden information in her head that had eaten away at her sanity without her knowing it until it was too late. She had been used. The Grey Knights had also been used to play their part in an unravelling plot Ghargatuloth had woven into the Trail of St Evisser since before the first time he was banished.

And now, with Ligeia gone, Alaric had to face it alone.

Ghargatuloth was not just the monster Mandulis had killed. He was knowledge planted in the minds of his followers, the same knowledge that could infect the minds of his pawns and force them to do insane things. Alaric had fought daemons and cultists in the past many times on the road to becoming a justicar, but they had always ultimately been enemies he could see and touch and kill. Ghargatuloth, on the other hand, was a power that did not have to fight the Ordo Malleus to win.

AFTER THE *Rubicon* had left Trepytos for Mimas, Alaric set about picking up the pieces of Ligeia's investigation. He had to have her chambers stripped and the contents burned; there was no way of knowing how many of the notes she left behind were tainted. But it was the only chance Alaric had. And if there was anyone in the Imperium who could follow up her investigation without falling prey to the call of Ghargatuloth, it was a Grey Knight.

Inquisitor Klaes had put all the resources of the Trepytos fortress at Alaric's command. Klaes's best ship, the one Ligeia's death cultists had used, was still impounded at the Naval fortress on Iapetus, but Klaes called in some favours. Within days Alaric had two armed merchantmen, the fastest ships on the Trail with veteran ex-Naval crews.

Alaric had sent Genhain on the *Rubicon* to escort Ligeia to Mimas. Genhain was to travel to Titan afterwards and, on Alaric's authority as acting Brother-Captain and commander of the strikeforce, recover the sword of Mandulis. If this really was the 'lightning bolt' Valinov had spoken of, then perhaps it was the only chance the Grey Knights had in the coming reckoning with Ghargatuloth.

Squad Santoro and Squad Tancred were now quartered in the fortress, taking up the training floor in makeshift cells and practising their combat drills in the duelling arena. The fortress had once been impressive but Alaric was acutely aware, as he prepared to take up the investigation that had cost Ligeia her mind, that the Trail of St Evisser had few resources he could commandeer compared to the millennia-old cult network of Ghargatuloth. The upsurge in cult activity had seen the Naval ships and Guardsmen stationed on the Trail increase in number, but it was still too small a force to cover the whole Trail.

Even if the Ecclesiarchy could be persuaded to put their Sisters of Battle – tough and motivated troops who demanded respect – at Alaric's disposal, there would never be enough manpower for anything other than one solid strike.

Most of the Grey Knights were at the Eye of Terror, fighting a tide of daemons pouring out of that huge warp storm into realpsace. The rest were stretched far too thinly, holding down the many daemonic blackspots across the Imperium – the Maelstrom, the Gates of Varl, Diocletian Nebula, a dozen other weeping sores in real space. There would be no reinforcements from Titan.

Alaric knew now why so many qualities were needed for a leader, qualities he was still not sure he had. He had to fight, win, never waver in his faith in the Emperor and lead his fellow Grey Knights in all these things. But more than that – he had to be able to do all this when he knew he was utterly alone.

ELEVEN
PECUNIAM OMNIS

The Pecuniam Omnis dragged its cargo painfully across the Segmentum Solar, its engines flaring badly where the exhaust vents had become caked in deposits, its ageing nav-cogitator wasting fuel by constantly correcting its course. The run between Jurn and Epsion Octarius was a hard one, too competitive to allow for capital to be wasted on maintaining a decaying cargo ship, nowhere near lucrative enough to be able to replace it.

Captain Yambe knew that he would probably die with the *Pecuniam Omnis*. He was forty-seven years old. It was a good age for a cargo crewman – most died in accidents or dockyard brawls long before then. Yambe had survived two major wrecks and Emperor knew how many rough nights at harbour, but having finally made captain of his own ship he knew he would never be able to break out. He owed too much to too many people to be able to walk away, and he would never amass enough credits to upgrade his corroded ship.

Yambes's crew, at least, knew what they were doing – thirty men manning the few habitable areas surrounding the ship's bloated metal abdomen. The huge airless cargo holds carried vast quantities of Jurnian industrial product, from pre-moulded STC habitats to crates of mass-produced lasguns. The crew were hard-bitten and tough, most of them probably criminals treating the *Pecuniam Omnis* as a place to hide. Yambe didn't care as long as they gave the tech-rituals at least some passing respect and knew one end of a hyperspanner from the other.

The bridge of the *Pecuniam* was cramped and hot, stinking of sweat and engine oil. Yambe himself was running to fat, filling the command chair and slowly saturating its tattered upholstery with sweat. A half-empty bottle of Jurnian Second Best, a foul but highly effective spirit that Yambe could no longer sleep without, teetered on the arm of the chair. In front of Yambe a transparent plasteel hemisphere was blistered out of the front of the *Pecuniam* like the bulbous eye of an insect, looking out onto the cold, hateful space in which Yambe had spent most of his life.

The *Pecuniam* had dropped out of the warp so the ship's second-rate Navigator, a skinny, twitchy guy from one of the Lower Houses, could meditate for a few days on the right path to take on the next warp jump. The Navigator was a joke, but his House's fee wasn't. The astropath, Gell, wasn't much cheaper but at least she had some idea of what she was doing.

Yambe hated space. That was why he couldn't stop looking at it. He knew that one day it would rear up and kill him, and that would be the day he had let his guard down. He had been centimetres away from hard vacuum, once, and had seen friends turned inside-out in a hull breach back when he still let himself have friends. Space had killed more men than women had, and that was saying something.

The crammed banks of comm-consoles and instrument cogitators beeped and hummed behind Yambe, occasionally belching plumes of steam from coolant leaks. He could hear the engines groaning as they pushed the *Pecuniam* slowly through overlapping gravity fields from an asteroid belt looping around ahead of it; his ship wouldn't last much longer.

Maybe when he got to Epsion Octarius he would just leave the *Pecuniam* to rot and jump planet, try to find some other way to live out a lifetime he didn't deserve. Screw the docking fees. Screw the creditors.

But he knew full well he would just load up with food and luxuries from Epsion Octarius and start hauling them back to Jurn.

'Boss,' came a vox, warped and distorted from the stern of the ship. It was Lestin, the head of the engine crew and the only man Yambe trusted to keep the *Pecuniam* moving. 'Got a problem.'

Yambe spat. 'What kind?'

'Impact. Looks like something took out the fourth cluster.'

'"Took it out" like you can fix it or "took it out" like it's gone for good?'

'Kerrel went to take a look. Hasn't come back.'

Yambe didn't need to lose a man. The margin on this cargo would be low enough without having to hire someone new. 'I'm coming down. Don't anyone die till I get there.'

Yambe struggled out of his captain's chair, knocking the bottle of Second Best down into the guts of the cogitator array around him where the alcohol fizzed and popped against a hot coolant pipe. He swore liberally as he clambered over the chair and through the door in the bulkhead, feeling the ship thrumming painfully through the stained metal under his hand. A previous owner had carved machine-litanies into the girders and pipes, High Gothic pleadings to the Machine God to keep the ship safe and working. They didn't seem to be doing much good.

Through portholes in the corridor Yambe could see the cargo nets cradling massive volumes of building materials, tools, and weaponry, things Epsion Octarius couldn't make for itself. He jogged towards the stern along the long, arching dorsal corridor, feeling all his years and all his weight.

Once, on an armed merchantman out of Balur, he had been there when a plasma reactor vented into three decks, and heard two thousand men boiled in liquid fire. As a captain he had lost seven men when an airlock seal gave way. With each death you see, he believed, a little part of you turns dark and cold, which was why born spacers were all such hard-hearted sons of grox.

The corridor narrowed and split again and again, forming a lattice like a net which held in the bulbous forms of the plasma reactors, engine vents and warp generators.

Yambe forced a vox-bead into one ear. 'Lestin?'

'Found him, boss,' came Lestin's reply. He didn't sound as if this was a good thing.

'Where was he?'

'In about twenty pieces. Someone got him at the airlock, looks like he was running from something.'

'Like what?'

'We're not hanging around to find out. I'm closing the bulkheads around the fourth vent cluster.'

Yambe reached the ship's armoury, a dark little room where the crew's motley collection of weapons were racked up against the walls. Yambe pulled a naval shotgun from the rack and hurriedly snapped six rounds into the weapon's magazine. Shotguns were the weapon of choice of spacecraft where firefights were at close range and guns with greater penetrating power could punch through a wall and damage some vital system. Yambe paused to drag a tattered mesh armour jacket out of a cupboard and pull it over his shoulders. He headed back out into the corridor – the mesh jacket didn't cover much of his bulging stomach but it was better than nothing.

'Lestin, make sure the boys in the reactor crew are pulled back,' voxed Yambe. 'There's enough coolant channels from the vents to the reactors that anything could climb through.'

There was no reply.

'Lestin?'

Static filtered through the vox-bead. The vox-net on the *Pecuniam Omnis* was on its last legs, and seemed to go on the blink whenever it was most needed. This was what Yambe told himself as he racked the slide on his shotgun and hurried forward.

He heard footsteps approaching, weak and arhythmical. A shadow flickered in the weak glowstrip light and Yambe nearly blew the head off the figure that stumbled towards him.

It was the ship's Navigator. All Navigators were a strain of human – it was impolite to call them mutants, but that's what they were – who could look on the warp and guide a ship through it, and who were universally spindly and weak. The Navigator on the *Pecuniam Omnis* was no exception, but he was more than just weak – he was wounded. His dark blue Lower House uniform was black with blood, pumping from a wound in his chest, dribbling from his mouth and spattered on the pale skin of his face.

The Navigator, whose name was Krevakalic, fell forward into his arms and nearly knocked him flat on his back.

'What is it?' said Yambe, breathing hard. 'Where?'

Krevakalic slumped to the ground and looked up at Yambe from beneath the headband covering the third eye in his forehead, the warp eye. '… it… she was in… she came for me and Gell first…'

'Gell's dead?'

Krevakalic nodded.

That was bad news. Gell, as ship's astropath, was the only person who could transmit a psychic distress signal.

Krevakalic coughed and sprayed a gout of warm blood over Yambe. Yambe had to leave him – in a few moments he would die. Yambe had seen it before. His lungs and guts were laid open. It would be crueller to try to save him than to just leave him.

Yambe, meanwhile, had to press on. Not just because he had to find Lestin or any of the other crew, but because the ship's only working saviour pod was towards the stern and Yambe knew he could well have to get off the ship in a hurry.

He left the Navigator sprawled and dying on the floor of the corridor. If Krevakalic begged for Yambe to stay, the words were lost in the froth of blood bubbling from his lips.

The corridor opened up ahead into a wide circle that surrounded one of the plasma reactors, a bulbous cylindrical chamber five storeys high where the ship's energy was generated. The plasma core growled deeply as it provided power to the ship's systems, and white clouds of coolant vapour spurted from the pipes running along the floor and up the curving walls.

There was a body slumped over the closest control console. It was Ranl, a kid the *Pecuniam Omnis* had picked up at their last maintenance stop. Ranl was young and stupid and probably a criminal on the run, but he did what he was told and kept his head down. He hadn't deserved to have his head sliced off and his torso cut clean open, but that was what someone had done to him.

Yambe had never seen a man dead like that, killed and bisected as cleanly as if a good butcher had gone to work on him. Yambe looked around and saw Ranl wasn't the only one – there was another body draped over the railings around the upper level of walkways surrounding the plasma generator core. Yambe couldn't recognise him but his arms had been cut off and a rust-coloured streak of blood ran down the wall beneath him.

Something moved near the ceiling, scurrying too quickly for Yambe to make out, sweeping up and down as if it were actually running along the curved outer wall instead of along the walkways. Yambe tried to train his shotgun on it but it was gone before he could bring the barrel up.

His men were dying. Something had come onto his ship with the intent of killing everyone they found. They had gone for the astropath and Navigator first – that meant no distress signal and no escape.

Pirates? Yambe had had his brushes with them. Maybe even xenos – every spacer had heard more than enough tales of heathen aliens preying on Imperial shipping, from the callous and degenerate eldar to the murderous greenskins.

Maybe a more primitive life form. They said that the tyranid hordes that had swarmed over whole planets used fast, deadly creatures with multiple arms as scouts and spies, which could hitch a ride on ships on transit and kill everything on board. There were things that could possess crew members and creatures that could claw their way through the hull, all illustrated in lurid detail in tales told in bars, brothels and holding cells in ports all over the Imperium.

It moved again. Closer this time, further down, scurrying through Yambe's peripheral vision. He knew he couldn't hit it – it had to be something alien, something deadly. He wouldn't end up like Ranl. Damn the ship. Gak the cargo. He wasn't going to die out here.

Yambe ran out of the core, ducking his head to get through the low door leading towards the ship's stern. There was one saviour pod that he trusted to work – if no one had taken it already and if a ship passed close enough to pick up the distress signal, it might enable him to survive.

The further into the engine section Yambe got, the more cramped and filthy the ship became. Coolant vapour swirled around his feet. The stinking, oily air clogged up his nose and made his head throb. His breathing was so heavy it hurt – he was too old for this.

There was something over the vox. The film of thin static broke up and a man's voice came through, low and strong, resonant, confident.

'Captain Yambe,' it said. 'How much fuel does your ship hold?'

Yambe stopped. Lestin had the vox-bead. That meant the speaker had Lestin, and Lestin had been heading for the stern. Whoever had killed Lestin was between Yambe and the saviour pod.

Yambe turned and ran back the way he had come, ducking into a service tunnel that branched off and was barely high enough to run down. He needed somewhere to hide. The shotgun in his hands felt heavy and useless. There had to be somewhere to go. The *Pecuniam Omnis* was an old and filthy ship, with cavernous cargo spaces you could get lost in. Yambe had once picked up a stowaway who had given the crew the run-around for seven months. He had to hide. He had to survive.

Yambe blundered out into the ship's shuttle bay. The bay was a large, flat cavity between two of the reactors, and held the ship's single battered shuttle that was used for skipping between ships while in orbital dock. The shuttle was squat, tarnished and ugly, but if Ranl had remembered to refuel it as he had been told, Yambe should be able to start it and get the bay doors open in time to take off.

It was useless as a way out. It had air for about seven hours, no food, no water, and the energy cells were shot so it had to burn promethium just to heat the cabin. Its comm-link had such a limited range that it would never be found.

But it would let Yambe choose how he died. He could hide in the ship and try to outwit the invaders, or he could flee on the shuttle and pick a death from cold, suffocation, or just walking out of the airlock.

Yambe was about to head for the shuttle when a man walked out from behind it. Yambe began to raise his shotgun but out of nowhere a silver slash punched through his hand, slicing through to pin both the gun and the hand to his thigh. The shotgun's barrel pointed uselessly at the ground. White shock rushed through Yambe, followed by a red tide of pain. He sunk to his knees. The tip of the blade ground against the bone of his leg but refused to come free.

The man walking towards him was tall and well-built, wearing a battered, stained voidsuit and somehow still looking noble. His face was harsh and angular, his head shaven, and the skin of his face and scalp were covered in thick, blocky tattoos. His eyes looked straight through Yambe, so piercing that for a moment the captain forgot the pain in his hand and leg, and the hot blood spattering onto the floor.

'How much fuel,' repeated the man in that same thick deep voice that had come over the vox, 'does your ship hold?'

'Gak you, groxbanger,' snarled Yambe. Defiance was the only thing keeping him conscious. He would not die here. He would not. He was supposed to jump ship at Epsion Octarius and start a new life, away from space. He would not die.

The man threw something at Yambe, something warm and horribly wet that smacked into the side of his head and knocked him to the greasy metal floor. Pain rifled through him, and when the spots cleared from in front of his eyes Yambe saw Lestin's severed head lying on the floor beside him, jaw hanging off, eyes still open.

'How much fuel is there on this ship? Your man said he did not know.'

Yambe looked up. The intruder had absolutely nothing behind his eyes. For a second, it was like looking
out into the warp, the endless Chaos that drove men
mad.

'Enough...' stammered Yambe. 'Enough to get to
Epsion Octarius from here. You could push the reactors for more.'

'Good,' said the man. He glanced to a point above
and behind where Yambe lay. 'Kill him.'

Yambe looked around. There was someone standing
over him – he hadn't heard them sneak up behind
him. It was woman wearing a glossy black bodyglove,
her face masked, her clothing tight over muscles like
snakes coiled around her limbs. Gold-flecked eyes
looked down at him, filled with disgust.

'I can't die here...' said Yambe, but that didn't stop
her from drawing a long, gleaming sword and cutting
Yambe clean in two.

ALARIC COULD NOT feel the state of the Trail, as Ligeia
had done, but it was clear enough from the reports
coming into the fortress on Trepytos. The forge world
of Magnos Omicron was in open civil war, where regiments of tech-guard loyal to the Imperium fought the
titan legions that followed the world's blasphemous
prophet. Volcanis Ultor was in a state of martial law,
with Cardinal Recoba using the Balurian heavy
infantry to patrol the streets and seal off the wealthy
upper levels from the cultist hordes sure to emerge
from the underhives.

The Trail's small battlefleet began harassing shipping
between the worlds, destroying any freighter that
could not give a satisfactory account of its crew and
cargo.

An apocalyptic malaise fell over many worlds. Imperial citizens flocked to the cathedrals as rumours spread. Preachers led massed prayers for deliverance and forgiveness for the sins of the people against the Emperor, and in places it was impossible to tell the cults of Ghargatuloth and the Imperium apart.

Alaric was beginning to realise just how powerful Ghargatuloth must be. He could cause suffering and horror simply by the rumour of his existence.

PERHAPS ALL THE information Alaric needed was locked up in the archives on Trepytos. But he couldn't root through the endless vaults of decaying ledgers to find what he needed. Inquisitor Klaes's entire staff had tried many times before, and they had failed. All Alaric had to work with were the reports coming in from the rest of the Trail, and a handful of properly catalogued works on the Trail's history.

The room at the head of the archives was high and draughty, with watery shafts of light seeping through the tall, thin arched windows to pierce the gloom. A few of the fortress staff were working at the bookshelves that lined the room, bringing down reference works that Alaric had requested. He knew he would not be able to find anything that Ligeia had not already examined and dismissed, but he had to cover all the possibilities. There was too much at stake to assume anything.

In front of Alaric were hundreds of report sheets, each detailing some atrocity committed by the cults of Ghargatuloth. Bomb blasts, assassinations, uprisings, and more sinister things – heretical broadcasts over vid-nets, raids on Imperial cathedrals, mass kidnappings.

Inquisitor Ligeia had delved straight into the heart of darkness, into the beliefs and insanities that drowned the minds of Ghargatuloth's followers. Alaric could not do the same – compared to Ligeia's, Alaric's mind was a closed room.

'Brother-Captain,' said a familiar, deep voice. Alaric looked up from the stack of papers to see Tancred walking towards him through the archive room. A couple of the fortress staff looked round in surprise at Tancred's sheer size – he wore his Terminator armour, and in it he stood almost twice as tall as some normal men. 'Fortress astropaths have received the message that Genhain has reached Titan.'

'Good.' Alaric still hadn't got used to being addressed as 'brother-captain'. 'I want us ready to head out as soon as the *Rubicon* returns. We don't have any time left. Ghargatuloth is already rising.'

Tancred nodded at the piles of papers. 'How bad is it?'

'Bad. There isn't a world free of corruption. Even Magnos Omicron is suffering. The Planetary Defence Forces are completely overwhelmed. Local law enforcement is the same. The Arbites are doing what they can but there are just too many cults to pin down.' Alaric shook his head. 'How long have they been there? Sophano Secundus was one thing, it's an isolated world, one tainted individual could last for centuries there. But we're talking millions of men and women, in hundreds of cults across almost every single world of the Trail. And they've all lain dormant until now.'

'The Navy could quarantine the place. Declare a crusade.' Tancred was serious – whole sectors of space had been purged before. The Sabbat Worlds, the Asclepian

Gap, a handful of others, each cleansed in a great crusade of Imperial armies and battlefleets.

'If the Trail was in open rebellion,' replied Alaric, 'and if the Eye of Terror wasn't tying up half of the Imperium's forces, then maybe the Malleus could do it. But not now. Ghargatuloth won't play his hand overtly enough to bring the whole of the Imperium down on him. It's up to us.'

'You sound as if you despair.' There was a dangerous note of steel in Tancred's voice.

'There is no despair, justicar,' replied Alaric. 'Not while one of us still lives. I am simply aware of how cunning our enemy is. Ghargatuloth has been planning this for some time, probably from before Mandulis banished him the first time. It might not even be an accident that he is returning at the same time the Eye of Terror is opening. And we have one advantage.'

Alaric picked up a handful of the reports, some of the worst. 'He's out in the open. All this is distraction, Tancred. He's trying to blind us, and as far as the Arbites and the PDFs are concerned it's working. But we are different. We know that until his cultists bring him fully back into real space, he will be vulnerable. Once he gets dug in like on Khorion IX it will take nothing short of a crusade to get to him, if we even keep track of him. But now he is vulnerable. He knows we are here, and he is afraid of us.'

'But how do we find him, brother-captain? We cannot fight what we cannot see.'

Alaric held out his arms, indicating the whole of the archives. 'It's here somewhere. Ghargatuloth's cultists have to make the preparations for the rituals that will bring him back, and most of the cults on the Trail are rising up just to distract the Imperium from those few who are making those preparations. Ligeia could have filtered out the real cult activity from the distractions, but she is not here, and so we must do it instead.'

'I should let you work, then. My men must stay sharp.'

'Of course. Emperor guide you, justicar.'

'Emperor guide you, brother-captain.'

Alaric watched Tancred leave. As far as Tancred was concerned, the Grey Knights should be fighting the vermin who were setting the Trail alight, not hunting through the archives for clues that probably weren't there. Tancred would never voice such doubts openly – he was too much a soldier, too aware of how he slotted in to the vital chain of command. But he could not hide his concerns from Alaric.

Alaric knew he could only ask obedience from his Grey Knights, and not control everything they thought. But he hoped that he could keep their trust for long enough to find a lead on Ghargatuloth, because Alaric could only fight one enemy.

TWELVE
THE VAULTS

THEY SAID you could feel the years on Titan, layers of history weighing you down. The truth was that Titan's gravity was slightly heavier than Terran standard due to the superdense core that had been injected into the moon some time during the lost Dark Age of Technology. But there was some truth to the saying – history was literally etched into the rock of Titan, faces of forgotten heroes, inscribed litanies of deeds once famous, murals depicting terrible battles against the forces of Chaos. The whole surface of Titan was inscribed as if by a huge chisel, forming a network of battlements and citadels, and it had been carved layer upon layer since before the dawn of the Imperium. There was so much history there that it would overfill all the libraries of the Inquisition, if only it could be unlocked.

Justicar Genhain wondered how much the Imperium could learn if its scholars could properly

read all the images and messages that covered the walls
of Titan's vaults. Beneath the upper levels of Titan,
where the Grey Knights lived and prayed, were the catacombs where their dead were buried. Down here,
there were vaults and tunnels carved by artisans from
before the Ordo Malleus had even been formed from
the fires of the Horus Heresy. As Genhain followed the
procession down to the vault where his battle-brothers
would be buried, he saw faces of Grey Knights in
archaic marks of power armour, locked in endless
combat with leering stone daemons. A column was
wrought to represent an unnamed saint of the
Imperium. The names of battle-brothers covered the
vaulted ceiling; Grey Knights who had died in action
but whose bodies had never been recovered for burial.

Genhain walked behind Chaplain Durendin. In full
black power armour, the face of his helmet a skull of
gunmetal grey, Durendin had walked these tunnels
many times before. As a chaplain, he was the guardian
of the dead just as he guarded the spiritual health of
the living brothers.

Behind Genhain, the battle-brothers of his squad
carried the biers on which lay the body of Brother
Krae, the dead Grey Knight from Squad Tancred that
Genhain had brought back to Titan on the *Rubicon*.
Brother Caanos had died on Sophano Secundus, too,
but his body had been left on the planet. Genhain
knew that if the Grey Knights were to close in on Ghargatuloth, there would be many more to bury beneath
Titan before it was over.

Krae was covered in a white death caul, draped
over the huge plates of his Terminator armour. The
shape of his Nemesis halberd was visible, placed on
his chest with his gauntleted hands folded over the

hilt. Behind Krae's bier, several novices walked. They were young trainees who had only just begun the transformation into Grey Knights – they carried the censers that filled the close air of the catacombs with the dark, spicy smell of sacred incense. Genhain remembered the time, almost hidden in the fog of psycho-doctrination and endless medical proce-dures, when he had walked behind the funeral procession of a dead Grey Knight and wondered how long it would be until it was his body on the bier, draped in white.

The procession moved in silence through the cata-combs. Here and there the walls opened up into cells cut into the stone, each holding the mouldering bones of a centuries-dead Grey Knight. Here and there were inscriptions on the floor, almost obliterated by the marching feet of countless funeral processions, detail-ing the names and histories of the battle-brothers lying nearby. Genhain read fragments of names as he passed. Some of the dead down here would not even be recorded in the histories of the Grey Knights, hav-ing fought and died in times skipped over by the earlier records.

Durendin reached the chamber where Krae was to be buried, and led Squad Genhain and the novices in. Several stone coffins lay on pedestals, perhaps fifty of them, ranged through the chamber. Three of the pedestals had no coffin, and it was onto one of these that Krae was placed.

Krae would lie there until Squad Tancred returned from the Trail, when Tancred and Krae's battle-brothers would remove Krae's armour and Nemesis weapon, ritually cleanse his body, and oversee the Chap-ter artificers as they built the coffin around the body.

In the earliest days, great heroes of the Grey Knights would be buried with their weapons and armour. But the valuable Terminator armour could not be spared, and soon it would be worn by a Marine newly inducted into one of the Chapter's Terminator squads. Krae's gene-seed, harvested from the body just after his death by Tancred himself, would be implanted into a novice and a new Grey Knight would take shape. His weapon would be handed to a Marine just receiving his first sacred blade, his bolter ammunition would be redistributed amongst the Chapter. In this way Krae would continue to fight the Great Enemy, and have his revenge against the foul forces that killed him.

'Before the sight of the Emperor most high, in the face of the Adversary, did Brother Krae fall in combat with the forces of corruption.' Durendin's voice was low and grim, and seemed to fill the whole catacomb. The *Liber Daemonicum* contained dozens of different funeral prayers, and Durendin had spoken each of them hundreds of times. Brother Krae had chosen one of the simplest to be spoken at his death – Genhain remembered Krae as a humble man, one who followed Justicar Tancred's orders absolutely, seeing himself as nothing more than an instrument of the Emperor's will.

Genhain and his Marines bowed their heads as Durendin continued. Behind them, the young novices hung on the chaplain's every word, seeking meaning for themselves in the eulogy for the fallen Krae. 'The Enemy found no purchase in his mind, and no mercy from his arm. In the Emperor's sight did he fall, and at the Emperor's side will he fight to destroy the Adversary at the end of time. In the name of the Golden Throne and the Lord of all mankind, let our Brother Krae live on through our fight.'

Durendin's prayer finished, the young novices filed out silently. They would return to their cells and meditate on all the battle-brothers like Krae who had fallen before, and whose gene-seed organs were now implanted in the novices to regulate their transformation into Grey Knights.

Genhain turned to Brother Ondurin, the Marine who carried his squad's incinerator and acted as unofficial second-in-command. 'Ondurin, take the squad back to the *Rubicon* and have the crew prepare to take off. I shall be with you shortly.'

Ondurin nodded and silently led the Marines of Squad Genhain back out of the chamber. It would take them two hours to reach the entrance to the catacombs.

Justicar Genhain was left alone in the chamber with Durendin.

'Brother-Captain Alaric did Brother Krae a great honour in delivering his body to Titan,' said Durendin. 'But he did not send you and the *Rubicon* just for that.'

'You're right, chaplain. He has sent me to make a request.'

Durendin nodded. 'I received your astropath's message. It is a rare request. I do not know of a similar request being made for many centuries. It is even rarer for such things to be granted. Alaric explained all of this?'

'He did. He also explained that he has the authority of an acting brother-captain and that he can demonstrate an urgent need for the item I am here to collect.'

Somewhere within the skull helmet, Durendin smiled. 'Of course, justicar. But you understand the meaning of what you ask. As one of the guardians of our dead, I must consider such things very carefully. Follow me, justicar.'

Durendin walked off between the pedestals. Genhain glanced down and saw stone faces looking back up at him. They were stern faces covered in scars, and Genhain knew that the spirits of these Grey Knights were not at peace – they were still fighting, battling the Adversary as the Emperor did from the Golden Throne, and they would carry on fighting until the end of everything.

An arched doorway led off into a corridor, and Durendin led the way down it. Genhain followed into the gloom. Lumoglobes down here were spaced far apart and many had failed. The niches in the walls held bodies that had been there for centuries.

The tunnel curved downwards, describing a tight spiral that corkscrewed into the crust of Titan. Sculptures so old the details had been ground away by time lined the walls. Durendin's armoured footsteps echoed against the smooth stone floor.

The air got warmer. Genhain saw glimpses of carved Grey Knights wearing long-obsolete marks of power armour, of which a handful of examples survived on display in the Chapter's chapels and scriptoria. Exposed skeletons were all but handfuls of dust and gleaming white teeth.

Some way down, the tunnel opened up into a huge underground chamber. It was so wide that the far wall was like a horizon, the roof like a sky of stone. Large, elaborate structures filled the chamber like the buildings of a wealthy, sombre city of marble and granite.

'Our dead were not always buried side by side as brothers,' said Durendin, his voice low in the silence. 'Few realise it, but the Chapter does change. These levels survive from a time when the Grey Knights were buried like heroes in these cities of the dead.'

'How long ago?' said Genhain, almost unwilling to speak. Like every Grey Knight he had fought truly terrible things and witnessed sights that would drive lesser men mad, but still the oppressive, silent necropolis struck him with awe.

'The last was just over nine hundred years ago,' replied Durendin. 'Follow, justicar.'

Durendin walked out beneath the stone sky, down a broad avenue tiled with gleaming granite. Tombs rose on either side, many several storeys high, each different. Carved reliefs of battles adorned some, others bore monumental carved symbols – the stylised 'I' of the Inquisition alongside the sword-and-book symbol of the Grey Knights. Genhain saw a painted mural, the colours faded, of a Grey Knight in archaic Terminator armour fending off a tremendous horde of pestilent, tentacled daemons. Another tomb was topped by a massive marble Thunderhawk gunship, poised as if to ascend at any moment carrying the soul of the Marine buried beneath it.

Durendin turned a corner and Genhain saw, at the far end of the avenue, a building shaped like an amphitheatre. Arches in the circular walls looked in onto an area where hundreds of stone figures sat silently watching the raised obsidian block in the centre.

Durendin entered the amphitheatre. It was huge, the size of one of the grand gladiatorial arenas that could be found in the Imperium's more brutal hive cities. The watching figures were hooded and cowled, and wore the symbols of the various Imperial organisations – the Inquisition, Adeptus Mechanicus, Ecclesiarchy, Administratum, even the Adeptus Terra. The symbolism was powerful – every man and woman of the Imperium, whether they knew it or not, owed an impossible debt to the Grey Knights.

'You see why we bury our dead as brothers now,' said Durendin. 'Not kings.'

Genhain was momentarily lost for words. Saying such things had seen more than one novice chastised for impiety.

'The Grey Knights have made their own mistakes, justicar,' said Durendin. 'Alaric trusted you enough to send here, so I trust you to understand. Whole Chapters of Marines have fallen to pride before. No Grey Knight has ever fallen from grace, partly because the chaplains have seen such sins as pride and tried to guide our brothers away from them. That is why we no longer bury our dead here.'

Durendin carried on down the steep steps, into the shadow of the obsidian tomb. Words in High Gothic were inscribed into the glossy black stone – names of worlds and crusades where the entombed Marine had fought, allusions to daemonic enemies he had vanquished, the honours bestowed on him by the lord inquisitors of the Ordo Malleus.

The last battle honour listed was Khorion IX.

Durendin spoke a whispered prayer. He passed a hand over a panel set into the sarcophagus and slowly, with a deep grinding noise from within, the obsidian lid slid open. The stone around the sarcophagus rose up to form marble steps leading up, and as the steps formed Durendin walked up them to stand over the head end of the sarcophagus. There was a strong smell of spices and chemicals, the resins and incense with which Grey Knight bodies were once prepared before burial.

Genhain followed Durendin up the steps. When he got to a level where he could see into the sarcophagus, he bowed his head with almost instinctive reverence.

Grand Master Mandulis had been buried without his armour, for he had died in a time when all precious suits of Terminator armour were passed on to Grey Knights who had just been granted Terminator honours. His shroud was old and yellowed and it clung tightly to the skeleton beneath, so the bones and the features of the skull were clearly visible. Genhain could see the surgical scars around the eye sockets and on the cranium, the breastplate of fused ribs, the holes where lifesign probes and nerve-fibre contacts had once connected to the body. Mandulis's warding, the anti-daemonic patterns woven into his armour, had burned so brightly in his final moments that they were still traced onto his bones in intricate spiralling paths.

Mandulis's skeletal hands were folded across his chest, and in them he still held his Nemesis sword. The lightning bolt design, wrought in gold, started at the crossbar and ran halfway up the blade. The gold and silver still glinted. The blade was so bright it reflected the distant stone sky, brighter and clearer, as if the weapon was so holy its very reflection was pure.

The more Genhain looked down at the grand master's body the more he could see what terrible damage had been wrought on it. Something corrosive had eaten away at the inside of the rib-plate, spilling over the clavicle to leave a scabrous honeycombed scar on the bones. Hairline cracks covered the limbs where they had been broken and then re-set by the apothecaries tending the body. The back of the skull was a web of fractures. Mandulis had died in the death throes of Ghargatuloth, and the daemon prince's malice was so great that he had shattered the body of a Grey Knight as if it were nothing.

'Were this anyone else,' said Durendin, 'Alaric's request would have been refused, brother-captain or not. But Mandulis died to banish Ghargatuloth. None of us could deny that he would make any sacrifice to help us do it again.'

Durendin reached down and unfolded Mandulis's fingers from around the hilt of the Nemesis sword, careful not to damage the old bones. He lifted the weapon, and handed it to Genhain. The blade was still as sharp as the day Mandulis had last drawn it.

It felt heavy in Genhain's hands. It had been made in an era when Nemesis weapons were handled differently – the blade was heavy, for chopping through armour and bone, while the Nemesis swords used by Genhain's battle-brothers were lighter and thinner for slashing and stabbing.

'It has been four hundred years since a tomb in the city of the dead was opened,' said Durendin. 'The Chapter wishes it could render Alaric more support, with Ligeia now gone. But Alaric knows as well as any of us that the Chapter is stretched woefully thin at the best of times, and with the Eye opening no Grey Knight can be spared. We know now that the threat of Ghargatuloth has been proven to be real, and we hope that the sword of Mandulis will help Alaric when his brothers at the Eye cannot. I wish I could impress this upon Alaric himself, but I trust you will convey my words.'

Genhain knew that Durendin could have spoken to Alaric himself, through astropathic relay. The fact that Durendin would not told Genhain that Durendin was not going to be on Titan for very much longer.

'Emperor be with you in the Eye, chaplain,' said Genhain.

'May his light guide you on the Trail, justicar,' replied Durendin.

They walked down from the sarcophagus, which ground closed again over the body of Mandulis. Silently, the two Grey Knights began the long walk back towards the surface of Titan.

THERE WERE NO chances taken with Ligeia.

As soon as the *Rubicon* had arrived at Iapetus, Ligeia had been sedated and kept in a stupor until the interrogator command on Mimas had locked her up in the most secure holding cells they had. Normally reserved for prisoners in the throes of full-blown daemonic possession, Ligeia's cell floated in close orbit above the dark side of Mimas, anchored to the surface by a long metal cable. The only way to get to the grim, pitted metallic cube was to take a servitor-transporter that crawled like some parasitic insect up the cable to dock with the underside of the cell. The cube contained the cell and an observation room, a supply of enough oxygen and heating fuel to keep the occupant alive (both of which could be switched off instantly), and a fully-furnished interrogation array that would allow for intensive questioning assisted by both physical and psychic pressure of anything up to the ninth degree of intensity. The cell had not been deemed a resource suitable for Valinov, since he had never shown any psychic ability. But considering the circumstances of his escape, the Conclave on Encaladus had insisted that Ligeia be kept in the most secure location Mimas had.

Inquisitor Nyxos knew Ligeia. For normal men, that would make him a poor choice to interrogate her. An

inquisitor, however, accepted that those he knew the
best could still fall from grace and become a danger to
the Imperium. Nyxos had been called in to break
friends before – there were still such colleagues, even
fellow inquisitors, rotting in the depths of Mimas. The
only tragedy worse than an Imperial servant fallen to
the Enemy, was one who fell and was not brought to
justice. Nyxos was the automatic choice to conduct
Ligeia's interrogation.

The servitor-transporter only had room for two pas-
sengers. Nyxos could taste the fear and desperation left
in this place, from all those inquisitors and interrogators who had made this journey to converse with
daemons bound in human flesh. The portholes looked
out across Mimas's barren, broken surface, and in the
black sky above hung the huge multicoloured orb of
Saturn.

'Mimas command have given the word, inquisitor,'
said Hawkespur beside him. Hawkespur was a brilliant
young woman, headhunted for Nyxos's staff from the
Collegia Tactica on St Jowen's Dock. Her face, normally youthful and flawless, was darkened by several
livid bruises and she now walked with a cane. She had
only narrowly avoided dying in the slaughter at Valinov's botched execution. Augmetic correction at
Nyxos's expense would render her wounds invisible,
but Hawkespur would be marked far more deeply by
witnessing the cunning of the Enemy at first hand.

Nyxos had nearly died, too. Were it not for several
redundant internal organs the death cultist's knife
would have killed him in a moment. Nyxos banished
the thought. There was no point in pondering how
close you are to death, otherwise you live all your life
in fear.

'Take us up,' said Nyxos. Hawkespur pressed the control stud and the transporter began to climb the cable, swaying as it went. Nyxos's servos whirred as they compensated for the movement. He had not been able to move under his own power for more than thirty years, not since he had been all but dismembered by cultists who had offered him up as a sacrifice to their gods. The experience had left his body broken, but his mind far sharper. He had seen what went on inside their heads. He had seen what the taint of Chaos did to a man, and glimpsed the sights they saw beyond the veil. Only an inquisitor had the strength of mind to understand such things and live.

The transporter reached the top of the cable and metallic grinding sounds indicated that it was docking with the cell.

'We're there,' Hawkespur voxed to Mimas interrogator command. There was a pause, and then the side of the passenger compartment slid open.

Through the door was a small monitoring room full of lifesign readouts and cogitator consoles, with a window looking out into the cell itself. The air was cold and heavily recycled – it tasted metallic and almost hurt to breathe. A single door led into the cell, so an interrogator could enter the cell and talk to the prisoner face to face.

The prisoner was Inquisitor Ligeia. She was curled up in one corner of the white-tiled cell, dressed in the plain bone-coloured coveralls that the Mimas interrogators issued to isolated prisoners. Her hair, which Nyxos remembered as always being elaborately fashionable, was long and straggly, clinging to her face in greying rats' tails. Nyxos had never seen her looking so old.

She was shaking. It was cold in the cell, and at Nyxos's request she hadn't been fed for some time. She was kept almost permanently sedated, but she was just aware enough of her situation to be uncomfortable.

Nyxos settled his augmented body into the observation chair. He could feel the wounds deep inside him, like dull knives still stabbing.

Ligeia's lifesigns were stable. Her heartbeat flickered on one of the cogitator screens. Other monitors showed blood sugar and temperature. She was cold, hungry and tired.

Good, thought Nyxos.

'Wake her up, Hawkespur,' said Nyxos coldly.

Hawkespur took an injector gun from a cabinet beside the door, then punched a code into the door lock and headed through into the cell. Nyxos watched as Hawkespur injected a dose of stimulants into Ligeia's throat. Ligeia spasmed, then gasped and rolled onto her back, eyes suddenly wide, mouth gaping.

'Get her up,' said Nyxos into the vox receiver in front of him.

Hawkespur grabbed Ligeia by the scruff of the neck and hauled her into a sitting position against the back of the cell, using her cane for extra balance. Ligeia shook her head, then stopped shaking and looked around her, lucid again.

Hawkespur returned to the monitoring room, locking the door behind her.

'Ligeia,' said Nyxos carefully. 'Do you know where you are?'

The window was one-way. Ligeia would see only her own reflection looking back at her.

'No,' she said faintly.

'Good. The only facts relevant to you are that you will suffer if you do not answer our questions.'

'I'll… I'll suffer anyway…'

'Once you tell us what we need we can dispose of you and all this will end. Until then, we own you and will do with you as we see fit. You are an object now. You are a receptacle for knowledge that we will wring out of you. That process will be easier if you co-operate. You ceased to be a human being when you betrayed your species and your Emperor, the only way out for you is death. I can make it quick but those who come after me will not be so generous.'

Nyxos let her wait for a while, He wanted her to be the one who spoke next.

'It's Nyxos, isn't it?' she said at last. 'You knew me. They think you'll open me up quicker.'

Ligeia was sharp, always had been. That was one of the reasons the Malleus had headhunted her from the Ordo Hereticus. 'That's right. And we both know they made a mistake. I can't do to you the things they want me to, Ligeia, not to a fellow inquisitor. So this is your only chance.'

Ligeia put her hand over her eyes and shook. Silently, she was laughing. 'No, no, Nyxos. You're not my friend. I don't have any friends.'

'Your cultists were your friends. They died for you.'

'Do you know why they served me? I should have had them executed! They were heretics, they should have burned and they knew it. They just wanted to kill and so they killed for me.'

Nyxos paused. There was a chance that Ligeia was doing to him what Valinov did to her. If that was the case he had ordered Hawkespur to kill him at the first sign of deviance, an order he was certain she would be capable of carrying out.

'What did he tell you to do?' asked Nyxos bluntly.

Ligeia was shaking her head mournfully. 'No one told me to do anything, Nyxos. Don't you even understand that much yet? I saw what would happen. I saw what I had to do. There was no one controlling me, I didn't make any decisions to be influenced.'

'What did you see?'

'I saw that Ghargatuloth would rise and that Valinov would bring him forth. It wasn't bad, it wasn't good, it just was. Once I saw beyond the veil and forced myself to understand, it was all clear.' Ligeia looked up suddenly. Her red-rimmed eyes were fierce. Though she could only be staring at her own reflection, her gaze seemed to reach out and punch right through Nyxos's soul. 'Nothing you do, inquisitor, nothing anyone does, has the least bit to do with what you want. You do not control any action you take, you simply react to the changes around you. You are a puppet of the universe. The only thing that has any power in this galaxy or any other, the only thing worth seeking or worshipping or even giving a moment's thought, is that change that controls you.'

'The Lord of Change,' said Nyxos. 'Tzeentch.' Nyxos saw out of the corner of his eye as Hawkespur flinched at the name. The officer was so straight-laced the forbidden names still sounded wrong to her coming from the mouth of an Imperial servant

'Men give it a name,' said Ligeia, sadness in her voice. 'But it doesn't need one. Nothing any of us do will make a difference. Change had decreed that Ghargatuloth will rise and Valinov will make it happen. I was the only one who could free Valinov, and so I did it. I didn't make a choice. The act was completed before I began it.'

Nyxos sat back in his chair, watching Ligeia's movements as she slumped against the wall and stared at the ceiling. That was how she had been broken, then. She had been convinced that all human actions were governed by fate instead of free will, and that nothing she did was of her own volition. She had been absolved of all responsibility for her actions and turned into a puppet of whatever had been talking to her. Possibly Ghargatuloth itself, maybe Valinov through some unknown means, maybe another intermediary no one had detected yet. In any case, the undermining of Ligeia's spirit had been complete. Nyxos had seen it before, and he knew how hard it would be to break her now.

'Where is Valinov, Ligeia? What is he planning? Is he still in contact with you?'

Ligeia said nothing.

'You will tell us. You know that. You know that we will break you eventually and you will answer all the questions I have just put to you. You might say that you have already broken down, it's just a matter of time. Isn't that how the universe works, Ligeia?'

'Her heart rate's going up, sir,' said Hawkespur.

Panic always accompanied doubt. Doubt was an inquisitor's weapon.

'It will happen, Ligeia,' continued Nyxos. 'We broke Valinov. Do you really think you will hold out when he could not?'

'We don't choose,' said Ligeia quietly, as if to herself. 'We only serve.'

'Where is Valinov? What will he do? How will we stop him? You have to tell us, but you do not have to suffer. You can see that, can't you? You know how all this will end.'

'We only serve!' said Ligeia again, loudly this time. 'We serve the Change and the Change is our fate! Hear its words! Kneel in the darkness and obey the light!'

'Heart rate rising. Anomalous brainwaves.' Hawkespur's face was lit sickly green by the monitor screens. 'Much more and we may have to revive her.'

'Fate has already broken you, Ligeia!' shouted Nyxos as Ligeia began to whimper pathetically. 'Fate wanted us to arrest you and bring you here. It wanted you tried and executed, and it wanted you to tell us everything you know. Otherwise, why are you here? Fate brought you to this cell so I could give you the chance to talk before the explicators started working on you. What else could fate want, if not for you to talk?'

'She's going,' said Hawkespur as the cogitator interpreting her lifesigns suddenly started beeping alarmingly. 'Her heart's stopped.'

Ligeia spasmed again and suddenly sat bolt upright.

'Tras'kleya'thallgryaa!' she screeched, in a hideous atonal voice that seemed to break through the walls of the cell and straight to the inside of Nyxos's head. 'Iak-the'landra'klaa…'

Nyxos smashed a fist down on the emergency shutter controls and a steel curtain fell down in front of the observation window. Ligeia's voice was cut off. Nyxos had felt something monstrous in the words, something old and terrible. Ligeia was speaking in tongues, and it was one of the worst signs – her head was so full of forbidden knowledge that it was flooding out of her. Emperor only knew what damage her words could do to an unprotected mind.

'She's gone,' said Hawkespur. Ligeia's vital signs were flat green lines running across the cogitator screens.

'Bring her back,' said Nyxos. 'We have to give the explicators something to work with.'

Hawkespur pulled a medicae pack from beside the door, punched in the code, and hurried into the cell, where Ligeia lay sprawled on the tiled floor, twitching.

Nyxos watched Hawkespur take out a narthecium unit and pump Ligeia full of chemicals to get her blood flowing. Both Hawkespur and Nyxos would have to undergo a thorough mind-cleansing to ensure that Ligeia had left no trace on them of whatever was in her head. Ligeia would be quarantined even more completely – interrogation would be performed by remote control, with only pain-servitors allowed to go near the prisoner.

Ligeia coughed once and drew a long, sputtering breath.

'Leave her, Hawkespur,' said Nyxos, and rose from his chair. 'She was lost to us a long time ago.'

There was nothing left now but to lock Ligeia's cell, call a servitor-medic to stabilise her, and head back to Enceladus. The woman Nyxos had known was gone, her personality swallowed up by a mind full of blasphemies.

She would suffer much. But that was Mimas's problem now.

THE RUBICON MADE good speed back to Trepytos, carrying Squad Genhain and the sword of Mandulis. It docked above the Trepytos fortress just as the last of Inquisitor Klaes's few small ships left to keep a closer eye on the Trail. Klaes had a handful of interrogators, mostly drawn from the Trail's Arbites and the brighter of the fortress personnel, and now they were all but immersed in the slow madness engulfing the Trail of St Evisser. Alaric had impressed on Klaes the importance of high-quality information about the cult activity rising everywhere, and so all the men Klaes had at his disposal were scattered throughout the Trail. Klaes himself left on the last ship, heading for Magnos Omicron where civil unrest was threatening to tear the forge world's great cities apart. Klaes's priority had to be the citizens of the Trail – the Grey Knights on the other hand were no use on the front lines, where their small numbers would ultimately mean nothing. Alaric had to concentrate on Ghargatuloth, and hope the authorities on the Trail of St Evisser could keep the systems in check long enough for the Grey Knights to make a difference.

Genhain found Alaric still in the archives, surrounded by spilling heaps of books and papers. Alaric had removed his armour and worked by candlelight – it was night on Trepytos and the lumoglobes high in the ceiling did nothing but tint the darkness yellow.

Alaric was absorbed in his work. Several data-slates lay on the table in front of him, amongst scores of open books and sheafs of loose papers. Numerous plates and empty cups were piled up, too – Alaric was spending so much time in the library he had ordered the remaining fortress staff to bring his food to him there. He was scribbling notes with an autoquill, the candlelight glinting in his eyes. A Space Marine could stay awake for more than a hundred hours without negative effects, but even so it looked like Alaric had gone without sleep for some time. It had taken more than three weeks for the *Rubicon* to make the return

journey to Saturn, and it seemed to Genhain that
Alaric had been awake almost the whole time.

'Brother-Captain,' said Genhain carefully.

Alaric paused a moment, then looked up. 'Justicar. It
is good to see you.'

Genhain held up the sword of Mandulis. Its heavy,
razor-sharp blade felt as if it were alive. The bright
blade seemed to make the whole room slightly
brighter, reflecting and magnifying the dim light.
'Durendin said Mandulis would have wanted you to
wield this.'

'I won't wield it, not if I can help it. Tancred is better
with a sword than I am.' Alaric put down his quill and
sat back in his chair. 'Forgive me, justicar. You have
done well. There was no guarantee the Chapter would
grant us this, thank you.'

Genhain walked up to Alaric and laid the sword on
the table. 'Brother Krae was lain out.'

'Good. I will let Tancred know. I only wish we could
have brought Brother Caanos back with us.'

The Grey Knights had left Brother Caanos behind on
Sophano Secundus, burying him after harvesting his
gene-seed.

Genhain looked around at the piles of books surrounding Alaric. 'Are we any closer?'

'Maybe,' said Alaric wearily. 'Ghargatuloth uses his
cultists to hide his true intentions. All this is misinformation.' He waved a hand over the piles of reports,
each one detailing some new atrocity. Persons
unknown had sabotaged the geothermal heatsinks on
Magnos Omicron, destroying several layers of the forge
world's capital hive. A group calling themselves the
Nascent Fate had taken control of the media transmit-
ters on an orbital station and filled the airwaves for

several systems around with non-stop broadcasts of blasphemous sermons. 'Ghargatuloth is talking to his followers, and they are doing everything they can to raise hell on the Trail so those who are doing his true work will go unnoticed.'

'Can we be sure what the Prince is doing?'

Alaric looked up at Genhain. 'Right now Ghargatuloth is weak, and he has to fight to survive. Ultimately, everyone fights the same. You hide your strengths, move them into position, and strike. Ghargatuloth might herald the Lord of Change but for the moment he's scrapping for survival just like all of us.'

Genhain leafed through a couple more of the reports. There was a rash of mutated births on Volcanis Ultor, and shipping throughout the Trail was reporting crewman driven suddenly insane for no reason. 'There is so much here. Ghargatuloth could be doing anything. That's why Ghargatuloth drove Ligeia mad – he knew she could sort through it all and find what really counted.'

Alaric sighed. For the first time, Genhain saw Alaric somewhere close to defeat. 'Mimas transmitted her interrogation logs. She's insane. Speaking in tongues. Klaes is helping, but it's all his staff can do to keep bringing the information in. I had wanted to leave as soon as you brought the *Rubicon* back but until we make some sense of this there is nowhere for us to go.' Alaric stood suddenly, and took hold of Mandulis's sword. Like every Space Marine, Alaric was a huge man, but even so the sword's long, broad blade made him look small. Emperor only knew what Mandulis must have looked like, wielding it in battle. Alaric held the blade, turned it in his hand, looked at his face staring back at him. The reflection picked out the hollows around his eyes, the lines in his face. The sword reflected more than just light – it was so pure that it saw the truth. After a thousand years buried on Titan, it was still as sacred as the day it had been forged.

'Inquisitor Klaes has given us the run of the fortress,' said Alaric with sudden determination. 'Levels seven through twelve are derelict – Tancred is running urban combat drills there with his squad. Have your men join him, I need them battle-fit. My men will join you later.'

'Yes, brother-captain. Where will you be?'

'Praying,' replied Alaric. 'I need to think without all this… this noise.' He indicated the piles of books and papers. 'Ghargatuloth does not have to corrupt us directly to fuddle our minds.'

'Durendin told me some truths I believe he would rather you heard directly,' said Genhain. 'It is not my place to repeat them, but… brother-captain, I feel Ligeia was right to choose you.'

'That remains to be seen, justicar. Now attend to your men, I hope I shall be able to call on them soon.'

'Yes, brother-captain.' Genhain turned to leave. 'Emperor guide you.'

'I hope he does, justicar,' replied Alaric. 'Without him we are lost.'

THIRTEEN
HIVE SUPERIOR

CARDINAL RECOBA'S OFFICES were alive with activity. The liaison officer from the Adeptus Arbites had taken over a side chapel and was yelling impassioned orders into a vox-relay as he moved Arbites units to support local law enforcement all over Volcanis Ultor. The three adepts who made up the chief Departmento Munitorum presence sat surrounded by reams of printouts and requisition forms, dozens of lesser adepts running messages to and from them as they tried to organise supply lines for the forces still arriving at the hive world. Representatives from various noble houses, including that of Volcanis Ultor's Imperial Governor, wandered the lower corridors and the anterooms trying to get someone to listen to them.

Cardinal Francendo Recoba had seen the crisis growing and had ensured that he would be in charge. Governor Livrianis was under effective house arrest, to prevent his potential corruption. He was a slow and cowardly man at heart – it took Recoba to manage a potential catastrophe like this. Volcanis Ultor was the primary hive world on the Trail, its population accounting for a good proportion of all the citizens of the Trail, and it had to be held against the hidden tide of heresy at all costs. Recoba was the only man with the respect and natural authority to lock the planet down, and organise a military defence for when the crisis truly broke and the legions of the Enemy rose from amongst them.

Recoba had long preached to his fellow clergy that the Ecclesiarchy could only enforce the true meaning of the Imperial cult if it had temporal as well as spiritual authority. Here was his proof – the Trail of St Evisser needed faith now more than anything, and its chief hive world had chosen Cardinal Recoba to lead its defence. This would be a battle for the spiritual survival of Volcanis Ultor and of the whole Trail, even more than it would be a physical conflict, and Recoba was determined to be in control.

Recoba's offices occupied several layers of Hive Superior, the capital hive of Volcanis Ultor. It was located in the secondary spire – the primary spire, where the governor's family and sub-families lived, was locked down completely with the troops of the hive's Municipal Order Regiment guarding every entrance. Recoba's private chambers occupied three layers, which he maintained as his personal realm where only trusted advisors and invited representatives could tread. The rest were divided into grand areas for receiving dignitaries and private chapels where Recoba normally ministered to the spiritual needs of Volcanis Ultor's elite, and it was in these layers that leaders from all the authorities active in Volcanis Ultor's defence had set up headquarters. Recoba had just received the canoness of the Order of the Bloody Rose, whose Battle Sisters were now reinforcing the defensive lines around Lake Rapax just outside Hive Superior. Several Imperial Guard officers were also trying to get a foothold in Recoba's realm, to coordinate the Guard regiments now policing the planet's hotspots and forming defensive positions.

At that moment, the crisis seemed some distance away. Recoba sat in his state room, reviewing some of the field reports coming in. The state room was furnished as a lavish bedchamber, though Recoba never slept here, only received his most trusted advisors. It did him good, he knew, to retire to his state rooms when everything around him was at its most hectic. He, above all, had to keep a clear head. It would be too easy to get drawn into the details – a hundred lives here, a hundred lives there. He took a sip of imported Dravian wine – a good vintage, something he had been saving for a crisis – and went back to reviewing the overall state of Volcanis Ultor.

Recoba saw that almost half the levels in Hive Tertius were still out of contact, having been overrun by factory workers under the influence of some kind of popular messianic movement. Recoba shook his head and tutted. He had hoped the sealing of the main exit routes would be the end of the troubles in the hive, but now it looked like the survivors were in danger of losing their minds to the tide of heresy. He would have to send the scout platoons of the Methalor 12th Regiment into the hive to keep the madness from spreading.

The next report he picked up from his writing desk was a communiqué from the colonel of the Salthenian

7th Infantry Regiment. He regretted that he was unable
to commit his regiment to the defence of Volcanis
Ultor, citing garrison duties on Salthen itself. Recoba
sighed. He would have to call in a few favours from the
clergy on Salthen, and show the colonel how a few
well-chosen words from the regimental preachers
could make his commission look very shaky indeed.

There was a knock on the chamber's hardwood door.
Recoba looked up in annoyance. 'Enter,' he said sharply.

A valet servitor opened the door with a polished
chrome hand. Deacon Oionias walked in, a young but
eager man who Recoba trusted as a messenger and
aide. 'Your blessedness,' said Oionias. 'There is someone who most urgently needs to speak with you.'

'Remind this someone that my office has protocols.
My time is valuable. Have him go through Abbot
Thorello if it's important.'

'That's just the thing, your blessedness,' said Oionias.
His plump face was slightly red. 'He says he has the
authority to address you directly.'

'I do not have the time to…'

'You have the time for *me*, cardinal,' said a resonant
voice from behind Oionias. A man walked in, breezing
past the young deacon – he was tall and well-built,
with a sharp, noble face and intelligent eyes. He wore
a splendid traveller's cloak of flakweave trimmed in
ermine over a dark green officer's uniform with several
sheathed knives worn across the breast. His synth-
leather boots shone like glass.

'Forgive my intrusion, your blessedness,' he began
graciously with slight bow, 'but we are better served by
dealing with one another directly. I bring news critical
to the defence of Volcanis Ultor, and to the survival of
the whole Trail.'

Recoba felt slightly less aggrieved. 'What authority do you represent?'

'I am honoured to bring the tidings of the Holy Orders of the Emperor's Inquisition,' said the visitor, taking a small Inquisitorial rosette from inside his cloak. 'I am Inquisitor Gholic Ren-Sar Valinov, and I fear our Enemy may be even more dangerous that you suppose.'

THE BATTLEMENTS OF the Trepytos fortress were bleak and cold. The dark granite blocks of the fortress formed grim, blunt teeth along the edge of the battlements and the dismal half-decrepit city around the fortress spread out towards a barren grey-brown plain. Trepytos used to be beautiful. Now, it was drained and dying. The fortress was still formidable, with sheer unscaleable walls and a massive set of gates protected by watchtowers and scores of gun emplacements – but the emplacements had rusted solid and the garrison that once permanently manned the walls was long gone. The fortress had been there since before the Ordo Hereticus chose it as the Inquisition headquarters for the Trail, but it was difficult to imagine anything for it now but slow, grim decay.

Alaric stood on the battlements, his augmented eyesight picking out the faint glimmer of the planet's weak sun on the edge of the ocean some distance away. The *Rubicon* was a sliver of silver in the sky directly overhead, and there were lights scattered throughout the inhabited parts of the city. The winds sheared across the battlements and most men would be chilled to the bone. Alaric barely noticed it.

He was so close. He knew it. He had an advantage Ghargatuloth had not expected the Grey Knights to get

– he had faced one of Ghargatuloth's chosen champions on Sophano Secundus, someone he was not supposed to find. That meant that the place that had led the Grey Knights there – the cult temple in the Administratum building on Victrix Sonora – was important, too.

'Brother-Captain!' called Justicar Tancred over the driving wind. He was walking towards Alaric in full armour, and he was taller even than the megalithic teeth of the battlements. 'The staff found what you needed.' There was a data-slate in Tancred's gauntlet.

'Good,' said Alaric, taking the slate. 'We may have to leave very soon. Are you ready?'

'Always, brother-captain.' Alaric saw Tancred was sweating and the sheen was off his armour – he had only recently finished training rites with his squad. Tancred had been training gradually harder and harder, Alaric had noticed, turning derelict floors of the fortress into warrens of kill-zones for the Grey Knights to battle through. Justicar Santoro had been driving his Marines hard, too, taking them on endless squad drills along the walls and through the fortress's upper levels. The Grey Knights needed to fight. The Trail was going insane around them, and to them it was blasphemy to just sit by and watch it happen.

'Do you know where to look?' asked Tancred.

'I know where to start,' said Alaric. 'I know why Ghargatuloth drove Ligeia mad. It is information that is his weakness. If we have too much of it, we can use it against him. Think about it. We hurt him on Sophano Secundus, because we found a part of his plan that had been there since before he was banished. That's where the link is.'

'The link?'

Alaric began flicking through the files on the data-slate. 'We know the cult on Victrix Sonora raided Ecclesiarchy sites and stole relics. They had been doing so for a long time, since before they were detected at all. The Arbites thought it was just spite, and with everything else the cultists did no one thought it was important.' Alaric paused. 'And... and on Sophano Secundus Missionary Crucien based his cult in the Imperial Mission. He could have hidden it anywhere in the forests, in the mountains – there was a whole planet to hide it in. But he stayed in the most obvious location there was, a place sanctified by the Imperial Church. Why?'

'The Enemy is perverse,' said Tancred simply. 'They need no logic.'

'But it's not just Sophano Secundus. Why here at all?' Alaric held his arms out wide, indicating everything around him. 'The last time Ghargatuloth reigned, he laired on Khorion IX. That was on the far edge of the Segmentum Pacificus, it took us a hundred years to find him. Why the Trail? There are backwaters more decrepit than the Trail, there are whole sectors of empty space where he could hide. What makes the Trail of St Evisser special?'

'Saint Evisser?' said Tancred.

'Saint Evisser. Ghargatuloth has his cults collecting Imperial relics. He needs the biggest relic of all to complete the ritual that will bring him back.' Alaric held up the data-slate. It was showing a set of planetary coordinates. 'The Hall of Remembrance on Farfallen was the biggest Ecclesiarchical archive on the Trail. As far as we know it's still there. We are going to find out where the body of Saint Evisser is buried, because that is where Ghargatuloth will rise.'

* * *

THE PRIMARY DEFENCES of Volcanis Ultor described a semicircle around the base of Hive Superior, several hundred kilometres of hastily-dug trenches, prefabricated bunkers and command posts, endless rolls of barbed wire, emplacements for Basilisk self-propelled guns and even an immense Ordinatus artillery piece manned by Volcanis Ultor's class of tech-priests. Hundreds of supply trenches zig-zagged back through the pollution-bleached ground into the outer reaches of the hive, crawling with thousands of men from the Balurian heavy infantry, Methalor 12th Scout Regiment, 197th Jhannian Assault Regiment and Volcanis Ultor's own PDF. Rearward positions were held by men and women drafted from Hive Superior's underhive gangers, who had answered the call of the Departmento Munitorum and joined the defence in return for being allowed to keep the weapons they were issued with. The strongpoint at the northern end of the line, where the broken plain met the shore of Lake Rapax, was held by the Sisters of the Order of the Bloody Rose, and Cardinal Recoba had personally sent hundreds of preachers and confessors to the front lines so spiritual leadership would never be far away from the troops.

The attack, when it surely came, would come from the plains in front of the defences. The jagged mountain ranges on the far side of Hive Superior meant that the plains were the only place an arriving army could gather, and the defences would be ready for them. Recoba knew that if Hive Superior was overrun, Volcanis Ultor would fall, and with it the keystone that held the whole Trail intact. He had drawn troops and resources from all over the planet and even off-world, sacrificing the smaller hives and inter-hive settlements to ensure that Hive Superior would survive.

The northern half of the line was served by a rearward command centre, a massive plasticrete arena of bunkers and parade grounds built along standard template lines and dropped from orbit by a Mechanicus transport just a few days before. Rings of overlapping gun emplacements surrounded it and Hydra anti-aircraft quad autocannon were mounted to cover central parade ground. Transport and staff shuttles zipped overhead, and the sky was patrolled by an occasional Thunderbolt fighter of which three squadrons had been scrambled to the surface. A pulpit and lectern had been set up in the centre of the parade ground, linked to vox-casters and to the comm-net that covered the entire hinterland of Hive Superior.

As the sun's murky morning light filtered through the clouds of pollution overhead, troops began filing into the parade ground. Several platoons of Balurian heavy infantry were first, smart and well-drilled. The Methalorian scouts were less polished in their parade ground skills, and they had a ragtag appearance with each carrying non-issue weapons and gear, from camocloaks to orkish combat knives. The Guardsmen were from units who were still waiting to be assigned to a section of the defences – every one of them would be heading to the front line within a few hours. There were even some of the conscripted hive gangers milling around towards the back of the parade ground, almost feral figures in clashing gang colours who carried trophies from gang-scraps in the depths of Hive Superior.

Officers yelled at the men to redress ranks and smarten up. A couple of commissars prowled, and everywhere they looked Guardsmen stiffened at attention. They all knew they could soon be in the thick of fighting against Emperor knew what kind of enemy. Even the gangers mostly fell silent.

Finally, Cardinal Recoba's staff arrived to take their places beside the pulpit. Recoba himself wore his full cardinal's regalia, the crimson and white standing out amongst the drab fatigues of the soldiers, the gold of his mitre glinting in the murky light of the rising sun. There were several deacons and preachers with him, along with the lexmechanics and protocol officers who followed senior officers everywhere.

Finally, alone, Inquisitor Valinov entered the parade ground, and ascended to the pulpit. Vox-casters would send his voice booming across the parade ground, and across the comm-link so that thousands of soldiers could hear his every word. Cardinal Recoba had required all officers to ensure their men were listening. The media of Hive Superior were broadcasting, too, because Recoba knew how important Valinov's words would be.

Valinov looked out over the thousands of men assembled on the parade ground. The eyes looking back at him didn't know who he was. That meant he could be whoever he wanted to be. It was something he had learned a long time ago, as an interrogator in the service of Inquisitor Barbillus. He wore polished carapace armour and an antique power sword, taken from the armoury of the Governor's household – today, Gholic Ren-Sar Valinov was a hero.

'Men and women of Volcanis Ultor,' he began. 'Soldiers, Sisters and citizens. All of you know that a dark time has come to the Trail of St Evisser, and that darker times still are yet to come. The Enemy, who we must now speak of freely, has come to the Trail. I have seen this Enemy, and fought it, and believe me when I tell

you it can be beaten. You will see things that may
make you despair, things that you cannot understand,
but you must fight. The Enemy fights with lies, and
will use confusion and dissent to break your resolve. It
cannot succeed. No matter what, you must fight, and
carry on fighting until the Trail is free. That is the order
I give you that supersedes all others, by the authority
of the Holy Orders of the Emperor's Inquisition.'

Valinov paused. The existence of the Inquisition was
officially suppressed, but rumours were the most uni-
versal currency of the Imperium. Guardsmen talked
over bottles of bootleg spirits about the figures who
could kill planets with a word and purge entire populations to root out the taint of corruption. Valinov
would be one such figure – a legend come to life, a
story made real. The soldiers had flinched when they
realised that an inquisitor was in command – a real,
genuine inquisitor! Even the lexmechanic scribbling
down a record of his words had paused.

'But there is a far darker truth that I must tell you.
You have all heard of the Adeptus Astartes, heroes of
the Imperium. The defenders of mankind.' Valinov
knew well that they had – the Balurians had fought
alongside the White Consuls at the Rhanna Crisis, and
the chapels of Hive Superior had stained glass windows depicting the Ultramarines who destroyed the
rebels of Hive Oceanis centuries before. If inquisitors
were figures in dark stories told on long nights, Space
Marines were the heroes of wide-eyed children's tales.
'And you have all been told of the Horus Heresy, when
the Enemy stole away the minds of billions and waged
a civil war against the Emperor-fearing people of the
Imperium. It is my duty to tell you that the Space
Marines were at the heart of this conflict. Fully half

their number fell to the Enemy and marched with Horus.'

Valinov let that sink in, too. Imperial histories – as told to the ordinary citizens who needed to know no more – glossed over the details of the Horus Heresy, and of the Traitor Legions of Space Marines who fell to Chaos.

Valinov let his voice rise. He could see the eyes of the soldiers growing wide. For one of them to say these things would be heresy – for an inquisitor to say them was a revelation.

'For ten thousand years those Traitor Marines have held their grudge. Now they are returning, for the Eye of Terror has opened and the eyes of the Enemy fall again on the galaxy. The Traitor Marines think that the Trail is the weak underbelly of the Imperium. They think that with so many of our forces at the Eye, they can do what they want with our worlds and our homes. If we stop them here, they will be thrown back into the darkness, and the touch of the Enemy that curses the Trail will go with them.

'I tell you this because the Traitor Marines are coming here, to Volcanis Ultor. I have been sent ahead of them by the daemon hunters of the Inquisition to ensure that you understand what you are fighting. In a few days they will be here. They were once the Imperium's finest soldiers, now corrupted beyond redemption, but they are expecting to meet no resistance. We have the advantage of surprise. That is why the battle will be here, and that is why it must be won.

'Recognition documents are being circulated to every officer now. Understand the form and markings of this enemy! In their arrogance they proudly display the marks of their heresy. The sword and the book is their symbol. To parody the nobility of what they once were, they call themselves the Grey Knights. They bring with them daemons and foul sorcery, but we have the hearts of Imperial citizens and the steel of the Emperor's will!'

Valinov could taste the heady mix of emotions. Fear, because every Guardsman had heard of Space Marines but never expected to see one, let alone have to go against their legendary strength in battle. Pride, because they were the ones trusted to stop them. Awe, because suddenly the defence of a single hive city had become a crusade against darkness, led by a hero of the Imperium.

'Take your positions, obey your commands, have faith in the Throne of Terra and show the Enemy no quarter! For here will the Enemy's will be broken, and here will be forged your future.'

Everyone had heard of Space Marines. Some had heard of the Inquisition. No one had heard of the Grey Knights. The Inquisition's own obsessive secrecy was its greatest failing, an irony Valinov enjoyed as he stepped down off the pulpit and turned his thoughts to the coming battle.

LIGEIA HAD ASKED for Valinov's execution to be stayed. There was no one left to ask for Ligeia.

Ligeia was still in her cell, anchored just above Mimas's upper atmosphere. All interrogations had elicited only the same garbled stream of syllables she had uttered when Nyxos had broken her. She was all but useless as an intelligence source, and her freeing of Valinov marked her as an enemy of the Imperium and an immediate moral threat.

The lord inquisitors came to the only conclusion they could. Ligeia had to die.

Inquisitor Nyxos stood in the interrogator command control room at the heart of the Mimas facility, waiting patiently as the interrogators, explicators and chief medicae staff made the last few checks on Ligeia. In the past, particularly corrupt prisoners had waited until the moment of their execution to display Chaos sorcery they had managed to hide until then. Ligeia, however, had not changed – she was still in a constant state of physical shock, her heart rate fluctuating, her brainwaves fractured and haphazard. Several pict-stealers watched her from many angles, but all she did was curl up in the corner of her cell and shiver. She had nearly died when Nyxos had interrogated her, and since then had been just a few steps from death.

'No lifesign change,' said one of the medicae as the final checks were completed.

'Negative brainwave change,' said another.

The chief medicae, an elderly, portly man who had taken on the role after the death of his predecessor at Valinov's botched execution, turned to Nyxos. 'Medical go.'

'Good,' said Nyxos. 'Explicator command?'

The chief explicator's voice was voxed from elsewhere in the facility. 'Psychic activity residual only. No change.'

Nyxos stepped up to the comm-pulpit, which was connected to Ligeia's cell via several warded filters that lessened the likelihood of her words corrupting the listener.

Nyxos opened the channel. His voice was fed directly into the cell.

'Ligeia,' began Nyxos, 'this is the end. I promised you it would be over and now it is. There is one last chance before you die. Tell us where Valinov is, tell us what he is doing. Do this and the Emperor may show you mercy where men cannot.'

Ligeia stirred. She lifted her head and looked up at one of the pict-stealers, and on the screen Nyxos could make out her deathly pale, almost translucent skin, her sunken red eyes, grey hair clinging to her damp skin. She shook and seemed to be choking on something, her fingers curling into claws, her jaw clenching and unclenching.

'Tras'kleya'thallgryaa!' she yelled suddenly, as if vomiting the words up from somewhere deep inside her. 'Iakthe'landra'klaa! Saphe'drekall'kry'aa!'

Nyxos snapped the sound feed off, leaving Ligeia screaming silently out of the monitor.

'She is lost. In the sight of the Emperor, witness her excommunication from the human race and the extinguishing of her corruption.'

Nyxos slammed his fist down on a large control stud on the pulpit. Soundlessly, the back wall of the cell blew out and the image shook violently as the air was torn away. Ligeia grabbed instinctively, digging thin fingers between the tiles, hanging on as suddenly the blackness of space was shockingly close. The cell was open to space, the barren frozen rock of Mimas below, the glowing banded disk of Saturn above, the blackness streaked with stars and the smears of dust that made up Saturn's rings.

Ligeia looked with horror at the void in front of her. For a few moments she tried to crawl towards the front of the cell, her eyes fixed on the endless darkness. But then something inside her finally realised it really was the end. She lay helpless on her back as the freezing cold seized up her limbs and the vacuum paralysed her lungs. Her eyes flooded red as blood vessels burst. She gasped silently for air that wasn't there. Then, she stopped moving altogether, red eyes wide, mouth frozen open.

Nyxos watched her for some minutes, trying to detect the slightest movement. There was nothing.

'Monitor her for three days,' he said eventually to the interrogator command staff. 'Then destroy the body.'

An inquisitor was due a proper burial, below the fortress on Enceladus if possible. But Ligeia wasn't an inquisitor any more. Aside from a warning footnote, she would be better off forgotten completely.

FOURTEEN
FARFALLEN

FARFALLEN WAS A dying world. It had once been a garden world, one of those rare breed of planets kept pristine as rewards and playgrounds for the Imperium's nobility. Retirement on a garden world tempted the most ambitious of planetary governors and rogue traders to toe the Imperial line. At the height of the Trail, when the mass pilgrimages had given plenty the opportunity to leach fortunes from the faithful, Farfallen had been a wondrous mixture of lush virgin forests and carefully manicured landscape gardens. White marble villas had nestled in the fronds of towering rainforests. Elaborate turreted castles of coral had looked out on an endless azure sea. Sky yachts plied the clouds and elderly nobles hunted imported big game on the vast rolling plains.

The Ecclesiarchy, who could claim the greatest credit for the Trail's prominence, maintained a great estate on Farfallen, and used it as the seat for the Hall of Remembrance where the Trail's religious legacy would be collected and compiled for posterity. The Administratum took a tithe of land from the garden world, so Consuls Majoris of the Administratum could themselves retire in splendour.

With a stable ecosystem, hardly any predators, a predictable temperate climate and the protection of the Adeptus Terra, Farfallen had been a rare paradise in the grimness of the Imperium. But that had been a long time ago.

Much of Farfallen was untended and overgrown. Landscaped gardens fell into disrepair and tree roots broke up the marble buildings. With fewer fortunes to be made on the Trail only a handful of noble families remained, ageing and cut off, retreating into their estates as Farfallen became wilder. Imported game predators could no longer be controlled by hunting and they turned the jungles into savage places. And somewhere, somehow, the uninvited had come to Farfallen – feral humans who infested the deepest jungles. For centuries no one noticed them, and they remained hidden from Farfallen's dwindling Imperial population.

Then Ghargatuloth's call went out across the Trail, and suddenly hundreds of thousands of savages poured from the forests to do the work of the Change God.

THE GREY KNIGHTS had lost two Thunderhawks on Sophano Secundus and so Alaric took only as many Marines as would fit into the remaining gunship – he chose his own unit and Squad Genhain. He might discover something unpalatable, and he trusted Genhain to cope with it best of all.

Alaric watched the surface of Farfallen from the Thunderhawk as it made its approach. It was late evening and the thick carpet of forest was dark green, the curling fronds of the trees like the bristles on an animal's hide. It was easy to see how the dense forests had hidden the feral tribes, and how they could be corrupted away from Imperial eyes.

The forest sped past beneath the Thunderhawk and on the horizon Alaric could see the Hall of Remembrance. It was built into a cliff that soared above the forest canopy, a massive blocky shape carved from the rock face. High arched windows like dead eyes looked out from beneath a deeply carved pediment depicting the heroic figures of past Ecclesiarchs, trampling the minions of Chaos beneath their feet.

As the Thunderhawk swooped lower for the final approach Alaric could pick out signs of the chaos on Farfallen. Lights from fires burning at ground level flickered on the stone. Charred tatters marked the places banners had once hung. The edges of the roof were scarred where crude catapults had slung stones and balls of fire at defenders firing down. The jungle on the top of the cliff just above the hall's roof was chewed and trampled – early on the ferals had tried to climb down the cliff, only to be shot off the rocks as they made the descent. Some broken, desiccated bodies were still wedged into cracks in the cliff face, a testament to the first moments of the attack. The Hall of Remembrance, the most visible Imperial bastion to remain on Farfallen, was under siege.

'The hall has responded to our comms,' said the Ordo Malleus pilot in the Thunderhawk's cockpit. If the Malleus crew on the *Rubicon* had mourned the loss of two of their pilots on Sophano Secundus, they hadn't shown it. 'We can land on the roof.'

'Do it,' said Alaric.

The Malleus-trained crews were a strange breed. All of them had emotional repression doctrination and Alaric knew some of them even had cortical detonators that would activate in extremes of terror or elation, so that even if some Chaos power corrupted them the experience would kill them before they did any harm. They were little more than servitors, denied the chance to ever develop a fully-fledged human personality. It seemed to Alaric that countless lives had to be wasted or destroyed just to make the fight against Chaos possible. Of course, that in itself was a victory for the Enemy.

The Thunderhawk passed over the roof of the hall and the top of the cliff, slewing round as it decelerated. Alaric could see the siege lines of the ferals – they had dug trenches in concentric circles and piles of spoil marked the places were they were undoubtedly digging tunnels in the hope of finding a way in through the foundations. There would be enough vaults and cellars beneath the Hall of Remembrance to make it more likely than not that they would succeed. To the rear of their lines huge bonfires burned, with wild-haired, paint-daubed figures dancing around them. Alaric was sure he made out mutations and flickers of sorcery among them as the Thunderhawk descended.

The ferals couldn't trouble the Thunderhawk. For ranged weaponry they had only catapults and bows. The Thunderhawk's landing gear lowered and the gunship touched down on the roof of the Hall of Remembrance, its engines leaving great scorch marks on the cliff face.

The exit ramp lowered, letting in the smell of old stone and burning forest. Squad Alaric and Squad Genhain dropped down onto the pockmarked marble tiles of the roof.

An old, barrel-chested, battle-scarred deacon ran over from a lookout position on the edge of the pediment. He carried a battered autogun and wore grimy, tattered Ecclesiarchical robes. A few young novice preachers and archivists with haunted eyes manned the walls, now looking in undisguised awe at the huge armoured warriors emerging from the Thunderhawk.

The deacon was the only one there who looked like he was worth a damn in a fight. The days of the Hall of Remembrance were numbered.

'Throne be praised!' bellowed the deacon as he approached the disembarking Marines. 'Long have we prayed for deliverance. We had begun to doubt that reinforcements would ever arrive. And yet we have been sent Space Marines in our plight! Truly the Emperor has heard our pleadings!'

'We're not reinforcements,' said Alaric bluntly. 'Are you in charge here?'

The deacon's shoulders dropped. If he had been hanging on to the possibility of the hall's survival, that hope was now gone. But servants of the Emperor did not bemoan their lot, and he did his best not to let it show. 'I am in command on the roof,' said the deacon.

'And below?'

The deacon sighed. 'No one is commanding the defence. We are not soldiers – I was, once, but I can't command a siege. With Confessor Arhelghast dead Senior Archivist Serevic has rank but he's just a scholar.'

'Good. I need to see him as soon as possible.'

'I'll have one of the novices show you down. But… brother… if one of you could stay. Just one of you. Think what could be lost here, think what the Enemy could do to us. One Marine could do the fighting of a hundred men, everyone knows it.'

'Farfallen stands or dies alone, deacon. I need all my battle-brothers for when we take the fight to the enemy. Do what you can to survive, but my Marines will not die here for you.'

The deacon looked like he was about to argue, but he bit back the words. He had not chosen to lead, but he was the only one here who could – now hope of survival was gone, perhaps he would be able to face death on its own terms and realise the only fight he had to win was against despair.

THE HALL OF Remembrance was cut deeply into the rock, a dense warren of vaulted corridors and high-ceilinged chapels that seemed to have been designed with no reason or purpose. Piles of ledgers and scrolls were crammed into every available room and alcove, and some corridors were lined with them. The hall, if it had been designed as anything, had not been designed as a library. Alaric picked one volume up as he passed – its cover identified it as a record of the tithes paid to one of the sub-chapels on Volcanis Ultor. The last entry was three hundred years old.

The whole place stank of rotting paper. The novice who led them down into the Hall – a gangly, hollow-eyed novice preacher carrying an antique lasgun he clearly didn't know how to use properly – took the Grey Knights lower and lower until the chanting of the ferals outside could be heard through the walls. The boy was terrified of the Grey Knights – very few

Imperial citizens indeed ever saw a Space Marine, let alone got this close to them. It must have been like a dream lain over the nightmare of the siege.

'How is all this organised?' Genhain asked, echoing Alaric's own thoughts.

'It's… it's not, really, sir,' answered the novice. 'The archivists keep it all in order, in their heads. They don't write it down. The word of the Emperor is in the hearts and minds of His subjects, not written down where heretics might twist it for their own use.'

Alaric sighed inwardly. Like all Imperial organisations the Ecclesiarchy matched its immense size with its enormous variety. Every preacher and confessor did things differently, and in spite of the zealously conservative synods on Earth and Ophelia VII, matters of dogma and interpretation sometimes made one branch of the Imperial cult look like a whole different religion to the next. The traditions by which the Hall of Remembrance did its sacred work evidently had more to do with the prominence Farfallen once had than with the Emperor's own will – the senior archivists had protected their own coveted position on the garden world by making sure only they understood the hall's archives.

The central levels of the hall contained the archivist's offices. Most were empty – the hall had by then lost most of its staff. Novices' cells led off from one wall, with exhausted novices recuperating in a couple of them. One hard bed contained a body, the bedclothes pulled up over the head, a well-thumbed copy of the *Hymnal Imperator* placed reverentially on the chest.

'Senior Archivist Serevic,' said the guide meekly, indicating a carved door of dark wood and standing aside. Alaric opened the door and a cloud of heavy purplish incense flowed out. The novice stifled a cough as Alaric entered.

Alaric's enhancements meant the incense and darkness didn't bother him. It was still a dispiriting sight – Serevic, an unassuming, scholarly man in late middle age, bent over a lectern as he pored over a huge illuminated tome, had evidently shut himself up in the room some time ago.

Serevic looked around at the intrusion, evidently about to remonstrate with whichever novice had dared to disturb him. When he saw Alaric filling the doorway his watery eyes widened in shock and he half-fell off his chair, stumbling back against the far wall and dislodging tottering piles of papers and books.

'Who…? Throne preserve us!'

Alaric stepped into the room. He noticed an unmade bed in the corners, scraps of paper everywhere, books heaped against the walls. 'Archivist Serevic?'

'Senior… Senior Archivist. Machas Lavanian Serevic.'

'Good. Acting Brother-Captain Alaric of the Grey Knights, in the service of the Emperor's Inquisition.'

'The Inquisition? We… we are Emperor-fearing servants here, there is no need…'

Alaric held up a hand. 'We are not here to judge you. Something dark has come to the Trail and we need information from you if we are to fight it.'

Serevic tried to compose himself, but his voice still wavered. 'I have heard them singing at night, even here. They say their Prince is here.'

'They are right. It is rising somewhere on the Trail, but if we are to fight it we must find out where. The violence here is happening all over the Trail and there is not much time left.'

'The other archivists are dead. There is so much that has been lost to us.'

'This will not be lost. The Prince of a Thousand Faces will rise at the burial place of Saint Evisser.'

There was a long pause. 'There is no burial place.'

Alaric stepped closer so he was looming right over Serevic. 'The Prince needs Evisser's body to come back. That is the only reason he is on the Trail at all.'

'Brother-Captain, there is no burial place. There is no Saint. That the Trail will soon die proves this. We were forsaken a long time ago.'

Serevic was steeling himself. This was a moment he had prepared for, which meant it was important to him since he was clearly not prepared to lead the defence of the Hall.

'What happened here?' asked Alaric.

'The Emperor's Inquisition cannot save us, brother-captain. The Emperor's Church must keep its own counsel.'

'Very well.' Alaric turned to Justicar Genhain, who waited just outside the door. 'Burn all this.'

Serevic gasped. 'Burn? But... this is sacred, this is our...'

'The Hall of Remembrance will fall. This knowledge will fall into the hands of the Enemy. If it is of no use to the Emperor, then it is nothing more than a weapon for his foes.'

'There is no reason! No reason! This is... this is sacrilege! The sacred word must remain! To destroy all this is no more than heresy!'

'I first thought,' said Alaric carefully, 'that the archivists only wanted to maintain their own positions here. But that's not why you keep all this knowledge organised only in your own memories. Is it, Serevic?'

Brother Ondurin had unslung his incinerator and a blue flame was flickering at its nozzle.

'You are here to guard this knowledge. You are here because the Ecclesiarchy knows something about the Trail, and St Evisser, and Ghargatuloth, and they want it kept secret. But we are offering to destroy it all, so that once the ferals tear you apart there will be no secrets left to find. So why shouldn't we burn it all? We would be helping you. Why do you care about saving any of this?'

Serevic's voice was a whimper. 'Because... I'm not finished...'

Alaric held up a hand. Ondurin lowered the barrel of his incinerator, which had been poised to send a gout of flame into the books piled up in the nearest cell. 'The Ecclesiarchy should have appointed a stronger-willed man to keep their secrets. Tell us what we need to know or it will all burn, and you will watch it.'

A fat tear rolled down Serevic's face. 'I can't tell you. Throne of Earth, they took me here as a child, and even when I didn't know anything they told me it is a mortal sin to tell...' Serevic looked up. His lip trembled. 'But... I can show you.'

KELKANNIS EVISSER WAS nobody. He was a novice adept sent to the tiny Administratum offices on Solshen XIX back when it was a newly-settled planet earmarked for use as an agri-world. He was no more than a name on a roster, just like trillions of men and women who would never amount to anything more.

It was late in Evisser's life when Solshen XIX found itself in the path of greenskin raiders. The orks belonged to just one of thousands of warbands who marauded through the frontiers of the Imperium, and their periodic bouts of carnage amongst scattered Imperial settlements were as much a part of an Imperial citizen's life as prayer, work and obedience.

Nothing remained when they left Solshen XIX. Nothing but burning ruins.

And Kelkannis Evisser.

Evisser was not the only sole survivor in the Imperium. Whole mythologies had grown up around them – to some they were unlucky, having used up the good luck of everyone around them. To others they were lucky charms, protected by the Emperor's grace. To the Administratum a sole survivor was just another adept, to be moved sideways while the settlement on Solshen XIX was rebuilt.

But Kelkannis Evisser would not be drawn back into the vast machine of the Administratum. He had seen the will of the Emperor as the greenskins butchered his colleagues. He had seen how even the orks were, in their own way, instruments of the Emperor's hand – they had been sent to show Evisser the Emperor's infinite mercy and strength, the blinding heat of His wrath, the endless depth of His belief in mankind's destiny to rule the stars. Kelkannis had been chosen to survive precisely because he was nobody, just like the trillions who made up the Emperor's flock, and it was Kelkannis's duty to show them all how the Emperor's message applied to the lowly and the exalted alike.

They thought him mad. He refused to prove them right. Those sent to denounce him listened, and in turn came to believe that it was something more than blind fortune that had saved him from the rampaging greenskins. The mere fact that the Administratum could not make him another part of their machine made him special. Even the faceless, endless bureaucracy of the Imperium could not crush his spirit.

He was more than just a man with divinely inspired grace who spread the word of the Emperor. He was hope itself – hope that the lowly men and women of the Imperium could play a meaningful part in the Emperor's plan for humanity, hope that a single soul could mean something to the Imperium.

If there was one thing the people of the Imperium needed, it was hope. Worlds clamoured for Evisser to visit them, and when he came the governors and Arbites were powerless to stop immense crowds flocking to hear him speak. It was not long before some started speaking of future sainthood.

Then came the miracles. A savage plague was decimating the lower city of one of Trepytos's port hives. Evisser went to the heart of the quarantined zone and stayed there for six months, easing the dying hours of thousands, giving to millions the comfort of knowing they died in the Emperor's grace. That was miracle enough, but in spite of spending every waking moment at the bedsides of the dying Evisser was untouched by the plague.

An uprising of mutant slaves on Magnos Omicron threatened to tip the forge world into anarchy. Evisser walked miraculously through the gunfire to speak with the rebellion's leaders and convince them, through nothing but the clarity of the Emperor's word as it was spoken through him, to lay down their arms and return beneath the Imperial yoke.

In the void between the star systems starships followed Evisser everywhere he went, for as he passed he left the warp cold and still. Not one ship was lost to warp storms or madness so long as they followed. In this way the Trail was first marked out, systems linked by the journeys of Evisser as he ministered to the despairing and the downtrodden.

He brought the Emperor's grace to deaths that would otherwise mean nothing. He left a wake of renewed faith and diligence everywhere he went. The citizens of the Trail adored him and began to celebrate him vociferously – within a year of his miracle at Trepytos there were festivals and parades in his name. Chapels were dedicated to his spirit. Soon, the speculations of sainthood were forgotten and people began to refer to Saint Evisser as a matter of course – for what else was a saint, but an individual made graceful and miraculous by the Emperor's will, an embodiment of His mastery over humanity?

And so as a living saint, Kelkannis Evisser did wonders that came to bear his name. He spent decades travelling to almost every system in the Trail, and wherever he trod shrines and chapels were built in celebration. The Hall of Remembrance itself was built where he first landed on Farfallen, for when he stepped off the exit ramp of his shuttle it was said that every flower on the planet suddenly bloomed in exaltation. He blessed the dark towers of Volcanis Ultor and the subterranean geothermal forges of Magnos Omicron, the fields of Victrix Sonora and the teeming oceans of Solshen XIX, the very stars that shone down on the Trail.

It was due to St Evisser that a tract of frontier space had become a populous and wealthy cluster of worlds. Pilgrims came and brought prosperity with them, and in thanks the wealthy and powerful built monuments to St Evisser. They refused any overtures of humility from the Ecclesiarchy and built gold-domed cathedrals, jewel-studded statues, museums of priceless art in Evisser's name.

A saint had been born to the Trail to show how the Emperor looked out as lord over all humanity – the wealthy and the poor, the powerful and the meaningless, those ministered by his church and those who toiled ignorant in the hives and the forges.

And while the Trail of Evisser endured, Evisser himself would never truly die.

ALARIC SNAPPED THE book shut crossly. Serevic had shown him to a locked vault beneath the hall, where books and scrolls lay strewn seemingly at random across the floor. But Serevic had known exactly what each one contained, and had picked out for Alaric only those that were relevant – the true and corroborated history of St Evisser.

And when the eulogising and myth-making were taken out, there was very little truth indeed. All Alaric had was a skeleton of a saint's life. No details. No description of Evisser's family, his companions, even what he looked like. Of course, the history of the Imperium had never been written down in its entirety – such a thing was impossible – and events of the distant past were coloured by interpretation and bias if they survived at all. But there had to be something more. Why else would the Hall of Remembrance have trained its archivists to maintain such secrecy over St Evisser?

Alaric was almost alone in the darkness of the vaults. A terrified novice waited by the door, attending on Alaric to show that the hall, though besieged, still observed the protocols that one Imperial servant deserved to receive from another. Genhain and Brother

Ondurin, his incinerator still held ready, waited just outside the door. Genhain and Alaric's Marines were in a defensive cordon around the vault, and they were not just there for show – Alaric was sure he could hear scratching beneath the vault where the ferals were tunnelling under the Hall. It was only a matter of time before they got in.

'Justicar Genhain,' said Alaric. Genhain walked in, leaving Ondurin at the door. 'What do you make of this?'

Genhain walked over to the table Alaric sat at, and looked at the pages lying open. They were from a sketchy, official history of the Trail, and Serevic had assured Alaric that this description of St Evisser, along with a few documents confirming some of his miracles, constituted the body of information the Ecclesiarchy had wanted to protect.

'It's not much,' said Genhain as he scanned it.

'It's all the truth we have.'

'Perhaps that's the point.'

Alaric thought for a moment. What did he know? There had been a man named Evisser who claimed inspiration from the Emperor and was proclaimed a saint. That was it.

And of course, that was the point.

Alaric stood up, grabbed the book, and strode out of the room, pausing only to glare at the novice who stood shivering just inside the door.

'Where is Serevic?'

The boy pointed nervously. Alaric headed in the indicated direction, walking into a long, low gallery where the walls and ceiling were covered in pages torn from books, pinned to wooden supports or stuck in a ragged patchwork to the stone. Serevic was standing in the middle of the gallery, gazing at the thousands of words as if he was looking out of a window at Far-fallen's landscape in its prime.

'There never was a Saint Evisser,' said Alaric simply, throwing the book down at Serevic's feet. 'The Ecclesiarchy never confirmed his ascension. He was proclaimed by the people and the Ecclesiarchy had to accept it, but to them he was nothing more than just another man.'

Serevic seemed to deflate, if anything looking even less imposing than before. He shook his head sadly. 'That so much good can come from a man we could never accept. It was shame that kept our secret.' He looked up at Alaric, and he seemed on the verge of tears. 'Can you think what harm would have come to the Trail, if the cardinals had denounced him? There would have been terrible strife. Hatred would be turned not on the Emperor's enemies but upon his faithful.'

'But he had miracles. He forged the Trail out of fron-tier space. He should have been a prime candidate for canonisation. What did they find?'

'It was too late then, you see,' continued Serevic. The knowledge had been bottled up inside him for so long that now he had committed the sin of revealing it, he had to get it all out. 'Evisser had been a saint to the people for decades before the Inquiry Beatificum was even begun. By the time it reported to the Holy Synod it was too late. Our own cardinals preached in cathe-drals built to his spirit. Men spoke his name in prayers. You cannot root out that kind of belief, not when it holds a place like the Trail together.'

Alaric knew now that Ghargatuloth had not just cho-sen the Trail. He had very probably made it in the first place. 'So the cardinals had their clergy cease his worship until the Trail decayed and Evisser could be forgotten. But why was he never a saint? What did they know about him?'

Serevic choked back a sob. Outside, the sound of foul chanting filtered through the walls as the ferals made ready for another attack.

'All this,' said Serevic in a near-whisper, 'all this will burn...'

Alaric picked up Serevic by the throat and slammed him up against the wall of the gallery, head against the ceiling. Alaric only had to will it and his gauntlet would crush the archivist.

Serevic forced his eyes to meet Alaric's. 'His... his home world. There was a taint there. If... if the cardinals had ignored it, and it was discovered, there could be even worse strife... Evisser a traitor, holy war, another Plague of Unbelief...'

Alaric let go and Serevic slipped down to the floor in an undignified heap.

'It's what you didn't write that betrays you,' said Alaric, kicking the book at Serevic. 'No home world. No burial place. No canonisation. Because the Ecclesiarchy knew that Evisser could be tainted, and that he could have been warped by some dark power. And they were right. But they would rather let it take root amongst Imperial worlds than admit they could not control this new prophet. Where was he born? Where is he buried?'

Serevic whimpered.

'Now! Or it all burns, and you will go with it!'

Serevic buried his head in his hands. He was broken. Since he was a novice, a child, he had been trained to keep the sacred knowledge of the Trail, remember and protect it in the Emperor's name. Now he had nothing left. Nothing at all. And knowing that no matter what, all that knowledge would burn eventually, he gave up.

'He was born on Sophano Secundus,' said Serevic weakly. 'But we buried him on Volcanis Ultor.'

FIFTEEN
VOLCANIS FAUSTUS

THREE DAYS AFTER Valinov escaped his execution on
Mimas, the Conclave on Encaladus sent a fast messenger ship to the Trail. The information it carried was too
sensitive to be transmitted by astropath – every Imperial organisation on the Trail was considered
compromised by the hidden cults rising up on every
system, and corrupted astropaths had leaked vital
Inquisitorial intelligence before. A messenger was the
only option.

Its message was simple. Valinov was probably heading for the Trail, and he was a man considered so
dangerous merely speaking with him carried an intol-
erable risk of corruption. Killing him on sight was the
only acceptable response.

The message was entrusted to Interrogator DuGrae,
an ace pilot and trusted agent of Lord Inquisitor
Coteaz, and she had been given multiple cortical

enhancements that allowed her to convey sensitive information in her head without the possibility of anyone retrieving it by psychic means. DuGrae was once a fighter pilot who had thrown a Thunderbolt across the skies of Armageddon, racking up scores of kills against the flying contraptions the greenskins used. The craft she now flew through space was as responsive as a fighter. It was a sleek, glossy black dart of a ship, the smallest and quickest warp-capable ship the Ordo Malleus could scramble at such short notice. It hit the warp like a knife, the sole crew members DuGrae and her Navigator.

The ship cut through the immaterium quickly at first, but three days out warp storms blew up without warning: a sudden flare of black madness in the warp that rippled in a wide crescent across the Segmentum Solar from Rhanna to V'Run. A clumsier craft would have been cut off completely but DuGrae, flying blindfold while her Navigator talked her through the warp currents, flung the sleek messenger ship through roiling banks of hatred towards the Trail.

But it used up time. Too much time – if Valinov got a big enough head start they might not catch him now.

DuGrae, without an astropath to contact Encaladus, had no way of reporting back or receiving news of the Trail. She had to trust that the Emperor would foil the Enemy's plans for a few hours more, and that she would fly fast enough.

DuGrae sliced out of the warp just beyond the edge of the Volcanis system, the light of the livid red star flooding the cockpit. Volcanis Ultor was the seat of authority on the Trail – once the cardinal and governor there had been warned, the next stop was the Inquisitorial headquarters on Trepytos.

Straight away it was obvious the state of the Trail had worsened. There were Imperial Naval ships in the system, doubtless drawn there by the rising tide of Chaotic activity. The Mars class battlecruiser *Unmerciful*, an old craft left over from when fighter-carrying warships were the weapons of choice, sent patrols of fighter-bombers out to sweep for marauding enemy ships. The Lunar class cruiser *Holy Flame* and the three Sword class escorts of Absolution Squadron kept close orbit around Volcanis Ultor itself.

With no astropath, DuGrae couldn't contact them until she flew in closer. But she was still uneasy. Were there Chaos ships prowling the system that would make short work of her lightly-armed ship if they found her? She held off approaching Volcanis Ultor until she could get more information from the ship-to-ship traffic picked up by her close-range comms. She sent her craft in a slingshot around Volcanis Faustus, the barren, baked rock planet closest to the star Volcanis. The scraps of information she picked up suggested very nervous captains waiting for an inevitable conflict, as if the chaos on the Trail was rising to critical mass that would explode into open warfare. Crews were pulling multiple maintenance shifts to get older craft battle-ready. Ordnance was at a premium and the Departmento Munitorum couldn't provide enough fuel for the fighters.

From out of the shadow of Volcanis Faustus drifted the battered, proud shape of the old warhorse *Unmerciful*. The proximity of the star warped communications and the carrier deployed three wings of fighter craft to get closer. When they were in range, they scanned DuGrae's ship and transmitted a simple message – the Volcanis system was not safe. The

Unmerciful's fighter wings would escort DuGrae into the spaceport on Volcanis Ultor's principal hive.

DuGrae thanked the squadron leader and shut down her engines while the fighters approached her to take up escort formation.

While she was hanging helpless in orbit, the captain of the *Unmerciful* gave the order and the fighter wings fired every missile they had, turning DuGrae's ship into an expanding cloud of plasma. And with her died the message she carried, that the man calling himself Inquisitor Valinov was in reality a servant of Chaos.

GHOLIC REN-SAR VALINOV watched the blinking triangle representing the messenger craft wink out. The blue squares representing the *Unmerciful*'s fighters whirled around for a couple of minutes, skirting around the debris field. The large orbital command display mounted in the suite Valinov had commandeered was set to depict the area around Volcanis Faustus, and as Valinov watched, the fighters scattered back to join their parent ship on the other side of the barren world. Recoba had thrown out two noble hangers-on to give Valinov free rein of an entire floor, and he had set himself up with cogitators, pict-consoles, several holomats and the orbital command display to ensure he knew as much about what was going on in the system as possible.

'Kill confirmed,' came the static-masked voice of the squadron leader.

'Good hunt, Squadron Theta,' was the captain's reply. The large blue rectangle of the *Unmerciful* began to bring its ponderous bulk around for the short journey back to the outer orbits of Volcanis Ultor. The fighters followed it, like pups hurrying back to their mother.

There was a commotion at the door and Cardinal Recoba entered, shrugging himself into his voluminous official robes, followed by a gaggle of lesser clergy.

'Inquisitor!' called Recoba. 'I just heard. Was it an intruder?'

'It was good we found them when we did,' said Valinov. 'If I had not been informed they might have been escorted straight here. The ways of the Enemy are many and foul, Emperor only knows what they could have done had they reached us.'

Recoba swallowed. 'It was an agent of the Dark Powers?'

Valinov nodded. 'As soon as the *Unmerciful*'s fighters scanned it, I knew. It was a sorcerer, I am sure. It was good the fighters could destroy it quickly, otherwise their crews might have been corrupted.'

Recoba shook his head. 'Then they were so close. Thank the Ever-Living that they were stopped. Indeed, the Throne protects.'

'The Throne protects, your blessedness,' said Valinov humbly.

They really had been close. Valinov wondered who had been sent – probably one of their best. Maybe Nyxos had sent someone, since he had probably survived Mimas and wanted to have a personal hand in stopping Valinov. No, more likely it was one of the lord inquisitors on Encaladus, taking matters into their own hands to cover up the mistakes they had made. Probably that showman Coteaz, preaching blood and thunder and sending off one of his star pilots to die. Valinov allowed himself a small smile – it was crusaders like Coteaz who could be the easiest to use. Of course they would send a messenger ship. And of course Valinov would use it to heighten the fears of the Trail's defenders.

It was as if the rest of the galaxy knew its role in the grand dance of Chaos, and obeyed its tune without complaint. And what was more pleasing to the Lord of Change, than letting his enemies forge the chains of their own slavery?

'Should I have the captains increase our patrols?' Recoba was asking. 'We have promised a dozen fighter wings to Magnos Omicron, but we could fly them out to the far orbit watch stations…'

Valinov held up a hand. 'No. Bring the captains into close orbit. But bring the extra fighters in, too. The rest of the Trail will have to fight their own battle, Volcanis Ultor itself is the keystone that must not fall. Put a wall of steel around our world, cardinal. It will not be long before it will be the only protection we have.'

'Of course, inquisitor,' said Recoba, sounding almost obedient. This pleased Valinov, as Recoba began snapping off orders to his hangers-on.

Gholic Ren-Sar Valinov glanced back at the orbital command display before he switched it off, knowing that the empty space where the messenger ship had been represented the death of the Trail's last hope.

CANONESS LUDMILLA OF the Order of the Bloody Rose looked through the magnoculars at the place the battle would be fought. Her Battle Sisters, the soldiers of the Ecclesiarchy, held a strongpoint of bunkers and trenches surrounding a chemical reclamation plant on the shores of Lake Rapax.

On her left flank were trenches held by the Balurian heavy infantry, well-armoured and well-drilled Guardsmen who could be trusted not to break and leave her Sisters vulnerable. On her right flank was Lake Rapax itself, an expanse of liquid so befouled by pollution that it couldn't be called water any more. Ludmilla commanded the extreme right flank of the defensive line in front of the capital hive, and she had hundreds of Battle Sisters to help her do it. Many considered the Sisters of the Adepta Sororitas to be the most effective troops the Imperium had save for the Space Marines themselves, and with power armour and disciplined bolter fire there were few who could fend off the hordes of Chaos any better.

The plains in front of the capital hive were barren and broken, stained the colour of livid wounds by centuries of pollution, drained and battered until fractured stony desert and dunes of ash were all that remained. In the dim distance foothills rose, framing the much smaller Hive Verdanus, but behind Ludmilla rose the true prize of Volcanis Ultor – Hive Superior, the seat of government for the planet, the system and the Trail.

The battle could be over in moments if the Ordinatus stationed amongst wasteland fringing the hive could home in on the landing enemy forces and send pinpoint salvoes of multiple warheads on top of them. Ludmilla, however, knew it would not happen that way. The attack would be spearheaded by Chaos Marines, the heretics of the Traitor Legions, who would use the speed and strength of all Space Marines to get amongst the defenders before most knew they had even landed. This battle would be won not on the plains but at the range of a bayonet, the attack dragged down and stifled by the ranks of defenders.

Ludmilla looked over her own defences, which had been built in admirable time by drafted hive citizen labourer gangs. The squat, ugly plascrete processing plant formed a bastion that went right up to the edge of the lake itself, and Ludmilla had placed several Retributor support squads on the plant's roof to cover it with heavy bolters and multi-meltas. Two Excorcist missile tanks guarded the sealed gates of the plant and several Sisters squads were in cover around rockcrete defences. They could not enter the plant itself because of the volatile open vats of chemicals, but nothing would get that far.

Around the plant looped long lines of trenches, bristling with razorwire. Rockcrete blocks studded the broken plains in front of the trenches to break up tank assaults, and there were points on the line where these defences had been removed to channel armoured assaults into crossfires from Retributor squads and anti-tank teams supplied by the Balurians. The Sisters who manned the front trenches could easily fall back into bunkers behind them that still sat in shallow craters where they had been dropped, pre-fabricated, from low orbit when the defences were first being marked out.

To break through, the attackers would have to push through several trenches, then bypass dozens of bunkers. The Balurians had a large body of reserves who could sweep from their own rear lines to meet any assault that got that far, pinning them down so the Sisters could emerge from their bunkers and charge into the attackers from behind.

That was the plan. Plans, as Ludmilla knew as well as anyone, only lasted as long as it took for the first trigger to be pulled. But it would take a massive assault indeed to shatter the line at this, probably its best-held point, where the resolute Sisters formed as impassable a barrier as the toxic waters of Lake Rapax.

Ludmilla watched the Balurians down the line presenting themselves for inspection to their regimental commissar, a black-uniformed figure who had the authority to execute anyone – man or officer – who was suspected of failing in his duty to the Emperor. Ludmilla could just catch his voice as he barked short speeches at each platoon he inspected. The enemy was coming, he was saying. It would try to take their minds even as it broke their bodies. Any man found wanting when his faith was put to the test would be lucky to get a bullet from his own squadmates. This was a war of the soul, not just of physical conflict.

Ludmilla closed up the magnoculars and climbed back down the short ladder into the interior of her command bunker. Two of her Celestians, elite Sisters who served as her command squad, stood to attention by the door and Sister Superior Lachryma was waiting to speak with the canoness.

'Canoness,' said Lachryma with a bow of the head. 'The Seraphim are in position.' Lachryma led the Seraphim squads, units of Sisters skilled in hand-to-hand combat who wore jump packs to charge into the thick of the fighting. They would be used as a rapid counterattacking force to charge any enemy getting past the first line of trenches.

'I want priority given to the join in the lines. The Balurians are good but the enemy will exploit the gap.'

'Of course. My Sisters positioned with the Balurians say the Guardsmen are getting nervous.'

'As well they might. Make sure you lead the battlehymns personally in that sector. The Balurians must hear our example.'

'And… Canoness, may I speak freely?'

'Go on.'

'Inquisitor Valinov's speech has caused some doubt amongst the Guardsmen and, I believe, in the Sisters too. Very few of us have met the Traitor Legions in battle before. The schola progenia taught us they didn't exist.'

'Pray that one day, that will be true.' Ludmilla thought for a moment. 'If any of the Balurians ask, let them pray with you. If they break we could be lost.'

'Understood.'

'And Sister?'

'Canoness?'

'The Traitor Legions fell because the Enemy exploited their sins of pride and arrogance. Those are sins we will not commit. Do not let the Enemy break your spirit before the battle has even begun.'

Lachryma saluted and left the bunker to join her Battle-Sisters. Ludmilla watched her go – Lachryma was a tall woman, given greater bulk by her power armour and the flaring jump pack mounted on her back. The black sleeves covering her glossy blood-red armour bore the bleeding rose symbol of the Order. In the days before the Horus Heresy, Space Marines had painted kill marks on their armour to proclaim their battle-prowess – the Sisters of Battle did nothing so vulgar.

One of Ludmilla's command staff, a Sister Dialogous manning the Sisters' communications, appeared from the lower level of the bunker. 'Canoness, Cardinal Recoba's staff have contacted us. Inquisitor Valinov wishes to review our defences in person.'

'Tell him we are honoured,' said Ludmilla, 'and that I trust our preparations will match his standards.'

The Sister hurried back down to relay the message.

Valinov is a born leader, thought Ludmilla. He had taken to commanding the defences without seeming

to even try. The Guardsmen hung on his every word
ever since he had told them the Traitor Legions were
real, and Ludmilla imagined that some of her Sisters
felt the same. Ludmilla was a fighter, not a politician,
but even she had to admire the way Valinov could take
such complete control so quickly, when the stakes
were so high.

And the presence of Valinov meant more than just
decent leadership. The Sisters often worked with the
Ordo Hereticus rather than the Ordo Malleus, but Ludmilla knew Valinov was probably a member of the
Malleus – for him to be involved, it meant that the
threat to Volcanis Ultor was daemonic in nature.

Traitor Marines and daemons. There were few more
potent forces in the Enemy's arsenal. She understood
why Valinov wanted to inspect the Sisters' preparations
– it was not just political showmanship, but a genuine
concern. The daemons would strike here, on the very
edge of the line in the hope of gaining a foothold and
then rolling up the defences before turning in towards
the hive. The Sisters had to hold.

And hold they would.

THE RUBICON HAD left the Hall of Remembrance to
burn. The ferals would tunnel into the lower vaults
soon and when they did, the defenders would die
alongside their books. Serevic would probably be one
of the last, cowering amongst his burning tomes. Alaric
knew all this and left anyway – he could spare no Grey
Knights to help the defenders fight a hopeless battle.
He was a leader, and leaders could not waste the lives
of their men on lost causes.

The bridge of the *Rubicon* was silent save for the distant thrumming of the engines and the clicking of the

bridge cogitators. The coordinates had been plotted and in a few moments the short warp jump would begin. It would take only a few more hours to make the jump to the Volcanis system, and the Malleus Navigator was good enough to put the *Rubicon* well within system space.

Alaric watched the quiet preparations for the jump from his command pulpit. The bridge doors hissed open and Justicar Santoro walked in.

'Brother-Captain? I had the crew bring up all the information they had on Volcanis Ultor.'

'And?'

'Nothing much we didn't know already. A hive world, controlled by the Ecclesiarchy with a nominal governorship. We looked up the location Serevic gave us – Lake Rapax is just outside the capital hive. It doesn't look like there's much there.'

'But we know different. Have they given us landing coordinates?'

'That's the problem. The astropaths say there is no one receiving messages.'

'Quarantine?'

'Possibly. Volcanis Ultor had some of the worst of the cult activity, a psychic quarantine would be a logical step.'

'Not very convenient for us, though. We'll just have to arrive unannounced. I want us on a battle footing just in case – if Volcanis Ultor has gone the way of Farfallen we might not have a friendly reception.'

'Understood. I'll brief my men.'

Alaric stepped down from the pulpit so he was on the same level as Santoro. The justicar's face, as always, betrayed little. 'Justicar, I know you are frustrated at not being able to fight. Ghargatuloth wants to use that as a weapon.'

'The Enemy will find no weapon in me, brother-captain.'

'I know, but he will try to find one. This fight will not be on our terms.'

'They never are. Not for Mandulis, not for us.'

'Make sure your men understand.'

Santoro saluted and walked out. Alaric knew the justicar didn't trust him completely as a leader yet – Alaric himself knew that the grand masters wouldn't have chosen him as brother-captain on his own merits, and it had taken the madness of Ligeia to put him in command. Ghargatuloth would be the sternest test of leadership possible, and no matter what else happened Alaric would find out if his core of faith would ever have been strong enough.

But of course, this battle was not about him. It was about billions of Imperial servants who would die, or worse, if the dark star of Ghargatuloth rose again.

'Navigation is go for warp jump,' said one of the crewmen at the nav helm.

'Engineering go,' was the vox from deep in the *Rubicon*'s stern.

The ship's commands counted off. The ship was ready.

'Take us in,' ordered Alaric, and the *Rubicon* dived headlong into the warp.

THE NAVAL DEFENCES around Volcanis Ultor were the strongest the system – the whole Trail – had seen in centuries. The *Unmerciful* was an old ship but a proven one, its multiple fighter decks crammed with Starhawk bombers and Avenger torpedo craft flown by battle-hardened pilots who had been expecting their next action to be around the Eye of Terror. The *Holy Flame* was newer and tougher, with a proud crew whose rapid gunnery could throw out broadsides massive enough to turn huge swathes of space into a shrapnel-filled killing zone. Absolution Squadron, comprising three Sword class escort craft, was almost brand new, paintwork gleaming as bright as the day they had first been launched from the dockyards of Hydraphur.

Drawn around Volcanis Ultor, the two warships and three escorts could cover the whole of the planet with ease, sensor fields overlapping over population centres, information from out-system monitoring stations flowing in constantly. All commercial shipping in the Volcanis system had been halted, and anything that moved was to be considered a threat.

Inquisitor Valinov's orders had been very clear. The enemy were coming. Everything else was secondary. They would try to make landfall, and the best way of destroying them was to engage their ships in high orbit where they would be vulnerable as they delivered their payloads.

Captain Grakinko of the *Unmerciful* liked the odds. Of the oldest Lastratan stock, Grakinko had seen dozens of engagements through a born officer's analytical eyes. The new-fangled tacticians said battleship broadsides were the ultimate weapon but Grakinko knew better – wave upon wave of fighters and bombers could achieve what no one battleship could, and in the close quarters of this coming engagement they would be as deadly and swift as a swarm of spitewings.

Grakinko waited in his gilded captain's throne, the bridge of his old proud ship so richly decorated and furnished it was more like the ballroom of a palace spire on his home hive than the functional heart of a warship. He waited in the satisfying knowledge that Volcanis Ultor was now the safest place on the Trail.

The *Holy Flame*, in contrast, was crewed by a well-drilled core of officers almost all of whom were graduates from the Imperial Navy Academy on Hydraphur, and were near-fanatical adherents to the belief that superior gunnery and discipline could overcome any enemy. Pryncos Gurveylan, ninth-year valedictorian and highest-scoring graduate for a decade, was the captain, but the whole officer corps on the *Holy Flame* functioned as one decision-making machine trained to analyse every situation and apply strict Naval doctrine. The fighter swarms of the *Unmerciful* would doubtless serve as a useful distraction but it was the guns of the *Holy Flame* that would win the day.

The captain of the *Holy Flame* shared a second cousin with the vice admiral who had commissioned the building of Absolution Squadron and so a quick private communication with the squadron's captains had ensured that they and the *Holy Flame* would fight as one. With the guns of the *Flame* firing at full rate and the escorts of Absolution Squadron to herd the enemy into range, nothing could approach Volcanis Ultor without being forced through a withering curtain of disciplined fire.

Pryncos Gurveylan was confident, as a captain must be, that every eventuality had been covered. The bridge of the *Holy Flame* was all wood panelling and upholstery, mirroring the old halls and lecture theatres of the Academy – the ship itself was an extension of the Academy, a repository for the best received wisdom the Navy had to offer. Gurveylan's fellow officers bustled efficiently, poring over large parchment system maps with compasses and rulers, relaying orders to engineering and ordnance, manning the constantly chattering communications helms.

It was just then that an urgent communication arrived from the outer system monitoring stations. A ship had just entered the Volcanis system unannounced, apparently at full battle-readiness. To all intents and purposes it was a Space Marine strike cruiser but its speed and ornate design were of unknown origin.

Both the *Unmerciful* and the *Holy Flame* received the message at the same time, and both knew there was only one explanation. Just as Valinov had said, the Traitor Legions had arrived.

Chapter 16
HOLY FLAME

'INCOMING!' YELLED SOMEONE from the nav helm as scores of angry red hostile blips appeared on the bridge viewscreen.

'What have you got, comms?' ordered Alaric.

The crewman on the comms helm looked up. 'We sent an acknowledgement message to Volcanis Ultor but there was no reply.'

Alaric gripped the sides of the pulpit. It didn't make sense. They had been in the Volcanis system less than an hour and suddenly, without even challenging the *Rubicon* over the comms, a carrier warship was steaming towards them and sending out waves of fighter-bombers, armed up and aggressive.

'Archivum, I want the class and designation of that ship. Any others in-system. Someone told them we were coming and they said we weren't friendly.'

The other justicars were listening in to the situation over the vox. 'Has the system fleet been compromised?' voxed Justicar Tancred.

'I don't know,' replied Alaric. It was a possibility. If Ghargatuloth had corrupted the crews of the warships in the Volcanis system, it would explain their aggression. But at the last count Volcanis Ultor was standing relatively firm, its defenders rallying around Cardinal Recoba – if the whole system had been corrupted then it had happened with impossible speed. 'More likely misinformation. If they think Ghargatuloth sent us then they'd attack on sight. Nothing we said would make a difference.'

How many Imperial citizens had heard of the Grey Knights? Very few. Even if the command crews on the warships could see the design and livery of the *Rubicon*, would they be able to recognise it?

Alaric felt that Ghargatuloth would like nothing better than for the Inquisition's own secrecy to be used against it. Whether the ships heading to engage the *Rubicon* were controlled by Chaos or not, the Grey Knights would have to fight this one through.

'How long do we have?' asked Alaric. Gradually the noise and bustle on the bridge was increasing as warning alarms sounded and the various command helms sent messengers to other parts of the ship.

'Less than twenty minutes,' came the reply from the navigation helm. 'Then the first wave will hit.'

'I want every defence we have in space. Chaff, ordnance, everything. Then we punch through them into upper atmosphere. We're not here to engage them, we're here to get a force onto Volcanis Ultor.'

Ordnance helm started barking orders and several Malleus crewmen and women began running as messengers off the bridge, heading down to the gunnery decks where torpedoes and anti-ordnance charges would be loaded and ready to fire. Short-fused torpedoes would fill space with enough debris to throw off the first fighter waves, but the *Rubicon* would be short of armaments if it had to tangle with another warship.

'All justicars, get to the launch bays now. I'll take the Thunderhawk. Tancred, you'll be with me. Genhain and Santoro, you'll have to go in by drop-pod. I want you loaded up before the fighters reach us.'

The justicars sounded off. They were already armoured up – the Grey Knights would take just minutes to reach the launch deck. Alaric would need to be with them soon.

Alaric spoke through the bridge vox-caster so the whole crew could hear him. 'Crew of the *Rubicon*, your objectives are clear. Your goal is to reach the upper atmosphere of Volcanis Ultor and allow for deployment. All other concerns are secondary. This includes the survival of this ship and yourselves. Sacrifice the *Rubicon* if you have to. You may also have to sacrifice yourselves. I know the Ordo Malleus has prepared you for this but you cannot know if you are truly prepared for death until you face it. The Emperor trusts that you will do your duty in this. I trust you, too. Helm commands, you have the bridge – use whatever means you deem fit but get us close to that planet.

'You do not need to know what is at stake. It is enough that I must ask you to do this. Go with the Emperor, as He goes with you.'

There was a brief moment of silence, a reaction of considerable emotion considering the mind-scrubbed and psycho-doctrinated nature of the crew. Then the bridge bustle kicked in again as the blips on the viewscreen display crept closer to the position of the *Rubicon*.

Alaric stepped down off the command pulpit. An officer from the navigation helm gave Alaric a quick salute as he took over the pulpit controls. Alaric watched as a messenger was sent to engineering to make sure the engines were primed ready for evasive action. The ordnance helm began counting off all the various stores of ammunition that would be expended when the first wave was upon them. Officers at navigation were plotting the positions of the other ships in-system – three escorts and a cruiser, lying in wait around Volcanis Ultor, ready to pounce on whatever the carrier left for them.

The archive helm, with a small crew of scholars surrounded by mem-banks, had identified the closest ship as the *Unmerciful*, a veteran of Port Maw in the Gothic War. That was good. It meant the ship was old, and old ships were usually slow. The *Rubicon* could skirt around her and her fighter swarms. Then the real battle would begin, where the air of Volcanis Ultor met the void.

Alaric had rarely even noticed the crew of the *Rubicon*, composed as they were of efficient but almost invisible men and women. Some had been literally bred for anonymity, the product of breeding programs that produced easily-doctrinated individuals. But Alaric was glad of them now. They were efficient and unshakeable. They could never have the leadership to take a ship through war on their own but now they didn't need it – they just had to do things by the numbers, keep the *Rubicon* going long enough for the Grey Knights to get onto the planet.

They didn't need Alaric now. He hurried off through the bridge doors to join his battle-brothers, and left the crew of the *Rubicon* to their work.

CAPTAIN GRAKINKO ON the bridge of the *Unmerciful* watched the huge holographic tactical display where the fighter blips swarmed towards the Chaos ship. To think, the enemy had even tried to claim they were Imperials, and asked to be allowed to land at Volcanis Ultor! Inquisitor Valinov had predicted their every move. If they thought an old ship like the *Unmerciful* was easy pickings, then they were woefully wrong.

'Fighter command! I want the torpedo ships to the front. Pull the Starhawks and the assault boats back, we'll soften them up first!'

'Aye, captain!' came the enthusiastic reply from the fighter command helm, manned by several dozen petty officers most of whom had been born on the ship during its long service history. The pitch of activity on the bridge was rising as the *Unmerciful* worked itself up to full battle-readiness. The medicae crew were manning triage stations near the engines and fighter decks where casualties were always highest, and the chapel staff were scattered throughout the ship leading prayers. Refuelling crews waited nervously on the decks, ready to re-fit and bomb up the first wave of fighters and bombers when they returned.

'It's beautiful, isn't it?' said Grakinko, beaming proudly. 'Damned beautiful.' He turned his considerable bulk in his seat and opened up a panel in the arm of his throne, pulling out a bottle of finest sparkling Chirosian wine. With a fleshy thumb he popped the cork out and held up the bottle in salute. 'To war!' he bellowed.

Several of the bridge crew returned the toast enthusiastically. A chatter rose from the fighter command crew as they gave final approach orders to the attack craft.

As the first orders to open fire were given, Captain Grakinko took a good swig to mark the beginning of the battle.

Good wine, he thought.

THE FIRST WAVE of torpedoes was met by a return salvo from the *Rubicon*. Short-fused ordnance from the Space Marine cruiser burst in a shower of debris, bright blossoms of flame imploding in the vacuum leaving storms of silver metal shards like a glittering curtain.

The first wave of attack craft, maybe thirty craft strong, launched their own torpedoes and banked sharply to avoid deterrent fire spattering from the *Rubicon*'s turrets. Most of the torpedoes were detonated by the wall of debris and massive pulses of exploding munitions ripped silently through space, sending ripples through the debris like stones thrown into water. Some torpedoes, inevitably, made it through, and great black flashes played over the hull of the strike cruiser as the ship's shielding absorbed the blasts.

The real damage was done. As the damage crews on the *Rubicon* fought to restore the shields to full strength the next waves approached, Starhawk fighter-bombers this time, sweeping in through the debris field. Many were lost as their engines were clogged by debris but most of them made it through, for the fighter pilots of the *Unmerciful* were veterans who had mostly done this many times before. Instead, the debris shielded them from the *Rubicon*'s turret fire and they emerged in formation, close enough to make their attack runs.

They banked into long swooping strafing runs and with nose-mounted turbolasers began spattering the gunmetal hull of the *Rubicon* with fire.

In the gun decks and maintenance runs of the strike cruiser, men and women began to die.

ALARIC HEARD THE strafing runs hitting home, dull chains of explosions rippling along the outside of the hull. He was inside the Grey Knights' remaining Thunderhawk, strapped into a grav-couch ready to launch, alongside his squad and Squad Tancred.

With Krae lying dead in Titan's vaults, Squad Tancred now numbered just Tancred himself and his remaining three Terminator brothers. Tancred cradled his Nemesis sword, Locath and Golven held halberds, and Karlin carried the squad's heavy incinerator. The Terminator Marines were much like Tancred himself – uncompromising assault troopers who lived to do the Emperor's work up close where their massive armour and Nemesis weapons would bring them the greatest advantage.

Karlin was a regular student in the chaplain's seminary, where his incandescent brand of faith echoed the blessed burning fuel he sprayed over enemies. Locath was as strong as Tancred himself, and the Nemesis halberd he carried was a powerful relic given to him by a brother-captain he had once attended on as a novice. Golven was a skilled halberd fighter who had earned his Crux Terminatus boarding abandoned spaceships and fighting Chaos-tainted genestealer cults.

Alaric carried the Nemesis sword of Mandulis under one arm.

'This is yours, justicar,' he said, handing the weapon to Tancred.

Tancred took the weapon and looked up at Alaric in surprise. 'Brother-Captain, I do not feel I have earned the...'

'You are our best soldier, Tancred,' said Alaric. 'It took Captain Stern to beat you. We need you to carry the Lightning Bolt. It's what you do the best of all of us.'

Tancred put his own Nemesis sword to one side and held the sword of Mandulis. It was an abnormally large weapon but it fitted Tancred perfectly – it was made more for strength than for finesse but in combat Tancred had plenty of both, and it looked as firm and balanced in his hand as it must have done when Mandulis held it. The inside of the Thunderhawk was lit by the gleam of its blade – Tancred seemed to loom even larger in the reflection from its blade, darker and stronger, a reflection of the spirit inside Tancred. 'The sword that banished Ghargatuloth,' said Tancred, almost to himself. 'I can believe it.'

He turned the blade, weighing its point of balance, checking the razor sharpness of its edge and the flawless surface of the blade. It seemed like an extension of Tancred, a weapon he had been born to hold. To Alaric it was a sacred relic, but to Tancred it was a sword the Emperor wielded through him.

Another sequence of dull ripping explosions echoed overhead, so close the strafing run must have scored hits along the side of the launch deck itself. Secondary explosions sounded somewhere in the ship. Alaric could hear the vibrations running through the deck as the *Rubicon*'s manoeuvring engines were fired up.

'Pray to the Emperor that you will get the chance to use it,' said Alaric, as the high resonant vibrations of failing shields thrummed through the hull.

* * *

THE ENGINES OF the *Rubicon* kicked in even as strafing runs tore ruby explosions from its hull. The strike cruiser, using its superior mobility, darted forward suddenly, ploughing forward through its own debris field and right into the upcoming fighter wings. Many pilots were forced to adopt new formations as the ship bore down on them, launching runs that impacted only against the *Rubicon*'s thick prow armour. Attacks down the side of the hull were shortened as the craft flashed by and those fighters who banked for a second run were targeted by the turrets now free of debris interference and reaping a harvest of burning fighter hulls. More than seventy craft were destroyed or disabled, their valuable pilots killed or stranded with little hope of rescue, munitions detonating in firing tubes before they could be fired, attacks scattered as the huge silver beak of the *Rubicon* ripped through space.

The strike cruiser's ordnance was depleted, and it was bleeding fire from scores of wounds. The Avengers and Starhawks had done their work, but they had not finished the *Rubicon* off.

Leaving shoals of attack craft whirling in its wake, and with the follow-up squadrons of attack boats and boarding torpedoes fleeing before it, the *Rubicon* headed at full speed towards Volcanis Ultor.

CAPTAIN GRAKINKO, ON the bridge of the *Unmerciful*, listened in to the sounds of his fighter assault breaking up. Crackling screams as cockpits filled with fire. Static-filled chains of explosions as ammunition cooked off. Transmissions cut short as power plants detonated. The crewmen operating the fighter command helm were used to hearing such long-range death and

Grakinko had lost thousands of men in naval engagements before, but it was still disheartening.

'Navigation!' bellowed Grakinko above the growing din on the bridge. 'Why are we standing still? Where are they going?'

'Heading for the planet, sir!' came the reply from somewhere in navigation, where dozens of junior officers were wrestling with system charts and compasses while the cogitators smoked with the effort of calculations.

Grakinko let out a barking, triumphant laugh. 'Then we'll get in front of 'em and give 'em a broadside! Let's see the gakkers run away from that!' He slammed his hand down on the arm of his throne. 'Gunnery! What are our rates?'

The gunnery officer – seventh-generation Naval man, Grakinko remembered playing three-board regicide with his father – stood up smartly. 'Fresh gangs and fully loaded, captain. At their speed I can give her three full volleys to the prow.'

'And if we hang about to get them in the backside?'

The gunnery officer thought. 'A good two half-volleys to the stern.'

'I've got a bottle of dry amasec older than I am. Give me three half-volleys to her stern and it's yours, you hear?'

'Yes, captain!'

The *Unmerciful* wasn't a pure gunnery ship, but it had been refitted (against Grakinko's wishes, he admitted) with plenty of guns after the Gothic War and by the Emperor it could give a decent volley when it had to. Three full volleys, and then three half-volleys from the depleted gun gangs, should be enough to cripple any ship at point blank range. Then it was a matter of bringing the surviving fighters in and bombing the gak out of the strike cruiser until it came apart.

Grakinko thought he might let the escorts of Absolution Squadron get a sniff of the kill, too. It was the done thing, a gesture of courtesy to fellow captains.

Those upstarts on the *Holy Flame* could go gak themselves, though.

'Navigation, get us side-on to them now!' ordered Grakinko. He felt the *Unmerciful* lurching as its engines turned its old creaking hull round and hauled it into the path of the strike cruiser.

The holographic tactical display on the viewscreen zoomed in, leaving the scattered attack craft out of its field of vision. Instead it concentrated on two blips – the shining blue symbol denoting the *Unmerciful*, and the red triangle of the Chaos strike cruiser, streaming burning fuel and debris as it hurtled towards Volcanis Ultor.

ALARIC WAS STRAPPING himself into the grav-restraints when he heard klaxons going off all over the *Rubicon*.

'Collision warnings,' he said to himself, as the ship's engines roared louder.

THE UNMERCIFUL OPENED up with a few straggling shots, range finders that streaked past the oncoming prow of the *Rubicon*. The gunnery sergeants denoted the target in range and closing, the officer at the gunnery helm concurred. With that order, every gun on the port side of the *Unmerciful* let loose.

Against a ship with full shields and the ability to return fire, the effect would have been damaging but ultimately unspectacular. Against a ship with few shields and in no position to return fire, the guns could pour volley after unanswered volley into the strike cruiser's prow. The massive armoured beak of the strike cruiser, shielded with layers of adamantium and covered in engraved prayers of warding, was first battered and then pierced by the munitions fired by the massive guns. Plates of armour were ripped off, flung spiralling through space, trailing fire. Secondary explosions sent walls of flame spurting from between the seams of hull plates. With a single titanic eruption the whole prow was blasted off, a rushing cowl of flame billowing out from the front of the *Rubicon*. The void swallowed the fire and an ugly, blackened ruin of metal was all that remained of the ship's prow.

The ship didn't slow but it did veer dangerously, systems without number damaged, fires coursing along maintenance ways and corridors, bulkheads bursting into hard vacuum. The bridge was rocked, and had it been set a few metres further forward it would have been torn apart, too. Thousands of Malleus crew died, immolated, blown apart or sucked out into space. The wrecked prow shed armour sections, plumes of debris, and broken, frozen bodies.

THE THUNDERHAWK WAS thrown sideways, slamming against its moorings as the *Rubicon* rocked.

'Injuries?' voxed Alaric.

'None,' said Genhain, whose men were loaded into one drop-pod alongside the Thunderhawk.

'None here,' echoed Santoro.

Alaric checked the Marines in the Thunderhawk with him – his Marines were unhurt and it took more than that to injure one of Tancred's Terminators.

Alaric voxed the bridge. 'What was that?'

'Took the prow off,' came the reply, warped by the damaged vox systems. 'All forward locations lost.'

'And the bridge?'

'Minor damage. Nav is correcting our course. We'll hit the atmosphere in twenty-two minutes.'

From the tone of the crewman's voice and the background noise on the bridge, Alaric knew he wasn't alone in thinking that was too long.

THE RUBICON PASSED close underneath the *Unmerciful*, close enough for the wreckage raining off it to spatter like iron rain against the *Unmerciful*'s underside.

Gun gangs on the starboard side of the *Unmerciful* were under-manned and under-munitioned compared to those on the opposite gun deck, but they had their part to play, too. As the stern of the *Rubicon* emerged from under them the ship tilted to give them a better firing angle before they poured everything they had into the aft section of the strike cruiser.

The massive engine exhausts were punctured again and again as red lances of fire fell in a burning hail. Jets of superheated gas kilometres long shot from the ruptured engines. One plasma reactor was cracked open and boiling plasma flooded out, forming a ragged smouldering ribbon where it hit the cold of space. The secondary explosions tore a hole in the upper hull four decks deep, exposing the primary engineering command centre to the void. The chief engineering officers stared up at the yawning hole above them where the ceiling of their aft bridge had once been, their breath stolen from their bodies, their blood frozen, the *Unmerciful* rolling slowly and pouring fire into them from above.

The bridge's primary link with the engine section of the *Rubicon* was gone. As far as the state of the engines went, the ship was flying blind.

The starboard guns of the *Unmerciful* ran dry. The *Rubicon* passed underneath it, prow gone, stern badly chewed, spewing air, plasma and wreckage. But it was not dead yet. The fleet records on Iapetus would witness that it had survived worse.

Plasma reactors thrumming with the strain, the *Rubicon* plummeted on towards the pale disc of Volcanis Ultor.

CAPTAIN GRAKINKO LOOKED up to see the gunnery officer standing on front of him, the buttons of his neat starched uniform gleaming.

'That was a few shots short of four half-volleys from the starboard guns,' said the officer.

Cocky little prig, Grakinko thought, taking the bottle of amasec from within the arm of his command throne. Never taking his eyes of the officer he smashed the neck of the bottle on the edge of the arm and poured the whole bottle down his throat, letting it spill down his chin and the front of his uniform. When it was empty he threw the bottle to smash on the bridge floor.

Heretics or not, those gakkers knew how to build themselves a damn spaceship.

CAPTAIN PRYNCOS GURVEYLAN, seated behind one of the many banks of cogitators that made up the bridge of the *Holy Flame*, watched the *Rubicon* trailing wreckage as it ploughed through the curtain of fire from the *Unmerciful*'s starboard batteries. The *Unmerciful* was not a ship known for its guns, but it had opened fire on a closing opponent at point blank range, with everything it had. It was a testament to the toughness of the enemy strike cruiser that it was still going.

Gurveylan was not a ship captain in the old sense. His word was not law on his ship – he left that privilege to Security Officer Lorn and Ship Commissar Gravic. He did not rule his bridge with an iron fist, since he could rely on his officers to do their duty. He was, instead, the executive arm of the *Holy Flame*'s officer corps. That was how they had done things at the Academy – teamwork, responsibility, obedience.

The giant holoprojection unit filled the bridge with the image of the enemy strike cruiser, its prow chewed off, ribbons of congealing plasma coiling from its engine section. The projection of the *Unmerciful* drifted through the ceiling of the bridge as the strike cruiser carried on, tracked by the *Holy Flame*'s sensors. It was headed directly for Volcanis Ultor – not taking any evasive action, just streaking towards the planet.

'I want a damage report on that ship,' said Gurveylan.

One of the several dozen engineering officers took the bridge vox-caster. 'The ship's an unknown marque, captain. It's a Space Marine strike cruiser. We don't have the specifications for it.'

'Give me your best guess.'

'Extensive prow damage, non-essential systems only. Command structures probably intact. One major plasma breach, engines down to seventy per cent. Crew casualties thirty to fifty per cent.'

'Gunnery and logistics!' snapped Gurveylan. 'If we match her speed and hit her with rolling broadside volleys, what is the probability she'll be crippled?'

There was a long pause as gunnery officers and lexmechanics scrabbled and calculated. 'Eighty per cent,' came the reply.

'Good. Comms, contact Absolution Squadron and have them take up high orbit in case the enemy gets through. Everyone else, I want us alongside the enemy ready to open fire in seven minutes. I think after this is done I shall shake Captain Grakinko's hand for softening her up for us. All stations, to your duties.'

At the order the hundred-strong officer corps of the *Holy Flame* snapped into action. The wood-panelled theatre of the bridge was full of activity. Navigation had to plan complex vectors. Gunnery and ordnance had to flood the gun decks with gangs to work the enormous broadside cannons. Engineering had to place damage control teams at strategic points because even the depleted firepower of the enemy strike cruiser could, with bad luck, cripple key systems of the *Holy Flame*.

A warship was a beautiful thing: every part and crewman directed at the same goal, bound by the same duty. From the short-lived labourers of the engine gangs to the command crew and Gurveylan himself, the whole of the *Holy Flame* was united towards a common purpose.

If all the Imperium were run like the *Holy Flame*, the Enemy would be thrown back into the darkness forever. But for now, Gurveylan was content to see the Chaos Marine strike cruiser reduced to flaming wreckage.

VALINOV COULD SEE, through a break in clouds of pollution, the white streaks of fire in the sky as the *Holy Flame* opened up on the *Rubicon*. He knew how much firepower the *Holy Flame* could bring to bear. If Valinov had pulled the right strings, if the threads all came together as they should, then the end was almost here.

Valinov was in an open-topped groundcar driving through the final dregs of ruins and shanty towns that marked the western edge of Hive Superior. In front of him the dry broken earth was cut through with lines of trenches edged with razorwire, and studded with large plasticrete bunkers. Even from some way behind the rear lines Valinov could see men hurrying to their positions, and hear the klaxons and vox-casters ordering them to full battle alert. Recoba had managed to put together a fairly cohesive defence and the word had spread quickly down the command chains that the enemy was in-system and, just as Valinov had predicted, were heading straight for Volcanis Ultor and Hive Superior.

The groundcar, driven by a liaison officer from the Balurian heavy infantry, rounded a rear supply post where pallets of lasgun power packs were being stacked, ready to go out to wherever the fighting required. Standing in the back of the car, Valinov watched as tiny crimson explosions blossomed in the sky as the battle in space raged on. The last of Ligeia's death cultists sat beside Valinov, her ever-taut muscles twitching now and then. Valinov had made sure the death cultist was hidden while he went about his business in Recoba's spire – she looked sinister and dangerous, and she could have compromised his attempts to be trusted. Out in the field, he didn't need to hide her any more. Valinov had to look like a warrior, and the death cultist certainly helped generate an air of lethality.

The groundcar turned north and Valinov saw they were driving just behind the Balurian lines. The Balurian heavy infantry were noted for their discipline, which was as much an asset to Valinov as the heavy half-carapace armour the Guardsmen wore or the lasguns they carried which were configured for high power and short range. The Balurians would do what they were told. That was all he needed of them.

Their officers were barking orders, shuffling units into position. Fields of fire were overlapping, counter-attacks were placed, key weak points were reinforced with heavy weapons posts. The regimental commissar prowled the ranks, bolt pistol in hand, but Valinov knew he wouldn't have to use it on his disciplined, faithful men.

Except perhaps towards the end. But by then it wouldn't matter.

The groundcar headed towards the northern end of the line, the processing plant and the bleached shore of Lake Rapax. The glossy red armour of the Sisters of the Bloody Rose glinted in the murky greyness that passed for the morning sun on Volcanis Ultor. Valinov spotted Sisters on the roof of the plant itself, Retributor squads with heavy bolters. Seraphim units, with their distinctive winged jump packs, were kneeling in prayer as their Sisters Superior prepared them to act as counter-attacking units when the enemy broke through. Canoness Ludmilla had brought a whole commandery of more than two hundred Sisters of Battle. It was them that Valinov was going to review, to thank the canoness personally for answering Volcanis Ultor's call, and to warn her further about the nature of the Enemy. Their leader, he would tell her, carried a powerful daemon weapon that must be captured so the Inquisition could have it destroyed. And she would believe him, of course, because in high orbit the blazing sheets of broadside fire were proving him right.

Valinov had already won. The Lord of Change himself had promised him that – all he had to do was to go through the motions and let the threads of fate twist into shape around him. He could feel it even now, the weight of fate lying on Volcanis Ultor, crushing the freedom out of it. Chaos was pure freedom, the glory of the soul's full potential, the realisation of what mankind could be under the tutelage of the Lord of Change – but for Chaos to rule, first the minds of the mortal had to be squeezed dry of their freedom so they could receive the full wisdom of Tzeentch. Mankind had to be enslaved to the will of Tzeentch, so it could eventually become free. The masses would never understand, even though it was the only possible truth, and so it fell to men like Valinov to act as instruments of the coming Chaos.

The shape of the *Rubicon* could just be made out now in the sky, a twisted splinter of silver trailing debris and vented plasma like a comet.

The groundcar arrived at the rear of the Sisters' lines. The Balurian driver stepped smartly out and held open the door for Valinov and the death cultist.

Valinov stepped onto the parched, dusty ground, gathering his long blastcoat around him, shoulders back and hand on the pommel of his power sword like a true gentleman. The death cultist stood just behind him, and Valinov wondered if she had any idea of what she was involved in. She didn't speak, and Valinov didn't even know her name, but he knew she would follow him to the death just as she had her previous mistress, Ligeia.

Which was just as well, because whatever fate Tzeentch had in store for Volcanis Ultor, it would involve a great deal of death.

'BRIDGE!' YELLED ALARIC into the vox, almost unable to hear his own voice over the din of the *Rubicon* coming apart under the vast waves of punishment. Shells were still crashing into the hull, screaming as they detonated, hull plates were howling as they were ripped off the ship, air was booming out into the vacuum.

Voices sounded through the static. '...damage reports in... thirty per cent...'

'Can we get to low orbit?' shouted Alaric.

'...systems down, engines... down to twenty...' Alaric couldn't tell which one of the Malleus crew was speaking. It sounded like the bridge itself had sustained damage. How many of the command crew were dead? How many would it take before the *Rubicon* was left blind and crippled?

The Thunderhawk shook violently in its moorings, as if it was flying through heavy turbulence. The Grey Knights were held fast by their grav-restraints as explosions groaned through the ship.

Suddenly the static on the vox was gone and a clear voice was layered over the sounds of the dying strike cruiser. 'Brother-Captain Alaric, we've lost the bridge. We've set the *Rubicon* on a final deployment run but control systems are gone so there's no one to correct if the approach is wrong.' Alaric recognised the voice of the officer who held the comms helm, a man Alaric couldn't name. 'We will hit high atmosphere in six minutes if the engines hold. We're heading down to your decks now to make sure the hangar doors open.'

'Good work, officer,' said Alaric as the vox filled back up with static. 'What's your name?'

'None of us have names,' came the faint reply. 'Deployment in six minutes, brother-captain. The Emperor protects.'

THE STRIKE CRUISERS used by the Chapters of the Adeptus Astartes weren't built for gunnery. They were built for speed and resilience, since their primary purpose was to move Space Marines quickly and safely and to take part in boarding actions. They could take a hell of a lot of punishment, the equivalent of Imperial Navy ships of far larger classes, and so the *Holy Flame* had calculated that it would take almost its whole stock of munitions for its starboard guns to destroy the *Rubicon*.

The *Rubicon*, however, was not just a Space Marine strike cruiser, as rare and remarkable as those were. It had been commissioned by the Ordo Malleus whose resources dwarfed those of the highest Naval admiral. The *Rubicon* had been built using alloys and construction techniques so advanced the Adeptus Mechanicus could no longer replicate them. The Ordo Malleus demanded the best of their Chamber Militant, the Grey Knights, and they provided the best as well. The *Rubicon* was as solid a ship as had flown since the Dark Age of Technology.

The slow dance of the *Holy Flame* and the *Rubicon* twirled into the first wisps of Volcanis Ultor's atmosphere, the thin air ignited into long bright ribbons by the shells that pumped from the *Holy Flame*'s starboard guns. The *Rubicon* blossomed into flame as it entered the atmosphere, fire rippling like liquid up its sides, pouring from the ruined prow and billowing in huge fluid plumes from its shattered engines. A second plasma generator exploded and sent superheated plasma flashing through the whole engineering section. A section of hull blew out so huge that the *Rubicon* was split down half its length, spilling wreckage and bodies like a gutted fish. When the ordnance magazine detonated, the explosion was like an afterthought compared to the shrieks and eruptions as the *Rubicon* began to come apart.

The *Holy Flame* disengaged, forced out of the dance by the thickening atmosphere that threatened to melt the underside of the hull. But the *Rubicon* was tougher, and the remaining engines kept it on course to enter the atmosphere shallow enough to deploy its payload.

To hit the *Rubicon* with another broadside, the *Holy Flame* would have to loop around, adopt a shallower trajectory to enter the atmosphere, and slide into step with the enemy strike cruiser. But that manoeuvre would take almost twenty minutes to achieve, and by then it would be too late. Captain Gurveylan ordered it anyway.

In the end it was Absolution Squadron, who had waited just inside the atmospheric envelope, who killed the *Rubicon*. The three Sword Class escorts had enough firepower between them to see off the crippled *Rubicon* – with a bit of luck just one of them could have done it. But there was not enough time. Any second the *Rubicon* would send down its drop-pods full of Traitor Marines and then it wouldn't matter what happened to the crippled ship.

To the captain of Absolution Beta, the lead ship in the escorts' formation, his duty was clear. Captain Masren Thal was a pious man who had been born into the Navy and earned his place on the bridge with a service record as long as his lifetime. Thal knew that one day he would have to die doing the Emperor's work, and he had given his vow to the Emperor (who always listened, always watched) that when that time came he would not be found wanting.

He knew that his officers and crew, had he had the time to explain it to them, would have agreed. So it was with no hesitation that Captain Thal ordered Absolution Beta to ramming speed.

THE THUNDERHAWK ENGINES opened up, barely audible over the near-deafening roar of Volcanis Ultor's atmosphere burning against the underside of the *Rubicon's* hull. Alaric would have voxed his Marines to be strong and have faith, but he didn't think they could hear him. It was better to leave them to their own prayers.

The Thunderhawk lurched forwards as its engines thrust it against its docking clamps, ready to shoot the ship forward when the clamps were released. The inside of the passenger compartment was bathed red as warning lights came on – Alaric could see the grim face of Justicar Tancred as he mouthed the Rites of Detestation, one hand touched to the copy of the *Liber Daemonicum* that was always locked in a compartment in his chest armour.

There was no way of contacting Santoro or Genhain. The vox was a screaming mess of interference. He couldn't even signal the Malleus crewman in the Thunderhawk's cockpit. Alaric realised the pilot was probably one of the few crewmen left alive on the *Rubicon*.

So many had to die just so the fight could continue. So many had to suffer so the Grey Knights could do their duty. It was as if Chaos had already won – but then that was the same thinking that drove men into the arms of Chaos in the first place. Alaric spat out a prayer of contrition.

An impossibly loud explosion ripped through the ship behind the Thunderhawk, an appalling crescendo of tortured metal. Something was tearing through the ship, something massive. Or perhaps the ship was finally splitting in two, the strain of entering the atmosphere too much for the shattered hull.

The Thunderhawk and the drop-pods wouldn't make it. The engines would send the gunship smashing into the flight deck doors because there was no one left alive to make sure they opened. The drop-pods would stay fixed in their clamps until they shattered when the *Rubicon* crashed into Volcanis Ultor. The Grey Knights would die, and Ghargatuloth had known all along it would end this way.

Alaric put a hand to his copy of the *Liber Daemonicum* locked in his breastplate, and prayed that someone would avenge him.

Alaric was slammed back into his grav-couch as the Thunderhawk shot forward. The viewport next to Alaric snapped open and he could see the flight deck rushing by – promethium tanks spewed flame, charred bodies lay in pieces, holes gaped into space streaked with fire.

Then the screams of the dying ship were gone, replaced by the pure roar of the Thunderhawk's engines. Alaric craned his neck to see the *Rubicon* shrinking behind the ship, a plume of flame gushing from the flight decks where the Thunderhawk had waited a moment before. The prow of another ship punched suddenly through the tortured hull of the *Rubicon*, cutting through the strike cruiser like a knife,

massive explosions erupting behind it as its own hull
was sheared in two by the force of the impact.

Alaric didn't see the *Rubicon* explode, but he felt it,
the shockwave thudding through the gunship as it
descended in its landing course. He knew that the final
plasma reactors had gone critical, and that the chain
reaction would have turned both ships into a ball of
expanding flame like a new star in the sky of Volcanis
Ultor.

'...pod down...' came a crackling vox from either
Santoro or Genhain. One of them had made it at least,
maybe both if the surviving Malleus crew had been
quick enough. Not that any of the crew survived now,
of course.

'Battle-brothers,' shouted Alaric over the noise of the
engines. His Grey Knights were all brought out of their
private prayers and looked to him. 'Ghargatuloth will
think we are probably dead. I have every intention of
showing him that we are not. And though we yet live
there is little chance that many of us will survive. Pray
now, then, as if this is your last word to the Emperor.'

The Grey Knights bowed their heads.

'I am the hammer,' began Alaric. 'I am the sword in
His hand...'

SEVENTEEN
LAKE RAPAX

CANONESS LUDMILLA HURRIED through the twisting, cramped trench towards the front line. She passed squads of Battle Sisters, and offered them a quick blessing as she passed. The hush over the front lines was chilling – Ludmilla had seen enough battles to associate it with the sudden unleashing of violence that was sure to follow.

She turned a corner and saw the front-line trench stretching before her, its forward edge snarled with razorwire. Ludmilla had almost a hundred Sisters in the front trench; they were the rock against which the attack would break. The Sisters were excellent troops for fighting off a massed assault – their power armour and bolters kept them alive long enough for the Seraphim counter-attacks.

The sound of murmured prayers was a quiet backdrop to the silence. Each Sister had endless pages of

321

prayers memorised, and many had those sacred words sewn into the cloth sleeves or tabards over their armour. Their faith was a shield, a weapon, a way of life.

Sisters were sheltering beneath the front wall of the trench. Trench junctions were held by isolated heavy weapons Sisters, carrying heavy bolters or multi-melta guns to turn enemy breakthroughs into killing zones. Several tanks were dug in to act as anti-tank bunkers – an Excorcist tank was positioned where it could send its payload of rockets streaking down the broad trench should the enemy take it.

Sisters Superior, quietly leading their units' final ministrations, saluted discreetly as the canoness walked down the trench to take her own position on the front line. Ludmilla switched onto the vox-channel that let her communicate with the whole commandery of more than two hundred Sisters, most of them soldiers about to join the fight.

'The Emperor is our father and our guardian,' began Ludmilla, quoting the Ecclesiastical Fundamentals of the revered Saint Mina herself, in whose name the Order of the Bloody Rose had been founded millennia before. 'But we must also guard the Emperor. For He is all Humankind, and Humankind is no more than its faith and diligence in the Emperor's name. An injury to that faith is an injury to the Emperor and to every citizen of the Imperium. It is through affirmation of that faith that our greatest duty lies, but sometimes mere affirmation does not suffice and we must act against those who would harm the faith of humanity through heresy. For we are engaged in an unending war for the soul of the Imperium. Though it may seem the fight will never end, there is victory even in the defeat we see threatening all around.

'There is no greater proclamation of faith than to offer up our very lives to guard the soul of humankind. In this we win a victory greater in magnitude than the harm that any heretic can inflict, and so every battle is a shining triumph that the traitor and the apostate can never take away from us.'

Ludmilla let her words hang in the air, the final words dictated by Saint Mina on her death-bed. Every Sister had heard them before. Now, in the calm before the slaughter, every Sister heard the words more clearly than ever before.

Then, in a low, mournful voice, Canoness Ludmilla began to sing.

'*A spiritus dominatus, domine, libra nos…*'

Recognising the High Gothic opening lines, the Sisters Superior joined their canoness in the invocation of the Fede Imperialis.

'*From the lightning and the tempest, our Emperor, deliver us…*'

The Fede Imperialis began to echo around the front line as the Battle Sisters took up the hymn.

'*From plague, deceit, temptation and war, our Emperor, deliver us…*'

The Sisters of the Seraphim squads behind the front line and the Retributor units stationed around the industrial plant joined in the hymn. The crews of the tanks and the Sisters Hospitaller setting up casualty stations along the rear lines sang, too, their voices ringing through the vox. Even the Sisters Famulous back in Cardinal Recoba's spire sang, steeling their hearts so their faith would be equal to the task.

'From the scourge of the Kraken, our Emperor, Deliver us…'

Those Guardsmen who knew the Fede Imperialis, the battle-hymn of the Ecclesiarchy, joined in. The singing rang out from the northern end of the line, hundreds of voices raised in affirmation forming a choir that filled the polluted air with faith and hope.

They were still singing when the remains of the *Rubicon* crashed into the Balurian line.

THE THUNDERHAWK WAS sweeping low over the broken plains of Volcanis Ultor to keep below the sensors of anti-aircraft guns. Alaric could see the plain streaking past below a murky sky, dirty pale earth drained of all its life, bleached by chemical pollutants, dried and cracked by aeons of merciless industry. It was barren and bleak, a place where men could not survive long amongst the ash dunes and toxic dribbles that passed for rivers.

Alaric checked the runes displayed on his forearm readout. The drop-pods' beacons were working – the pods of Santoro and Genhain had both made it down, landing close enough to one another for the point between them to serve as a rendezvous. The Thunder-hawk could not get close to the defences and the Grey Knights had no armour to transport them – they would have to reach Lake Rapax on foot. What little Alaric had seen of the defences from the *Rubicon*'s bridge indicated that the end of the line was very well-defended. It would not be easy. Ghargatuloth had seen to that.

All Alaric knew about the resting place of St Evisser was that it was on the shore of Lake Rapax. That much Serevic had told him. Everything else he would have to find out the hard way.

'How long?' yelled Alaric over the engines.

'Thirty seconds!' shouted the Malleus pilot in reply. Alaric tried to imagine what the man must be thinking, knowing that all his colleagues had died in the fireball the Thunderhawk had only just escaped. But who could know what such a man was thinking when he didn't even have a name to call his own, when he had been stripped of everything that made him human so he could better serve the Ordo Malleus?

The Thunderhawk ramp rolled down and Alaric saw the ground speeding past beneath it, the Thunderhawk's wake kicking up spirals of ash. They were going in fast – there would be more than enough artillery, perhaps even Ordinatus, to destroy the Grey Knights before they could even launch their attack. They had to move fast, for every moment until they got to Lake Rapax was a moment they were intolerably exposed.

The *Rubicon* had tried to contact Volcanis Ultor to claim the Grey Knights were on Imperial business, but after the first few exchanges, all communications were cut. The defenders were convinced the Grey Knights were the heralds of a Chaos attack, and had sealed their vox-nets and other communications in case the imaginary enemy tried to infect their minds. The only way to get through the defences would be to fight through them, and Alaric could feel the Imperial blood on his hands already.

'We're going in hot, prepare to deploy!' shouted Alaric, the acrid chemical smell of Volcanis Ultor filling the Thunderhawk. Squad Alaric and Squad Tancred snapped off their grav-restraints. The Thunderhawk slewed around and decelerated, the Grey Knights inside holding on tight as the ground loomed close.

Alaric jumped first, followed by the men of his squad. Squad Tancred was next, their armoured bodies smashing craters in the ground as they landed. Justicar Tancred himself held the sword of Mandulis, its mirror-polished blade shining incongruously in the swirling dust and murky light.

'Get away from here,' voxed Alaric to the Malleus pilot, possibly the last survivor of the *Rubicon*. 'Head west.'

The pilot didn't answer. The Thunderhawk swooped down as it turned, then its engines gunned and it shot off leaving the swirling trail of ash.

Alaric glanced at the runes on his readout. They pulsed brightly – the drop-pods were a short jog away.

'Genhain, Santoro, we're down,' voxed Alaric.

'Genhain down,' came one justicar's voice. 'Ready to move out.'

'Santoro down,' said the other.

'We're heading your way. Stay defensive and be ready to…'

Alaric was cut off as he saw a rose-red light burning through the gauze of dust. Something had punched through Volcanis Ultor's mantle of bruise-coloured cloud, burning red. It seemed to be falling incredibly slowly, its underside white-hot, huge sheets of fire trailing behind. Alaric could hear a roar like a hurricane and he recognised, stripped bare and melting, the shape of one of the *Rubicon*'s engines.

'All Marines take cover!' yelled Alaric into the vox, and dropped down to the fractured ground.

A great white flash of heat burst like a wave. A roar followed, a shockwave running through the earth like the blast from a huge bomb, a hot blast of air washing across the plain. The sound was appalling, like an army of daemons howling. Suddenly the fire in the sky was gone and a mantle of ash and pulverised rock was drawn across the plain like a thick black blanket, turning Volcanis Ultor as dark as night. The hot, dry storm ripped over Alaric's Grey Knights as they took cover, the shockwaves rippling back and forth. The vox was a wall of interference, the feeble sun was shut out, the sky replaced by a grimy swirling mass of dust and ash

Alaric yelled at the top of his lungs. 'To me, Grey Knights! Press on! Stay close!'

The Grey Knights could not stay where they were. They were vulnerable – man-to-man they were some of the best soldiers in the galaxy, but trapped in the open they were just so many targets.

Tancred lumbered out of the darkness, the sword of Mandulis shining so bright it seemed to be on fire. His Terminator-armoured battle-brothers followed him. 'At your side, brother-captain,' he shouted grimly.

Alaric gathered his men and plunged on into the storm, heading for Squads Santoro and Genhain, and Lake Rapax.

AN INTACT STRIKE cruiser at full speed would have been like a meteor hitting Volcanis Ultor, forging a winter decades long, exterminating whole ecosystems. The falling section of the *Rubicon* represented a fraction of its weight and it had decelerated dramatically to deploy its payload, and so it did not annihilate most of Hive Superior and a fair chunk of the plains surrounding it.

To the city's defenders, that was little consolation. The engine section landed towards the southern end of the line held by the Balurian heavy infantry and it hit with a force larger than a shell from one of the huge

Ordinatus artillery pieces built by the Adeptus Mechanicus. A full orbital strike from a battleship would scarcely have done more damage.

The heat and shockwave released by the impact vaporised a good portion of the Balurian regiment, and hundreds of men drowned in the flood of ash and dust that coursed through their trenches. Three kilometres of trench were destroyed, from the front line to the rearward assembly areas. The command post was wiped out, killing the Balurian colonel Gortz and almost his entire staff. Sisters Hospitaller perished at their medical posts. Supply posts full of equipment and munitions were crushed, exploding into flat sheets of fire and shrapnel.

The Ordinatus deployed behind the Balurian lines was destroyed, its immense cannon barrel and titanic loader systems ripped apart by the flood of wreckage that spewed from the engine section as it disintegrated.

The engines did not explode, for the plasma reactors had bled their contents into the upper atmosphere when the Absolution Beta had torn the strike cruiser apart. Instead there was a terrible eruption of darkness, a pall of black ash and earth that boiled up almost as high as Hive Superior's outer spires and billowed out across the plain. It swept out over the no-man's-land beyond the front lines, down through the sections south of the Balurians and north to halfway across Lake Rapax. It boiled into Hive Superior's outer reaches. Some were buried, others suffocated, while others dug themselves out of drifts of ash that gathered everywhere.

The whole north end of the defences was buried under a blanket of blackness, as if night had fallen. Further south disruption was immense – communications cut, bunkers undermined by the shockwave, eardrums burst, unstable munitions and fuel dumps detonated. Confusion paralysed the defences, and only the most well-equipped and disciplined troops could hope to fight with anything approaching full effectiveness.

Those troops were the Battle Sisters of the Adepta Sororitas.

ALARIC SAW JUSTICAR Santoro through the gloom, crouched with his storm bolter ready to fire. The other four Marines of his squad were in a tight formation around the drop-pod site, hunkered down behind the opened steel petals of the pod.

Alaric clapped Santoro on the back. 'Good to see you got down.'

Santoro nodded grimly. 'Night has fallen early. It looks like we're in the right place.'

Genhain loomed out of the darkness. Were it not for Alaric's enhanced vision he would not have been able to see the justicar at all. 'Lachis is hurt,' he said – the vox was still down so vocal communication was the only option.

'How bad?'

'Mangled a leg in the landing. He'll lose it.'

Alaric saw Brother Grenn and Ondurin helping Lachis along – the lower part of his right leg was severely mangled, bone jutting from the sundered armour plates. Anyone other than a Space Marine would have been unconscious.

'Marine, can you fight?' said Alaric.

'Always,' said Lachis. He was a relatively young Grey Knight, having been promoted from a novice into Genhain's squad just over two years before. 'But not run.'

'Your brothers will help you until we reach the front line. After that you move under your own power. We'll need your covering fire.'

'Understood, Brother-Captain.'

'We'll leave you behind. You won't survive.'

'Understood.'

Alaric looked through the dust storm. He couldn't make out the processing plant that marked the end of the line and the shore of Lake Rapax but he could sense it there, the centre of a web spun by Ghargatuloth, drawing them near.

'The vox is out and we won't be getting it back, so we stay close and stay in communication. The defences are manned by Imperial citizens but while Ghargatuloth lives they are the enemy. When we reach the Prince of a Thousand Faces, we will have our revenge for their deaths.'

With that Alaric ran into the darkness, his Grey Knights following him, every thought turned towards how many would have had to die before this fight was done, and how every death would be visited on Ghargatuloth.

CANONESS LUDMILLA CROUCHED down in the front line, feeling her filtration implants grinding in her throat as they cleaned out the dust and ash that would otherwise flood her lungs. Several Sisters had put on their Sabbat pattern helms, keeping the storm out of their eyes; Ludmilla rarely wore hers, preferring to see the enemy as plainly as possible the better to hate them.

Sister Lachryma, the leader of Ludmilla's Seraphim, hurried down the trench towards the canoness.

'It hit the Balurians!' Lachryma called out. 'They're in disarray. Gortz's staff is gone. It's just us now.'

'Did you see what it was?'

Lachryma was standing right beside Ludmilla now. The veteran Seraphim's face was streaked with sweat and grime, and the glossy red of her armour was dull with ash. 'It fell from the sky. Some Sisters think the Ordinatus crew has betrayed us. It looked more like a meteor. Some foul weapon of the Enemy.'

'With the Emperor's grace the Enemy will have died beneath it, too.'

'His plan is rarely so simple,' said Lachryma grimly.

'I have heard few words truer,' replied Ludmilla, drawing her inferno pistol.

Somewhere down the trench, ranging shots snapped from a heavy bolter, sharp gunshots stitching through the dim roar of the storm.

'Enemy sighted!' came the call down the trench.

'Give me range!' yelled back Ludmilla at the Sisters.

'Close! Visibility's nothing, but they're Marines!'

Chaos Marines. And with the visibility so bad, the Sisters would have to fight them toe-to-toe, without fields of fire from the Retributor squads at the plant.

'Lachryma, bring your Sisters forward. We can't fall back, the fight will be here.'

'Yes, canoness.'

Sisters Superior were calling out final battle-rites. Ludmilla could feel the tension, perceived not by her senses but by her years of battlefield experience – the tension before every battle, now about to break in a shower of blood beneath the darkness that had fallen over Volcanis Ultor.

Marine bolter fire erupted and heavy bolters opened up in return, snapping back at half-glimpsed targets. Marines had full auto-senses that would give them a crucial advantage here, when the Sisters couldn't make out targets at long bolter range.

'Sisters!' yelled Ludmilla. 'For the Throne and the end of time! Charge!'

ALARIC SAW THE first defenders rising out of the trench in front of him, trampling through the razorwire, heavy bolter fire snapping in red-white tracers from behind them. He saw red armour and black cloth, an Imagifer's banner depicting the symbol of the Bloody Rose.

Sisters. Ghargatuloth had put them up against the Sisters of Battle. The foulness of the daemon prince's plan just got deeper – the Sisters were dedicated, faithful, noble, soldiers of the Imperial church who had fought under Inquisitorial command innumerable times.

There was no room for doubt. No mercy, not even here. Here, they were the enemy.

When the first bolter shells rang off his armour, Alaric broke into a sprint, charging headlong for the front line. Bolter fire opened up all around him and his armour was battered terribly, waves of shells ripping through the air. Alaric dived into the fray, Nemesis halberd swinging, smashing one Sister back and slicing off the arm of another. Hate-filled eyes looked through the darkness, and Alaric could hear prayers to the Emperor yelled over the howling of the storm and the drumming of the gunfire. Dvorn was beside Alaric and there was a flash like a lightning strike as his hammer swatted one Sister backwards.

Tancred battered his way through the Sisters who charged against him, swatting them aside. Brother Karlin's Incinerator sent a gout of flame out to clear a path and a Sister's flamer roared in reply, illuminating Squad Tancred in a sea of fire so they seemed to be battling the Sisters across the surface of hell.

Alaric's Marines were charging forward with him now. Brother Clostus was fighting, halberd to power sword, with a Sister Superior who yelled the Catechisms of Righteous Loathing as she fought.

She sliced down and cut deep into Clostus's chest, punching her free hand hard into his face and barging him back into the swirling ash.

Alaric couldn't stop now. He had to press on.

Fire was streaking from all sides. Heavy psycannon rounds punched through the air from Genhain's squad who were following Alaric in. Somewhere back there the wounded Brother Lachis was left by Squad Genhain, to cover his battle-brothers with storm bolter fire while he crouched down for cover on his shattered leg.

Squad Santoro, beyond Tancred, reached the lines first, leaping into a trench junction that would have been covered by heavy weapons Sisters had they been able to see him. Alaric saw the clusters of bolter fire like chains of firecrackers where a short-range firefight developed. Alaric himself was still out in the open and exposed, trying to follow the trail literally blazed by Squad Tancred. Alaric ran towards the glow of flamers and saw Tancred, wading knee-deep in burning promethium streaking from several flamer-armed Sisters firing from the trench itself.

Clostus's rune was gone from Alaric's retinal display – either the Marine was dead or he was too far away for his armour's life sign readings to get through the interference. Either way he was lost to them now.

Alaric saw one of Squad Santoro, probably Brother Jaeknos, on his knees, his armour pocked and smoking by a dozen bolter wounds. He was still firing but his Nemesis halberd was on the ground – Alaric saw the hand he normally used to wield it was reduced to useless bloody rags. The ash closed in on him as vengeful Sisters bore down on him, bolters blazing.

'Forward, Knights!' yelled Alaric. 'Forward!'

Shells ripped into his shoulder pad and hot pain blossomed there. Tancred, silhouetted in the blazing fire, kicked his way through a bank of razorwire and dropped into the trench, bellowing war-prayers as he did so. Alaric shook off the pain and followed – a Sister charged from behind the cover of the razorwire and ducked Alaric's first blow, grabbing one shoulder pad and smashing him in the face with the butt of her bolter.

Alaric grabbed the collar of her power armour, lifted her up, and pitched her into the fire at his feet. She scrambled to her knees, blazing horribly from head to toe, and Alaric swiped her head off with his halberd as she moved to fire.

Lesser men would break. Not a Grey Knight. For if Alaric gave in to despair at killing Sisters, then Ghargatuloth would win yet again.

He clawed through the razorwire and dropped into the trench. Bodies were already choking the trench section, battered with bolter fire or cut open by Nemesis weapons. Tancred was still fighting, the sword of Mandulis mirror-bright in spite of the dust, sprays of blood frozen in the strobing gunfire as Brother Locath plunged his halberd blade through the chest of a Sister Superior.

The trench was their best chance, away from the gunfire of the Sisters charging forward from the rear lines, where the Grey Knights' superior armour and close combat skills would help them the most.

'North!' yelled Alaric. 'North! Now!'

Heavy bolter fire streaked down from ahead. Santoro yelled for his Marines to take cover in alcoves and dugouts as Tancred stomped forward to take the brunt of the fire on his Terminator's superior armour. Alaric, even with his enhanced Marine's senses, could barely see what was going on ahead – his superior hearing picked out the different sounds of storm bolter shells smacking through the air and heavy bolter fire thudding into the sides of the trench. Ceramite armour cracked. The sword of Mandulis cut the air and the low roar of burning promethium swirled from somewhere ahead.

A new sound suddenly cut through the din – engines shrieking in an arc overhead, plunging down towards Squads Alaric and Genhain to the rear of the Grey Knights' spearhead.

Alaric knew jump packs when he heard them. He knew the Seraphim would hit home before he saw them plunging through the black ceiling of ash, he knew their twin bolt pistols would fill the confined trench with a wall of shrapnel. He knew that the elite close combat Sisters were the hardest-hitting shock troops the Ecclesiarchy had, and that the Grey Knights would have to kill these brave, zealous servants of the Emperor if they were to survive.

The Seraphim Superior dived, power sword-first, streaking through the darkness. Alaric turned the point of her sword but the Seraphim slammed into him, her face against his, her breath hot through gritted teeth. Alaric stumbled and fell onto his back, the thrust of the Seraphim's jump pack driving him into the mud. He pinned the Sister's blade under his halberd arm but she got a knee down on his storm bolter hand. Her free hand pistoned up and slammed down an elbow into Alaric's jaw – the blow made him reel but he held on, trying to break the Sister's hold, throw her off him before the other Seraphim now battling Squad Genhain could come to her aid and riddle Alaric with bolt pistol fire.

'From the blasphemy of the fallen…' she snarled as she struck again and again.

'… our Emperor, deliver us…' gasped Alaric.

The Seraphim Superior paused for a split-second as Alaric spoke the words of the Fede Imperialis. In that moment Alaric wrenched his hand free and punched the Seraphim so hard she was flung against the side of the trench. He felt her jaw give way – had it not broken the blow would probably have snapped her neck.

Dvorn shattered a Seraphim's hand but the pistol in her other hand stitched heavy bolts into his breastplate, raising showers of sparks as he was battered backwards. Brother Lykkos, hampered at close quarters by his psycannon, kicked a Seraphim's legs out from under her only for her to squirm away from under his aim, so he blasted a crater of glowing mud out of the trench floor. Sisters were firing blindly into the trench from above, and gunfire was spitting in from everywhere. Squad Genhain was holding off another Seraphim squad – explosions sounded from the north as Tancred and Santoro faced heavy weapons from Retributor squads and dug-in tanks.

The air stank of blood, propellant and sweat. Ash was everywhere, the darkness lit from beneath by flame and muzzle flashes like the heart of a hellish thunderstorm.

The Seraphim Superior was dragging herself to her feet, blood running from her mouth.

'From the begetting of daemons!' shouted Alaric above the gunfire, his storm bolter levelled at the Sister. 'Our Emperor, deliver us!'

There was a commotion behind Alaric and he saw a figure vaulting over the razorwire into the middle of the Grey Knights – Vien tried to fend her off but the Sister was quicker, blocking Vien's halberd with a forearm and swinging him behind her to close with Alaric. Alaric swung his aim around but suddenly he himself was staring into the barrel of an inferno pistol.

'From the curse of the mutant...' said Alaric levelly. He saw the Sister's armour was detailed in gold with the symbols of the Ecclesiarchy. High Gothic words were embroidered into the cloth of her sleeves and the red rose of her Order was tattooed onto her cheek. Her face was lined and bore several faint scars, left over from reconstruction by a good medicae, he guessed.

'Grey Knight,' said the canoness. 'Show me the book.'

Alaric let his aim fall and he opened up the small compartment in his chest armour. He took out the small volume of the *Liber Daemonicum*.

'Read from it.'

Alaric opened the book at a well-thumbed page. 'The nature of the daemon is such that righteous men may not know it, and yet know it we must to fight it...' read Alaric hurriedly, feeling the death around him, the storm bolters of his Grey Knights firing, the clash of blades on ceramite, the explosions from up ahead. 'And so the Enemy must be known not through direct discourse and study but through allegory and parable...'

'Sisters!' shouted the canoness, and Alaric knew she was talking over the vox – the Sisters must have had a robust vox-relay station somewhere in the rear lines, that kept their vox-net intact. 'Cease fire! Now, all of you!'

'Grey Knights cease fire!' echoed Alaric. An explosion sounded from Tancred's spearhead down the trench. 'Now, Tancred! Cease fire and fall back to me!'

Alaric glanced around. The Seraphim were standing back, bolt pistols aimed. Several Sisters appeared at the edge of the trench training their bolters on Alaric. The Grey Knights moved warily towards Alaric, storm bolters levelled, Nemesis weapons held ready. Alaric saw Lykkos was bleeding from several rents in his armour and Dvorn's chestplate was pockmarked and smoking. Squad Genhain had fared better but every Marine was looking the worse for wear, covered in wounds and bullet scars. Several Sisters lay wounded or dead, and the mud of the trench was soaked with blood.

The Seraphim Superior was helped to her feet by one of her Sisters. Her skin was pallid with shock but there was no hiding the hate in her eyes.

'Justicar?' said the canoness.

'Brother-Captain,' replied Alaric. 'Acting.'

'I fear there has been a terrible error of judgement.' The canoness looked down at the Sororitas bodies in the trench. She could rein in her emotions when so much was at stake, but she could not completely hide her sorrow.

'There was no error,' said Alaric. 'The source of the suffering on the Trail is here on Volcanis Ultor. The Enemy has used Imperial troops to guard it. The same Enemy was counting on none of the defenders having heard of the Grey Knights, in which respect I am assuming he was wrong.'

'My Order served with Lord Inquisitor Karamazov at the Tigurian Flow. The Grey Knights were there, too, though I never fought with them. You were fortunate I recognised you at all.' The canoness lowered her inferno pistol. 'Canoness Carmina Ludmilla, Order of the Bloody Rose.'

'Brother-Captain Alaric. Are your Sisters defending Lake Rapax?'

'It hardly seems worth defending. We are holding the end of the line, the only thing here is the processing plant.'

'Is there anything else on the lake?'

'No, just the plant.'

'Have you been inside?'

Ludmilla shook her head. 'Valinov warned us the chemicals inside were volatile.'

Alaric started. 'Inquisitor Valinov?'

'Yes. Did he send you?'

Alaric paused. How could he begin to explain? But seeing the noble canoness waiting for an answer, he knew the only choice was to tell her the truth. 'Valinov is the enemy. He was sentenced to death by the Ordo Malleus and escaped. The confusion is his doing. He ordered you to defend the plant because it conceals the place where his master will rise.'

'Valinov is an inquisitor.' Ludmilla's voice was stern – Alaric could tell he hadn't yet completely earned her trust. 'He has the blessing of Cardinal Recoba and everyone else on Volcanis Ultor. You, however, have killed my Sisters and very nearly killed me. Grey Knight or not you are asking me to believe a great deal in a very short time.'

'We are not aggressors here,' said Alaric. 'Your Sisters fired the first shot.'

Ludmilla glanced to the south, where the inferno of the blast site glowed dully through the ash. 'The

Balurian heavy infantry would argue otherwise, brother-captain.'

Tancred stomped through the trench towards Alaric. Smoke was pouring off him – the servos of his Terminator armour were working hard and the ceramite plates were charred and stank of promethium. 'Canoness,' he said darkly. 'Your Sisters fight well. I wish I had found out another way.'

Ludmilla glared at him.

'Where is Valinov now?' asked Alaric.

'He has offices in Cardinal Recoba's spire,' replied Ludmilla. 'But he was due to review our positions when the crash happened.'

'Then he's here already.' Alaric looked down at the dead Sisters, brave soldiers and servants the Imperium could not afford to replace. Sisters Hospitaller were hurrying from the rearward lines to tend to the wounded and take away the dead. 'I am sick of being too late. canoness, I need you and your Sisters. Valinov is raising something terrible on the shore of Lake Rapax and he has created our conflict to cover his tracks. He assumed that we would fight each other to a standstill, but he was wrong. I intend to prove him wrong with or without you, Sister, but I fear we cannot prevail on our own.'

'I cannot help you if I do not know what we are fighting, brother-captain.'

Alaric took a breath. How could he articulate something like this, an evil composed of pure knowledge that used insanity and corruption as its weapon, that could not be fought or killed or understood, that once risen would ingrain itself into the fabric of the Imperium until it would take another thousand years to find?

'Sister,' began Alaric carefully, 'There is no time, so I cannot make you begin to truly understand. But it calls itself Ghargatuloth...'

EIGHTEEN
THE STATUE GARDEN

THE BALURIAN HEAVY infantry had lost a third of its men, wiped out by a crash that turned them into dust that swirled over the mantle of ash and mud. Colonel Gortz was dead and communications were gone, so another third were cut off and helpless, stranded blind and out of contact, forced to hunker down and hold their defences against an enemy they could not see.

The rest of the Balurians, more than seven hundred troops, gathered towards the northern end of the Imperial lines. The Balurians were exceptionally disciplined troops but with so many officers dead there was no one to lead them against the enemy that would surely attack in the wake of the catastrophe.

But the Imperial Guard could fight on without officers. Because when officers could not lead – whether through incompetence, corruption, lack of willpower or, as at Volcanis Ultor, sheer magnitude of casualties, the Guard had another command structure that took over.

A commissar was not a tactician. He was not a strategist. He could not fine-tune an assault or design the perfect defence. But when the Guard needed leadership, such things were irrelevant. Commissars led when the Guardsmen needed to be led from the front into the teeth of a foe a colonel and his officers could not face. When there was no room for tactics or skill or anything but sheer bloody-minded, fanatical bravery, the commissars took the lead.

Commissar Thanatal had always known he might have to take the Balurians into combat when there was no one else to do it. It was what he had been trained for since he first came to the schola progenium, an orphan of one of innumerable Imperial wars. In many years of harsh tutelage he had learned that duty was a sword that would kill you as surely as it could be wielded against the enemy, a sword it was his destiny to wield. He did not care about the lives of his men or the cleanness of the victory, or even his own wellbeing. He cared about punishing the enemies of the Emperor for the sin of daring to exist in His sight, in bringing the souls of his Guardsmen to the embrace of the Emperor in the holy light of war.

He believed in culling the cowardly and the weak-willed, so the Balurians could count only true Imperial spirits in their number when the time came to die for the Emperor's glory.

The hem of Thanatal's long black leather coat dragged in the clotted mud of the trenches and his mesh armour was heavy as he struggled northwards through the blinding ash. He heard men yelling their comrades' names, screaming in pain, praying out loud.

He stumbled over choking bodies. The commissar took off his peaked cap and pulled his rebreather over his head, breathing deeply as the filter screened out the worst of the ash.

The clouds parted and Thanatal could see, just, as if in the dead of night. Torchlight cut through the swirling gloom. Men, dim struggling shapes, were scrambling over the ruined defences, heading back in the direction of Volcanis Ultor.

Thanatal saw a sergeant directing a gaggle of men. 'Sergeant!' he yelled. 'Where are you going?'

'They're coming at us through the Sisters' lines. We're gathering at the rearward trenches. We're going to hold the supply trenches, set up another line…'

Thanatal drew his bolt pistol and shot the sergeant through the throat. The soldiers nearby stopped dead.

'The regiment!' yelled Thanatal as if he were bawling orders on the parade ground, 'Will advance to the north! The enemy has assaulted us to cut us off from his objective, but he has failed! While Balurians still live, the enemy will be punished!'

Men tried to scramble through the darkness away from Thanatal. Two more shots barked out and a Guardsmen fell, draped over the razorwire. No one else ran.

'The enemy is to the north! The regiment will advance!'

Men were gathering around him. Thanatal strode as best he could through the bodies and mud, clambering over the crumbling edge of the trench so all the men could see him. He grabbed a torch off one of the men and held it high, casting a finger of light that pointed upwards through the ash.

'The enemy is trying to surround us and cut us off! Even now he butchers our brothers and plots our deaths! Even now he thinks he has won! But if he wants victory then by the Emperor, he will have to kill us all! While one Balurian lives the Emperor will suffer no defeat!' Thanatal fired again, at random this time into the murk. More Balurians were scrambling towards him. He walked north, through the wreckage and razorwire, and gradually the pull of the crowd drew more and more with him.

'To the north!' men were shouting. 'They're gonna get behind us! Follow me!'

Out of the chaos was forged a growing crowd of men, stumbling through the darkness, Thanatal never letting up as he commanded their attention. He told them of the revenge they were seeking. He fired at men who tried to crawl away as he approached. He took the anger of the Balurians and turned it into something that drowned out their fear, and his heart swelled as he thought of all those loyal minds turned upon him when they could have been seeking refuge in despair.

He was their salvation. He was walking the path that led them away from the sin of cowardice and into the blinding light of the Emperor.

The enemy was here. They had to be. The devastating crash was the first gambit in an all-out attack, and Thanatal would not let his Balurian charges lose the chance to be in the heart of it.

'Commissar!' came a voice from up ahead. Thanatal saw the shape of an armoured car through the ash. A figure jumped down from it and hurried over the mud. It was a tall, lean figure in a long flak-coat, holding a power sword. As the blade leapt to life it shone a pale blue and Thanatal could make out a proud, noble face, eyes burning with determination.

'Commissar, praise the Emperor! I had thought the Balurians were lost!'

'Not while one still breathes,' said Thanatal, making sure his men could hear. 'Not when we can still make the enemy suffer!'

'Then your men will be my honour guard, commissar. The enemy is here and they are foul indeed, but with you I can bring them the justice they crave.' The man saluted with the blade of his sword. 'Inquisitor Gholic Ren-Sar Valinov, commissar, honoured to serve alongside the men of Balur.'

Thanatal gripped Valinov's hand in a firm leader's handshake. 'What do you want of us, inquisitor?'

'Steel and guts, commissar. It's the only way.' Valinov held up his sword so the men could see it, a sparkling beacon like harnessed lightning. 'For the Throne and the Balurian dead! Vengeance and justice, sons of the Emperor! Vengeance!'

'Vengeance!' men yelled back, and soon the men took it up as a chant led by Thanatal. 'Vengeance!'

Vengeance. Everyone knew it was the only thing worth fighting for. Commissar Thanatal knew his duty would be done, for under him the sons of Balur would have the chance to fight for it.

THE PROCESSING PLANT loomed up through the darkness, squat and ugly, its sheer plasticrete sides streaked with grime. Alaric could just make out Retributor squads on the roof, trying to train their heavy bolters on the defences around the plant. Large rockcrete anti-tank blocks and several bunkers were ranged around the plant, offering plenty of cover to the Grey Knights and Sisters moving into position at the front of the plant.

The plant itself was on the very edge of Lake Rapax, the foul waters lapping at its rear wall. The squat blocky shapes that made up the plant were streaked with chemicals that had condensed on the walls. The whole plant looked filthy and neglected, like a prison – no windows, no markings, just the single rusted entrance serving the whole bloated building.

The stench of Lake Rapax cut through everything – harsh and metallic, a terrible chemical smell. The oily glint of the lake's surface was just visible, still rippling from the shock of the impact. Foul greasy mist rose off the lake, mingling with the ash to form a grim drizzle of corruption.

Alaric jogged through the defences towards the plant, his squad and Justicar Santoro's Marines around him, Ludmilla close behind.

Ludmilla had brought almost a hundred Sisters of Battle with her – she had seen many of the atrocities committed throughout the Trail, and now she knew that Ghargatuloth was behind them she understood why the Grey Knights were there.

She could now understand the web of lies and manipulation that had turned her Sisters into instruments of the Enemy, and Alaric thought it must have made her feel so unclean that only pure bloody revenge could get her soul clean.

'Sister Heloise,' ordered Ludmilla, her voice raised to get over the static still fouling all communications. 'Bring your multi-meltas to ground level, now!'

The rusted steel front doors of the plant wouldn't have opened even if the Sisters could have unlocked them. The Excorcist tanks stationed at the front of the plant could have blasted through them but the Sisters and Grey Knights would have had to hang back to avoid the explosion – the multi-meltas could cut through the metal and let them charge in much more quickly.

Ghargatuloth would know they were coming. Whatever they found, the Sisters and the Grey Knights had to strike before it could fight back.

The Seraphim Superior, Sister Lachryma, brought her Seraphim to the front. Two squads had lost so many Sisters that they now fought as one, seven Seraphim under Lachryma whose jaw was now a large purple bruise.

She nodded once in salute as she led her Sisters behind a buttress on the plant wall for cover. Tancred stomped forward to the other side of the doors. These two squads, without having to be ordered, would be the first in.

The Retributor squad of Sister Heloise were down off the walls, lugging their multi-meltas and massive heavy bolters with their chains of explosive ammunition. Alaric saw Heloise had a bionic arm and her shaven scalp was half-covered in an ugly burn scar.

'Anything from inside?' asked Ludmilla.

'Nothing,' said Heloise.

'Open it up,' ordered Ludmilla. 'Sisters, ready! Lachryma and the Knights will lead. Steel your souls, for the Enemy will try to take you first.' Ludmilla turned to Alaric. 'I know the Grey Knights have never had a Marine lose their mind to Chaos. But the Adepta Sororitas have lost Sisters to the Enemy before. It is rare, and no one will admit to it, but…'

'It is bad enough that Ghargatuloth has used you,' said Alaric. 'I would not let any of you live on with your minds violated.'

Ludmilla nodded in thanks. Then, she turned back to Heloise. 'Fire!'

The melta beams cut through the steel, sending showers of sparks that cast huge, sinister shadows through the mantle of ash. A section of the doors fell away, and even to Alaric's superior sight there was only blackness inside.

Lachryma hurried out of cover and charged into the darkness, sword drawn. Her Seraphim followed, pistols out, and Tancred's squad followed. Their Terminator armour barely fit through the gap.

'Clear,' voxed Tancred after a few seconds.

'Move in!' called Alaric and ran for the gap, halberd ready. Santoro and Genhain followed him in. Ludmilla was next along with several squads of Battle Sisters, leaving Heloise outside to back them up.

It was pure blackness inside, not just an absence of light but a veil of obscuring darkness. Alaric couldn't make out the walls or the ceiling. The floor was ancient broken marble, once covered in exquisite mosaics but now fragmented and crumbling. There were no chemical vats or processing turbines – the plant was silent and cold, and the air smelled only of age. The place had been completely sealed against the corrosion from Lake Rapax.

Alaric advanced carefully, the faint shaft of pallid light from the doorway his only point of reference. He spotted Lachryma's Seraphim up ahead, Tancred's Terminators holding a loose line in front of them. The sword of Mandulis glowed faintly in Tancred's hand, gleaming bright and clean in spite of the blood and ash that covered it – casting a faint pool of pale light around the justicar.

Alaric approached Tancred and saw why they had stopped. Looming through the darkness, stretching as far as Alaric could see, was a sinister forest of immense

statues. They seemed to grow from the marble floor
like trees, many times the height of a man, each one
cracked and ancient. Many leaned at awkward angles.
They were figures carved in sweeping robes or elaborate finery, turned by darkness and age into indistinct
half-glimpsed shapes. Alaric jogged up behind Tancred
and saw the face of the nearest statue was gone, eaten
away as if by corrosion, blank pits where eyes should
have been, the faint outlines of bare teeth instead of a
mouth. The figure had once been a cardinal or a deacon in long robes, but now it leaned precariously as if
about to topple down on whoever approached.

'Forward,' said Alaric. 'Spread out but stay in sight'

He passed the faceless cardinal and saw there were
dozens of statues, forming a field of monuments that
seemed to fill the shell of the processing plant. Here
there was a dashing figure in a naval uniform whose
head had crumbled into a featureless twist of stone. An
astropath reached out to make the sign of the aquila,
but his hand was a pile of broken stone on the floor
beneath him.

There was even a Space Marine, the titanic stone form
toppled completely to the floor and half-shattered.
Lachryma's Seraphims skirted around the fallen
Marine, using its broken forearms as cover, picking
their way through the debris that remained of its torso
and backpack.

Alaric could make out tarnished blackened gold
inlaid into the floor, marking out elaborate patterns of
mosaic that were broken and obliterated by age.

'I have something,' voxed Lachryma, her voice thick-
ened by her injury. Ludmilla and Alaric had ordered their
troops to use the same vox-channel, so the Sisters and the
Grey Knights could fight as one force. 'Up ahead.'

'Tancred, check it out. We're behind you,' said Alaric. He heard Ludmilla order Battle Sisters squads to move forward on either flank, surrounding any potential enemy.

Alaric followed Tancred past a giant stone Sister Hospitaller, mostly intact except for her missing hands. Ahead, the floor of the statue forest rose into a pyramid of steps leading upwards towards what looked like a temple, bathed in a very faint pale glow from above. Alaric peered through the gloom and made out columns holding up a pediment whose sculptures had long since crumbled, an inscribed frieze with a few remaining letters of High Gothic, the remains of smaller statues at the corner of every step. He saw these statues had completely eroded until they were just vaguely humanoid forms.

There was only one word still legible on the frieze below the pediment.

EVISSER.

'We've found it. It's the tomb,' said Alaric.

'Looks like we're the only ones who have been here in a long time,' replied Ludmilla. 'No one's here.'

'Valinov is on Volcanis Ultor. This has to be the reason.' Alaric was certain as he said it. It all made such perfect sense. The Trail of St Evisser was a puzzle created by Ghargatuloth, and this was the final piece.

'We can storm the place,' said Lachryma, waiting with her Sisters at the base of the steps. 'We'll take the rear, the Terminators go in the front.'

'Good,' said Alaric. 'Santoro, go with her. Genhain, follow us in and cover us if we need it. I need to see what's in there. I'll go in with Tancred.' He turned to Ludmilla, who was directing her Battle Sisters to skirt around the steps and surround the temple. 'Back us up,

Sister. This is a multi-point assault on a location we have to assume is defended and there is no way to know what is inside. You may all have to think on your feet.'

'That's what we're good at, brother-captain. You and me both. Face the unknown when no one else can? Fight the darkness itself? It's what they made us for.'

The canoness was right. Sisters, like the Grey Knights, were in their own way created. Trained from childhood, saturated in the word of Imperial clerics just as Grey Knights were indoctrinated, very little remained of the woman every Sister might otherwise have become. They had, in many ways, already made the ultimate sacrifice – their lives were not their own, for they had been moulded into the only soldiers that could do the Emperor's work when it really mattered. The Grey Knights and the Sisters of Battle had more in common than a mutual enemy.

'For the Throne, Sister,' said Alaric as he went to join Tancred on the steps.

'The Emperor deliver us, brother,' said Ludmilla.

Squad Alaric and Squad Tancred moved up the steps towards the looming temple. Black threads of corruption had snaked up the columns and the top steps were riddled with dark oily veins. The whole building seemed diseased when he saw it close up, and it was huge – its colonnaded sides stretched out into the darkness where Lachryma was poised to charge into the rear of the building.

There were more rows of columns beyond the first, staggered so it was impossible to see into the inside. At the top of the steps the air was cold and wet, as if something had drawn the life out of it. Alaric could feel his senses heightened and his muscles tensed by the malice that saturated the air – his psychic core was thrumming with alarm, as forces he could not see surrounded him.

Something inside the temple screamed. It was the screaming of daemons.

'Go!' yelled Alaric, and began the charge into the Tomb of St Evisser.

COMMISSAR THANATAL SAW the broken bodies of dead Sisters lying in the trench and knew he was right. The enemy had come over the lip of the trench, fending off a spirited counter-attack from Sisters who now lay butchered on the blood-soaked ground in front of the first line. Bodies in the red power armour of the Order of the Bloody Rose lay draped on coils of razorwire or battered into the ground – the wounds were from bolters or power weapons, speaking of a murderous short-ranged struggle.

The Balurians were moving rapidly up the trenches once held by the Sisters, Thanatal and Valinov at their head. One of the regimental preachers had survived and now spoke the words of the Hymnal Odium Omnis, a High Gothic prayer of hate that most of the Balurians had learned as boys in the temples of their homeworld.

'Got one!' shouted a sergeant on the Balurian left. He was aiming his lasgun at the huge battered corpse of a Chaos Marine, its grey metal armour stained with blood, one leg folded and mangled beneath it. Thanatal could see the ornate patterning on its armour and the huge halberd it had fought with, lying spattered with Sisters' blood on the ground beside it.

'Stay back!' yelled Valinov. 'Their very bodies are corrupt!' The sergeant barked an order and his men skirted carefully around the body, the Balurian who followed giving it a wide berth.

It was just like the Enemy to threaten Imperial servants even after death, thought Thanatal bitterly. Death was too good for them – but death was what they would receive.

'Sir? Where are all the Sisters?' The question came from a young officer who was hurrying along just behind Thanatal.

Valinov interrupted. 'The Sisters are lost,' he said simply.

'Remember, son of Balur,' said Thanatal. 'Vengeance.'

The officer nodded briskly and turned to make sure his men were following.

Lost? What could wipe out so many Sisters of Battle? Many of the Balurians to the north of the line had joined the Sisters in their prayers, and all the Balurians were aware just how effective the Sisters could be. What could destroy them? And where were the rest of the bodies?

Those kinds of questions could unsettle the men. Thanatal could not let them be asked.

'By their sacrifice the Sisters of Battle have weakened the enemy!' he called out to anyone who could hear him, knowing the nervous soldiers would pass the message between them as quickly as a vox-cast. 'Through their deaths the foe has been left bloodied, and it is up to us to deliver the killing blow!'

'There!' shouted Valinov from the head of the column, pointing with his power sword. Up ahead, on the very shore of Lake Rapax, the processing plant loomed, its monstrous form a squat shadow through the clouds of ash. 'That is where they lie!'

Thanatal was thankful. The Balurians could have become too wrapped up in the idea of the missing

Sisters to retain cohesion. Now they had something to charge at. 'See, sons of Balur! See how the enemy cowers! Now, strike when he is still weak! Strike for vengeance, for your comrades and for the Sisters! Vengeance, Balurians! Vengeance! Charge!'

'Charge!' yelled the old preacher, holding up his holy book and scrambling out of the trench as nimbly as a younger man to shame the soldiers who might lag behind.

'You heard the man!' shouted an officer in the mass. 'Double-time, loaded and ready to kill!'

The Balurians were alive again, filled with the fire. Thanatal broke into a run and he didn't need to lead them any more – he just had to be the first in, leading by example, Inquisitor Valinov alongside him. The Balurians surged forward, scrambling through the trenches and running along the bloodstained earth, charging towards the processing plant.

Whatever happens, Thanatal told himself, we have already won. When the time comes and they are given the chance to offer themselves up on the altar of war, the Balurians will thank me for leading them here, into the last fight.

A Chaos Marine was worth ten loyal Guardsmen, Thanatal knew that. But with enough spirit and no fear in their veins, the Balurians could even those odds. They would buy time for the rest of the defenders. They might even break the Enemy there on the shore of Lake Rapax. Either way, the Emperor's will would be done.

Valinov ran full-tilt, sword drawn, Thanatal following him. The Balurians yelled war-cries as they charged, and when the first heavy bolter shots rang out from the heretics holding the plant, there was nothing that could have stopped the Balurians from fighting back.

NINETEEN
THE TOMB OF ST EVISSER

THE SEVENTY-SEVEN SCREAMING masques of the Hidden One were born in the depths of Volcanis Ultor six hundred years before Ghargatuloth awoke. Amongst the gangs of the underhive, where a lucky man lived to twenty and guns were as valuable as food or clean water, a prophet arose who claimed he knew each of the seventy-seven faces of death and could promise any devoted follower of his that they would be immune to each form of death that stalked the under-hive. For one face was the hot buzzing steel of bullets, another the cold red pain of a knife.

The thick strangling death of drowning, the pallid crushing face of starvation – each of the seventy-seven masques lusted for death, and only by understanding them and worshipping them could death be cheated. The prophet (his name forgotten, his face remembered) told them that death itself was the object of their devotion – a study, a religion, a way of life.

His followers formed the most formidable gang in the underhive, for each one was immune to many forms of death. Eventually there was only one option left. The gangs buried their enmities for one long night of slaughter, and the prophet's followers were butchered in the twisting streets below Volcanis Ultor. Few stories came from the gang war for few survived to tell them.

No one knew where the prophet went. That he survived is not in doubt because the seventy-seven masques reappeared, worshipped in secret by those who remembered the tales of men who knew death so well they could not be killed. Gradually, the masques were revealed to be just aspects of the one – the Hidden One, a force so powerful that death itself was just one facet of its being. The cult spread, taking in the embittered and the fearful, those crushed by the weight of revenge or tainted by madness. All were welcome. The most devoted few became servants of the Hidden One himself, and his voice spoke to them through the centuries-old prophet.

Eventually, they understood.

The final masque of death was the most complete. It was utter destruction, dissolution of the body, evisceration of the soul, crushing of breath, the very cessation of existence. Once this masque was understood the follower would become something beyond death, something to whom life and death were just shadows cast by the true light of existence. A purity, a glory beyond the grasp of the living or the dreams of the dead – this was what the Hidden One promised.

The final masque could be realised only in the place where the underhive's legends spoke of destruction and chaos – Lake Rapax, a seething pit of pure corruption where the sin and hatred of thousands of years had seeped into the earth. They said it was alive, and hungry. They said monsters roamed its depths and ghosts reached helplessly from its oily surface. Beneath Volcanis Ultor they said many things, and the followers of the seventy-seven masques knew that they were all correct.

One terrible night the followers left their hovels and gathered in the streets of the underhive, following the call of their prophet. No one tried to stop them – fear gripped every heart beneath the city and the underhivers could only watch, horrified, as the insane took over the streets.

They marched out through the city's broken hinterland right to the edge of Lake Rapax, where the skeletal form of the prophet waited, howling insanely the praises of the Hidden One and recounting the seventy-seven masques that had reaped such a bounty in the underhive. His followers rejoiced as they walked in a huge crowd into the lake, the corrosive waters stripping them clean of skin and muscle, sucking the breath from their lungs, worming its way through their eyes and eating out their minds.

The lake boiled and seethed as it swallowed them up, its thick shining waters closing over the heads of the faithful, its shore foaming pink with blood. Finally the prophet himself walked upon the lake's surface, right into its very centre where, slowly, always singing the litany of the masques, he sunk beneath the waters.

The underhivers gave their thanks that the insane and the benighted had left them. Had they known the truth, they would have despaired.

The seventy-seven screaming masques did not let their followers die for nothing. The cultists really did become something else beneath the surface of Lake Rapax – with bodies of corrosive pollution and minds rebuilt in the image of the masques, they were beings so pure the Hidden One could speak to their hearts directly from beyond the veil of the warp.

And as they reformed in the toxic silt of the lake bed, their new cause was made clear to them. They were the Hidden One's children, devout followers who had transcended the boundaries of life and death. They would be given the most important task the Hidden One had – they were to travel to the forgotten place on the lake's shore, make their home there, and stay vigilant for the day when the Hidden One would bring seventy-seven shades of suffering into the galaxy.

They went to guard the great forgotten tomb, wherein lay the bones of St Evisser.

ALARIC HAD NEVER felt such a wall of pure hatred, solid and terrible. It was like charging in slow motion, the weight of malice dragging him down. It was that, more than anything, which told him he was in the presence of Ghargatuloth. That purity of emotion could only be product of the warp, ripped from the minds of humanity and layered thick over this place where the sea of souls intersected with real space. He could feel it battering against his mind, and his psychic shield felt a precariously thin barrier. If his will broke, what would flood into his mind? Would he see the madness of warp and go insane? Would Ghargatuloth himself dig his talons in and turn Alaric into a servant of Chaos? For the first time, Alaric felt he could fall. A Grey Knight could become one of the

Enemy, and the Grey Knights would never be forgiven for their failure.

Then Alaric banished the doubt. He would not fall. The Emperor was with him. He stumbled onwards and clawed himself through the wall of hate, feeling the veil pulled off him. The darkness peeled away and he saw what had happened to the resting place of St Evisser.

Past the columns of the entrance the space within the tomb warped horribly, forming a gigantic landscape with a sky of veined marble and a sun that hung in a giant censer, swinging backwards and forwards casting shadows across a hellish landscape. The tomb was several kilometres across, impossibly, like a warped mockery of a planet's surface, monstrous and wrong.

It could only be pure Chaos, the kind that had saturated Khorion IX. The land was of splintered stone, jagged plates of dark marble balancing between deep black chasms. Sprays of black water gushed upwards at random, like geysers, and large black creatures circled over the landscape like vultures. Alaric could hear screams that seemed to come from everywhere at once, and the air stank of a hundred things – sweat, blood, sulphur, burning meat, gunfire, decay, disease, pollution, incense.

Broken walls cut through the stone, becoming thicker towards the centre of the scene until they formed what looked like a skeletal city. The city clung like a parasite to a rise in the stone, as if something huge was forcing its way up from below. Empty shells of temples and basilica seemed to ooze from the mountain, forming a nightmarish labyrinth, dark and broken, a place of unalloyed death. The stone peak of the mountain pushed up through the buildings and terminated in a stark, white plateau forming the acropolis of the city. On a massive slab of the summit was a block of pure white marble, incongruous and shining, bathed in a pool of golden light. The marble sarcophagus was like the lynchpin that held everything in place, the heart of the tomb, the point to which all paths led.

Alaric tore his eyes away. He saw his Marines following him, shaking the terrible veil of hatred from their shielded minds – Lykkos carrying his psycannon, Vien, Haulvarn, Clostus, Dvorn with his Nemesis hammer. Tancred and his Marines – Locath, Karlin and Golven – were close behind, their massive forms dwarfed by the scale of the evil in front of them.

Tancred made the sign of the aquila. It seemed a futile gesture here, a tiny drop of virtue in a sea of sin.

'I don't think the Sisters will make it,' said Alaric. There was regret in his voice, but they all knew it was true. 'It's up to us. Santoro and Genhain will follow, we keep moving.'

'What's our objective?' Tancred, like Alaric, knew they could not go back. Ghargatuloth knew they were there. It had to end now.

Alaric pointed to the sarcophagus, high up on the acropolis above the city. 'Throne be with us, for otherwise we are alone.'

Squad Tancred and Squad Alaric moved out, leaving the columns behind them and moving quickly onto the shattered landscape. Chasms gaped everywhere and the tortured ground formed insane angles and sharp gradients. There were a thousand places for ambushers to hide, a hundred ways to get lost. Were it not for the beacon of the sarcophagus shining up ahead, the maze of shattered marble could form a labyrinth no man would ever escape.

The screams were deeper the further in they went, like layers of suffering bearing down on them. Skeletal trees loomed between the jagged peaks of marble and somehow it didn't surprise Alaric that they had once been human beings, warped by corruption and deformed until their skeletons spread into branches and their faces screamed hopelessly from twisted trunks of skin and muscle. Sinister black shapes flapped overhead – Alaric could make out hollow rotted eye sockets tracking them through the rocks.

Alaric glanced back and saw Genhain following, hurrying to keep Alaric and Tancred in sight. Covering fire hadn't been needed yet but Alaric knew that very soon it probably would, and he would be relying on Genhain to keep enemies pinned down while the other Grey Knights pressed home the attack.

He wondered if Santoro would make it, far across on the other side of the tomb. He feared for Lachryma's Seraphim, and for Ludmilla's Sisters that would probably try to follow them in. Would they make it inside the tomb at all? Would they be warped by Ghargatuloth's presence and turn into another enemy the Grey Knights had to fight?

Whatever happened, happened. The Grey Knights were trained to be ready for any weapon the Enemy threw at them – and that included their own allies.

The vox, Alaric wasn't surprised to learn, didn't work in the tomb. 'Anything in sight?' he asked his Marines.

'They're watching us,' said Dvorn bleakly, gripping his Nemesis hammer in two hands. Lykkos was scanning rapidly for targets, sweeping the barrel of his psycannon through the shadows.

The ground was crunching underfoot. Alaric glanced down and saw finger bones mixed in with the gravelly surface of crumbled marble.

The Grey Knights could smell the enemy before they saw them – it was a cold, foul stink, as if all the corruption that saturated the tomb coagulated and solidified into a wall of repugnance that all but forced the Grey Knights back. It was the sharp odour of toxic pollution and the sickly taint of decay, a force bearing down on them from all directions.

'Genhain! Covering fire, now!' yelled Alaric and suddenly the shadows were alive, the traces of bolter and psycannon bullets picking out tall, loping shapes between the rocks. Gunfire streaked from Genhain and Tancred's Marines, and through the storm of gunfire forms leapt from the darkness to attack.

Alaric's first parry was more reflex than decision, the kind Tancred had taught him in long sparing sessions. It was just as well because even he might have faltered had he seen his enemy before he acted – it was only vaguely humanoid. Its skin was dark grey and translucent so organs could be seen squirming in its torso, writhing up its neck and down its arms and legs. A foul curtain of transparent slime coated it, and its arms ended in long whip-like tentacles, one spraying corrosive slime as Alaric batted it away with his halberd. The thing's face was barely a face at all – a high thin mouth lolled wildly open, blind pale smears passed for eyes, and it emitted a horrible low howling as it pounced.

Alaric fired wildly, spraying storm bolter shells around the creature and the other following it. The attacker moved with fluid speed, whipping its tentacle around the halberd and dragging it down, drawing itself up plastically to its full height and bearing down on Alaric with that mindless gaping mouth.

Alaric plunged his free arm down the creature's throat and rattled off a solid volley of shells, blasting the back of the creature's head into flying globs of stinking gore. The creature shrieked and powerful muscles closed around Alaric's arm, trying to suck him in. Through the stench Alaric could smell burning and knew the outer layers of his armour were being eaten away by the creature's corrosive substance. Alaric pulled hard and lifted the creature off its feet, swinging it into the attackers following it, batting one aside and firing another volley. The creature came apart in a spray of acidic gore, and Alaric was free to move.

His Marines were right behind him, forming a tight circle as the corrosive attackers leapt at them from every side. Alaric saw Clostus holding one up high on the point of his halberd so one of the psycannon Marines in Squad Genhain could blow its head clean off with a single shot. Dvorn swung his hammer down straight through the closest enemy, reducing the creature to a slime-filled crater in the marble ground.

Alaric turned and saw Tancred, easy to pick out because of the bright lightning flash of the sword of Mandulis as it lashed out time and time again. Writhing tendrils of slime fell oozing to the ground but the fluid creatures reformed even as Tancred sliced through their bodies. One leapt on Tancred, trying to wrestle him to the ground – Tancred flipped it over his head, turned deftly and stamped down on it so hard it burst apart in a welter of toxic filth.

'Blades won't work!' yelled Alaric over the unearthly howling. 'Dvorn! Take them apart!'

Squad Alaric turned, forming a wedge with Dvorn at the head, facing down the dozen more enemies charging from the darkness. Dvorn swung his hammer in wide arcs, battering the creatures back or ripping the hammer's head right through them, while Squad Alaric concentrated on blazing away with their storm bolters and holding the enemy back.

'In war and abandonment!' Tancred was bellowing, 'Be thou my shield and my steed! Be thou retribution, and I shall be your hand in the darkness! Light from the shadows! Death from the dying! Vengeance from the lost!'

Alaric could feel the buzzing in the back of his mind as Tancred's remaining Marines tried to focus their willpower.

It was the Holocaust – the expression of the Grey Knights' faith, focused through Tancred's mind and forged into a weapon worthy of the Emperor's finest. Alaric knew it was hard enough to do with a full squad – with only Tancred and three battle-brothers, the power would require almost everything they had.

'Vengeance from the lost!' echoed Alaric, giving Tancred all the help he could. 'And from the void shall rise only the pure!'

The sudden psychic crescendo nearly knocked Alaric off his feet – a pure white flame of faith, bursting out from the sword of Mandulis like a shockwave, rippling across the stone. Alaric saw the closest creatures blasted into ash, the after-images of their twisted forms ghosted against the light as they came apart.

The creatures facing Dvorn shrieked and whipped their tendrils around their faces as if trying to block out the light. Alaric's auto-senses were overloaded and he could see nothing, just pure whiteness, the sword of Mandulis at its centre like a shard of lightning.

'Down!' yelled a voice from behind Alaric and he instinctively dropped to the ground. He felt his battle-brothers doing the same an instant before heavy thudding impacts ripped overhead. Blessed bolts from Genhain's two psycannon Marines thudded into viscous flesh, their psychic detonations ripping through corrupted bodies.

Alaric's sight came back. He was face-down on the ground, which was spattered with stinking, steaming blood. He quickly got to his feet to see the area covered in smouldering patches of gore, and heard Squad Genhain walking down the slope behind Alaric snapping off shots at any enemy that still moved. Brother Ondurin poured gouts of holy promethium from his incinerator into the shadows, and Alaric heard the screams as he immolated the creatures lurking there.

The armour of Alaric's squad was smoking and corroded, its gunmetal covered in patches of smouldering black.

Tancred's Marines had fared worse. Tancred himself was on his knees, sagging with fatigue. The use of the Holocaust power had drained him terribly – even he had not expected the strength of his Marines' hatred to be that great. The sword of Mandulis still shone, smoke coiling off its blade.

Brother Golven, one of Tancred's Terminators, lay face-down and limp. Brother Karlin turned him over and saw the whole front of Golven's armour had been rotted away, exposing blackened, oozing flesh. Karlin dropped Golven back down. It was obvious the Grey Knight was dead – he must have been dragged down almost right away and had his armour corroded by the attackers. Even blessed Terminator armour wasn't proof against the guardians of St Evisser.

Tancred turned to Karlin, who was armed with the squad's incinerator.

'Burn our brother,' he said, and Karlin dutifully scoured Golven's body clean with a spray of flame. It took a few seconds for Golven's corpse to be reduced to a guttering shell of charred armour.

They wouldn't even be able to take his gene-seed for return to the Chapter. But Alaric, if he survived, would ensure that Golven would be remembered.

'Move on,' said Alaric. 'Stay tight. The Emperor is with us.'

As the Grey Knights moved on into the stunted outskirts of the skeletal city, Alaric could see the carrion beasts circling in greater and greater numbers overhead.

Commissar Thanatal had almost given in to despair when he had seen what surrounded the processing plant on the shore of Lake Rapax. Creatures were writhing out of the ground all around the plant, faces and clawing limbs reaching from the earth, moaning and gibbering in a thousand tongues. There were hundreds and hundreds of them, foul things with massive mouths full of teeth, grasping hands with fingers that ended in razor-sharp talons, all dragging themselves from the earth to defend the plant.

Thanatal had felt then that the Emperor's duty lay not in death, that being torn apart by the maddening horde was too great a price to pay for duty. The sin of doubt had clawed at him, and he had felt his resolve eroded by the sight. The men around him stopped as the ash parted and the scene was laid out before them and the cries of daemons reached their ears.

But Inquisitor Valinov was not afraid. Thanatal's fears were banished as he watched awestruck – Valinov walked out into the boiling sea of daemons, sword held out, and they recoiled from his presence, shrieking in fear as he approached.

Valinov bellowed out words in a strange, sibilant language – a prayer, Thanatal guessed, an ancient rite dedicated to the Emperor – and the daemons parted before him. Valinov walked out into the very centre of them, calling out words of power as he did so, making sharp arcane signs with his free hand that sent daemons reeling back into the earth.

'Be thy cowed in the presence of your Master's work!' called Valinov in High Gothic. 'Fear His touch, be burned by His words! Back, back, servants of decay, back into the earth, back beneath the notice of the pure!'

The daemons were forced back beneath the ground by Valinov's words, his commanding presence spreading out in a ripple through the sea of daemons, forcing them down until a path was cleared between the Balurians and the tomb.

'See!' shouted Thanatal. 'See how the word of Emperor cows the Enemy! He is with us! Press on, servants of the Emperor, for the work of mankind has yet to be done!'

'The Enemy recoils!' echoed Valinov from up ahead as he began to lead the Balurians towards the processing plant. 'We are but the tip of the Emperor's spear. Feel His spirit as he drives us home, rejoice as we pierce the heart of corruption!'

Their faces alight with wonder, the Balurians moved across the sea of daemons who were now whimpering

in defeat, their faces turned away, the shimmering iridescence of their skin now dull and defeated.

The ash was parting and a shaft of pure, bright sunlight, such as had not shone on Volcanis Ultor for
centuries, illuminated the processing plant, turning its
grey plasteel walls golden, lining it with a white light
of purity.

The Emperor's eyes were on this place. The gates of
the plant stood blasted open, as if entreating the
Balurians to enter and purge it of corruption. Valinov
strode boldly towards it with hundreds of Balurians
behind him, Thanatal at their head.

Without prompting, the Balurians began to sing an
old, popular marching-tune they had sung as boys on
their first parade grounds on Balur. It was a song about
duty, bravery, longing for home, yet adventuring
through the stars. Their valour crushed the daemons
down further until they were cloaked in shadow, weak
and pathetic, cowed into helplessness by the light of
the Emperor filling the Balurian hearts.

The doors of the plant were up ahead. The darkness
within was pleading to be filled with light. Valinov
didn't have to urge the men on any more – he just
broke into a run and plunged through the burst doors.
Thanatal followed and the Balurians poured after him,
lasguns ready, not one man faltering in his step.

Light streamed in with them, illuminating a place of
ancient stone. Statues of Imperial heroes looked down
with approval on these servants of the Emperor. A temple was up ahead, covered in gold and shining like a
beacon – this was the place the Balurians had to liber-
ate from enemy hands.

And ranged in front of the temple were the enemies. They were shimmering and indistinct, their very

existence threatened by the sudden appearance of the faithful Balurians. Their red-painted armour would not help them, neither would the guns in their hands. The Balurians had the Emperor, and his most faithful servant, Inquisitor Valinov. They would not fail.

Thanatal didn't even realise he was singing along with the Balurians as he drew his chainsword and, along with hundreds of his men, charged.

CANONESS LUDMILLA HAD expected the threat to come from the temple. The vox was cut off completely and she had no way of knowing what was happening inside the temple, but she knew the Grey Knights and Lachryma's Seraphim had gone in intending to secure the place rapidly, and no one had come out. She was about to order her Sisters in after the Grey Knights when Sister Heloise, the Superior of the Retributor squad holding the plant's gates, reported there was some sorcery afoot – the ground outside the plant was seething and creatures were trying to force their way up.

Heloise was halfway across the statue graveyard, heading for Ludmilla's position, when the enemy force burst in.

'Sisters! To the front of the temple, now! Heloise, get into cover and fire at will! The rest, rapid fire and prepare to engage!'

'Looks like Guardsmen, my canoness,' said Heloise over the static-filled vox. 'Maybe we should…'

Thousands of las-shots ripped through the air from hundreds of lasguns on full auto. Ludmilla watched in horror as the ruby-coloured lances of fire filled the air with crimson threads, riddling the statues until they crumbled and fell, scoring chunks out of the ground, whipping around the temple steps and spattering against Sisters' armour. Somewhere heavy bolters and multi-meltas opened up from Heloise but they were soon drowned out by the sound of las-fire and – obscenely – of singing, a parade-ground tune carried by hundreds of hoarse throats as the Guardsmen charged closer.

Ludmilla's inferno pistol was in her hand and she could see Battle Sister squads converging at the foot of the steps to form a firing line. About half of them were in position and just beginning to fire volleys when the Guardsmen hit.

Heavy chains of bolter fire punched through deep royal blue body armour, sending out sprays of blood frozen in the strobing las-fire. The lasgun fire blasting back riddled the marble steps and Ludmilla saw Sisters spasming as las-bolts found weak points in their armour. One shot burst against Ludmilla's lower leg and nearly knocked her flat on her face, another thudded into her breastplate, and she felt the sleeves over her armour fluttering as shots streaked through the material.

She saw a tide of men, teeth gritted. A commissar led them, bolt pistol in one hand and a chainsword in the other. The front rank of Guardsmen was chewed up before her eyes by the Sisters' bolter fire but there were hundreds of them, trampling their wounded as they charged. She heard their voices raised in anger and loathing.

And she saw Inquisitor Valinov, his face lit by the glow from his power sword, striding tall and heedless of danger in front of the horde.

The Guardsmen crashed into them and Ludmilla's world suddenly shrunk into a tiny painful place of pressed bodies, stabbing bayonets and swinging las-gun stocks. It was full of the smell of sweating bodies and smoking barrels. Ludmilla held firm as Guards-men scrambled all around her, and she struck left and right. She fired her inferno pistol point-blank into the press and she was sure its superheated blast must have bored through three or four bodies – the weight less-ened and she pushed bodies off her.

She couldn't lead her troops now, as a canoness should. It was every Sister for herself.

'In the name of the Throne!' someone was yelling in the thick of the fight, his voice carrying over the yells of anger and the screams of the wounded, the sound of blades against armour and bolter fire muf-fled by the press of bodies. 'For the saints! For vengeance!'

A Guardsmen reared up over the throng, his bayonet slashing down at Ludmilla. She grabbed the barrel of the gun and dragged the man over her head, wrapping an arm around his neck and wrenching it until his neck broke. She kicked out and felt bones break beneath her ceramite boot. She fired again and saw a Guardsman's torso come apart in front of her, his body collapsing in on the ragged burning hole bored through its centre.

Blood was slick on her face, thick in her hair. The din of the fight was becoming a wall of white noise, like a dream. Men and Sisters were dying – Sister Superior Annalise cut an officer's legs out from under him with her chainsword, sending out a crescent of blood and shredded flak armour. Sister Gloriana fell back clutch-ing her face, blood spurting between her fingers. Sister squads were falling back up the steps unloading bolter clips into the tide, while others were in the thick of the fight trying to beat back the Balurians with combat knives and bolter stocks.

There was a flash of light and Ludmilla saw it was a power sword – the one carried by Valinov. A Sister's head flew through the air, teeth still gritted in defiance as the sword flashed by.

Valinov. Alaric had told her the inquisitor had betrayed them, and this was the proof. Inquisitor or not he had killed her Sisters and in the Emperor's name he would pay.

Ludmilla clambered through the throng, blasting a path with her inferno pistol, battering her way through. In the dark rabid mass of heaving bodies she could only see that power sword as it stabbed and slashed, its power field carving through ceramite in showers of white sparks. Valinov had a sneer on his face as he killed, a picture of utter arrogance. Ludmilla felt that same holy anger boiling up inside her that had filled her when she heard the tales of the Emperor's foes from the pulpit, that had driven her on her first missions as a Battle Sister and fuelled her ascent to the position of canoness.

It was hate that kept her going, even as a lasbolt burned right through her thigh and a bolter stock cracked against her forehead. She pressed on as her eye filled up with blood and the screams of dying Sisters cut through the din. She could hear the commissar urging his men on and it spurred her on, too, because it reminded her that the Balurians had been betrayed as well.

She could see Valinov now, cutting a space around him, forcing a squad of Battle Sisters back up the steps as Guardsmen died all around him. Ludmilla made one last charge, barrelling headlong through the

Balurians, feeling them fall back as she threw them aside and trampled them under her feet.

Then she was free, and she launched herself right at Valinov, inferno pistol held out in front of her.

Ludmilla was an excellent markswoman. She would not miss, not now. Through her hate the Emperor guided her hand – she could feel His strength filling her, for He had listened to every prayer she had made throughout her whole life. Now He was rewarding His faithful with the honour of being the instrument of His vengeance.

The melta-coils burst into life. The barrel flared and a bolt of energy leapt from the weapon, carving through the air right towards the centre of Valinov's chest.

A sudden flash of white light burst and Ludmilla felt heat wash over her. The after-image of Valinov was burned into her retina, framed in light as the conversion field around him dissipated the energy of the shot and crowned him with an outline of white fire.

An energy field. Expensive, rare, coveted. Probably taken from the Imperial Governor's armoury in Hive Superior, like the power sword. Ludmilla should have guessed, and the awful cold knowledge of failure was so strong it was like a punch to her stomach.

Ludmilla hit the marble steps hard. Valinov slashed his sword in a wide arc as she fell and sliced her arm off at the elbow, her hand still gripping the pistol as it spiralled away.

Ludmilla tried to scramble to her feet but as she rose, the inquisitor reversed his grip and plunged his sword straight through her midriff. She felt the blade shearing through her spine – red electric pain flared and dragged the breath from her lungs, and she even forgot her severed arm as pure freezing agony flooded right through her, cold as the blade in her guts, sharp as its edge. For a single endless moment, all she could think of was the pain. Las-bolts froze in the air. The screams became a blank wall of noise. The Emperor, her Sisters, the galaxy she had sworn to protect, were all gone, all replaced by agony.

When Valinov twisted the blade Ludmilla felt a great blackness open up in her mind as her life spilled out onto the steps. Valinov withdrew the sword and turned his attention back to the Sisters in front of the temple.

He didn't even bother to check if Ludmilla was really dead. He didn't need to. Ludmilla crashed back down onto the steps and knew that she was dead already – her senses just hadn't realised yet. She saw flak-armoured Guardsmen swarming over her as they charged, feet stamping down on her, warm blood flooding out of her and leaving only a huge black coldness that grew and grew.

Then it grew so big it swallowed her whole, and the tomb of St Evisser was left behind as Canoness Ludmilla died.

TWENTY
ACROPOLIS

THE CITY SWARMED with cultists.

At least, they had once been cultists, followers of Ghargatuloth in one of his many forms. Now they were debased and devolved, infused with the filth of Lake Rapax and animated by the will of the Prince of a Thousand Faces. The city itself was just as much a servant of the Prince as they were – its walls were contorted into bloated biological shapes or wrought into daemonic faces, its streets treacherous slabs of shifting marble. It was outlined in the light from the sarcophagus and drowned in the deepest shadow.

Tentacles reached from between chunks of fallen masonry. Cultists leapt from gaping windows or sagging roofs, spewing corrosive venom, lashing out with tendrils to drag down and smother.

Tancred led the way, the sword of Mandulis cutting a cultist in half with every stroke, the massive bodies of his Terminators charging through the crumbling walls. Alaric's Marines followed, fending off the cultists that tried to force their way between the Grey Knights, trying to surround them and cut them off from one another. Alaric's halberd cut through slime-covered muscular bodies, sliced off foul gibbering heads. Dvorn's hammer smashed through walls and Genhain's psycannon Marines riddled fire through the cultists lurking behind them.

Somewhere in the slaughter Brother Vien died, dragged back down the slope by arms that snaked up from the ground and dissolved their way through his leg armour. Vien had been a part of Alaric's squad since Alaric had been chosen as a justicar – Alaric knew him as a Grey Knight whose personal prayers were brief and incisive, an intelligent and studious soldier who spent as much time immersed in Imperial history and philosophy as he did performing bolter and close combat drills. He would probably have become a justicar himself, and now, in a flash of shadow and a final bitter prayer spat through dying lips, he was gone.

The Grey Knights struggled up the slope, the city becoming a tight warren of stone with cultists around every corner. Faces began to leer from the walls. The marble sky overhead bowed and rippled as if reality itself only had a tenuous hold over the acropolis. Voices gibbered in the back of Alaric's mind, his psychic shield muffling them until he could not make out the words.

The wards woven into his armour were freezing cold against his skin, reacting to the malice that infused the tomb. His breath was cold in his throat, and even with his Space Marine's metabolism it hurt him to draw breath. The place was sucking the life out of him. There was pure death at it centre.

The acropolis was just above the Grey Knights, a final encrustation of parasitic buildings between the Knights and the summit. The roofs of the buildings were edged in gold but all around the Grey Knights was deepest shadow. There were no roads between the looming buildings – the Grey Knights would have to make their own path up. One more row of buildings, and they would be there. One last place of shelter before they reached the top.

Alaric led the way into a tattered basilica, a domed building that seemed to ooze out of the steepening slope. Its steps crumbled beneath his feet and once inside the shadows swallowed him, turning his vision dark and grey. High above, indistinct writhing figures were carved, covering the dome in an illusion of movement. Words in a language Alaric couldn't read were inlaid into the floor and walls, and they squirmed as he watched. The place was a drained shell, devoid of life, but the hatred suffusing the tomb kept it alive. Alaric felt the floor recoiling as he stepped on it, his wards flaring in a cold spiral around his body, the carved figures turning their heads away in disgust at his piety.

His depleted squad followed him in, Tancred close behind. Alaric saw Tancred's armour was battered and scraped, and blood was running from one shoulder joint. Tancred himself was breathing heavily like an exhausted animal. His Terminators had born the brunt of the charge, battering through walls and stumbling into nests of cultists – only Tancred, Locath and Karlin with his incinerator remained. The use of the Holocaust had drained them, and Alaric knew they could not call on it again.

'We are close,' said Tancred. 'I can feel it. The sword knows it.' Impossibly, given how much toxic slime and gore it had carved through, the sword of Mandulis was still bright. Its mirror-polished surface reflected light where there should have been darkness.

'One more,' said Genhain, his Marines coming up the steps into the basilica. 'One more step.'

There was nowhere to hide in the basilica and for the moment the cultists were regrouping somewhere. The Grey Knights had a few seconds here to pause.

'If I were a proper brother-captain,' said Alaric as he caught his breath. 'I would know the prayer we are supposed to say. But I think you all know what we have to do. We do not know what our chances of survival are, so we fight as if they were zero. We do not know what we are facing, so we fight as if it was the dark gods themselves. No one will remember us now and we may never be buried beneath Titan, so we will build our own memorial here. The Chapter might lose us and the Imperium might never know we existed, but the Enemy – the Enemy will know. The Enemy will remember. We will hurt it so badly that it will never forget us until the stars burn out and the Emperor vanquishes it at the end of time. When Chaos is dying, its last thought will be of us. That is our memorial – carved into the heart of Chaos. We cannot lose, Grey Knights. We have already won.'

There was silence for a moment, broken only by the breathing of the Grey Knights, the psychic babble of the tomb far away beneath it.

Dvorn hefted his Nemesis hammer and walked across the basilica to the far wall, where faceless carved figures squirmed around each other to get away from him. Tancred followed, Locath and Karlin ready for one final charge. Dvorn mouthed a silent prayer and swung the hammer.

The back wall came apart beneath the impact and light flooded in, silhouetting Dvorn and Squad Tancred in shocking brightness.

'You'll make a leader yet, Alaric!' called Tancred, and charged into the glare. Alaric and Genhain followed, their auto-senses straining to keep from burning out.

Alaric ran through the back wall, up the steep marble slope, and out onto the acropolis.

The psychic din was replaced by a single, strident note, like a vast choir singing. Light streamed down from above. Alaric glimpsed cherubim, such as those depicted attending on Imperial saints, fluttering above a huge block of white marble that shone so brightly to look at it was like staring at the sun.

There were no cultists up here. The light would have taken them apart.

Tancred walked across the smooth stone, Genhain and Alaric covering him. The sarcophagus was so huge it even dwarfed Tancred.

Tancred waved forward Karlin and Locath, who stomped up to the sarcophagus itself. They reached high above their head, digging their fingers into the stone seam between the body of the sarcophagus and its lid.

Their enhanced musculature and the servo-assisted Terminator armour gave them even greater strength than a power-armoured Grey Knight. Slowly, as they heaved, the lid broke free.

Squad Tancred helped lift the lid and pushed it to one side. It fell with a crash onto the stone of the acropolis, shattering into fragments.

The light cut out instantly. The sound of the choir turned into a scream.

Something stirred within the open sarcophagus. Squad Tancred opened fire with storm bolters, Genhain followed suit. The bursts of bolter fire were drowned out by the howl blaring down from overhead. Alaric lifted up his arm to take aim and fire but he knew, deep within him, that bolter shells wouldn't make any difference.

A skeletal hand, each finger as long as a Marine's arm, reached blindly out of the sarcophagus. A huge dark shape shifted and the head of St Evisser emerged, huge and decayed, its face stretched, tattered skin over dark bone, the remains of its death shroud clinging to it in rot-coloured tatters. Blind, dripping orbs seethed in its eye sockets. Gnarled teeth grinned. The hand planted itself on the ground and St Evisser rose from the sarcophagus, an enormous, twisted monster, his once-human form saturated with corruption.

The mouth opened and St Evisser bellowed, the sound sending cracks through the marble sarcophagus. Bolter fire spattered off its face – teeth shattered, fragments of bone flew. Its other hand reached out and grabbed Brother Locath, picking up the Terminator and, with a screech, dashing him against the stone ground so hard he impacted in a shattered crater and his armour split open. St Evisser lifted what remained and threw it to the ground again, and this time blood spattered across the ground.

Tancred charged, as Alaric knew he would – St Evisser swung an arm and Tancred was sent flying. Alaric watched as the justicar was hurled through the air and straight through the wall of the basilica below. Karlin, the last member of Squad Tancred, drenched St Evisser with fire from his incinerator but the fallen saint ignored the flames.

St Evisser stepped out of the sarcophagus. At full height it was four of five times as tall as a Grey Knight. Its foot slammed down and a chasm ripped across the whole acropolis, the stone tipping inwards. Squad Alaric and Squad Genhain fought to keep their footing, scrambling as they slid towards the creature. It picked up a man-sized shard of marble and, with a bestial shriek, hurled it into Squad Genhain – Alaric saw Brother Grenn sliced in two and Brother Salkin's severed arm go cartwheeling away.

Alaric couldn't hear them yelling in defiance as they died. He couldn't hear Genhain ordering his Marines to fire, or even hear himself calling for vengeance and holy anger from his own squad. Alaric regained his footing and, his senses close to overloading, charged down the shifting slope at St Evisser. The saint swung a hand at him but Alaric ducked it, coming up swiftly to slash with the blade of his halberd.

The blade passed between mouldering ribs, glancing off bone, cutting through dried tattered organs and death robes. Alaric withdrew the halberd and stabbed, the blade passing through St Evisser's body and lodging in its spine.

Alaric twisted the halberd to get his blade free. St Evisser's enormous hand closed over his head and he felt himself lifted – he lashed out with the halberd, hoping to sever the skeletal wrist, but all he could see between St Evisser's fingers were those revolting liquid eyes, pale pools of malevolence, full of madness and Chaos.

His wards were overloading, blazing with cold fire inside his armour and cutting into his skin. It was only the pain that reminded him he was still alive. He squeezed down on the firing stud in his bolter hand, knowing that the volley would do no good, but knowing that he had to fight on as he died.

A flash burst just beyond Alaric's vision and St Evisser's head snapped to the side, bone shards flying. The hand let go and Alaric thudded onto the ground to see St Evisser throwing Justicar Santoro off its back, where the justicar had just landed a massive blow with his Nemesis mace. The side of St Evisser's skull was coming apart and Alaric could see the reddish fibrous mess inside that had once been the brain of an Imperial saint.

Fire rippled up St Evisser's torso – Sister Lachryma, her faced streaked with blood and grime, her jaw swollen and bleeding, was clambering through the shattered stone of the acropolis as her Seraphim attacked. One Sister with twin hand flamers was pouring fire up into the fallen saint, drawing his attention as bolt pistol fire from the other Seraphim thudded into its head.

Alaric dragged himself away from St Evisser. Brother Mykros, the Marine who carried Squad Santoro's incinerator, slammed into the ground beside him, one side of his armour caved in by the impact. Alaric rolled to the side as Santoro hit the ground beside him – Santoro was battered but alive, his mace smouldering with the unholy flesh that clung to it.

Alaric grabbed Santoro and the two helped each other to their feet, moving as quickly as they could up the broken slope as St Evisser lashed this way and that, trying to scatter the Sisters and Grey Knights. Sister Lachryma narrowly dodged a blow that shattered the arm of one of her Seraphim, and Brother Marl was trying to crawl away, his leg clearly broken.

Suddenly, the huge shape of Justicar Tancred appeared at the edge of the crater St Evisser had formed. His armour was battered and the ceramite plates were bent out of shape – sparks spat from ruptured servos and blood leaked from a dozen rents. The whites of his eyes were tiny glints in a mask of blood. The storm bolter on the back of his wrist had been wrecked by the impact as he smashed through the basilica wall but in his other hand was the sword of Mandulis.

St Evisser kicked out and another Seraphim went flying, her shattered jump pack spurting burning fuel. The fallen saint turned back towards Alaric and Santoro, and beyond them Squad Genhain was still trying to pin it down with a constant stream of fire.

Alaric knew what had to be done. Santoro, too.

Alaric ignored the pain and the screaming in his head and charged once again. St Evisser knocked the blade of his halberd aside and Alaric barely kept his footing, but Santoro was behind him, smashing Evisser's hand away with his mace. Alaric stabbed upwards again and felt monstrous ribs turning the blow away, but he wasn't trying to kill St Evisser this time.

St Evisser reached down and Alaric rolled out of the way of the gigantic fist that slammed into the rock behind him. He heard the impact of Santoro's mace against the saint's ribcage and knew the creature would be reeling – Alaric cut down at Evisser's leg and was rewarded with a shower of bone.

'I am the hammer…' intoned Tancred, his deep level voice somehow cutting through the din. 'I am the sword in His hand, I am the point of His spear…'

Tancred was walking carefully towards St Evisser, judging its every movement. Alaric and Santoro had to keep it busy. They had to stay alive for a few moments more, because St Evisser was the vessel through which Ghargatuloth would be born and only Tancred could kill it now.

St Evisser ripped a slab of marble up from the ground, straight and pointed like a blade. It swung it like a two-handed sword – Alaric pivoted to one side to avoid it and Santoro met the blade with his Nemesis mace, shattering the marble into a thousand stone splinters.

Evisser bent down to pick up Santoro and tear him apart, but Alaric was quicker – he dived at the fallen saint, both hands on the haft of his halberd, and planted the blade through one of Evisser's seething eyes.

Evisser shrieked so loudly Alaric thought his auto-senses would short out against the white wall of noise. Evisser flicked its head and Alaric was thrown hard against the broken marble slope, the bruised sky of the tomb reeling around him. The saint kicked out and Santoro hurtled through the air, cracking against the lip of the crater, his body cartwheeling brokenly out of sight.

'I am the gauntlet about His fist! I am the bane of His foes and the woes of the treacherous! I am the end!'

Tancred was the best swordsman Alaric had ever fought alongside. It had taken Brother-Captain Stern to best him. St Evisser was brimming with Chaotic strength but Tancred was a wily and merciless attacker. The sword of Mandulis flashed and Evisser's hand was sheared clean off its massive skeletal arm, falling to the ground in a spray of bone, light streamed from the wound. Tancred slashed again and the mirror-bright blade plunged into Evisser's torso, gouging again and again, hacking through ribs. Splinters of bone showered Tancred, chunks of vertebrae flew like bullets.

St Evisser was on its knees, Justicar Tancred battering it back with every strike. Evisser lifted its head to howl and the sword of Mandulis lashed out in a bright crescent, shearing right through the neck of the fallen saint.

St Evisser's head, its face twisted in the shock of a second death, toppled to the side. From the stump of the neck a shaft of pure light leap upwards, piercing the dark sky.

The screaming rose to a shriek almost too high-pitched to hear, spearing right down into Alaric's soul.

With a sound too loud to be heard, the acropolis exploded in a starburst of white light.

GHOLIC REN-SAR VALINOV reached the inside of the tomb in time to witness the rebirth of his lord.

Behind him, the Balurians stumbled and faltered in horror as they saw the sprawling, corrupt world that Chaos had built around St Evisser's corpse. The rotted shell of a city that crawled with the seventy-seven masques, the heaving stone sky heavy with destiny, the shattered marble and hungry chasms, and the daemon carrion creatures that circled over the shining acropolis.

Many of the Balurians lost their minds there and then, even before the acropolis exploded. Valinov had already bent them to breaking point, using the subtleties of his words and actions to whip them into a frenzy and direct them to the tomb. Now they had served their purpose he didn't need them, so he let them go insane. Ghargatuloth had erected a shield of pure emotion around his tomb to keep out the unwary who might somehow find their way here, protecting his sacred site with madness – most of the Balurians quickly succumbed, but Valinov was not so weak.

Some Balurians saw only beauty and light as their minds were divorced from any sense of morality. They saw a world of glory and bounty, and ran open-armed into it only to fall down unseen chasms or be snatched into the shadows by the few cultists the Grey Knights had left behind. Others collapsed at the sight, their subconscious minds preferring to cut them off from their senses rather than risk the deeper madness that might follow. Some turned on their friends, convinced that anyone around them must be corrupt – lasguns barked and knife blades hissed through flesh.

The commissar stayed true to his duty to the last, accusing everyone near him of heresy and daemonancy in an attempt to explain where such corruption had come from. He fired at random into the Balurians, and those still composed enough to act leapt on him, dragging him to the ground so he disappeared beneath a heap of insane Guardsmen. Bolt pistol shots thudded out of the mass as the commissar enacted the Emperor's justice even as he was crushed and beaten to death against the fractured marble floor.

Valinov was untouched. The part of him that might have once gone insane had long since left him along with the weak spirit that could be levered open by psykers and the lake of despair that could boil over in lesser men's minds. Valinov had once prayed to anyone who would listen that those parts of him would shrivel and die, because they had caused him such torture when he did the grim, violent work of the Inquisition under Barbillus. Ghargatuloth had listened and stripped away Valinov's weaknesses until he was free of conscience and doubt. It was the greatest gift a man could receive. It was no hardship for Valinov to repay the Prince of a Thousand Faces with his servitude, and now he was going to join his master at last.

The explosion tore the acropolis apart in a tidal wave of white life, the birthing pains of Ghargatuloth shattering stone and wiping out the crumbling city, vaporising the seventy-seven masques in an instant, a shockwave coursed through the marble like a ripple through water. The whole tomb bulged outwards with the psychic force of the blast and the Balurians were thrown backwards, some smashing against the columns, others hurled right out back into the statue garden. Valinov was sure he saw the armoured body of a Grey Knight as it shot through the air like a bullet and slammed into the distant wall of the tomb.

Valinov was untouched. Ghargatuloth would protect him.

A massive crater like a giant gaping mouth was all that remained of the city.

And then, at long last, the Prince of a Thousand Faces was complete, and in an eruption of glory he was brought back into real space.

THE SHORE OF Lake Rapax rippled like water. That was all the warning there was, before the roof was ripped off the processing plant by a column of shimmering iridescent flesh several hundred metres across and a kilometre high, erupting like a volcano into the sky of Volcanis Ultor.

The outer spires of Hive Superior were dwarfed by the column as it tore up from the tomb of St Evisser, shimmering in colours that didn't exist outside of the warp. Reality twisted and folded around it as it forced itself into dimensions real space couldn't hold. As it poured upwards thunderheads of sorcery formed around it, shining nebulae that spat multicoloured lightning. Great writhing tentacles split off from its mass, spasming with new-found freedom, lashing out and demolishing the processing plant and the defences around it.

The ground in its shadow was boiling. The daemons that served as Ghargatuloth's heralds were following it out of the warp, dragging themselves up through the earth.

From the bleached empty plains to the depths of the underhive to the tips of the noble spires, fatal sorcery sparked into life. Many went mad. Others were struck down, hearts stopped by fear. A panic gripped everyone in Hive Superior – the Prince of a Thousand Faces brought fear with him, so pure that those who had never seen the sky of Volcanis Ultor were overcome with terror of the daemon prince manifesting outside the city.

Hatred became liquid and dripped down the walls. Suffering was a cold, lethal mist that rolled out across the plains. Deceit rained down in fingers of black malice over the remains of the trenches, and minds snapped all along the defences.

The column rippled and shifted, and on the end of each squirming tentacle monstrous, maddening features were formed from the flesh. A thousand new faces were looking down on Volcanis Ultor.

ALARIC HIT THE wall, and time stopped.

He watched as Ghargatuloth erupted from the ground, unfolding in horrifying slow motion, oceans of iridescent flesh moulded into a single daemon spear that punched up through the sky of the tomb and out into the air of Volcanis Ultor. The landscape of the tomb crumbled. The skeletal city and the foothills of marble were shattered into dust as the daemonic flesh ripped out from beneath them.

Alaric was falling, slowly. Broken bones were recoiling inside him. The tomb was being destroyed a stone at a time and the full hideous spectacle of Ghargatuloth was being played for him so he could experience every maddening moment of it.

Alaric was in awe of the sheer scale of it. He had faced daemons before, but nothing that spoke of such power. His mind was full of Ghargatuloth's horror, the mindless strength of the tentacles that tore out from its flesh, the enormity of its explosion into real space.

'How small your mind is,' said a voice, 'to be impressed by such a little show of my power.'

Alaric tried to look round but his muscles, locked in agonising slowness, couldn't respond. The voice was so familiar it started somewhere inside his head and worked its way out.

A figure coalesced from the air in front of Alaric, as a portion of Ghargatuloth's immense knowledge shifted into a physical form. The Prince of a Thousand Faces appeared as a tall, muscular, strong-featured man, wearing clothes of skins and hide. He had a hard-won physique that spoke of short, brutal lives, war, survival and the hunt. His long black hair was tied back with strings of finger bones and feathers, and he carried a spear with a head of flint.

Every cultist who worshipped Ghargatuloth saw a different face. This was the face that Alaric saw, taken from somewhere deep beneath him, ripped from the lowest levels of his mind to tell him how he was going to die.

'Is this how you appear to me?' said Alaric, for his lips were the only part of him that he could force to move. 'One of the thousand faces?'

'I have many more than a thousand.'

Alaric could not read the expression on the man's face – it kept slipping away from his sight, as if focusing on it made it change. 'On this world I was the Seventy-Seventh Masque, the death beyond death. On Farfallen I was the God of the Last Hunt. To you, I am just the face you yourself see in me.'

Behind the Prince, his daemonic body was billowing up from the ground to form a lance of flesh now reaching up high into the sky through the shattered roof. Thick writhing tendrils were laying waste to the walls of the tomb, reaching in exultation towards the sky.

The Prince turned to watch it, seemingly in admiration or even nostalgia. 'The Changer of the Ways granted me that body. Holy Tzeentch himself. A vessel for what I am, which is knowledge, the most sacred weapon of the Change. Every man I kill, every secret I force a follower to divulge, every moment of suffering I cause, I learn more and I become more. I have learned a great deal in the last few months. I am more now than I have ever been. When Mandulis banished me I was like a child, and now I understand so much more. The galaxy needs me, Grey Knight. Time and space are prisons. The minds of mankind are the bars that keep everything inside. Break their souls, and they will become free, and freedom is the essence of Chaos.'

'Lie to me,' said Alaric. 'Go on. Lie. Prove to me that I am right.'

The Prince turned back to Alaric, his face still a vague swimming hint of an expression. 'You are very interesting to me, Alaric. You embody what I first tasted in

Mandulis when he died. You run from the very elements that once made you human. You have become less than human – you have shut away the only parts of you that could ever be enlightened by the Changer of the Ways. You call it faith, but if you understood the true nature of what Tzeentch promises to the galaxy then you would realise how grave a crime it is to render a mind so inert.'

'We found you once, daemon. We will find you again.'

'And then what?' Ghargatuloth's voice was mocking. 'Where would I be if Mandulis had not found me? Here, Grey Knight, here and now, with my followers and the work of my Master well under way. Banishing me changed nothing. Why must you refuse to understand? Chaos cannot be defeated, you must know that.'

Clouds were gathering in the sky as Ghargatuloth's body shrieked up into Volcanis Ultor's upper atmosphere, and sparks of blue lightning reflected off the shining flesh. The face of the Prince in front of Alaric hung in the air ignoring the destruction behind it, as more and more of the tomb was sucked into the searing column of flesh.

'You just had to look around you, Grey Knight, and you'd have seen it. What is Chaos? Suffering, you might say. Oppression. Deceit. But could not all these things be said of your Imperium? You hunt down the talented and the strong-willed. You break them or sacrifice them. You lie to your citizens and wage war on those who dare speak out. The inquisitors you call masters assume guilt and execute millions on a whim. And why? Why do you do this? Because you know Chaos is there but you do not know how to fight it, so you crush your own citizens for fear that they might aid the Enemy. The Imperium suffers because of Chaos. No matter how hard you fight, that will never change. Chaos exists in a state of permanent victory over you – you dance to our tune, mortal one, you butcher and torture and repress one another because the gods of the warp require you to. The Imperium is founded on Chaos. My lord Tzeentch won your war a long, long time ago.'

Alaric could feel the blasphemous words hitting his shield of faith like broadsides from a battleship. The Prince's words cut more deeply that any sorcery ever had, worming their way through the layers of doctrination. He felt naked – he had never been this vulnerable, even when he had been surrounded and outgunned, even when Ligeia had been lost and Alaric had been left alone in the hunt for Ghargatuloth. He let his anger burn hotter, to drown out the fear.

'We killed, daemon!' spat Alaric furiously. 'We killed you with the sword of Mandulis! The lightning bolt!'

'"Only the lightning bolt will cleanse this reality of Ghargatuloth's presence",' said the Prince. 'Valinov told you that, I suppose? When you broke him on Mimas? Must I really explain to you that Valinov cannot be broken? I removed those weak parts from him when I made him my own. So pleasing it is, Grey Knight, to deceive by telling the truth. So ironic, so beloved of Tzeentch. You see, Valinov was right. I cannot be killed, I cannot be stopped. The only way I can be cleansed from the galaxy is if I finish Tzeentch's work and turn the galaxy into a thing of pure Chaos. Then I shall become one with my lord, and then will I cease to exist. The weapon that banished me was the one with the power to bring me back, so I could do this work of Chaos. Valinov was telling the truth – you simply chose to hear a different truth.'

Of course, it was true. Every daemon had a condition that had to be fulfilled before it could return – a particular date, a location, a specific sacrifice or spell. Ghargatuloth, a being of great power, had many. He had to be born through a corrupted Imperial relic, the body of Saint Evisser. It had to be on the Trail, and it had to be now. And the vessel through which he was reborn had to be killed with the weapon that had first banished him.

Gharghatuloth could create them all – the Saint, the Trail, the cultists to serve him and the plots to bring the threads into place. But he could not create the sword of Mandulis. That had to be brought to him, and the Grey Knights had done exactly that.

Alaric's mind burned with conflict. The Grey Knights had not been used. They had fought and killed and done their duty. They were not a part of this plan, they were not the instrument of the Enemy...

'It was the way it had to be,' he said, teeth gritted with anger. 'You did not use us like you used Ligeia. We had to fight you face to face, to do what Mandulis did... we freed you so you could be fought...'

'Desperation, Grey Knight. You were with me from the beginning. It had to be you, you see. I find you Grey Knights so fascinating, with your unbreakable souls. Such wonderful tools. Impossible to discourage, some of the best soldiers the Imperium can muster, completely devoted to whatever cause I can plant in you. I just have to point you in the right direction and I know you will do what I want. *You* brought the sword of Mandulis to me, *you* helped fuel the carnage on the Trail, *you* turned Volcanis Ultor into the kind of bloodbath I needed to hide my preparations until it was time for me to fully awaken. And the challenge of breaking you afterwards is more than I can resist.'

Alaric saw the Balurians dying, a tiny swarm of dark blue figures by the entrance to the tomb, seething as they killed one another in their madness. He saw Valinov, hands raised in praise.

'Like all humans you have your flaws,' continued Ghargatuloth, 'but you are so proud you cannot see them. Your fault is fear, Alaric. You know the Grey Knights have never lost one of their own to corruption by the Enemy, and somewhere deep inside you is the fear that you will be the first. It is this that makes you feel so helpless in your unguarded moments. It is why you could never have been a leader. Why else do you see this face of me?' Ghargatuloth indicated his current form, the fierce tribesman. 'I appear to you as what you could have been. I am what you fear – I appear as what you could have been, if this fragile reality had not delivered you into the Grey Knights. Beneath your conscious mind you remember your old life on that savage world, and it reminds you that you could change again – you could change into someone who worships me. And I shall make sure that fear comes true, Alaric. I shall spend a long time breaking you, and when you fall you will be one of my dearest trophies.'

Alaric was silent. He didn't have long to live. He might only have one chance, but it was more than he could have hoped for. He had to make it count. For his fallen brothers, and for Ligeia. For Mandulis, who had given more than his life a thousand years ago.

Ghargatuloth hadn't brought him here. Alaric had made all those decisions himself. The sword of Mandulis, battling the Sisters, hunting Ghargatuloth to Lake Rapax – it was all his own choice. He was following his plan, not Ghargatuloth's. And there was one last chance to prove it.

His shield of faith was failing. He had to act now, before it fell and Ghargatuloth saw what he kept hidden there.

'Then it really is the end,' he said. 'But a death defying the Enemy is a victory in itself. You cannot take that away.'

'Perhaps not,' replied Ghargatuloth. 'But after death, you will be mine. I will have an eternity to make you fall.'

'You had to use the whole Trail,' continued Alaric. 'Saint Evisser, the cardinals, every single citizen, you had to move them all into position to beat us. Remember that. You put your plan in motion before the Trail even existed, because you knew it would take nothing less. We made you work, daemon. You feared us so much you had to move star systems to make us dance to your tune.'

'Keep that pride, Alaric. It gives you so much more to lose.'

'Well then,' said Alaric resignedly. 'Let us go through the motions. A Grey Knight should have some heroic last words, that's what the stories tell us. A final denial of the Enemy.'

'Indeed. Something to remind you of how futile your death was.'

'Good.' Alaric forced himself to focus on the figure's face. He concentrated until Ghargatuloth's eyes were drawn into view – they were hard, expressive, determined. A lot like Alaric's.

'Tras'kleya'thallgryaa…' began Alaric, and suddenly the world shifted back to full speed as the face of Ghargatuloth shattered.

A TENTACLE OF daemon flesh reached out from the column, bending gracefully over the wreckage of the disintegrating tomb towards where Valinov stood, surrounded by dying Balurians. Hundreds of hands reached out from the shimmering skin and lifted Valinov up, drawing him face-first into the body of Ghargatuloth, bestowing on him the ultimate reward for his devotion to the Lord of Change and his herald.

Valinov felt the power all around him – the power of pure knowledge, a perception so intense it seeped through his skin and began to eat him away, reducing him, too, to the pure substance of the knowledge that made him. Ideas of skin and bone were freed from their prisons. Valinov's organs began to dissolve in the shining liquid mass of Ghargatuloth. Faces beyond human description were staring out of the tentacle now as Valinov was drawn into it, watching their master's greatest servant becoming one of them – a new Face for the Prince, an idol before which countless cultists would bow. When Tzeentch swallowed up the galaxy and all was Chaos, Valinov would be a god.

ABOVE VOLCANIS ULTOR the thousand faces of Ghargatuloth suddenly recoiled, slipping back into the column of flesh. Tentacles writhed, looping in tortured knots around the pulsing central column. The clouds flared with angry lightning, the daemon's pain made solid, arcing in brutal red streaks to the ground. The iridescent flesh rippled with mottled dark colours, like wounds beneath the skin.

Daemons shrieked and were thrown back, their flesh becoming unstable, one daemon flowing into another and dying as their burning blood and organs spilled out onto the bleached stone. The sound was awful, like a million death-rattles at once.

Against the shattered wall of the tomb, destruction all around him and Ghargatuloth towering over him, was Alaric of the Grey Knights. His body was battered and broken, his armour split and torn. But he was alive, and he was conscious. He was shouting out the same words that Inquisitor Ligeia had, over and over again, in the run-up to her execution.

The Inquisition had believed she was speaking in tongues, her mind ruined by Ghargatuloth's influence. But Alaric knew how strong her mind was, and he had found it in him to trust her one last time. He had taken the transcripts of her interrogations and memorised the phrase she repeated over and over again.

It was not a stream of meaningless syllables. It was Ligeia's last desperate message to her captors, her last attempt at getting revenge against the Prince of a Thousand Faces.

'Iakthe'landra'klaa…' shouted Alaric, and the flesh of Ghargatuloth was shocked into dullness, flakes of it shearing off and falling like grisly grey snow.

Every daemon was ultimately a servant. Every one had a master, even one as powerful as Ghargatuloth whose master was Tzeentch himself. But for daemons to serve unquestioningly, a master had to have power over them. And so every daemon had a name. Men might know them by any number of names, but only one was the True Name.

Inquisitor Ligeia had known her mind was being invaded by Ghargatuloth. She had known her fall was inevitable, and so she had left herself as open as she possibly could. Her psychic power drew information out of any source, and Ghargatuloth was pure information – she had let him course through her, giving up her sanity and ultimately her life, searching for the knowledge she needed. She had found it, and in her final moments she had stayed just lucid enough to communicate it to her captors.

Of all of them, only Alaric trusted her enough to listen.

Syllable by painful syllable, just as Ligeia had done even in her dying moments, Alaric recounted the True Name of Ghargatuloth.

THE SYLLABLES BURNED Alaric's lips. Had it not been for his faith, he could not have survived saying the True Name at all. It was hundreds of syllables long and Alaric knew that if he made the slightest mistake he would fail, and so he pushed through the pain flowing through him and carried on.

The immense form of Ghargatuloth was flashing black and sickly green, blotches of purplish decay rippling up it. The faces writhed beneath the skin, fighting to get to the core of Ghargatuloth's body and away from the words that were burning their way through the daemon prince's flesh. Skin was flaking off in great slabs now, falling to earth in a terrible hail of dead flesh. Tentacles became dry, grey arches of flesh that cracked and fell to crash against the ground far below.

Alaric forced the last syllable out of himself, a sound he thought he could never make, ripping up through his throat. He thought he would die with the effort – he fell forward and landed face-first in the drift of shattered marble at the base of the ruined wall

Unconsciousness pulled at him. Blackness flashed at the edge of his vision. The death cry of Ghargatuloth cut through the pain – it was a low, hideous keening, at once pathetic and full of rage. It was hatred and pain. It was a raging against the agony of death.

Alaric forced his eyes open. Over the shattered shell of the tomb, the column was showering dead flesh and leaning drunkenly. Tight masts of flesh near its base snapped and Ghargatuloth toppled sideways, towards the plains that lay to the east of the processing plant and the line once held by the Sisters of the Bloody Rose. Slowly, appallingly, Ghargatuloth fell with a terrible sound as thousands of tendons snapped in sequence.

Alaric forced himself to his feet. The air was thick with falling scraps of desiccated flesh like black snow. His Nemesis halberd lay nearby. He stumbled over to it and picked it up as he heard the massive crash of Ghargatuloth hitting the ground.

Alaric clambered up the wreckage until he could see out from the remains of the tomb, painkillers flooding through his system but failing to cut off the ache that came from everywhere at once. Ghargatuloth was a huge, dying drift of flesh. Daemons were dissolving back into the ground.

Justicar Genhain stumbled across the wreckage towards Alaric. A couple of other Grey Knights could also be seen – Alaric recognised one of the Terminators and realised it must be Brother Karlin, for Tancred must surely be dead.

There were perhaps ten Grey Knights left – Karlin, a couple of Genhain's men, a couple of Alaric's. Alaric couldn't see any of Squad Santoro – he wasn't even sure how many had made it to the acropolis at all. Lachryma and her Sisters were gone.

Alaric turned back to Ghargatuloth. The True Name had weakened it, for so soon after its birth the shock of having a new, mortal master had made its very fabric unstable. But the Prince of a Thousand Faces wasn't dead yet.

Alaric began to walk towards the fallen daemon prince, followed by the remains of his command. He still had work to do.

In the end, it wasn't the Grey Knights who killed Ghargatuloth. It was mostly the Balurian heavy infantry, who marched in a cloud of ash wheeling anti-tank guns to finish the job the Grey Knights had started. None of them knew what had happened or that the Grey Knights were even there – all they knew was that immense destruction had been unleashed on Volcanis Ultor, that many of their regiment were dead, and that the fallen beast was responsible. A couple of Leman Russ tanks were brought up and the few surviving officers began to direct their fire into Ghargatuloth.

Tank shells and heavy weapons fire ripped into the daemon's flesh. Many-coloured blood soaked the earth, turning the ash-choked ground into a foul swamp and running off into Lake Rapax.

The surviving Sisters of the Bloody Rose added their firepower, too, their one remaining Exorcist tank sending rockets streaking into Ghargatuloth. The Methalor 12th Scout Regiment made the long march up from their positions on the south of the line and added what little long-range firepower they had, too, until Ghargatuloth was a pulpy burning mess of oozing flesh.

The Balurians advanced, the Methalorians by their side. Lasgun fire flashed in a crimson storm, turning

Ghargatuloth's blood into clouds of foul steam. Both regiments fixed bayonets and, filled with the hatred they had felt when Ghargatuloth first erupted from beneath the ground, set to hacking it to pieces. The Sisters joined in, intoning prayers of righteous wrath as they blasted Ghargatuloth to pulp with their bolter fire and the Sisters Superior laid into it with their chainswords.

Few noticed the Grey Knights. There were few of them, and everything was obscured by clouds of smoke and steam. Alaric and Genhain stood side by side as they hacked with their halberds, grimly and methodically reducing Ghargatuloth's daemonic body into a filthy viscous lake of daemon's blood.

THE SUN OF Volcanis Ultor was setting somewhere behind the ever-present clouds. Alaric could feel Ghargatuloth's life draining away and he stayed on the shore of Lake Rapax, waiting until his psychic core told him the daemon prince was gone.

He had several severe injuries – his storm bolter arm was broken somewhere, his rib-plate was fractured and shards of bone were loose inside his chest cavity. His third lung was the only thing keeping him breathing. Lesser men would have died. But the medicae facilities in Hive Superior could wait – Alaric would not go anywhere until he was sure Ghargatuloth was dead. And the faint throb of willpower was dying out. Alaric didn't have long to wait, leaning on the shaft of his halberd, feeling the night-time cold settle over the plain.

Justicar Genhain was trying to find all the surviving Grey Knights, and locate as many bodies of the fallen brethren as he could. He had found Santoro's body, broken almost beyond recognition by the explosion of the acropolis. He had been only metres away from Alaric – it could so easily have been Alaric who had died. Some of Santoro's Marines had died earlier without Alaric knowing anything about it, killed by Ghagratuloth's cultists on the way to the acropolis along with several of Lachryma's Seraphim. Tancred's body could not be found – Alaric knew that it never would be.

The sword of Mandulis had survived, glinting brightly at the bottom of the crater where the processing plant had once been. Genhain held it now, wrapped up so its blade would not reflect the drab destruction around it. It would be Genhain who returned with Durendin to the tomb of Mandulis, to re-inter the weapon beneath Titan. Until then the sword would be kept wrapped, its work now done.

The Sisters of the Bloody Rose were recovering their own dead, and Alaric had watched as they took away the body of their canoness from what remained of the steps up to the tomb. The whole of the processing plant was now just a crater filled with rubble, and it was impossible to see where the normal dimensions of the plant had ended and the abnormality of the tomb had begun. Balurian dead lay everywhere, and a Chimera troop transporter had been commandeered to carry loads of bodies back towards the rear lines.

So many had to die. So many that could not be replaced.

Something stirred in the dark stain of Ghargatuloth's blood. Alaric painfully walked over to it and saw, writhing in the filth, a human body.

Its skin was gone, eaten away as if by acid. It was covered in slime, its lidless eyes rolling madly, its hands wrapped around its entrails to keep them from spilling out.

At first Alaric thought it was a Balurian. But then he recognised the power sword that still hung on a tattered sword belt around the figure's waist, the same sword that Alaric had seen on Valinov as he welcomed Ghargatuloth into real space.

Alaric almost wished Valinov could still speak, so he could hear Valinov's taunts. But it didn't matter. As Alaric had recounted the True Name, Ghargatuloth had rejected his servant. Valinov had devoted his life – more than his life, his soul, his very existence – to Ghargatuloth, and it had been snatched away from him at the very last second. The pain of dying would mean nothing to Valinov, but the agony of failure when he had come so close was a torture of which Ghargatuloth himself would have been proud.

Perhaps it would have been fitting to let Valinov carry on despairing. But the Ordo Hereticus had already executed Valinov once, and Alaric knew they would expect the job to be finished.

'By the authority of the Holy Orders of the Emperor's Inquisition,' said Alaric, 'and as a brother-captain of the Grey Knights, Chamber Militant of the Ordo Malleus, I enact the judgement of Encaladus and place your soul before the Emperor for judgement.' Alaric bent down and picked up Valinov by the scruff of the neck. Valinov stared wildly at him, shivering, vile slime oozing out of his red wet body.

'But then,' said Alaric, 'you don't have a soul. So this is the end of everything, Gholic Ren-Sar Valinov. This is oblivion.'

Alaric walked slowly away from Ghargatuloth's dissolved corpse, up to the edge of Lake Rapax, which shone a multitude of sickly colours in the faint pale moonlight that filtered through the clouds. He knelt down at the lake's edge and plunged Valinov into the polluted waters.

Valinov struggled weakly. Slowly he stopped kicking. Alaric waited long enough to be sure that Valinov was dead, and then waited some more, alone and silent on the shore of the lake.

DAY WAS BREAKING by the time Justicar Genhain came to find him. Genhain had taken a Chimera from the Methalor regiment and was using it to take the surviving Grey Knights back to Hive Superior, where along with the Sisters they would tend their wounded until transports came to take them to proper apothecarion facilities.

Karlin had survived – he still held his incinerator in spite of the shrapnel wounds that covered him. Justicar Genhain along with Tharn, Ondurin and Salkin (who had lost an arm, sheared clean off). Alaric's Marines Haulvarn, Dvorn and Lykkos. Alaric himself. No one from Squad Santoro.

As the Chimera trundled across the battlefield towards Hive Superior, Alaric looked back, once, at the huge dark stain that remained of Ghargatuloth.

It wasn't over, of course. Ghargatuloth couldn't be permanently killed. But the Grey Knights – and Mandulis, and Ligeia – had shown that he could be beaten. And it was the duty of the Ordo Malleus to make sure that he stayed beaten.

The sun broke through the clouds, but it only shone on death and pollution, the piles of wreckage, the heaps of the dead. Slowly, very slowly, the long and gruelling task began of purging Ghargatuloth's influence from the Trail of St Evisser.

ON A RIDGE deep into the plain, the death cultist Xiang watched Ghargatuloth dissolve. Xiang had finally completed the last orders of her mistress Inquisitor Ligeia, and ensured that the daemon prince was brought into real space so that the Grey Knights could have their chance to destroy it.

Xiang was in a situation she had never been before. She had no master. She had once served the sect of the Imperial church that demanded blood sacrifice for the Emperor, and after that had sworn allegiance to Ligeia. Xiang had never been without a master, and it was a strange feeling – her thoughts, her movements, her decisions were her own now. She was not an instrument of another's will. There was only her own will to obey.

Perhaps she would find a new master eventually, and suborn herself to his commands. But perhaps she would explore this feeling more. Volcanis Ultor was as good a place to start as any – bleak wilderness to explore, layers of lawless underhive in which to test her skills, all manner of Imperial citizens to learn from, to observe, perhaps to obey.

She turned away from the dead daemon prince and looked across the plain, towards Hive Verdanus just visible far to the east. Xiang wondered if she would ever find a master like Ligeia again. Then she wondered if she wanted to.

Her taut muscles barely registering the effort, Xiang began the long walk.

* * *

THE AIR WAS cold deep beneath Titan. The psych-warded chamber was small and bleak, lit only by a single guttering candle. The chamber had been excavated only a few days before to serve as a secret, secure repository for information that had to be kept secure – and more importantly, that should never be forgotten. It was hidden in the bowels of Titan's catacombs, guarded by the legions of dead Marines, where only the chaplains of the Grey Knight would know where to find it.

A single large desk dominated the room, and a scribe-servitor sat hunched over a large open book. The book was new, only recently bound, its pages white and blank. The servitor's quill arm hovered over the page.

Chaplain Durendin and Inquisitor Nyxos stood towards the back wall of the room. Durendin had led Nyxos down to this place, because it was on Nyxos's insistence that the chamber had been built. Nyxos was recovering from the injuries he had suffered at Valinov's execution but he still looked weak and drawn, aged even beyond his advanced years, his every movement supplemented by the servos of his exoskeleton.

'You may begin,' said Nyxos, and the scribe-servitor began scratching a title onto the page.

Second Book of the Codicium Aeternum, it began in perfect flowing script. *Being a description and naming of Daemons, the Dates and Durations of the Banishments and Details thereof, that the Enemy might be known before his Machinations are complete...*

Inquisitor Nyxos began to dictate the details of the report Alaric had given in the apothecarion, about Ghargatuloth's elaborate plans to create a fallen saint to act as the centrepiece for the ritual that would revive him, to use the Grey Knights to deliver the weapon that had first banished him, and to suborn unnumbered cultists and demagogues to cover his tracks. Those same cultists were even now being purged from the Trail of St Evisser in an operation commanded by Inquisitor Klaes and Provost Marechal, and it would not be finished for decades, if ever.

He made sure to mention Inquisitor Ligeia, and how Alaric was the only one who trusted her in the end. He mentioned the many, many Imperial citizens that died, and the many that were still to die as Ghargatuloth's influence was scoured from the Trail.

Finally, the scribe-servitor noted down that Ordo Malleus research and readings of the Imperial tarot had suggested the duration of Ghargatuloth's banishment. He would be able enter real space again in one thousand years. But this time, the Malleus would not give him the chance to succeed.

'Note this exactly,' dictated Inquisitor Nyxos, 'for every syllable must be pronounced perfectly lest the banishment fail. Know that the True Name of the daemon Ghargatuloth is Tras'kleya'thallgryaa...'

For several minutes Inquisitor Nyxos forced the syllables out of his throat. When it was done, the servitor-scribe was taken away to be destroyed to ensure that hearing the True Name had not implanted some corruption in its biological brain.

Then Inquisitor Nyxos left Titan for Iapetus, to head for the Eye of Terror and continue the Emperor's fight. One chapter of Ghargatuloth's story was done, and by the time the next one began, Nyxos and all those who had fought the Prince would be long gone.

* * *

When it was done, when the bodies recovered had been buried beneath Titan, the reports had been made to the Ordo Malleus and the survivors had been thoroughly purified, Alaric was granted a few days of convalescence to himself while it was decided if he should retain his rank of brother-captain.

He was given permission to make the short journey to Mimas, and there he was guided by the interrogator staff to the place where Inquisitor Ligeia had died.

There was nothing left. The cell had been dismantled – only the clamp remained bored into the rock where the cable had once been fixed to the surface.

Ligeia's body had been cremated and scattered in orbit, to ensure there would be nothing left of her. All Alaric could do was say a prayer for her passing, but it was still more than anyone else had done – Ligeia had died a traitor, so no one had seen to it that her soul was commended to the Emperor's side. It wasn't much, just a few sacred words pitted against the horror of heresy. But it was enough.

So many had to die, thought Alaric as he looked out over the barren surface of Mimas, the huge glowing disc of Saturn overhead. So many had to suffer.

But sometimes, the fight was worth it. That was why the Grey Knights existed. The fight would never be over, but sometimes, it could be won.

ABOUT THE AUTHOR

Ben Counter has made several contributions to the Black Library's *Inferno!* magazine, and has been published in 2000 AD and the UK small press. An Ancient History graduate and avid miniature painter, he is also secretary of the Comics Creators Guild.

LET THE GALAXY BURN!